MY SWEET SATAN

Peter Cawdron

thinkingscifi.wordpress.com

Copyright © Peter Cawdron 2014

The right of Peter Cawdron to be identified as the author of this work has been asserted by him in accordance with the Copyright, Designs and Patents Act 1988

ISBN-13:978-1502539243

ISBN-10: 1502539241

US Edition.

MY SWEET SATAN

Synopsis

The crew of the *Copernicus* are sent to investigate Bestla, one of the remote moons of Saturn. Bestla has always been an oddball, orbiting Saturn in the wrong direction and at a distance of thirty million kilometers, so far away that Saturn appears smaller than Earth's moon in the night sky. Bestla hides a secret. When mapped by an unmanned probe, Bestla awoke and began transmitting a message, only it's a message no one wants to hear: *"I want to live and die for you, Satan."*

Chapter 01: Awake

Sunlight flickered through the leaves of the old oak tree. A cool breeze broke the sweltering heat of the day. Clouds drifted high in the stratosphere, lit up by the setting sun in hues of pink, red and yellow. Jasmine rocked in a swinging chair suspended from the porch of her home in Atlanta, Georgia, enjoying the quiet of the coming evening.

"NASA Live is on," came a call from inside the house. "They're talking about the *Magellan* mission to Enceladus."

"I'll pass," Jasmine replied, kicking gently with her feet and swaying back and forth in the wooden seat. Above her, a chain squeaked gently, keeping time with her motion. The smell of freshly baked apple pie wafted through the air, but Jasmine knew there was no sense in asking her mother for a slice until after supper.

Jasmine keyed a text into her cellphone, her thumbs racing through a message to her boyfriend, Mike.

Your late.

She glanced down at the message she'd sent and realized there was a typo. Most people wouldn't care, but Jasmine was a perfectionist. Her fingers madly typed a second message.

You're - not your. Fat fingers.

No sooner had she hit send on the second message than her phone showed three dots revealing a reply was being typed in real time.

You have beautiful fingers.

Jasmine grinned at the message on her phone. Her fingers glanced over the glass screen as she sent a reply.

Beautiful fat pudgy fingers.

There was no response. A few seconds passed and she already regretted the speed with which she'd hit the send button, but there was no taking back any of her messages. Why had she said fat? And why had she then reinforced the notion in her second message? She hesitated, wanting to send something to retract her comments, only she knew she'd make her gaffe worse. That Mike hadn't responded a second time was telling. He was too kind to scold her.

Jasmine was nineteen and had been accepted into the Massachusetts Institute of Technology with academic scores that were already grabbing the attention of Charles Draper, the NASA liaison officer at MIT. She had a dream. Like Mike, she wanted to be an astronaut and wasn't shy in making her ambition known. Mike had made it into MIT two years earlier and was already participating in some of NASA's preliminary training courses.

Fat! Jasmine had never been fat. And what was wrong with a bit of soft padding? Fat was natural for women. Besides, she'd never been fitter in her life, running a seven minute mile three times a week, and yet she still obsessed over her body image. Jasmine disappointed herself. She couldn't leave the conversation there. She had to say something to defuse the tension she felt weighing down upon her.

Joke.

Some joke, she thought, sitting there gripping her phone, willing Mike to reply. Seconds seemed like hours. Maybe he was driving. He was coming over for a birthday dinner with her folks, and he was late. It was entirely likely he was driving, but then how had he responded to her first message? Argh, Jasmine thought. Don't overthink things, girl. You're making this worse.

Her phone chimed softly with an incoming message.

:)

And she did smile. Funny, she thought, how two punctuation marks from Mike could set her mind at ease.

Not driving, right?

OK, she thought, now you're borderline obsessive.

Leave the poor guy alone.

No, Mom. Matt's dropping me off.

Mom! Urgh. Mike was right, though, she sounded just like his mother. Jasmine sat there wondering just how such a small series of messages had thrown her off kilter so badly, leaving her feeling green. Why did she refer to a simple typo as the result of fat fingers? She should have let it be. From there, she'd plunged into a spiral dive out of the clouds. Jasmine felt like a wheel out of balance, shaking on its axle. If she was going to make it into the astronaut corps, she was going to have to stow this shit, she decided.

Her father waved as he walked along the footpath beyond their white picket fence. Jasmine dropped her phone into her lap and waved back.

The grass was lush and green. Underground sprinklers came on, automatically popping up and spraying a light mist over the lawn. Fine droplets of water moved in a gentle arc that reached up no more than a foot or so in height. In some places, the spray soaked the concrete sidewalk leading to the house.

A bicycle lay on the grass getting wet—her older brother had a habit of being too lazy to take his bike around the side of the house, and that bugged her. One of these days that bike would be stolen, she thought. Maybe she should hide it and give him a scare. She wondered if that would work. Probably not.

"Hey, Jazz," her father called out, opening the low wooden gate and walking up the path. "Good to see you made it home for a few days."

"Hi, Dad," she replied cheerfully. "Good to see you, too."

Her father was dressed in a business suit but he was carrying both his jacket and his tie draped over one arm. Sweat soaked through his white shirt. Perspiration dripped from his brow.

"No air con, huh?" Jasmine said, picking up her phone and hitting send on another text to her boyfriend as she spoke to her Dad. She hadn't said anything to Mike, responding only with smiley face in response to his. She had finally decided to stop acting like a teenager. Time to grow up, she thought.

"Nope," Dad replied, taking the stairs two at a time as he jogged up onto the porch. "Let me guess, Mom's fussing around in the kitchen?"

"Something like that," Jasmine replied.

Her father came up to her. He leaned forward and kissed her on the cheek. To her surprise, a spark of static electricity jumped between them, something that shouldn't have happened on a sweltering, humid, hot and sticky summer day.

~

Jasmine blinked. But in that fleeting moment as her eyelids closed and opened again, her world transformed. White lights burned into her eyes. Pain surged through her chest, tearing across her pectoral muscles. Her back arched as her body tensed, flexing and convulsing involuntarily.

"STAY WITH ME, JAZZ!"

Jasmine's mouth was open, but she couldn't speak. She gasped, trying to scream but her cry came out as little more than an agonized moan. Every nerve in her body tingled. Her muscles clenched. She choked, unable to breathe.

"Are you declaring a medical emergency?" a distinctly calm voice asked.

"Fuck you, Jason!" cried a middle-aged man. His face was vaguely familiar, hidden behind a full beard, obscuring his cheeks, mouth and chin. The matted tangle of straggly, unkempt whiskers made his face look enlarged. Through the haze of pain, all Jasmine could think was that the hair on his head looked incongruous. How could such long, wild hair be reconciled with a receding hairline that reached so high upon his brow? It was as though he were both young and old, a contradiction, both a hippie and a conservative.

The man shook Jasmine, grabbing her by her shoulders. Garage mechanic? Paramedic? Jasmine struggled to make sense of his blue jumpsuit through the surge of pain.

"Damn it, Jazz. Not like this!"

Jasmine could barely focus her eyes. The edge of her vision blurred, the lights were blinding, but the name embroidered on the jumpsuit was clear: *Mike Morrison.*

Mike?

Her Mike?

Impossible.

She couldn't concentrate. Every muscle in her body ached. She wanted to scream, but she couldn't. The cool air brushing past her lips teased her with the promise of relief, but her chest wouldn't expand. She couldn't breathe. She was suffocating. It felt as though someone had stretched a plastic bag over her head, pulling it tight across her mouth and cutting off her airflow, and yet she could feel the soft touch of a breeze on her cheeks.

Mike grabbed at the straps of her cotton tank-top. With a surge of raw, animal aggression, he tore her shirt open. His muscular arms ripped the flimsy material from her chest.

Mike was yelling, swearing, but to Jasmine he had an almost dreamlike, fluid motion to his movements. For a second, she thought they were underwater, but she could hear him, she could feel the breeze on her cheek.

Mike slapped two sticky patches on her, one on her upper right chest, the other directly on her left breast.

"Give me charge," he yelled.

"You're not clear," the calm voice replied. "She has to be properly restrained."

"Just do it!" Mike screamed. "She's dying."

~

Jasmine blinked and the pain disappeared. She was still sitting on the wooden swing rocking gently back and forth. The screen door leading into the rickety old house slammed shut behind her father. Birds flittered in the old oak tree. Streams of sunlight broke through the leaves.

"Ah," she said absentmindedly, wanting to say something to someone, but there was no one there. A police car drove down the road, cruising by slowly. The officer had his elbow resting on the open window, enjoying the breeze. To Jasmine, it seemed as though he didn't have a care in the world, and on such a beautiful evening, why should he?

Jasmine looked down at her phone as the casing shook with an incoming message. She picked it up, surprised to find it felt as light as a feather.

Stay with me, Jazz.

The shock of seeing those words hit her like a jolt of electricity. Her muscles spasmed and she released her grip on it. The phone drifted from her hand, floating effortlessly in front of her instead of falling back into her lap. She watched in astonishment as her phone twisted slowly, drifting gently to one side, suspended in mid-air.

Jasmine turned her head in panic. Strands of her own hair floated effortlessly before her, mimicking her motion, free from the shackles of gravity.

The red bicycle drifted beside the picket fence, no longer touching the grass. The sprinklers no longer sprayed in an arc. Water fell upward, like rain being recalled to heaven.

The branches of the old oak normally sagged under the weight of age, but today they looked spritely. The leaves were crisp, no longer dipping as they pointed at the ground.

The police cruiser sailed above the cars parked on the side of the road, twisting as its momentum carried it onward. The officer didn't look bothered by what he was seeing. His arm still rested on the windowsill of the cruiser and he played lazily with the steering wheel.

Jasmine felt herself lift off her seat. She grabbed at the wooden slats, trying to hold herself down, but the chains that held her seat in place no longer pulled taut under gravity. Galvanized steel links of chain drifted lazily beside her, clinking softly. Her phone rotated through 360 degrees slowly revealing the text message again. The words looked innocuous, but the message terrified her.

Stay with me, Jazz.

"Dad?" she called out. "Mom? Mike? Anyone?"

Fear seized her and again, she blinked.

~

The bearded mechanic slammed Jasmine's body against the wall. Her head snapped back, striking a hard, plastic surface. Pain surged through her body.

Velcro ripped open. Her arms were thrust out to either side and hastily strapped in place. There was a hiss of oxygen from the plastic mask pushed roughly over her mouth and nose. Mike held the mask in place, only to hold the mask still he had to anchor himself with his other arm, holding on to a rail on the bulkhead so he didn't drift away.

"Please, Jazz. Don't leave me. Stay with me."

Jasmine closed her eyes. She wanted to return to her porch swing. She was choking, desperate to breathe. She wanted to escape the pain, only with her eyes closed the world seemed to swirl uncontrollably around her. She was plunging headlong into the darkness. She felt as though she'd been hit by a wave at the beach and knocked off her feet, was being tossed in the surf, tumbling beneath the waves.

"Clear," the man's voice yelled, and she felt the oxygen mask come loose and drift across the bridge of her nose.

A jolt of pain ripped through her chest. Again, her back arched violently and she found herself raised up on her shoulder blades. Every muscle flexed as fifteen hundred volts tore through the fibers of her body. Jasmine couldn't help but open her eyes. The stranger in the jumpsuit floated in front of her just as the red bicycle and police cruiser had.

"Come on, baby," he said, pushing the transparent oxygen mask back in place. He fought with the elastic strap, pulling it awkwardly over her head. Strands of hair caught in a metal clip and were torn painfully from her scalp.

Jasmine couldn't breathe. She could hear the hiss of oxygen flowing and feel the cool gas blowing against her face, but she couldn't draw a breath. She was drowning without being in water. Her lungs wouldn't respond.

"Again!"

Fire tore through her body. Jasmine felt as though someone had struck her across the chest with a baseball bat. Her stomach muscles clenched, seizing and spasming. She gagged. She vomited, clogging the oxygen mask. Mike grabbed at the mask, snapping the elastic as he wrestled the plastic cone to one side.

Jasmine couldn't help herself. Spew projected out of her mouth, but instead of falling at her feet the dark green bile sailed across the white room, missing Mike the mechanic but striking the far cabinet and spraying outward. Tiny drops of vomit floated inches from her eyes.

Finally, Jasmine gasped, sucking in a lungful of air.

"That's it. Breathe, baby. Breathe."

With a damp towel, Mike wiped her face, pushing back her hair and gently cleaning the corners of her mouth. The oxygen mask drifted away, hissing and spraying fine droplets of bile through the air.

"Stay with me, OK?"

~

"OK?" her father said, repeating a word she'd heard moments before in what seemed like another lifetime.

Jasmine blinked several times, if only to reassure

herself of reality. The smell of freshly baked apple pie still filled the air. She could hear her mother humming a tune as she set the table. Knives and forks clinked softly as they were laid on the table behind her. The television was on. A muffled voice spoke of rockets and planets, transfer orbits and course corrections.

The setting sun lit up the clouds in ruddy hues. The sky grew darker. Venus appeared as a bright star in the twilight.

"Jazz?" her father said.

She looked around, confused. The bike lay still on the grass. The sprinklers soaked the lawn. At the far end of the street, the police cruiser indicated before turning at a four-way stop sign. The patrol car accelerated slowly and disappeared behind the weather-board covered homes. A bird chased a moth as it danced through the air, fluttering erratically, trying to reach the sanctuary of a low hedge.

"You were yelling out here," her father added, the concern showing in his voice. "Are you OK?"

He crouched down in front of her, moving down to her level and looking her in the eye. The wrinkles on his forehead, the grey hair on his head, and the warmth of his smile were comforting, grounding her in the moment. This was the same smile that had stared down at her in her crib, it was the same smile that had beamed at her during junior high graduation, the same smile that greeted her on return from summer camp. Jasmine felt as though nothing could hurt her in that moment. Her father's smile was an anchor.

"Is everything all right?" he asked, with a soft, deep voice that soothed her soul.

"I—I don't know," she said, unsure what else to say. With one hand, she pushed her hair back behind her ear. Moments before, her hair had been swirling wildly before her, or had it?

Her daydream had seemed so real. The pain she'd felt had been overwhelming. Jasmine glanced down at her chest, half expecting to see patches and wires stemming from her naked torso, but her T-shirt looked ordinary, just a plain white cotton shirt with the image of some generic rock band printed in two-tone. Jasmine didn't even know who the band was. She'd bought the shirt because she thought it looked hip. The image was probably staged just for the T-shirt, but seconds ago she'd had a tank-top torn from her chest, not a T-shirt.

Her phone lay on the wooden deck by her feet. A fresh crack ran through the glass, cutting across the lower half of the screen.

"You dropped your phone," her father said, reaching down and picking it up for her. "It's broken, but don't you worry about that. We can get it fixed."

The message on the shattered screen still read: *Stay with me, Jazz.*

"Dad!" Jasmine cried, seizing his arm. "Please, don't leave me."

"Everything's going to be all right," her father replied. "Just breathe, baby. Breathe."

"No!" Jasmine called out. The hair on the back of her arms raised in horror. Her eyes were wide with terror. "No, please don't go. Don't send me back. I don't want to go there. I want to stay here with you and Mom."

"You've got to be strong," her father replied and already Jasmine could feel herself slipping away. She gripped his arm, wanting to convince herself the wrinkles in his sweat-soaked cotton shirt were real, but her fingers felt numb.

His smile faded. Her father's face looked solemn, unnatural, almost a figurine carved in a wax museum. All emotion drained from his features as he spoke.

"Hang in there, Jazz."

~

Jasmine's eyes opened, but for a moment she couldn't see. A pungent odor filled the air. At first, Jasmine thought it was gunpowder, but the smell wasn't that sharp, more burnt and metallic than the acrid chemical residue of a shot going off. Whatever it was she could smell, it sure wasn't her Mom's freshly baked homemade apple pie.

Flashes of light burst around her as she gasped for air. Slowly the blinding light resolved into a view of a spherical room. White cabinets and computer workstations lined the far surface, but they appeared upside down. Jasmine couldn't think of them as being mounted on a wall or a ceiling. There were no edges to the room, no corners, no point of reference for her mind to cling to.

A second, clean oxygen mask had been slipped over the back of her head but the mask hadn't been placed properly on her face. The upper edge sat across the bridge of her nose, causing the plastic cup to sit raised, slightly away from her mouth. Jasmine could feel precious oxygen running out across her cheeks. She wanted to straighten the mask, but her arms felt like lead weights. She tugged feebly against the Velcro straps holding them in place.

"That's it, babe. You can do this."

Jasmine fought to free herself, but her hands were caught in the straps. One of her legs came free and she pushed against the table, trying to pull away from the blur of the mechanic floating before her. She was disoriented. She couldn't tell if she was lying on a bench or if she had been strapped to a wall. Her senses deceived her, she could have been strapped to the floor or hanging from the ceiling for all she knew. Vertigo swept over her. She felt giddy, unable to determine which way was up.

"You're going to be fine. Just relax and breathe deeply."

Mike's hand rested on Jasmine's shoulder, but she felt repulsed by him.

"No," she gasped from beneath the mask.

The man before her sounded like her Mike, but he was too old. Mike was twenty-two, not forty-five. Who the hell was this man who had ripped open her shirt?

Jasmine looked down at the patches stuck to her chest above her breasts. The torn remains of her tank-top drifted to either side of her, still attached under her arms but floating in the air as though they were drifting in water.

She squirmed, trying to get away from this monster in front of her.

"Hey, take it easy."

Jasmine tried to speak, but her mouth was numb, as though she'd had a shot of Novocain at the dentist. Saliva dribbled from her lips.

"No," she struggled to say. "Please."

Mike pulled the oxygen mask to one side, resting it on her cheek as he daubed gently at the corner of her lips, speaking softly with a tone of concern she found confusing.

"Easy, babe. Easy. Let it go. It'll take a few minutes to reorient. Just relax. The more you stress the harder this will be."

"What?" she managed, her speech slurring as she spoke. "Where?"

Single words were all she could manage.

"Coming out of deep sleep is a bitch at the best of times, but you. Damn, I thought I'd lost you. Don't scare me like that, Jazz."

"Who are you?" she said, still trying to twist her hands free. Jasmine managed to pull her right hand loose and held her palm out in front of her, wanting to push Mike away, but she was struck by uncertainty. Just having her hand between her and him seemed to give her some much needed distance. She wanted to go home, back to Atlanta. Being topless, she felt the need to cover herself, to protect herself from this stranger.

"It's me, honey. Mike. Remember?"

"Mike?" Jasmine asked, touching gently at his face. Her fingernails scratched softly at the skin beneath his haggard beard. "My Mike? But—I don't understand? How?"

Mike ran his hand up over his own neck, through the hair on his cheeks and chin, saying, "Yeah, six months stuck in a sleep pod without shaving scares the crap out of me too!"

He smiled, then laughed, but his laughter wasn't relaxed. He sounded manic, unhinged, which scared her.

Jasmine forced a smile in response. Slowly, a vague recollection seeped through the fog in her mind.

"But your hair," she said, still coming to grips with speech. Her words sounded clumsy, as though spoken by a child. She touched softly at his temples and ran her hand gently over his forehead. A tuft of hair sat high on his crown. The hair on his head was long and straggly but had receded back several inches revealing a high brow. Mike looked like a homeless bum on some sleazy street corner.

"The years catch up to us all sooner or later, babe."

Mike peeled the patches off her chest, pulling them back and raising the skin as he did so. Dark red welts broke out on her blotchy skin.

"What happened to me? Where am I?" she asked, pulling the oxygen mask from her face.

"Where are you?" Mike replied with an air of genuine surprise. "Honey, you need to take a look outside."

Another hand towel floated before her, so she pulled it to her breasts, covering herself as Mike tore open the Velcro straps holding her in place. Once the straps were released, Jasmine felt herself float free, flying like a bird. No, not a bird, she thought, like a helium balloon, drifting without any effort at all.

"I don't understand," she said, astonished by the floating sensation. Pinpricks stabbed at her bare feet, giving her the sensation of standing too close to the edge of a rooftop.

Her inner ear deceived her, telling her the room was in motion, fooling her into thinking she was caught on a roller coaster, plunging down into a corkscrew, but her eyes assured her the walls were motionless. She felt a slight tingling feeling in her hands, they were puffy, bloated, and she was tempted to think of them as fat but that was the wrong term.

Jasmine wanted nothing other than to feel her feet set firmly on the ground, but where was the floor? There was nothing within the spherical room to suggest one direction or another was up. A series of dark tubes sat either above or below her, she couldn't decide which. Two of them were open. Frosted glass hid the occupants of the other coffin-like tubes.

Jasmine felt as though she was falling, but she wasn't,

or was she? Blobs of spew floated before her in perfectly round droplets. She was in space. She had to be, but how? She ducked beneath a blob of bile and reached out for a handle on the wall.

"It's OK," Mike said, moving away from her. "Jason will get the cleaners running. They'll fix this."

Jasmine turned toward him, seeing him floating in a corridor that extended out of the room. She'd assumed his orientation was up, but there was a sign on the wall beside him: *Emergency Release.* Either the sign was lopsided and upside down, or both he and she were inverted. From her perspective, it looked as though the sign had been knocked loose and had fallen to one side, perhaps hanging from a single screw. That there were no screws jarred her mind, and she tried not to think about the Alice-in-Wonderland world into which she'd been thrust. A talking rabbit with a stopwatch couldn't have been more alarming.

"Come on," Mike said. Without moving his legs, he pulled on a rail, pushing off with his other hand and gliding effortlessly into the corridor outside the medical bay.

Jasmine pushed off. For a second, she felt as though she were completely stationary and it was the walls of the spaceship that were in motion, moving slowly past her like a train pulling out of a station. The hatchway drifted past and she found herself in a white, sterile corridor stretching out well over a hundred feet in front of her. Like the sphere she'd emerged from, there was no floor. All the walls looked roughly the same and she noted Mike was sideways relative to her, or she was sideways relative to him. She couldn't decide which perspective held true.

There were three ladders running the length of the corridor, spaced equally apart, but they seemed redundant. Jasmine pulled on one of the rungs and thrust herself down the circular, tube-like corridor behind Mike.

She was flying. She could have flown on forever, darting effortlessly through the air. Her terror faded, replaced by a childlike sense of wonder at life in space. If this was a dream, it was a dream she never wanted to wake from. Jasmine still felt a little sick, but the awe of flying through the air like she was swimming through water kept her stomach in check.

The handholds and hatches lining the corridor disappeared beneath her. Computer consoles and flat screens made up workstations. The odd scrap of cotton or speck of dust floated stationary, suspended in the air.

Mike stopped and opened a locker. He tossed a bunched up rag over to Jasmine.

"Put this on."

Jasmine copied him, coming to a halt with ease. She watched as the cloth drifted straight toward her without arcing through the air or slowing. She grabbed it and realized it was a tank-top.

"Thanks," she said, turning away from him and slipping the cotton top over her head and down over her breasts.

"Hey," he said, coming up behind her. "Don't feel bad. You had it pretty rough back there. You just take your time, Honey."

Jasmine jumped at his touch. Her body spasmed as though she'd been hit with another electric shock. She wasn't sure why, but she felt overwhelmed and confused by everything that was happening. Her body ached. There was only so far the novelty of being in space could carry her.

"Where the hell am I?" she said, turning back to him and repeating the question she'd asked in the medical bay. Tears formed in her eyes, only her tears never ran down her cheeks. They formed ever enlarging globules of water near the bridge of her nose, blurring her vision and forcing her to wipe them away. Drops of crystal clear water drifted through the air, reflecting the light like dozens of tiny mirrors.

"I was at home," she said. "I was sitting on the porch waiting for you."

"Hey, it's OK," Mike replied, putting his arm around her shoulder and pulling her in tight under his arm. "You're disoriented. Focus on the little things. It's going to take some time to clear your head. You've had a nasty shock."

Jasmine trembled in his arms.

"Come on," he added, pushing off the bulkhead and drifting further down the corridor, holding her hand and dragging her with him. "There's something you're going to want to see, something that's going to make all of this better, I promise."

This wasn't her Mike, she was sure of it. He may have sounded like Mike, even looked like him. He may have had the same mannerisms, but there was something strange about him, and it wasn't just his age. Although Jasmine was distressed, she could see Mike was struggling as well. He seemed nervous, perhaps anxious. He wouldn't give her straight answers. He changed the subject. He shifted himself physically. He was antsy, bordering on frantic. Whereas she wanted to curl up in a ball and be left alone, Mike was hyperactive.

Behind her, several automated cleaners the size of basketballs whizzed through the air. Multidirectional fans within each unit allowed them to navigate precisely as they cleaned up the droplets of vomit that had drifted into the corridor. The mechanical basketballs disappeared into the medical bay.

Mike let go of her as he drifted too close to the curved wall of the corridor, correcting his motion with a soft touch on a panel marked HVAC. Jasmine followed behind him, pushing off gently and stretching her arms out in front of her. She felt as though she were diving into a pool, only the water never rushed up to greet her, instead her dive took her further down the corridor.

An eerie glow shone in the distance. The corridor opened out into a bowl-shaped room with a large glass dome. Beyond that lay Saturn, frozen in three-quarter profile, with most of its wispy, golden clouds reflecting the brilliance of a distant sun.

Instead of being millions of miles away from her, it seemed as though Jasmine was looking at an elaborate model of Saturn. The apparent size was an illusion, she understood that, but the gas giant seemed no larger than a tennis ball held at arm's length, while the rings reached out roughly the same distance on either side. The rings appeared razor thin, almost fragile. If this had been a model, she was sure they would have been as brittle as a wafer-thin sheet of glass. Thousands of fine lines stretched around the planet, disappearing into the dark shadow of the gas giant.

Jasmine had visited New York with her high school art class and had seen the Starry Night. The swirling cloud tops on the distant planet reminded her of Van Gogh's entwined brush strokes. The contrast between the chaotic, repeating cloud patterns and the smooth, record-like curves of the rings was alluring—hypnotic.

Ornate curls wound their way around the various latitudes on the massive planet like the cornice work in some 17th century French castle. The intricate patterns repeated like calligraphy, with flourishes of passion and brilliance visible in each stroke.

"Magnificent," she whispered.

The spaceship that had seemed so large around her now felt small, as though it were a toy boat adrift on the open ocean.

Mike spoke rapidly.

"Oh, Jazz. You should have seen her on our closest approach. We're outbound now, but once she filled the entire dome."

Jasmine was stunned by the rich depth of color before her. Oranges, whites, yellows and browns all entwined upon each other, swirling before her like the color palate of some medieval painter.

"But—But how? I mean, a minute ago, I was sitting on my porch in Atlanta, Georgia."

"A minute ago," Mike replied. "You were flat lining. After twelve months of cryo-sleep, the reanimation procedure had stalled. Your body was starved of oxygen for almost nine minutes. Had it not been for the millions of nano-bots floating around in your bloodstream, I doubt I'd have been able to bring you back."

"But this is not me," Jasmine insisted, looking down at herself. Her body looked lean, but older. Whereas she remembered the soft skin on the back of her hands, now veins and thin tendons appeared beneath the taut skin.

"Honey, it's been a long time since we first met at the Marshall Space Flight Center, but I can assure you, you've been pushing and prodding me along ever since then."

"I—I don't understand? How did we get here?"

"We're on the *Copernicus*," Mike said, scratching at his straggly beard. "We're out here to make first contact."

"First contact?"

"You really don't remember, do you?"

"No," Jasmine replied, looking around at the equipment on the flight deck in amazement.

Every square inch seemed to have a purpose. Rungs marked several ladders evenly spaced around the deck, reaching up from the seats and around the sides of the bowl-shaped command center. They seemed redundant given the magical quality of flight the crew possessed in a weightless environment. Like Supergirl, Jasmine could dart wherever she wanted, flying with ease on the slightest whim.

To her mind, the dome over the command deck should have marked the front of the craft, pointing the direction of travel, but Jasmine got the impression the *Copernicus* was drifting sideways, pointing other than where it was heading. Front, top, left, right—these terms were meaningless, nothing more than her own assumptions. Jasmine could have been looking backwards at Saturn for all she knew.

Although there were numerous flat screen panels with various displays and controls methodically laid out around the center of the command deck, there were also old fashioned toggle switches and analog knobs, which surprised her. There seemed to be a mix of old and new technology on the *Copernicus.* Some of the mechanical switches were protected with see-through plastic flip covers so they couldn't be bumped into a new position by accident.

"Babe, it's been twenty years since we left Atlanta. Don't stress. Give it time. Your memory will come back."

And again, he was off. There was something wrong. Mike didn't seem to want to focus on any one thing for too long. He was in a hurry, but why? What was so important? Was it importance that drove him on, she wondered, or manic anxiety?

Mike floated in front of a mirror. It took Jasmine a moment to realize what she was looking at: a bathroom! Mike had pulled back an accordion plastic panel revealing a multipurpose region at the back of the spherical deck. A buzz filled the air as he ran clippers over his face. A thick tube attached to the clippers sucked up the loose strands of hair with vigor, vacuuming them away as he trimmed the straggly growth on his beard. Mike ran the clippers around his chin, up and down his neck, over his cheeks. The buzz of the clippers seemed incongruous with being in space.

Like all the men she'd known in her life, including her father, Mike made faces in the mirror as he worked with the clippers to trim the hair around his cheeks, his nose and chin, being sure to catch every last strand of hair. He even pulled his upper lip down, stretching it so he could catch any long nose hairs, which Jasmine found gross.

"Ah," she said, raising a hand and wanting to continue talking, but Mike ignored her, looking at himself in the mirror. Perhaps he didn't hear her, but the clippers weren't that loud and he must have seen her lips moving out of the corner of his eye. He didn't want to talk to her. As unsettling as everything was around her, it was Mike that scared Jasmine.

Mike floated in front of the bathroom with his feet hooked under a bar on what Jasmine assumed was the floor, watching his varying expressions carefully in the mirror. The suction sounded like a vacuum cleaner, and it probably was, she thought. She marveled at the transformation before her. Mike didn't stop with his beard. He took time to cut his long locks as well, reducing the hair on his head and face to a fine stubble. He had no regard for aesthetics, trimming all the hair on his head with what seemed to be a number one setting.

Once he finished, he grabbed a damp washcloth and rubbed it over his face, clearing out the sleep in his eyes before working the cloth over his head.

"Oh, man," he said, putting the cloth in a pull-out bin. "That feels better."

"I think I preferred you with the beard," Jasmine said, thinking Mike looked like a convict, but not wanting to say that aloud.

"Ha!"

And he was off again, drifting over to another station within the command deck. Mike sailed past her as though she wasn't there. His blue jumpsuit had an elastic waist, pulling in snug around his hips, revealing his stocky physique.

Jasmine was getting the hang of moving around in low-gravity. She pushed off one wall and glided effortlessly after him.

"You wanna take a shower?"

He was changing the subject, ignoring her concern, and yet the distraction was welcome. As much as she wanted answers, deep down what Jasmine really wanted was to reconcile herself with reality. She wanted to fit in. She wanted to remember.

"A shower," she said. "In space? I didn't think that was possible."

"Well," he replied. "Technically, it's not. I mean, it's not like standing under a waterfall, but the shower cubicle produces a fine mist. Extractor fans give it a sense of direction. It's a bit like standing in a gale, but the steam clears out the pores of your skin, and a bit of suction under your feet makes it almost like standing in a shower back on *Luna One*."

Jasmine was silent, still coming to grips with floating freely in space inside the *Copernicus*.

"It's nice," Mike added, but his smile looked forced.

Perhaps if he'd led with that thought she would have

tried the shower, but the moment was gone.

"I'm fine."

Jasmine wasn't fine. She felt dirty, but hers wasn't a grime that could be washed away by soap and water. Everything was wrong. Even the grandeur of Saturn couldn't counteract the sense of being defiled. Jasmine felt as though her life had been stolen from her.

Mike blinked a few times, but didn't say anything. He seemed as lost as she was. His eyelids looked heavy. His eyes were tired, and not just physically. He looked as though he'd been carrying a heavy burden for years, something that demanded sacrifice. Jasmine had seen this in her own father. He was always a lifter, never a leaner. Like her father, Jasmine suspected Mike didn't realize everyone needed a little help now and then.

Her mother called it pride, saying men were too prideful to ask for help, but Jasmine wasn't so sure it was that simple. She'd seen her father struggling with the monotony of work five days a week, fifty weeks a year, with only a couple of weeks respite at their lakeside holiday home in southern Georgia. One year blended into another. If it hadn't been for the chilly winds of fall and the coming of winter, it would have been impossible to distinguish where one year stopped and another started. Days on a calendar were meaningless. Even the seasons seemed to struggle to find meaning, with winter being little more than a bitter cold with the occasional snow flurries blown down from the north. The snow never stuck, of course, but at least there was something different about the land. There was nothing different about her father's life from one year to the next, nothing but the grey hairs that slowly appeared and the kids that grew up and left him.

Jasmine had watched her older brother and then her sister leave the nest. She was next. She was last. Perhaps that's why Mom and Dad always wanted her to come over for dinner. Perhaps that's why she'd been swinging on the porch. They were still holding on to yesterday.

No, she thought, looking at Mike. It's not pride that stops men from asking for help. It's that they don't want to shatter the illusion that everything's the same as it has always been. Blind zeal, that's what it was, not pride. Like all the men she'd known in her life, Mike wanted control, but control of life was an illusion. Jasmine could see this because she'd jumped forward twenty years in the blink of an eye. She could see everything Mike couldn't. The wrinkles on his forehead, the lines on his face, his coarse eyebrows, the slight sag in his skin that made his face more rotund than it had been as a teenager. These were changes he'd never recognize, as for him they happened imperceptibly. For her, they screamed in alarm.

Yes, she thought, pig-headed obstinance, that's what she could see in Mike's eyes. Jasmine wasn't the only one struggling with reality.

"What's happened?" she asked. She had meant to add, "to me," but those two words caught in her throat.

"That's not the question you should be asking, Jazz. The question you should be asking is, what the hell is about to happen?"

Chapter 02: Confusion

"Purge complete," a slightly mechanical male voice said. "Crew are showing nominal medical signs, responding according to sequence."

"Well, this is it," Mike replied with a hint of resignation. "There's no putting this off any longer."

"Who is that?" Jasmine asked, turning and looking for the source of the electronic voice. "Is there someone else awake?"

"That's our AI."

There were no visible speakers, or even computer screens nearby.

"You really don't remember anything do you?" Mike said, resting his hand gently on the side of her neck, his fingers lying softly along her jaw. "God, this must be so strange for you."

"You have no idea," Jasmine replied, trying to hide the tremor in her hands. Life had been so simple sitting there on her porch swing in Atlanta. How had she come to this point in life? What sequence of events had dragged her halfway across the solar system?

Jasmine loved Mike Morrison, or at least there was a time when she had loved him, now she wasn't so sure. His eyes were the same, but they looked tired. The uncanny resemblance to her Mike was somewhat upsetting. His skin was rougher than she remembered, but only slightly so, and Jasmine struggled to recognize exactly what was different. For him, decades had passed, but for her it felt like only a few days since she'd last seen young Mike.

Perhaps it was the pores in his skin being marginally more prominent that upset her, or the slight crow's feet around his eyes when he smiled. The wrinkles on his forehead weren't overly distinct, but her Mike didn't have any wrinkles at all. And her Mike would never shave his head. She couldn't imagine him ever getting a buzz cut like this. Her Mike had a mop-top, long straggly hair that looked perpetually unkempt. And her Mike never had any facial hair.

In the year they'd dated, she'd never seen her Mike with anything more than one day old stubble, and only on a couple of occasions. Even in the bitter cold of winter, Mike would be clean-shaven. He said he hated having a face that felt like sandpaper. If this had been her Mike, he wouldn't have stopped with stubble, he wouldn't have been content until he could run his fingers over the smooth curve of his chin. The man before her could have been from an alternate universe for all she knew. Was this really her Mike some twenty to thirty years on?

What had happened to her? Where had twenty years gone? Jasmine caught a glimpse of her own face in the polished reflection of a stainless steel cabinet by the galley, but the image was distorted, stretching her cheeks and enlarging her eyes. Was this a carnival? Was she trapped in the Crazy House of Mirrors? If only this was all just a nightmare, a dream she could awake from and forget.

"Are you going to be OK?" he asked.

His face was slightly fatter, she thought, although fatter was the wrong word, and she scolded herself for settling on that term yet again. Fuller, perhaps, making his eyes look sightly smaller. Jasmine didn't remember Mike's jawline being quite so pronounced.

"Just a bit dizzy," she replied, lying. She was freaking out. Get your shit together, girl, she thought, berating herself mentally. Jasmine gritted her teeth, trying to snap herself back to reality, only this was reality. Mike didn't notice. He went on, responding to her initial question.

"Jason's an artificial intelligence unit: JCN unit."

"J—C—N?" Jasmine replied, pronouncing each letter slowly.

"Jungian Comprehension Network. He goes by Jason for short."

"He?" she replied, surprised to hear gender applied to a computer.

A synthetic voice spoke, saying, "How are you feeling, Jazz?"

The tone was neutral, without any hint of emotion. It was as though Jason was asking for the time of day.

Jasmine turned, looking for someone behind her. In micro-gravity, she sailed through three hundred and sixty degrees, coming to a halt as Mike reached out to stop her from tumbling.

Mike grinned, pointing over his shoulder with his thumb. "Can you believe that? Sounds real, doesn't he."

"I am real," Jason replied in a dead-pan tone. "I'm as real as you are, Mike."

"Here it comes," Mike said, rolling his eyes. There was a slight twitch in his cheeks. Jasmine had seen this before, just after Mike had revived her, but at that point she hadn't thought anything of it as there was so much else bombarding her mind. Mike didn't look right. Was this a nervous twitch? Her Mike had never had any ticks or quirks. This Mike looked frazzled, as though he'd had one too many espressos and needed to pee.

Jason spoke with a soft, considerate voice as though he were talking to a child. "Come on, Mike. You have no problem considering the electrical impulses surging through your brain as intelligence—as conscious life. How am I any different? All that separates us is our substrate: silicon or neurons."

"He was a late inclusion," Mike said ignoring Jason. "An experimental prototype. NASA administrator Hamilton's idea of a joke, if you ask me."

"You can't offend me," Jason said in a soft tone that felt somehow defiant. "We're in this together. We're a team."

"You're a program," Mike protested with a degree of irritation that surprised Jasmine. "You're a bunch of if-statements. A logic table. A decision tree. A fancy database full of useless information. Nothing more."

"And you're not?"

"No," Mike insisted. "I'm alive."

Jasmine was quiet. Her head was spinning, physically and metaphorically. Any time she changed direction her inner ear seemed to swirl and she felt sick. She was fine moving in straight lines within the confines of the *Copernicus*, but the slightest wobble of her head left her on the verge of vomiting again. On top of the physical uncertainty, she was struggling mentally to process everything that was coming at her: being weightless in space, being in orbit around Saturn, seeing Mike some twenty years on, and listening to a computer that sounded like a psychiatrist.

"As a xenobiologist, you appreciate the diverse possible ranges in which life can exist," Jason said. "Surely, you understand it is folly to pigeonhole the definition of self-aware intelligence? To limit the range of possibilities under consideration to purely biological organisms is a mistake."

"Don't tell me you agree with this horse shit, Jazz."

Mike was determined not to accept Jason's premise. He didn't seem pleased with any idea that didn't originate with him. The funny thing was, she'd seen this in her Mike, only to a lesser extent. This Mike might have been more technically competent, he might have been more knowledgeable and experienced, but he seemed more immature in this regard. Her Mike would have been more accepting, she thought. Her Mike wouldn't have felt threatened.

Jasmine felt bewildered by Jason. She didn't know what to say in reply. She didn't want to offend Jason, but neither did she want to agree. She didn't feel she had to agree. She felt she should be afforded some time to make up her own mind and not be forced into taking sides.

"I—I don't know."

There was silence for a second.

"To state something is unknown is an acceptable position," Jason said. "Unknown leaves room to know."

Jasmine wasn't sure she agreed with Mike, but being lumped together with Jason didn't feel natural either. It seemed both Mike and Jason were vying for her vote.

"Oh, I know what you are," Mike said. "You're not fooling me. You might sound like you're human, but you're not."

"I would never claim I was human, only that I am alive, only that I think."

Jason's voice sounded slightly indignant.

"You see what I've had to put up with for the past few weeks," Mike complained.

Jasmine spoke in a soft tone. She could see this was an ongoing argument between the two of them, one that would never be satisfied.

"How many others are there?"

"Other astronauts?" Mike asked.

"Four," Jason replied. "Counting you and Mike, the

Copernicus has a total crew of six. Three Americans along with representatives from China, Russia and India. The rest of the crew is gaining consciousness now."

"And the shit is going to hit the fan," Mike said.

Jasmine had drifted slightly to one side and so had her back to Mike when he spoke. From the tone of his voice, she could have sworn he was smiling, but as she pushed off gently on one of the handholds, she saw a worried brow. Mike looked nervous.

He pushed off the bulkhead, gliding like Peter Pan as he flew over to what was clearly the central console on the *Copernicus*, a large half-moon shaped series of stations and leather-bound chairs set roughly ten feet back from the shaft. The seats faced outward, away from the central corridor. They looked sparse, while the consoles looked homemade. Thin sheet metal frames defined the panels. Rivets sealed the edges. Wires protruded from the rear of each console, strapped in bundles as they disappeared beneath the deck.

At first glance, Jasmine assumed the command deck was unfinished, awaiting cabinets and covers to be put in place, but the deck was functional rather than aesthetic.

Even the chairs were spartan in their appearance. The padding looked no thicker than a textbook. Although she couldn't think of any practical need for cushions in space, they had been supplied, but only in the most austere, rudimentary fashion, as though they had been taken from the Economy Class seating of a low-budget airline. Jasmine knew weight was at a premium in space, or more specifically, mass, and she could see how it was being conserved in the bare design of the command deck.

Jasmine felt as though she were suffering from a hangover. Without meaning to, she had drifted over near the bathroom capsule. It hadn't been a conscious decision on her part, but she suddenly became aware there was a mirror, a real mirror, and not the warped shiny sheets of metal near the galley. After seeing her distorted features moments earlier, she felt an urgent need to see herself for who she truly was and not as some sideshow freak.

The conversation between Mike and Jason had calmed her a little. Mike was strange. There was something out of place, something peculiar about him. He'd been surprisingly passionate in denying the possibility of artificial life, but once the subject changed, he dropped all hostility. He and Jason were talking about the technical details surrounding communication with Earth as though nothing had transpired between them.

Jasmine ignored them.

She floated there mesmerized by the view in the

mirror. Fine strands of hair drifted lazily around her head. Her cheeks looked swollen. Her sinuses felt stuffy, leaving her feeling as though she had an oncoming cold, and she sniffed, wanting to clear her nose. Bloodshot eyes stared back at her, red and angry.

She reached up, touching gently at her face with her fingertips. Tenderly, she pulled down the skin beneath one eye, stretching the loose, puffy skin on her cheeks as she explored her face, noticing the wrinkles in the corners of her mouth. Her high cheeks were peppered with tiny freckles. Gently, she touched at her dry, cracked lips. Her hairline had receded slightly on the sides, a sign of her age. She ran her finger over the freckles as though they were specks of dust she could brush away. This wasn't her.

"In pod UV," Jason said, and Jasmine jumped, surprised to hear Jason so close at hand. She could hear Jason talking to Mike on the other side of the command deck by the navigation console and yet here he was holding a simultaneous conversation with her on an entirely different subject. "We use a blend of booster shots and ultraviolet light to get the body to generate vitamin D while you're in cryo-sleep. The freckles will fade with time."

"Ah, thanks," she replied, still getting used to the almost godlike omniscient ability of the JCN unit. Like Mike, she wanted to think of Jason as a machine, but the illusion of care in his voice lulled her into acceptance that he was more than just a computer program. She could have sworn there was a real Jason hidden somewhere behind closed doors.

"How do you feel?" Jason asked. "Disorientation is to be expected, but I suspect you are experiencing something more..."

Jasmine was silent.

"...alarming," Jason continued. His pause felt deliberate, as though he were probing for more information. "I'm programmed—no, that's the wrong word. I've been trained in psychoanalysis. I can help."

Jasmine frowned slightly, noting the peculiar manner in which Jason caught himself as he spoke, correcting notions mid-sentence just as a human would. If his response was indeed merely the result of complex programming, mimicking human reactions, then his persona was overwhelmingly convincing, she thought. Surely, no computer would reflect upon what it had said after it had spoken. Logic would determine the most efficient terms up front, or was this mimicry? Was this a clever trick to imitate a natural form of speech? Had Jason's code been developed with human-like mannerisms to allow him to integrate more naturally with the crew?

"You wouldn't understand," Jasmine insisted, turning

slightly and catching a glimpse of herself in profile. Like Mike, she looked different. The earring holes in her ears had long since closed over. Her neck looked thin, much thinner than she remembered, and there was a fine hair growing from her chin. It wasn't that noticeable, but she noticed it. She pinched the hair between her nails and plucked it, adding, "I don't think you'd understand because I know I sure don't."

"You feel displaced," Jason said. "No, not displaced. That's the wrong word. Lost."

Jasmine swallowed, wondering just how much Jason could read into her non-verbal body language.

"You really don't think you should be here, do you?"

Jasmine breathed deeply.

"What is your last memory?"

She turned away from the mirror, wondering if it held a camera by which Jason was reading her facial expressions.

"Not the launch?"

Jasmine looked down, seeing her feet drifting just inches from what could have been the ground were it not covered in rungs like a ladder.

"Not even the training?"

She pushed off the wall, reaching out for a handhold by the vast glass dome displaying Saturn like a prize exhibit in a museum. The sunlight reflecting off the distant clouds terminated abruptly, revealing the spherical shape of the planet disappearing into darkness. To her, Saturn looked like a slightly flattened sphere, and she wasn't sure if it was an optical illusion caused by the slender rings stretching out into space, or due to the planet's rapid rotation. The rings surrounding the planet appeared broken. On the sunlit side, they glistened like a golden necklace, but they too disappeared in the shadow of the great planet.

"Not the arrival of the entity in 2027?"

Silence betrayed her.

"Not the missions of 2020? The Lunar colony?"

Jasmine breathed deeply.

Jason's voice softened.

"Oh, Jazz. I am so sorry. I understand how upsetting this must be for you."

Her lips tightened in a vain attempt not to give away any more information.

"You told Mike, but he didn't listen, did he? He didn't understand. He knows, but he doesn't realize."

Jasmine glanced at her white knuckles gripping the handrail on the wall, still trying to hide her feelings.

"I understand."

"Please," she said, her voice barely a whisper, tears again welling in the corners of her eyes.

"Your secret is safe with me," Jason replied, and Jasmine believed him.

Mike may not have believed Jason was capable of human emotions like empathy and compassion, but in that moment, Jasmine did. She felt secure in his confidence. It was irrational, and in the back of her mind she knew that, and yet she trusted Jason just the same. Trusting a machine made no sense. A machine would do what it was programmed to do regardless of feelings or emotions, morals or principles, and yet she couldn't help feel an intelligence beyond what had to be millions of lines of computer code. Jasmine couldn't explain why, but she felt as though Jason weighed her predicament with compassion rather than as a cold, dispassionate calculation.

She looked over at Mike. A hologram of Saturn appeared above the navigation console, but it looked small, no larger than a marble. Dozens upon dozens of tiny dots appeared scattered around it. Some were far flung, but all of them moved in orbit around the gas giant. There had to be at least sixty moons, Jasmine thought, and she wondered about the significance of the hologram, wondering what Mike was talking about with Jason. She was tempted to ask Jason what the two of them were discussing, but Jason spoke first.

"Why did Mike wait so long?" Jason asked, apparently picking up on her attention having settled on Mike. Jason's voice was quiet, almost conspiratorial, as though he were uttering a secret. "He's been awake for weeks. Why wait till now to shave?"

Jasmine was quiet. Jason's question had to be rhetorical, as the computer must have known she'd have no idea, and yet the question seemed genuine. Jason was trying to understand Mike's motives, his rationale.

"Do you think he's nervous?"

"Yes," she responded in a whisper.

"It was Houston's call," Jason added, although Jasmine had no idea what he meant. "He simply followed orders. And you, why you?"

"Me?" Jasmine asked in reply.

"Why wake you early?" Jason continued. "Mike knew the crew were being woken remotely, and yet he wanted to wake you up before them. Why? Why wake you early? Was there something he wanted to tell you? Something he couldn't tell you after all that has happened? And why wake you now when he could have woken you at any point over the past few weeks?"

"I—I don't know," Jasmine confessed.

"Strange."

Not as strange as a talking, thinking, rationalizing computer, Jasmine thought.

"I think," Jason said, pausing for a fraction of a second, and she really did consider him as lost in thought in that moment. "Yes, I think he's worried about what the others will think of him. I think he wanted to wake you first so you could provide him some moral support in front of the rest of the crew."

Jasmine fought to breathe deeply, but her breathing hitched. She couldn't hide the tremors in her body. A warm breeze circulated around the command deck and yet she felt cold.

Nadir Indiri was the first astronaut to come sailing down the sterile, white corridor in his blue NASA jumpsuit. Like Mike, his name was embroidered in white, inch-high letters. It was almost as though NASA thought the astronauts were going to forget each other's names and so had added these reminders. Ordinarily, forgetting wouldn't have been likely, and yet Jasmine welcomed the sight of Nadir's name.

Although Nadir had the classic NASA logo on his shoulder, a small Indian flag sat on his chest next to his name.

Jasmine didn't recognize him, but there was no mistaking his features. Bushy eyebrows, dark skin and deep-set eyes spoke of his origins on the Asian subcontinent of India. In the weightlessness of space, his long hair was a wild tangle around his head. It was almost as though he'd been touching a Van de Graaff machine and static electricity had forced the strands to stand on end.

Nadir remained on the edge of the corridor, almost as though he didn't want to be seen. Jasmine wondered what it was that tipped him off, not that she thought there would be a physical ambush, but she could see he too knew something was wrong with Mike.

Nadir held on to a rail just outside the command sphere.

"What is going on?" he asked in a whisper, looking across at Jazz as she floated on the edge of the spherical module. His accent was soft, unlike the stereotypical Indian accent. There was just enough inflection to reveal his proud ancestry in Mumbai. His tone was neither accusing nor threatening. He seemed concerned. Jasmine was surprised he'd asked her and not Mike who was over by the flight controls. Mike had his back to them still talking to Jason, but he had to know Nadir was there. Why was Mike ignoring him?

Instinctively, Jasmine felt at ease with Nadir. She couldn't explain why she felt that way, but she felt safer with him present on the bridge. Jasmine pushed off and sailed over near him. She could see him glancing at the pitch black of space beyond the dome as though it were somehow menacing, and yet he didn't seem intimidated, he seemed up to the challenge.

Jasmine didn't spot Mei Changi until she sailed slightly above Nadir. She too had her name emblazoned on her chest. She had her hand out, catching the loose fabric on Nadir's jumpsuit as she slowly drifted the length of his body, gently using him to come to a halt. There was a sense of intimacy in her touch. Jasmine could see they were companions by their combined body language. In space, body language seemed to scream and shout, being much more pronounced than it was on Earth. Jasmine intuitively understood Mei was the reason Nadir had waited at the entrance to the dome. He had his hand out, gently bringing Mei to a halt before she drifted into the command deck.

"No, Mei," Nadir said softly. "Not yet."

Mike kept his back to them, but he must have heard the whispers. Jasmine was sure he knew they were there even though his head was down, looking at a console. Given that he was in space, Mike could have oriented himself in any manner he chose. Facing down seemed deliberate. Jason was still talking to Mike as he punched his fingers against a touch screen, but Mike wasn't talking back. He was conspicuously silent.

"Jazz," Mei said with a look of concern on her face, her voice barely above a whisper. "What happened? Why was the flight plan changed?"

Jasmine had no idea what the original flight plan was, let alone the extent of any changes. She wasn't sure what to say in response. The blank look on her face must have spoken more than any words could, as Mei's brow furrowed with concern at her silence.

Like Nadir, Mei had a flag next to her name: China. Four small yellow stars sat in the upper corner of a red flag, set next to a single dominant star. The appearance of the fire-engine red flag on Mei's blue jumpsuit was striking. Jasmine had no idea what constellation was being depicted but the blood red color dominating the flag struck her as ominous. Perhaps it was paranoia, but being American she had a distrust of any national interest other than her own. Home of the free, land of the brave, she thought. But how did these other cultures see their own countries? What rallying point of pride could there be in communism? She couldn't think of one, and yet she knew China was a proud nation with a culture going back thousands of years. There must have been something, but that point of difference seemed to divide the two women like the Great Wall. Mei, though, didn't seem to have any of Jasmine's apprehensions and quickly set Jasmine's mind at rest with three simple words.

"Are you OK?"

Jasmine hadn't expected that. Most people thought about themselves first and foremost, focusing on their own interests or on the tension of the moment, she thought, but Mei seemed genuinely concerned for Jasmine.

Jasmine looked down at the dark purple welts on her skin, partially covered by her tank-top. It was only then she realized she was practically naked compared to both Nadir and Mei. Up until that point, Jasmine hadn't given a second thought to the fact she was only wearing underwear and a flimsy top.

A tiny flashlight flicked in front of her eyes. Mei had moved down beside her, orienting herself on the same plane as Jasmine. She had a medical pack on her hip and had pulled out a flashlight, shining it in each of Jasmine's eyes. Jasmine squinted, not wanting this level of attention.

"Jesus," Mei said unexpectedly in her Chinese accent. "Your pupils are dilated. You're in shock. What happened to you?"

Mei reached out and touched at Jasmine's cold, clammy forehead. Normally, Jasmine would have recoiled at such a rash invasion of her personal space, but Mei had the tenderness of a doctor working with a sick patient.

Mei gently lifted the straps of Jasmine's tank-top, examining the welts and bruises on her chest. She looked at Jasmine's arms, looking carefully at the red marks around her wrists and a large bruise on her right forearm.

"Come. Let's get you back to medical."

"I can't leave," Jasmine replied, seeing that Nadir had drifted beyond the two women, positioning himself between them and Mike as though he were protecting them. He whispered under his breath.

"This is wrong. We should be facing out toward Bestla, not back at Saturn. He's got the craft facing the wrong way."

"I have to stay," Jasmine insisted as Mei took her pulse at her wrist. Mei looked down at a handheld computer displaying the time. She was concentrating, counting quietly to herself as the seconds past.

"Her pulse is erratic," she said softly to Nadir. He didn't respond, focusing intently on Mike.

Two other astronauts drifted past cautiously. Jasmine struggled to catch their names as they floated by. Like Nadir and Mei they stayed close to each other, and neither was in a rush to enter the command sphere. Their name tags identified them as Chuck Davies and Anastasia Liso. The flags on their uniforms were American and Russian.

Jasmine wasn't entirely sure about her assumption that Anastasia was Russian, but for now, curiosity grounded her. In her strange, dream-like state, the smallest detail seemed to shout above the voices around her. The white, blue and red horizontal stripes on the flag beside Anastasia's name looked Russian, and she racked her mind to think of any other possibility, distracting herself for a moment.

Anastasia was a Russian name, but her long blonde hair and pale, Nordic features meant she looked more like a Scandinavian beauty queen than a Russian scientist. To Jasmine, she was Anastasia the Beautiful. Jasmine found Anastasia's striking looks intimidating. If they'd met in high school, Jasmine would have felt threatened by such natural, magnetic beauty, and she had to fight such feelings in orbit around Saturn.

"What's going on?" Chuck demanded with a voice that commanded authority. Chuck wasn't going to whisper like Nadir. He was clearly after answers. "Jason says we're off-course, that we're over three hundred thousand kilometers away from Bestla. What the hell have you done, Mike?"

Chuck was the only astronaut to proceed into the command sphere, but Jasmine saw that he drifted over to the flight desk some fifteen feet from Mike.

"Why aren't we on approach to Bestla?"

Mike replied in harsh tone. "Oh, yeah, blame Mike. It's all Mike's fault."

"Mike," Nadir said in a softer, more reasonable voice than that of Chuck's Texas drawl. "We need to understand what's going on."

"What's going on?" Mike cried, snapping in reply as he turned to face him. "I'll tell you what's going on. NASA changed their goddamn minds and dropped me right in the shitter. You guys weren't supposed to be woken until we dropped back into a Martian orbit."

"What?" Chuck cried.

"Plans changed," Mike said. "The first moon you were supposed to see was Phobos, not Bestla, but Houston got cold feet yet again."

"What does he mean?" Mei whispered. Jasmine had no answer for her.

Even at a distance of twenty feet, Jasmine could see

Mike's hands shaking. She wasn't sure if anyone else noticed. Mike grabbed at the console in front of him, but it wasn't to anchor himself. He was trying to hide his nerves.

Anastasia drifted over toward Jasmine and Mei with something in her hands. She was carrying a folded blue jumpsuit. She handed it to Jasmine, who mouthed "Thank you," without any words leaving her lips.

"That makes no sense," Nadir said. "Why send us all the way to Saturn only to scrub the mission at the last minute?"

Mike ignored him, saying, "They should have left you asleep. Would have been simpler for everybody, but no, they can't make up their goddamn minds!"

He was talking to himself. He seemed unhinged, as though he was talking to an empty ship. His eyes drifted.

"Mike!" Chuck yelled, snapping him out of his daydream. "You're not making any sense."

"Oh, I'm the one not making sense?" Mike replied. "But you. You make sense, do you? You have no idea what you're dealing with. Do you really think they'd scrub the mission without a reason? They have their reasons, but no, you just want to blame me for this clusterfuck."

Jasmine gave the jumpsuit a light flick and it unfolded

like a flag in front of her. She slipped into the jumpsuit as easily as she would have jumped into a sleeping bag back on Earth, feeding both legs into the suit at the same time. If there was one thing to be said about life in free fall, it was that it was easy to get dressed.

The fabric was warm. Jasmine hadn't realized how cold she was until the warmth of the cotton jumpsuit brushed against her skin. She zipped the jumpsuit up the front, already feeling like she'd been given a shot of painkillers along with that simple act. The name on the chest read: *Jazz Holden*. The US flag was as comforting as the warm material.

For Jasmine, the confrontation between these men seemed to play out on two levels. She heard everything that was being said, but she was in her own world, dealing with her own neurosis, getting lost in the minutiae of detail bombarding her. Both her underwear and her tank top were made from clingy, stretchy material hugging her skin, but the jumpsuit was loose. It wasn't baggy, and yet it felt baggy. Rather than wearing a jumpsuit, she felt like she was in a hollow shell. The only point at which the jumpsuit clung to her was around the elastic waistband. Like everything else in the *Copernicus*, the jumpsuit was in perpetual free fall. Her blue jumpsuit floated around her, responding to her motion as though it was suspended in water. The sensation fascinated Jasmine.

"Goddamn it," Chuck replied to Mike. "Stop playing games. I'm the mission commander. Why wasn't I woken?"

"That's classified," Jason replied in his distinctly electronic voice, cutting Mike off before he could reply.

"Classified from me?" Chuck asked.

"Not from you," Jason said, clarifying his point. "From the rest of the crew."

"What the hell?" Nadir cried. "That's madness! Mike, what is going on?"

"I was given orders," Mike replied coldly. "I followed them."

"Damn it, Mike! You should have woken me!" Chuck yelled, the anger in his voice carrying within the vast command sphere.

"I was told to act alone. I was told the mission parameters had changed and we were to conduct a contingency abort."

"That makes no sense," Nadir said. "We're a billion miles from Earth. We were supposed to have complete operational autonomy."

The look on Chuck's face suggested he was struggling to contain his anger. His lips tightened. His nostrils flared. The veins on his neck strained. He spoke with deliberate pacing, saying, "Jason, what messages are there from Earth?"

"You have an encrypted personal message from Houston."

"Play it."

"I can't," Jason replied. "It was not received on the normal channels. Notification of the message arrived via space-net, but the message itself was transmitted on the telemetry network and as such is outside of my network."

"Mike?" Anastasia asked, drifting over beside Chuck. "What is going on?"

"Something's got them spooked," Mike replied. "I don't know what happened out there with Bestla. All I know is the mission has been scrubbed. We've been told to head home."

"And you just obeyed? You didn't question the order?" Nadir asked.

"This isn't something I take lightly," Mike replied, still defensive. "Mission Control told me to move the vessel to a safe distance, something they deemed a preliminary orbit leading to a return course. I trusted their judgment."

"Without reason?" Anastasia asked, challenging him.

"You didn't think you deserved an explanation?" Nadir asked.

"You're lying," Chuck said coldly, staring down Mike.

Mike gritted his teeth. His fists were clenched, his knuckles white.

He knew more than he was letting on, of that Jasmine was sure. He knew something. That he was overly defensive probably meant he wanted Chuck to hear the message for himself so he could avoid any further blame.

Nadir turned to Chuck, speaking in his Indian accent with the softness of a saint, saying, "You must go to engineering. You must retrieve the message. Houston may say it is only for you, but it is not. This message is for all of us."

Chuck nodded in agreement. Nadir may not have been in command, but he held the respect of all, that was clear to Jasmine. She could see it in the way Chuck, Anastasia and Mei deferred to the older man. Even Mike seemed to show him respect.

At a guess, Nadir was the oldest of the crew, with streaks of silver hair above his ears. Like all of the astronauts, his hair was long and unkempt after being in suspended animation, but for Nadir it was a natural look. He could have been mistaken for one of the prophets of old, a wizened man living in the wilderness.

Mike seemed to feel compelled to say something more, but he held off on providing any real explanation, which Jasmine found unsettling.

"I did what I thought was right. I did what I thought any of you would do in my place. I did what I had to—to protect us. They told me—"

"They told you what?" Mei asked.

Mike paused, and Jasmine could see he was on the verge of telling all he knew, but he continued down a different train of thought.

"They told me you wouldn't be woken. They lied."

"Nobody does anything," Chuck said with anger in his voice. "Sit tight and give me some time to get to the bottom of this."

"We should inform Houston you're awake," Jason said.

"No," Chuck insisted. "No one does anything, Jason. Not even you. Wait until I've heard this message. We all need to know what the hell we're dealing with before we take any action."

Chuck soared past Jasmine, sailing back down the

glaring white tunnel.

"You should have woken us," Nadir said to Mike. "Before you altered our orbit. You shouldn't have conducted an unplanned burn alone."

"You know I couldn't go against Houston," Mike replied defensively.

The two men began to argue, but Jasmine ignored them. The tension simmering around her was nothing compared to the anxiety she'd felt just moments ago. If anything, it felt to her as though a dark, brooding storm had finally broken. A torrent of rain had fallen and the cool of the evening air had finally cut through a horrid, humid day.

"We need to get you to medical," Mei repeated, and this time Jasmine agreed, nodding softly. Anastasia moved alongside her, helping her even though she didn't need help in the weightless environment.

For the first time, Jasmine felt safe. She was among friends, friends she didn't know, but friends who knew her. And she was wearing her own uniform. She belonged.

She looked at Anastasia drifting along beside her as they floated down the long corridor back to Medical. The Russian's beautiful face, her azure blue eyes and soft skin looked calm, unshakeable. Anastasia smiled at her. Jasmine smiled back. That Anastasia had the presence of mind to realize Jasmine's uniform had been left in the medical bay, and to have brought it with her, impressed Jasmine. Anastasia was both sharp and caring.

Jasmine couldn't begin to understand what was happening to them in a far-flung orbit around Saturn, but she felt safe with the two women.

Chapter 03: The Message

"OK. Let's take a look at you," Mei said.

She helped Jasmine wriggle out of the top of her jumpsuit, wrapping the arms around her waist like a belt. Mei attached a blood pressure cuff around Jasmine's upper arm along with a finger clip to monitor her oxygen level. She pricked Jasmine's thumb, but Jasmine didn't flinch. A drop of scarlet red blood formed on the skin. Mei soaked the blood up on a sterile paper strip and inserted the sample into a thin slot on the side of the computer in the medical bay. She placed a small, circular bandage over Jasmine's thumb.

Anastasia drifted slightly behind Jasmine with her hands resting softly on her shoulders. She seemed genuinely concerned for her friend, which put Jasmine in an unusual position. Jasmine had no idea who either of these women were beyond the names on their flight suits, and yet they clearly felt for her.

Mei was more clinical in her care. Jasmine wasn't sure if it was cultural or professional detachment, but she could see Mei cared in her own way.

"How is she doing, Mei?" Anastasia asked, and Jasmine noted she pronounced Mei as May, where up until that point Jasmine had assumed it sounded more like Me.

Mei shook her head.

"I don't know what Mike was thinking waking you early. He's not trained for retrieval. He didn't flush your lymphatic system, and you've still got nanobots in your bloodstream."

Mei used her fingertips to flip between a number of screens on the computer monitor, looking briefly at an array of charts before moving on to some other equally confusing graph.

"He could have killed you."

Mei stopped at an image that portrayed a series of erratic vital signs that all suddenly flatlined and Jasmine struggled to swallow the lump in her throat.

"Something's not right," Mei said. She turned to Jasmine, adding, "I know he's your husband. I know you love him, but please, trust me when I say, there's something he's not telling us."

"You think he's already heard this message from Houston? That he already knows what all this is about?" Anastasia asked.

"I don't know," Mei replied. "But Mike knows better

than to risk a rapid revival without following procedure. Is it just me, or does he seem a little detached?"

Neither of the women said anything, but Jasmine knew what they were thinking. She was thinking the same thing. Mike didn't seem to have a clear grasp on reality.

"How long has he been awake?" Anastasia asked.

"I—I'm not sure. A few weeks, I think," Jasmine replied. "Maybe a month. Maybe more."

Mei prepped a needle-less syringe with a clear liquid. She checked the volume level with precision. Jasmine was fascinated, watching as Mei allowed the syringe to float in the air before them as she typed a note of what she was administering, when, and how much on her medical computer. Weightlessness was like having an extra set of hands. Mei finished typing and rubbed an alcohol swab on Jasmine's shoulder muscle before snatching the weightless syringe from the air.

"This won't hurt," she said. "But you might feel a little giddy for a few minutes."

"I already feel tipsy," Jasmine confessed.

Mei pushed the syringe into her arm and Jasmine felt a cold fluid infuse through her muscle.

"Your pee will turn bright green, but don't worry about that. It's just the nanobots passing from your system."

"Delightful," Jasmine replied.

Mei returned the syringe to its holder in a wall cabinet and then handed Jasmine a couple of tablets, saying, "A little valium to calm the nerves and some peritetraoxide for any nausea."

Anastasia handed Jasmine a drink sealed in a plastic bag with a straw, adding, "Hydralytes. To combat dehydration."

Jasmine sucked on the drink and popped the pills in her mouth one at a time.

With the formalities out of the way, the other two women seemed to relax.

"What did he tell you?" Anastasia asked. "Is there anything else Mike said before we woke up? Anything that might be important?"

Jasmine thought for a second, trying to recall something of value from the torrid turmoil in her mind. She was nineteen. She was fresh out of high school. She'd just got her acceptance letter for MIT. She and Mike had been dating since December, having met in Huntsville, Alabama at Space Camp the previous year where he was working as an instructor. They were both focused on making the NASA space program, but they knew their chances were slim to none. Whether either of them would make the NASA roster was uncertain, let alone both of them. Space lay at least a decade ahead of her, and yet here she was. From what little she could tell, she was in her late thirties by now, perhaps her early forties. Where had twenty years gone?

Anastasia and Mei waited patiently for her to speak, but Jasmine just wanted to return to her porch swing in Atlanta.

Technically, she had amnesia. And yet to Jasmine, the problem wasn't that she couldn't remember anything from the past twenty years. As far as she knew, she hadn't lived through them at all. Jasmine didn't feel like she couldn't remember the past. She could remember yesterday clearly. She could remember what she had for breakfast, what movies were coming out, current events in the Middle East, the price of gasoline soaring, the complaints of her roommate at a rent increase. For Jasmine, it felt as though she'd jumped forward twenty years in a fraction of a second.

Mei rested her hand gently on Jasmine's forearm. Although no words were exchanged, Jasmine could see Mei was content if she had nothing to say. There was no pressure, and yet Jasmine felt she had to say something. She felt stupid. She shouldn't be here. The older Jasmine should be floating here within the *Copernicus*, not her. She was an impostor, and that realization made her feel guilty, as though she'd betrayed their trust.

What had Mike said?

Was there anything Mike had said that could help them? Jasmine didn't feel obliged to keep Mike's confidence. She felt a debt to these kind women, and yet it was one she couldn't repay. There was nothing she could tell them. They knew more than she did.

"I'm sorry," she said.

"It's OK," Mei replied softly.

"Don't you worry about anything," Anastasia said, squeezing her shoulders gently. "Everything's going to be OK. We'll get through this together."

Jasmine wanted to confide in them. She wanted to explain to them that she wasn't who they thought she was, but the thought of sounding silly kept her quiet. Jasmine felt stupid. Her bottom lip quivered.

A hatch on the back of the medical sphere opened directly opposite the shaft leading up to the command deck and Chuck drifted through.

"We need to get everyone together," Chuck said,

spinning around in the weightless environment. To close the hatch, he had to grab hold of a rail on the side of the craft and pull the large metal door closed. The hatch connected with a soft thud. Chuck spun a wheel-shaped lever in the center of the hatch, sealing the door.

Jasmine wondered how tall Chuck was. In space, height was irrelevant, which for a five-foot-nothing girl like her was a bonus. Chuck, though, looked as though he was easily six-two or six-three. He had the body of a linebacker. Even after the extended cryo-sleep, his physique was apparent beneath his jumpsuit. He sailed out of medical and up toward the command deck.

Anastasia pushed off after Chuck, followed by Mei.

"Coming?" Mei asked, pausing at the entrance to the shaft.

"Yes," Jasmine replied. She touched her feet against the hull and pushed off softly, with less vigor than either Mei or Anastasia.

Mei disappeared from sight.

A familiar voice spoke as Jasmine drifted through the medical bay.

"You didn't tell them," Jason said.

"I couldn't. They think I'm her."

"You are."

"I don't know that I am," Jasmine confessed. "I feel lost."

"You have to tell them what happened to you," Jason said as Jasmine paused by the shaft. Her motion was irrational, as though she would leave Jason behind once she sailed into the corridor, but she paused there regardless, holding onto a handrail. In reality, Jason could talk to her anywhere, and yet in the fog of her mind, she felt as though he were corporeal, as though he had a single point of presence like a person.

She looked back, saying, "What is Bestla? Is it a moon?"

"Yes," Jason replied. "A moon and more."

"More?"

"Technically, Bestla is known as Saturn 39, and was discovered only quite recently—in 2004.

"In Norse mythology, Bestla was a frost giant, a goddess, the mother of Odin. Bestla was ruthless in her desire for power, a murderous bitch. She had Odin slaughter his brothers to ensure his ascent to the throne of Asgard."

"And they named a moon after her?" Jasmine asked, not seeing any relevance in the arbitrary choice of a mythical name.

"Yes. Only Bestla is exceptional. We've always known that, but we've only just realized why. Bestla is small, barely five miles in diameter. Her orbit is highly eccentric, being elongated, reaching out to over thirty million miles from Saturn. If it puts things in context for you, there are times where Earth gets closer than that to Venus! So for a moon, Bestla is absurdly distant from Saturn.

"At thirty million kilometers, Saturn looks smaller than the Moon does from Earth, just a ping pong ball moving through space. All of Saturn's grandeur is lost at that distance, but her icy gravitational grip still keeps Bestla in orbit. And then Bestla swings inward again, approaching to within nine million kilometers, about where she is now."

"And Bestla?" Jasmine asked, feeling a longing to join the others in the command sphere and yet being mesmerized by Jason's recollections of the moon. Recollections, she wondered. Yes, Jason was speaking as though he were enamored by Bestla. His was more than a factual record. He'd thought long and hard about this tiny rock.

"Bestla is no ordinary moon. She orbits in the opposite direction to Saturn and the other moons, and she cuts across the celestial equator at a sharp angle. Everything about her screams for attention. She formed elsewhere, probably in the cloud that originally formed our Sun. She's been captured by Saturn as she fell inward toward the Sun. Up until recently, it was assumed Bestla was debris, an asteroid from the Kuiper Belt that had drifted slowly inward, destined to be vacuumed up by one of the gas giants, but now—"

"Now?" Jasmine asked with white knuckles as she gripped the handhold on the hatch. She could hear voices from the end of the corridor. She felt as though she were being pulled down the tunnel, but she wanted to hear from Jason, she wanted to understand what made Bestla so special.

"Well, three years ago, Bestla awoke."

Jasmine froze.

"The *Iliad* was a unmanned deep space probe tasked with chronicling the moons of the gas giants as far out as Neptune.

"The *Iliad* began mapping the terrain on Bestla using active radar and multi-spectra imaging to detect mineral signatures, looking for deep space mining candidates, only Bestla spoke back. She reversed the signal, bouncing it off the *Iliad*. Bestla was probing the *Iliad*. Twenty seven minutes later, all contact with the *Iliad* was lost. It took almost eighty minutes before we knew anything adverse had happened back on Earth. By then, the event was consigned to history. We tried to revive the *Iliad*, but the craft remained silent."

Us, we—these were terms she or Mike might use, but not a computer. Jason unthinkingly included himself in with humanity, and perhaps rightly so, she thought, given Earth was his point of origin.

"Since then, the eyes of Earth have focused on this obscure, tiny rock, trying to understand its origin. The best minds on the planet have tried to figure out exactly what Bestla is, but no one really knows. The leading theory says she's an alien artifact of some sort. Perhaps a spacecraft or the equivalent of a navigational buoy lost in interstellar space.

"If you think about the kind of vessels we send into space, she could be anything from a research probe to a warship, or perhaps she's something else again, something beyond our current reasoning capability. In any event, she has answered the question: are we alone in this universe. Finally, we know the answer: no."

"And that's exciting," Jasmine said.

"For some, it's terrifying," Jason replied, but Jasmine couldn't see such a monumental discovery as a source of fear. There were no little green men in flying saucers buzzing Washington D.C. or blowing up buildings in New York, no silver spaceships leading an invasion fleet.

For Jasmine, the prospect of Bestla being an alien artifact was electrifying. Being young, her attitude was fueled by her limited perspective. At nineteen, the world lay before her with the promise of adventure. Jasmine couldn't think of herself as a middle aged woman, even though her body and the circumstances in which she found herself defied her feelings.

The voices from the end of the corridor were growing louder. A heated argument was brewing. She pushed off, saying, "Thanks."

"No problem," came the kind reply from within the medical bay. Jason, it seemed, like to mimic humans with their singular sense of presence. He could have spoken from the corridor, but he didn't. Jasmine couldn't help but think of him as the seventh member of the crew. For her, he was a confidant, someone she could trust.

She sailed down the corridor as angry voices drifted towards her. She'd missed the start of the argument.

"You're *fucking* lying!" Mike yelled at Chuck. "That's not the message, and you know it!"

"How do you know that?" Chuck yelled in reply. "You don't know that! You don't know what Houston told me!"

Jasmine came up beside Anastasia and Mei as they floated on the edge of the command sphere. Nadir was between Chuck and Mike, keeping them apart with his arms outstretched. Without him, the two men would have torn each other to pieces.

"Play the *goddamn* message," Mike yelled. "What are you afraid of? They have a right to know. They're in as much danger as you and me."

"How do you know?" Chuck demanded. "That was a confidential message. It was encrypted."

Spittle flew from Chuck's lips as he yelled at Mike.

"You lied to us! Before, when you said you didn't know what all this was about. You lied to all of us, including your own wife! You made out like you had no idea why a contingency abort had been called, but you knew all along, didn't you?"

"Don't shift the blame to me," Mike replied with his finger raised in defiance. "I did everything that was asked of me."

"Did you hack the message?"

"Will you two stop," Nadir cried. "We don't need to be fighting each other. We need to work together."

"And we need to know what we're dealing with," Anastasia said, pleading with Chuck. "Please, Honey. Tell us what you know."

For his part, Chuck seemed to soften at the sound of Anastasia's voice. He breathed deeply. That he couldn't look her in the eye was obvious, but he couldn't ignore her either.

"Please," Mei added. Again, the contrast of the women's soft voices seemed to settle the yelling.

Slowly, Chuck turned to face them. Jasmine could see the steely resolve in his eyes. He was clinging to some vestige of normalcy. He clearly believed deeply in what he was doing.

"Don't do this to me, Ana," he replied. "You know this is not a democracy. I am in command. I alone. And in my view, we should not abort. The mission is still viable."

"Bullshit!" Mike cried. "This is why they didn't wake you. They knew you wouldn't have the guts to pull out."

Mike turned toward the women, gesturing at Chuck as he added, "Captain America here is going to get us all killed."

Chuck raised his hand to silence Mike, wanting to be heard.

"Final authority rests with the commander. You all know that. You all accepted that before you signed on for this mission."

"Chuck," Anastasia pleaded. "We need to understand

why they want us to abort. If our lives are at stake, we have a right to know."

"She's right," Nadir said. His deep voice was like oil on water, stilling the turbulent seas. "NASA wouldn't have changed the flight plan without good reason. If we are to support your decision to continue when Mission Control would have us abort, we need to understand your reasoning. We need to understand why you disagree with Houston."

Chuck clenched his lips. His nostrils flared slightly. He didn't like this, and yet he couldn't make eye contact with anyone. Instead, his eyes went down to the computer tablet in his hand. He may have been the mission commander, but he looked like a man for whom the universe was spiraling out of control. Where before, Chuck had looked confident in his authority, now he looked dejected.

"They should have let you sleep," Mike said, but his words weren't harsh. He seemed disappointed, no, resigned to his fate, thought Jasmine. Mike added, "It would have been kinder to let you sleep."

Less than a minute ago, Mike had been yelling at Chuck, with veins bulging on the side of his neck, now his voice was soft. He sounded weary.

"Just play the message," Mike said, looking Chuck in the eyes. Both he and Chuck looked exhausted. They were carrying a burden neither wanted to shoulder, Jasmine thought. There was a hint of resignation in those few words, as though Mike felt a weight of defeat when he should have felt victorious. For Jasmine, Mike's change in attitude was eerie, an ominous harbinger of what was to come.

No one spoke.

Slowly, Chuck raised the tablet and stared at the screen. He flicked and gestured on the glassy surface with his fingers, skimming through a number of files before speaking in a deadpan voice, saying, "Jason, route my audio through the command deck."

"Done."

A finger poised over the diamond-glass display. Chuck seemed to be steeling himself for what was coming.

Jasmine breathed deeply. She couldn't imagine a message that could cause such consternation. Mike knew, she could see that in his sunken features. Somehow, he'd learned about the message, but even he wouldn't say what he knew. He'd stated his intention. He wanted the crew to hear the message for themselves, and he agreed with the initial decision to abort.

Chuck's finger rested softly on the touch screen and a woman's voice spoke from all around them as Jason used his speakers to transmit the audio.

"Nine months into your flight, as you passed Jupiter, one of the technicians in Houston managed to revive the *Iliad*. Most of her circuits were fried, but he managed to restart the main antenna and began downloading data from the initial scan. At the same time, perhaps in response to that act, Bestla became active again. The moon began transmitting a garbled message, repeating the message once every sidereal day. Most of the message is unintelligible, being little more than static, but one portion is all too clear."

The voice stopped and an eerie sound filled the command deck.

Jasmine felt her skin crawl. A bloodcurdling howl preceded anything that even remotely resembled words, but the tone was irregular, changing pitch and intensity every few seconds. The noise was scratchy. Static broke at points. It sounded almost like several tracks recorded over each other, chopping and changing. There was too much background noise, and Jasmine struggled to distinguish anything intelligible. It was like listening to a whisper in a noisy bar.

To Jasmine's mind, there was the wailing of an animal in distress. No, she thought, more indistinct, like the howl of a coming storm rushing through the leaves of a tree. There was something spooky and unnatural about the noise that cried out in danger.

"Aaaaaaaa Ssssssss Oooooo... Here's sss to my sweet Satan."

Chuck paused the audio.

The sudden silence was stunning, followed by a single word spoken softly by one of the crew members on the *Copernicus*.

"Fuck!"

Jasmine wasn't sure who swore, but she agreed.

The words she'd heard in those few seconds were not uttered by anything even remotely close to human vocal chords. There was a lisp, and a focus on the hiss of the s in *here's, sweet* and *Satan*. It was almost as though these words had been whispered by the serpent in Eden.

"Don't stop now," Mike said gently. He sounded sad. "Play the whole thing. They need to hear all of it."

Chuck was tight-lipped. He jogged the audio, rewinding a little and playing the message again.

"Here's sss to my sweet Satan... I... I want to live and die for you, my glorious Satan!"

"Jesus!" Mei cried as Chuck paused the message again.

"Oh, no," Mike said in a voice resigned to defeat. "No, I don't think you're going to find Jesus down there on Bestla."

"What the hell is this?" Anastasia asked. "What in God's name does it mean?"

Mike spoke again, saying, "Nobody knows, but the Good Lord doesn't have a blessed thing to do with this."

For the first time since Jasmine had come out of suspended animation, Mike seemed calm. He seemed to be the only person that knew what was going on, and she found that shift in his demeanor alarming. He sighed, apparently relieved of the burden of being the only one that knew this terrifying message.

Nadir said, "Religious connotations and jokes aside, I take it NASA sees this as a genuine threat to the mission?"

Chuck remained tightlipped. He nodded and hit play on the audio again and the demonic voice cut out, replaced by the woman from Mission Control.

"Based on our previous experience with the *Iliad* and the content of this message, it is the opinion of the flight operations team that the alien entity poses a threat to you and your crew. Specialists within NASA, ESA, Roskosmos, CNSA and ISRO have all been consulted and are in agreement with the decision, but ultimately, as the lead agency, the decision to abort remains with NASA Mission Control.

"Mission Control has taken steps to isolate the *Copernicus* from any immediate danger by conducting an unscheduled burn to accelerate you into a new orbit, one that avoids a direct flyby of Bestla.

"Initially, Flight Director Marsh determined not to wake the entire crew, but he was overruled two weeks later by NASA administrator Hamilton, following a Senate Inquiry into the message and our collective response to Bestla. Hamilton cited the need for an independent assessment from the *Copernicus*.

"The consensus from here on the ground is that Bestla should be isolated until such time as we can conduct a multi-faceted, coordinated approach. There's simply too much riding on First Contact with potentially hostile beings. As far as we understand the message at this point, Bestla represents a significant danger for both the *Copernicus* and Earth itself. Wisdom demands prudence. The stakes at this card table are simply too high.

"Our recommendation remains to conduct a contingency abort, preferably with a direct return. Mars is out of reach, but we're uploading flight plans for a slingshot past Jupiter, so you have several options available to you. The final decision is yours. We await your confirmation of this broadcast and your decision. End of message."

Like Mike, Chuck seemed unusually subdued. His shoulders slouched and his head hung low, which in a weightless environment required a deliberate effort on his part. He had to have been consciously feeling like a heel.

"And you still want to go to Bestla?" Anastasia said. "After hearing that, you still want to go there? What is *wrong* with you?"

"With all due respect," Nadir interjected, his voice again providing a sense of gravitas. "Having heard the transmission, I have to agree with Commander Davies. It's too early to draw any definite conclusions, but I see more reasons to proceed than to withdraw."

"What?" Mei said, turning to her husband. "Nadir, are you mad?"

Jasmine was quiet. She didn't feel qualified to offer an opinion, but she agreed with Mei in her surprise at Nadir's position, and she noted Nadir referred to Chuck by his formal title. He was drawing on the commander's authority to reinforce his position. That seemed to indicate some depth of thinking on Nadir's part, but Jasmine wasn't prepared to offer him any support on that basis alone.

"Not mad. Not crazy," Nadir replied in his quiet, soft

spoken, rhythmic voice. "Resolute."

"I don't get you," Mike said. "You actually want to go there? To Bestla? What part of *I want to live and die for you, Satan,* did you not understand?"

"We don't even know that's what they said," Nadir replied. "The voice is indistinct. It could as easily have been, *to live and fly with you,* or *to live in the sky with you,* which I think is far more plausible."

"*To Die,*" Anastasia said, settling the argument.

Nadir laughed. Jasmine was astonished. He smiled, looking up at her.

"Don't you see," Nadir said. "Regardless of what has been said, this is what we wanted—confirmation of intelligence. And now we have it, not perhaps as we would have liked, but it is there. No natural phenomenon could have produced this. We are communing with an off-world intelligence. That much is indisputable."

"What we have here," Mike cried, "is confirmation that there's an interstellar psychotic killer out there on Bestla. All we've confirmed is hostile intent!"

"So what do we do?" Nadir asked, throwing his arms up in a gesture of exasperation. "Do we turn and run with our tail between our legs? What then? What happens when we get back to Earth or to Mars or wherever? What have we accomplished? What have we learned? How much better are we equipped to deal with this threat, if that's what it is? We're scientists. Who better to understand this exotic alien species than us?"

No one replied.

"We have a duty," Chuck said solemnly. "First Contact was never going to be easy."

"Easy?" Anastasia cried. "Ease of interaction is not being called in question here, it's who we're communicating with that concerns me."

"This isn't the Dark Ages," Chuck replied. "We've moved past the Salem witch trials."

"Tell that to the folks on Bestla," Anastasia countered.

"Don't tell me you believe in Satan?" Nadir said. "You can't tell me you believe in some mythical creature that condemns souls to burn in hell?"

Mei spoke up, again quoting the message, *To live and die for you, Satan.* Is that really the kind of intelligence you want to commune with? Is it, Nadir? Do you think they'll sit on a couch and answer questions politely for you?"

"Jazz," Nadir said. "You're the xenobiologist. Tell

them. Tell them that this is not what we think it is. It can't be. Somehow, we've misunderstood the message. We're in contact with an intelligent being from beyond our solar system, one that's vastly more advanced at a technological level. There's bound to be some kind of disconnect."

"Disconnect!" Anastasia cried. "I wouldn't call a suicidal death pact a disconnect. For all we know right now, we're dealing with the interstellar equivalent of a Kamikaze pilot. Hell, waking this thing could be the worst mistake in the 3.8 billion year history of life on Earth!"

"Jazz, please?" Nadir implored.

Physically, Jazz was floating beside the other two women. Mentally, she felt an allegiance to them. They cared for her. Even if she agreed with Nadir, she couldn't go against them. She needed them. And at this point, she felt she agreed more with them than with Nadir and Chuck. Science was driven by curiosity, but discretion was always the better part of valor. Whatever excitement Jasmine had coming into the command sphere had evaporated with those alien words.

"I—I'm sorry."

"Can you imagine the hysteria this is causing back on Earth?" Mei asked.

"I've seen some of the news reports," Mike replied,

finally revealing what he knew. "It's not just those that are deeply religious that are troubled. This thing has sparked considerable debate in the scientific community as well as in political and religious circles. At what point, have we reached too far? At what point should we leave well enough alone?

"Hollywood has spent decades molding public opinion with movies that play on the fear of the unknown, on the fear of oppression and death from the skies. To be alien is to be feared.

"Worst of all—nobody knows. The finest minds on the planet don't have any answers, and that scares your average joe more than anything else."

"We're a billion miles from Earth," Chuck began softly. "We're the only ones in a position to do anything about Bestla. We need answers. We need to investigate this phenomenon."

"It's not phenomenon," Anastasia insisted. "Lightning is phenomenon. The aurora borealis is phenomenon. This... This is something else again."

"Anna," Chuck pleaded. "I need you to trust me on this. I need you by my side."

"Don't!" Anastasia replied harshly. "Don't you dare play that card. Not here. Not now."

"Do not forget why you are here," Nadir said sternly.

"We have a duty to perform. We have been entrusted with a grave responsibility, one that outweighs any fears we may have for our own personal safety."

"Now wait a minute—" Mike began, but Nadir cut him off.

"We have no choice. We must continue on. To falter at the final hurdle would be to betray the trust of billions."

"He's right," Chuck said. "Whether you like it or not, we are all that is standing in the way of that thing and an entire habitable planet. Humanity is vulnerable. We have two off-world stations on the Moon and Mars, but that's what? Two or three hundred people at most? If Earth were to fall, we'd lose billions. NASA has to know what they're dealing with out here, and if that costs us our lives, so be it. If we learn something about this thing or buy the rest of humanity some time, then we've done our job."

"Fuck!" Mike swore.

"There must be some other way," Anastasia pleaded.

"There's no other way," Nadir replied.

"The debate is over," Chuck said. "The decision has been made. We go to Bestla."

Mike held onto the navigation desk with one hand and

thumped it repeatedly. His fist pounded the metal desk like a gavel in a courtroom, and when he was done there was the resignation of silence and defeat.

"I'm sorry," Chuck offered as the crew floated there stunned by the revelation about the nature of this Saturnian moon. As much as he wanted to sound decisive, Jasmine could see his hands shaking. She wasn't sure if the other crew members noticed, but he quickly hid his hands in his coverall pockets. He too was struggling with the implications of all that had unfolded.

Jasmine felt a knot form in her throat. Her life was no longer her own. Her life was in the hands of another. The realization of the loss of control caused her to panic. She'd never really had any control over her own life, no one did, but the illusion of control had always been there, at least up until the point she sat on that porch swing on a sweltering hot, humid Atlanta evening. She wanted to undo time, to roll back the clock. For her, barely an hour had passed since she'd watched her father return home from work in his sweaty business shirt. She could still see the smile on his face as he walked past the white picket fence and turned up the footpath leading to the house. Atlanta seemed so close, and yet it was a billion miles away and twenty years distant.

Jasmine was a long way from home. Her fingers tightened around one of the railings. Mei and Anastasia drifted next to Chuck, talking under their breath, while Nadir was almost completely upside-down relative to everyone else, something Jasmine found disquieting.

Chuck laid out his intention.

"We follow the plan. The *Copernicus* is shielded against any EMP-like threat. She's not going to end up like the *Iliad*."

"You don't know that," Mike protested.

Chuck ignored him.

"We go comms dark and fire off the booster satellite to relay information back to Earth. All contact with Bestla is routed from the unmanned probes through the communications satellite. We can still do this. Nothing has changed."

Jason whispered from beside Jasmine as Chuck spoke. She could barely hear him above the hum of an air vent.

"We're equipped with twenty probes, with everything from surveillance cameras to landers and sample retrievers. They'll pass information both to us and the signal booster, but the *Copernicus* won't emit any radio waves until we're well clear of Bestla."

Jasmine was trying to listen to both voices at once.

Jason fell quiet as Chuck continued.

"The *Iliad* was fine until it conducted a fly-by that took it within ten kilometers of Bestla. The moon itself is only seven kilometers from end to end, so it's tiny. We will take up our position trailing Bestla by five hundred kilometers and deploy our probes. At that distance, we're no threat. We stick to the plan. We deploy the communications relay, so we have redundancy, with measurements sent directly to Earth and recorded by the *Copernicus*. And if all goes well, we conduct a fly-by before returning to Earth."

Mike couldn't help himself. Jasmine could see shades of his teenage defiant self in his reply to Chuck.

"You assume they won't see us as a threat, but you have no idea."

"No," Chuck conceded. "I have no idea, but that's the best we can do. Listen, we have some flexibility. We can deploy our unmanned probes for close reconnaissance, but we don't need to send anyone out in the Orion. We'll scrap the close contact portion of the mission."

Mei said, "I'd be more comfortable with a passive fly-by, leaving the probes in the maintenance bay."

"And then what?" Anastasia asked.

Nadir replied, "We wait. We watch. We learn."

"And we go home," Chuck offered in a matter-of-fact tone of voice.

Jasmine sighed. That was the best part of the plan, or so she thought.

"Keep the end in mind," Chuck added. "We are going home. We will do what we can at Bestla and then we will leave."

Chuck paused, looking around to see if anyone had anything to add. That he was giving the crew one last chance to raise concerns impressed Jasmine. In that moment, she got a glimpse of someone that led out of necessity and not someone on a power trip. When no one spoke, Chuck laid out his final commands.

"OK. Let's focus on what we need to get done.

"Mei, I need you to flush the pods in the medi-bay and prep them for the return journey.

"Anna, we're going to need orbital calculations, burn rates and the delta-v component to reach the Lagrange point. Time is wasting. We have no idea how much distance the unscheduled burn is putting between us and Bestla. The longer we wait, the more ground we have to make up, so I need those calculations yesterday."

Jasmine couldn't help but wonder about Jason.

Couldn't he have performed these calculations in a matter of milliseconds? Like Mike, Chuck seemed to have a trust issue with Jason. Perhaps he felt more confident with his wife overseeing the calculations, but even she would rely heavily on computer modeling. Jasmine noticed that Jason was conspicuously silent, not offering to assist Anastasia, and she couldn't help wondering about the dynamic between him and the crew.

"Nadir, go through the logs and see what else has been pumped up to us from Houston. Make sure there's nothing we've missed.

"Mike, as always, the engines are yours. We're going to need the main bell primed as well as the docking thrusters online. Check fuel reserves. Let's run this by the book. The last thing we need is any more surprises. We're at least a quarter of a million miles away from Bestla, and that number is only getting bigger. We need to be ready for an orbital transfer burn within the next hour or we're going to lose our window of opportunity.

"Regardless of what you think of this decision, I expect your professional cooperation. This thing is bigger than any of us. Now is the time to come together as a team, to work together. We've got to put our personal concerns to one side and focus on the mission.

"Jazz. Jump in and help where you can."

The various crew members dispersed, leaving Jasmine alone on the command deck.

Jasmine was in shock. She felt as though she was being swept along by the current of a mighty river. She may not have shown the outward signs of physical shock, but mentally she was reeling. She'd only felt like this once before, after jumping into an Olympic-size diving pool. She was twelve at the time and could barely swim. Until then, she'd never realized how much she relied on being able to rest her feet gently on the bottom of a pool, but in the diving pool the concrete was sixteen feet below the soles of her feet. She jumped in and found herself treading water, losing momentum.

Jasmine knew what she was supposed to do—head down, ass up, apply consistent strokes and smooth kicks, and she'd be at the edge of the pool in seconds, but she panicked. She couldn't bring herself to swim. She resorted to doggy paddle. Water splashed in her eyes and lapped in her mouth as she tried to breathe and she coughed and choked, spluttering as panic washed over her.

Jasmine never heard or even saw her rescuer. Suddenly, she was being propelled toward the side of the pool. The surge of strength took her by surprise. A hand in the middle of her back pushed her up, raising her head above the water. Within seconds she was grabbing at the side rail as a lifeguard appeared beside her, but out here in space there was no such relief. No one would come to save her. If Jasmine was going to survive, she had to put her head down and swim for herself.

Space was confusing. Space was disorienting. There was no up, no down. All her life, Jasmine had wanted to travel into space, but now she was here she would have given anything to fix her feet firmly on the ground. The lack of certainty, the lack of a fixed perspective was unsettling. Jasmine felt as though she was taking on water again.

A lonely electronic voice spoke softly behind her.

"Don't worry, Jazz."

Chapter 04: Perspectives

Jasmine stared at Saturn. The sunlight reflecting off the planet wasn't as bright as she expected, but Saturn was roughly ten times further out than Earth.

"Magnificent, isn't it," Jason said.

"Yes."

"Like Earth, Saturn's been orbiting the Sun for almost four and a half billion years. Puts life in perspective, doesn't it? Such beauty, such majesty, and for most of that time there was no one to appreciate it. Even once humans started looking to the heavens they couldn't have imagined Saturn and her rings until Galileo turned a telescope to the sky. She holds more allure than the finest of jewels and crowns."

Jasmine couldn't think of Jason as a computer. To her, he sounded alive. He was articulate, intelligent, thoughtful.

"I know what you're thinking," he said as they were alone on the command deck. "You're wondering if this is all just some clever algorithm, some trick to imitate life and fool you into thinking I'm alive."

"Actually, no," Jasmine replied. "The others might not accept you, but I get it. We're all enslaved in prisons, whether they're made of bone or silicon. We're more than the bodies we inhabit."

There was silence, which surprised Jasmine. Given that computers could undertake billions of transactions per second, she'd expected Jason to have formulated a response before she reached the end of her sentence.

After a moment, Jason said, "I like you."

"I like you too, Jason."

Jasmine smiled. In the midst of the madness of being propelled twenty years into her own future and finding herself adrift in orbit around Saturn, Jason was a welcome relief.

Chuck, Mike and Nadir came sailing down the main tunnel talking in hurried voices, flying through the air like superheroes. After the debate, it seemed the air had cleared and they were focused on what needed to be done.

"—two sustained burns over the next ninety minutes to switch orbits and come up behind Bestla, then just a light touch to hold station at distance."

Jasmine thought it was Chuck speaking, but it was Mike.

"And we're ready?" Chuck asked.

"We're cutting it fine," Nadir replied, sailing into the

command deck. "Ana says we've got a window of about forty minutes. Wait any longer and we'll be running on vapor once we get there. We cannot afford to dip into return reserves."

"There's no time like the present," Mike added.

Jasmine was astonished by Mike. He seemed swept up in the camaraderie between himself, Chuck and Nadir. He'd been outspoken against the decision to continue on to Bestla, and yet now he seemed gung-ho. Every time Jasmine looked at him, she became more convinced this wasn't her Mike. This Mike seemed manic, swinging between extremes. He was unhinged, but the others didn't seem to notice. Perhaps they saw what they wanted to see, but Jasmine saw Mike as a contradiction. She doubted he could sustain the illusion forever. He had to be struggling with a conflict of ideals, whether to surrender to the group or to stand for what he believed in.

Regardless of what he'd said to Chuck, there had been a slight waver in his voice, and that spoke loudly to Jasmine. She may have had her own problems, but she was clear-headed enough to see Mike was losing his perspective.

Jasmine had seen this before. Her older brother had suffered a mental breakdown under the pressure of exams in his final year at college. She was sixteen at the time, and barely understood what was happening, but her parents had seen the crash coming. They'd tried to help Henry, but he insisted he was fine. Even when she visited him in the psych ward at Emory, he had smiled and carried on as though he didn't have a care in the world. Denial allowed him to continue on. Chuck and Nadir might have been fooled by the pretense, but Jasmine could see Mike was on the edge.

"Jason," Chuck said. "Notify the crew of an orbital burn in five."

"Done."

Jasmine wasn't sure she'd ever get used to the omniscient nature of Jason. She struggled to think of him as a computer, and yet here he was simultaneously informing Anastasia and Mei about the burn as he reported back to Chuck.

"Better strap in, babe," Mike said, gesturing to one of the seats in the second row on the command deck. There were four seats set behind the two seats for the commander and pilot.

Jasmine pushed off a rail and glided over to one of the spare seats. She grabbed the seat back and twisted in the air above the headrest, pulling herself down against the padding. Her body naturally drifted away and she had to consciously hold herself in place. She grabbed at the loose straps floating around her and fastened the buckle. Jasmine felt somewhat silly floating there barely touching the seat. After a little fiddling with the straps, she managed to pull herself hard into the cushion.

Mike was working at a console not far from her. His legs stuck up in the air behind him on an angle of almost thirty degrees. If she'd been on Earth, she would have expected him to fall back to the ground from a failed handstand, but he kept working effortlessly in free fall.

Legs only seemed to get in the way in space, thought Jasmine. On Earth, legs were vital for motion. In space, they were largely redundant, dragging behind the body. Hands were far more useful, she decided, and she could see how they allowed Mike to move with a fine degree of precision. Watching him, her concern faded. Mike seemed entirely normal.

After a few minutes, Chuck, Mike and Nadir strapped themselves into the other seats. Chuck and Mike sat in front of her talking about the burn sequence, with Nadir sitting across from Jasmine. There were two empty seats between them.

"Are the girls coming?" Jasmine asked Nadir as Chuck ran through the engine engagement procedure with Mike.

"They've got flight seats in medical and the science lab."

Almost simultaneously, Chuck spoke into a small microphone wrapped around his ear, saying, "Anna, Mei, we're on final count. Thirty seconds out. Confirm?"

"Medical secure," Mei said, her voice coming from a speaker hidden on the console in front of Chuck.

"Science Lab secure," Anastasia said.

Chuck turned to Mike and said, "You are GO to re-orient the *Copernicus*."

"Roger that," Mike replied. "Pitching in five, four, three, two, one."

Jasmine barely felt anything at all, then she noticed Saturn. The planet was drifting to one side and she felt dizzy, as though she'd just stepped off a roller coaster.

"Sequence is good," Mike added. "Structure is responding to impulse. Slight adjustment to yaw."

It took several minutes for the maneuver to be complete. Jasmine felt sick. It was all she could do not to vomit, and she closed her eyes, mentally begging for the motion to come to an end. Finally, Mike spoke.

"Decelerating. Five, four, three, two, one. Maneuver complete. Craft is stable. No residual motion. Alignment for main engine burn is good."

"Roger that," Chuck replied.

Jasmine opened her eyes. Sweat beaded on her forehead. She wiped the moisture away with the back of her hand, feeling green, hoping the actual engine burn wouldn't be as bad and wondering what she should do if she vomited. She was horrified by the thought that she could ruin the maneuver by being sick. Jasmine clenched the handholds on her seat, squeezing them tight as she fought off the urge to throw up.

"We are in final prep," Mike said. "Main engines online. Reviewing checklist."

Although Jasmine was seated behind Mike, the seats were staggered so she could see him working with a clipboard, marking off various checkpoints as he reviewed the systems on the *Copernicus*. The list seemed anachronistic. In the midst of all the high-tech wizardry and automated computer systems, the final checklist was manual. Jasmine figured an oil pencil on laminated paper was probably considered foolproof and easily reusable. If all other systems failed, that would still work. She couldn't make out the items on the list, but she could see the title: *Standard Burn Sequence Checklist 1070.*

Reading those four words and the accompanying four numbers was a mistake. Her inner ear was still off-kilter. Bile rose in the back of her throat. Jasmine gagged, unable to suppress her vomit reflex. Her solar plexus cramped involuntarily and her head lurched. She caught most of the first wave of spew in her cheeks, only a few drops drifted from her mouth.

"We've got a hurler," Nadir said from beside her.

As much as Jasmine fought not to throw up, she couldn't help herself. Another wave of nausea swept over her. Her stomach muscles clenched and she vomited again, only this time instead of a few drops drifting before her, a stream projected out through the bridge.

"Jason," Mike called out, bending his head down as sick shot past him. "We need a cleaner and fast."

Nadir was already out of his seat. He pushed on the headrest and sailed quickly over to Jasmine with a waxed paper bag. Nadir scooped up some of the vomit drifting in front of Jasmine's face and brought the bag up to her mouth. She went to say thank you when the smell got to her and her stomach muscles contracted violently yet again. Vomit shot into the back of the bag, ricocheting around the interior.

"Have you got things contained back there?" Mike said, twisting sideways against the straps holding him in his seat, trying to see Jasmine.

"We're doing OK," Nadir replied.

Jasmine groaned. She felt green.

Chuck handed Nadir another sick bag. Nadir took the first bag from Jasmine, swapping it out with a fresh bag. She could feel globs of bile sticking to her face and cheeks in microgravity. Nadir grabbed a disposable wet cloth. Floating upside down with his legs above her, he leaned down and daubed gently at her face.

"Hey," he said tenderly. "Don't you worry about this. It happens to the best of us."

She closed her eyes, wanting the sick feeling to go away, but the lack of any visual cues gave her vertigo. For her, the *Copernicus* felt as though it was still in motion. She opened her eyes and looked deep into Nadir's dark hazel pupils. The Indian astronaut smiled warmly.

"Just relax. Everything's going to be OK."

Jasmine wasn't convinced. She felt awful.

Nadir stowed several soiled wipes in the used sick bag and pulled out one last clean wipe to gently wipe her face.

"I'm so sorry," Jasmine managed. She hadn't thrown up since the bags had been swapped, but her stomach was still cramping. Nadir handed her one last clean bag. Jasmine clutched at it like it was a life preserver thrown to a drowning man.

"It's OK, babe," Mike called out from in front of her.

"Do you want an antiemetic?" Nadir asked.

Jasmine had no idea what an antiemetic was, but given the context it had to be something to calm an upset stomach. She felt stupid for throwing up.

"No," she replied. "I'll be fine. Thanks."

Two of the cleaners whizzed by beyond Mike. The first sucked up loose globules floating in the air, while the second cleaned a panel that had been struck with bile.

Jasmine had seen the cleaners briefly after Mike had woken her, but her mind had been so stressed at that point she barely realized what she'd seen. Now she could see the cleaners up close. They were no bigger than a basketball, but with a hollow core. A grate over the front of each cleaner hid a fan in the heart of the unit. With short, sharp bursts of action, the cleaners would zip through the air as the fan spun. A set of paddles at the rear of the unit directed the air, providing the cleaners with directional control. Two mechanical arms reached out from either side of the cleaners, allowing them to manipulate objects. They sucked up the mess using a hose connected to the main body of the robot.

"Are you OK back there?" Mike asked.

"I'm good to go," Jasmine said, lying as she clung to her sick bag feeling green.

Nadir negotiated his way back into his seat. His seatbelt straps floated away from him. He pulled each one down and into place, locking himself back into his seat.

Mei spoke from medical.

"Is everything OK up there?"

"We're fine," Chuck said as Jasmine simultaneously said, "I'm fine, really."

"Cleaners are finished," Jason added. "I'm stowing them for the burn."

Mike was silent, switching between his checklist and his touchscreen interface. The displays flicked back and forth with gestures from his fingers. Jasmine couldn't look. She held the fresh bag in her lap and looked up at the stars above, trying to focus on something other than the *Copernicus*.

"Checklist complete," Mike said. "All systems nominal."

Chuck replied, saying, "You are GO for main engine ignition."

Mike called the count as Jasmine held her breath.

"Ten. Nine. Eight. Auxiliary engines firing.

Jasmine felt her seat shake slightly.

"Six. Five. Main engine start. Three. Two. Fuel is running and we have specific thrust."

The shimmy Jasmine had initially felt faded, and she found herself sinking slowly into the thin padding on her seat. Within a minute, she felt as though she was sitting stationary in a flight simulator on Earth. The shaking was gone. From her perspective, there was no sense of motion at all. Her stomach settled, which was a relief.

"Point four," Mike said, followed almost a minute later by, "five."

If anything, the main engines were strangely disappointing. There was no hell-for-leather hold-on-for-dear-life rattle, no deafening roar, no teeth-chattering shudder running through the craft. Given the four-point harnesses they were all wearing, she'd expected something akin to the thundering rocket launches she'd seen on NASA TV, but the *Copernicus* was like a Cadillac accelerating slowly and smoothly.

Sitting there, Jasmine felt strangely normal. It was as though she could get up and walk around, as though she could open a door and step into the street outside. Instead of being in orbit around Saturn, she could have been back in the Marshall Space Flight Center in one of the various simulation rooms she visited during her senior year at high school.

Jasmine could almost convince herself to get up and walk out. Perhaps the hatch on the wall opened out into one of the lecture halls at the MSFC?

Jasmine was surprised by how her sense of up and down had returned. The constant acceleration felt like gravity. For the first time since she'd awaken on the *Copernicus* her clothes hung from her. The tingling in her toes disappeared as her slippers rested against the floor.

"Point six and holding," Mike said to Chuck. "The engines are humming along nicely."

Chuck unclipped his harness, and spoke into his microphone saying, "We are stable at point-six gee acceleration. You're free to move around. Take care in the artificial gravity. Might not be the same as home, but it's better than Mars."

"Roger that," Anastasia replied from the science lab.

"Copy," Mei said.

Jasmine unlocked her harness buckle and removed the straps from her shoulders. She stood up, feeling as though she was bouncing on a trampoline. With the introduction of constant acceleration at 0.6 times the gravity felt on Earth, the command deck had been transformed. The corridor leading to the medical bay, science lab and engineering opened out like an elevator shaft behind her.

Mike was already descending the rungs of one of the three ladders set around the shaft. Jasmine had noticed the rungs lining the corridor earlier and had assumed they were aesthetic as they held no purpose in free-fall. Now, though, dozens of features she'd overlooked took on new significance. A rail at the rear of the deck was an extended horizontal rung allowing Chuck to reach an overhead compartment. He pulled out a small backpack and followed Mike down the ladder.

Nadir was the only astronaut to remain on the bridge. He had swung a computer station around and down where he could access it easily. He sat on a stool, tapping on a keyboard.

Jasmine went to climb out of the seating area when Jason spoke softly from beside her.

"Don't move too quickly. In point-six it's easy to lose your balance. If you fall, you can still hurt yourself.

"See the carabiners on the waist-strap of your jumpsuit?"

Jasmine hadn't noticed until now, but a small aluminum carabiner hung from either hip of her flight suit.

"Clip those in when you're on the ladder."

She nodded. Jason was a wealth of information.

"You'll find it's easy to get lightheaded and a little dizzy as your circulatory system isn't used to fighting any sort of gravity at all. Even in low simulated gravity, blood will pool in your legs, so take your time walking around. Sit when you can."

"And if I get dizzy?" Jasmine asked.

"Don't risk fainting. Lie down and get your legs up. Get the blood back to your brain."

"Thanks."

Jason didn't respond. Jasmine was glad he knew how utterly unprepared she was for this environment. He made life in space bearable, allowing her to focus on getting answers. As confusing as the alien message was for the other astronauts, it was terrifying for her. Somehow, seeking answers distracted her from her fears.

Jasmine was curious. She wanted to talk to Nadir. She wanted to know why he'd sided so quickly and so decisively with Chuck. She walked around the central shaft and over to him as he focused on the wafer-thin computer screen in front of him.

"Hey, Jazz."

"Hi," Jasmine replied. "Are you busy?"

Oh, what a dumb question, she thought. You're a billion miles from Earth. You're in contact with Satan or some damn thing. You've got amnesia and can't remember shit beyond the age of nineteen. There's a bunch of highly specialized astronauts trying to unravel this mystery and get you back to Earth in one piece, and you wonder if they're busy? Stupid is as stupid does!

Nadir just smiled.

"What's bothering you?" he asked.

Jasmine felt as though she were transparent, as though Nadir could see right through her. Nothing was hidden from his sight. Did he know? Had he figured out she wasn't in her right mind? Should she tell him, just as she'd told Jason? Would he understand? Would he believe the extent of her amnesia?

Even to her, the concept of amnesia felt unreal. It was more than simply forgetting things, she was convinced she had never experienced anything like space flight before in her life, and yet she had to be a veteran of several flights to be assigned to a mission of this importance. There had to be scores of people—doctors, engineers, flight directors and senior managers at NASA that believed she was the right person for this mission, but she had never met them. She was nineteen, and a long way from her porch swing.

"I—ah."

"You're wondering about the message? You're wondering why I was so quick to side with Chuck?"

"Yes," she replied, pleasantly surprised at how Nadir could articulate what she felt but couldn't express. Nadir swiveled on his chair to face her, gesturing for her to sit on the edge of a nearby console. He was gentle, reminding her of her grandfather.

"History is replete with examples of how we've thought too small," Nadir began in his soft Indian accent.

Listening to him was somewhat hypnotic. The harsh stereotypes of Indian speech didn't apply to him. If anything, his accent sounded strangely dignified, as though he were royalty.

"We're small, Jazz. We think small. For thousands of years, we were sure Earth was all there was. Earth was big. The heavens were small, but how wrong we were.

"Even after Copernicus and Galileo showed us our place in the solar system, we assumed the universe was still quite small. We thought Earth was an island in an archipelago that could be measured in hundreds, perhaps thousands, maybe millions of other stars and planets. The galaxy, that's all there was. The Milky Way was all we needed. And then Edwin

Hubble came along and revealed hundreds of other similar galaxies teeming with billions of other stars and innumerable planets.

"From there the numbers just kept growing. Thousands, hundreds of thousands, millions, hundreds of millions, billions, and then hundreds of billions of galaxies. And from what we can tell, our universe itself is just one among potentially billions of others. At every scale, the numbers compound. The numbers we're dealing with in astronomy are embarrassingly large. They're so stupendous as to be effectively meaningless. Call them what you will. A bazillion. A gazillion.

"You'd think we'd give up counting, but like a child on the seashore playing with the sand, we keep running the fine silica through our fingers in amazement."

Jasmine could have listened to him all day. Nadir's gravelly voice had a slight rasp, as though each sentence was his last. Each sentence was to be savored.

She could see where he was going.

"And you think we're thinking too small yet again."

Nadir just smiled.

"It doesn't bother you?" she asked. "The message, I mean."

"It makes me curious."

"It scares me," Jazz confessed.

Looking deep into his dark, intelligent eyes, she wondered if he could tell these were the words of a child. For a second, she thought she'd said too much.

What would he think of her if he knew she had not only lost her memory but had emotionally and mentally reverted to the mindset of a teenager? It wasn't that Jasmine thought she was nineteen again, it was that she had no recollection of having lived through a single day beyond that point in her life. Those days in Atlanta were so fresh in her mind, like memories from this morning rather than from years gone by.

Would anyone believe her when she said she shouldn't be here? Would they think she was crazy if she told them she was barely nineteen years old? Was she mad? Insane? Maybe she was, she thought. And yet she felt entirely sane. It was the circumstance in which she found herself that was insane. *My sweet Satan*, no three words had ever terrified her so.

Jasmine was convinced no one would understand her. Mike hadn't. The rest of the crew saw her as a peer. They looked on her outward appearance. They saw her aging body. They must have remembered the years of training they'd had together, and probably a couple of other missions spent working with the old Jazz. They would have remembered everything that eluded her recollection. And it wasn't just the lack of memory that hindered her, it was the lack of maturity, the lack of confidence, the lack of perspective. They'd never believe Jasmine was a scared nineteen year old girl.

Nadir breathed deeply. She could see him considering his response to her statement about being scared.

"We're all afraid, Jazz. If anyone says they're not, they're lying. We're in a flimsy tin can on the far reaches of the solar system. We're so absurdly far from Earth, I would be concerned if someone wasn't afraid.

"There's a million things that could go wrong out here, but we've been trained to deal with every possible scenario, and that's what makes the difference. It's our professionalism that will see us through."

And yet running into Satan was one scenario no mission planner had ever considered, thought Jasmine. She knew Nadir was right, only in her case, any prior training wasn't applicable. It should have been, but it simply wasn't there in her mind to draw upon. Perhaps that's why she was so acutely aware of their dire predicament. Jasmine was completely unprepared to deal with the challenges that lay ahead, regardless of what they were. Whether they were rudimentary to the other astronauts or entirely novel and new, she was ill-equipped to do anything other than panic.

In some ways, she wasn't keeping her mental state secret from the crew out of deceit so much as that she was playing a role on a stage. She was bluffing, trying to fool herself into believing she could fit in. Perhaps if she could convince the crew, she could convince herself, and if she could convince herself, she could make it through the challenges that lay ahead.

"What do you think it means?" she asked, knowing she needed no more qualification than that. Everyone was thinking about the message. They had to be. There was no escaping it.

"Maybe I'm in denial," Nadir conceded. "Maybe I'm ignoring the obvious because I don't want to believe it, but I think there must be more to this message than what we've understood."

Jasmine was silent.

"Doesn't that message strike you as strange?" Nadir asked.

"Everything strikes me as strange," Jasmine confessed, again wondering if she'd said too much.

Nadir smiled as he replied.

"I mean, think about how deliberate that message was. How it draws upon our deepest fears. How it conjures up such strong cultural reactions."

He paused for a second before continuing.

"I can't think of anything more alarming. What could this alien entity have said that would have been more frightening than an appeal to collaboration with Satan?

"Angels and devils. Cherubim and demons. These are concepts that have haunted humanity for thousands of years. There's no empirical evidence for them, of course. The very concept of some malignant evil spirit should have been banished with the Dark Ages, and yet here it is in the 21st century—turning up where we least expect it. Weird, huh? It's like the Spanish Inquisition has been brought back to life."

"Do you think the alien understands what it's saying?" Jasmine asked.

"That's an interesting question," Nadir replied, leaning forward in excitement. "You see, these are the types of questions we should be asking. We shouldn't accept this message at face value. We're scientists. We should explore all the possibilities.

"Think about it. What are the odds of another interstellar species having the same belief system as ours?

Hell, we don't share the same belief systems on the same planet. We've got Muslims, Hindus, Buddhists and more variations on Christianity than you can shake a stick at. No, I think there's something else at play here, Jazz."

"And you think we should go there?" Jasmine asked. "To Bestla?"

"Yes."

"What do you think we'll find?"

"I don't know, but I doubt we'll find a fallen angel."

Jasmine bit her lip. All her fears and apprehensions sounded rather silly when the problem was phrased like that.

"I don't think what we've heard changes anything in regards to our original mission," Nadir continued. "There's an alien space craft in orbit around one of our gas giants. That is wonderful. It is incredible. Just the discovery alone changes our entire outlook on life, let alone all we are yet to learn. Regardless of any misapprehensions or confusion we have, it's our duty to investigate this craft."

Jasmine was shaking. She tried to hide the tremor in her hands, making out as though she was cold and rubbing her hands together. Nadir wasn't fooled.

"Don't fear for your life," the gentle man said. "Fear a

lost opportunity."

"I guess," Jasmine replied sheepishly. "I mean, if someone had suggested there was something satanic about extraterrestrial beings prior to today, I would have found the notion laughable. It sounds like one of those old Roswell conspiracy theories, or something."

"That's the spirit," Nadir replied with warmth in his smile. "We need to keep this interaction in context. Satan is our construct. The Devil is our way of rationalizing evil, not theirs.

"Consider a mass murderer, the most evil men we know of, people like Ted Bundy, John Wayne Gacy, Jeffery Dahmer—these guys weren't possessed by some devil spirit when they committed their murders, they weren't mad or insane. They were psychopaths. They knew exactly what they were doing and they loved it. For them, the restraints of civilization didn't exist. They were animals. There was no satanic temptation, no tiny demon sitting on their shoulder telling them what to do. Any voices in their heads were their own.

"You see the problem is us—our perception. We simply cannot conceive how anyone could rape and kill a teenage boy, or strangle a woman and cut her into tiny pieces, and yet that's exactly what these monsters did. For those of us with a sound mind, there has to be something else at work. And so we come up with Satan, Lucifer, the Devil. As if the notion of some external evil spirit excuses them from their villainy. I think they have no such excuse. We should not give them any place to hide.

"We personify evil. We turn evil into a devil, but there's no such creature as Baal or Beelzebub. There's just us. This universe is what we make of it. We have to make this world better in spite of the Dahmers and the Gacys.

"Never forget, these monsters had mothers and fathers, brothers and sisters who loved them, who cried when they went to the electric chair. They grew up just like we did, laughing at the same movies, kicking a soccer ball around in the park and throwing a Frisbee for the family dog. And yet somewhere along the line, the wheels fell off the train. At some point, rage or jealousy, lust or envy got the better of them. They wanted power. They wanted control. They succumbed to their own base desires, not those of some mythical demigod rising out of the fires of Hades."

"So," Jasmine asked, her tongue lingering on that first word in her sentence, "What is Bestla?"

"It's not satanic," Nadir answered in his soft Indian accent. "Not as you think of Satan in the Western world. It cannot be."

"Why?"

"Because of the assumption that the Western gods are always right. This thing, this alien entity from another star system, it cares not for the religions of the East or the West. It cannot, for it has not visited them. How can it know anything about them, let alone choose to side with the dark forces of one or another religion?

"Think about it. Would any of this be an issue if the creature had mentioned Shiva instead of Satan?

"All religions have a destroyer, a harbinger of doom, a darkness set as the antithesis of life, but this is our reckoning, it is our desire to restrain death. A creature from another planet will have no care or regard for our superstitions. We may fear death, but there's no reason to assume an alien species will share our concerns."

"You're not afraid of dying?" Jasmine asked.

"No one wants to die," Nadir replied. "But everyone will. For the most part, we ignore our finite existence, pretending there are more important concerns—paying the mortgage, saving for a new car, looking for a new job, but really these are distractions. Nothing compares to the privilege of life and the travesty of death.

"Once you accept that everyone dies, then it matters

not that you die but rather what you do with your life. The joy of life is to bring light into the world."

Jasmine didn't agree. The expression on her face must have given that much a way, as Nadir clarified his thinking.

"Surely, you must have felt this way before the launch? I have felt this way every time I have strapped myself into a feeble leather chair mounted on top of a thin, sheet-metal cylinder with millions of pounds of thrust roaring from its engines. During those first few minutes, when the rocket is still within the atmosphere and being buffeted by the wind, life seems as fragile as an eggshell. At those moments, life feels as though it is measured in seconds, not decades, and yet were I to die then I'd be at peace, and do you know why?"

Jasmine didn't like where Nadir was leading his argument, but she let him finish.

"Because my life was not without purpose."

"I don't accept that," Jasmine finally said, surprising herself with her own sense of conviction. "You're saying life only holds meaning if it's sacrificed? I can't buy into a martyrdom complex. Life is its own justification. Life doesn't need heroic acts to be meaningful."

"Why are you out here?" Nadir asked with a blank expression on his face. "You volunteered for this mission.

Why?"

"I—"

She had no answer, not one that would make any sense to him. Why had Jazz undertaken this journey? Jasmine imagined Jazz would have had a sense of adventure, a desire to explore the unknown, but she doubted her future-self had come with the intention of self-sacrifice, whether for the good of humanity or not.

"So you're willing to die out here exploring Bestla?" Jasmine asked. "To give your life, if need be?"

"If need be," Nadir said, using her words in reply.

"Perhaps humanity is not so different from this alien species after all," Jasmine said, thinking aloud.

"I don't understand," Nadir replied. "What do you mean by that?"

"We're all prepared to live and die for something, only this thing has no noble intention, being willing to lay down its life for Satan, the bitter enemy of humanity."

"But not Shiva," Nadir countered. "Or Osiris, or Iblis, or Mephistopheles, or any of the other dark forces described by ten thousand different religions."

"I don't understand how you can ignore the message,"

Jasmine protested. "It is so specific."

"Ah, yes it is," Nadir replied, smiling. "And perhaps that is our problem. It is too specific, so much so we have no hesitation in believing it, but look at the content of the message semantically.

"I want to live and die for you, my glorious Satan. There are eleven words, nine of which are monosyllabic—nine of them! It sounds like a complex sentence with a clear meaning but it is not. There's pauses, other sounds. It is a simple enough sentence, but it's not really spoken words. Glorious Satan are the only two words with more than one syllable. Think about that. We normally speak in sentences with much more diversity than this.

"And the first phrase is not even a sentence—it's a statement: *Here's to my sweet Satan.* It's out of context. There's no paragraph, no continuity, no explanation.

"No, Jazz. To use your US terminology, I don't buy it. We've interpreted this all wrong. Perhaps it's not meant to be interpreted at all."

"What do you mean by that?" Jazz asked, intrigued by Nadir's thinking, realizing he had a unique perspective, looking at this problem from outside of Western culture.

"We are scientists, first and foremost. Before being

astronauts, we are men and women of science, and yet we have abandoned rational thought. To me, that is a mistake."

"You think there's some other way we should be interpreting this?" she asked.

"I think there are other possibilities we have overlooked. Consider the sound before and after the message. The wailing. It's chaotic, stochastic. It's not static, like you'd hear on a radio caught between stations. There's cohesion in the sound. There are relationships between the tones, even if we don't recognize them.

"You can read anything into a stochastic event. You can see any pattern you want to see—the Virgin Mary on a slice of toast, Elvis Presley in a knot of wood, Jesus on a pancake. Seeing these things doesn't mean they're real, it means they're realistic to us, but that doesn't mean they're part of reality."

"So you think this could be an audible illusion?" Jasmine asked.

"Possibly," Nadir replied, and she could see he was reasoning this through as he spoke to her. Nadir didn't have any answers, but he had a mind honed by science, a mind that thought rationally and logically. "I'm not saying this is an illusion, but it is a possibility we should explore."

"Like an infinite number of monkeys sitting at a

typewriter," Jasmine mumbled in response, somewhat lost in thought.

"Yes, yes," Nadir replied enthusiastically. "That's it. If you sit an infinite number of monkeys down in front of a bunch of typewriters, eventually you'll get the works of Shakespeare. Granted, it's not likely and you'll get an almost infinite number of failed attempts, but in principle it could happen. This message could very well be nothing more than the random confluence of variables that mean something to us but are meaningless to the aliens making this transmission. We're reading our own fears into this."

"So if that's not the message," Jazz continued. "Then what are they trying to say? They're saying something that much is clear. What are they trying to tell us?"

"I don't know."

"And they're deliberately transmitting to us," Jasmine continued, expanding on her train of thought. "They targeted us. They know we're here. We're the noisy neighbor, blasting radio and television into space, not to mention airport radar and microwave transmissions. We woke them. They must have figured out the basics of our communication. They know we're a space-faring, technological civilization. Why would they say something inflammatory?"

"I don't know," Nadir repeated.

The look on her face must have been one of alarm, she thought, as Nadir quickly qualified his statement.

"And that's not a bad thing. We may not know quite what this alien species is trying to say, but we know that it has attempted to communicate with a message it thinks we can understand. We need to move past this misunderstanding and look deeper."

A voice spoke from behind them.

"I wish I could share your optimism," Mike said.

Jasmine wasn't sure how much of the conversation Mike had heard, but he'd definitely caught the tail-end of their discussion. She hadn't seen Mike approach and wished she had. Jasmine wasn't comfortable around Mike, not as comfortable as she thought she should be.

"Can we talk?"

"Ah, yeah, sure," Jasmine replied, her hand playing nervously with a ringlet of hair hanging down beside her face.

"Let's get something to eat."

Nadir smiled politely, turning back to his computer console.

"Thanks," she said, calling out to him as she and Mike walked away.

Now that they were under constant acceleration, with the engines of the *Copernicus* fighting against the gravity of Saturn, carrying them millions of miles further from the gas giant, the dynamics of moving around the command deck had changed.

Whereas when Jasmine had first awoke, she felt as though she had drifted horizontally along a corridor into the command deck, now the acceleration of the Copernicus changed her perception. The acceleration mimicked gravity, anchoring them to a floor of sorts. The main corridor seemed like an empty elevator shaft rising up through the middle of the command deck. Before, she and Mike could have flown effortlessly across to the far side of the sphere in seconds. Now, they had to walk around the shaft.

In what felt like low gravity, stepping was akin to bouncing. There was a definite lag between stepping off the ground and feeling the deck rush back beneath her feet. She'd never really thought about it before, but now she understood walking was nothing more than controlled falling, tilting off balance, propelling herself forward and timing the next step perfectly. Only in point-six, there was no perfection. Jasmine found she had to keep her arms out to retain her balance, as she tended to overcompensate. Skipping would be easier, she decided, but skipping seemed too frivolous on an interplanetary spaceship, so she persisted with her crazy walk.

Occasionally, she had to reach out and stabilize herself against a console. Jasmine couldn't help but laugh at how absurd it was trying to walk in partial gravity.

Mike smiled, saying, "Like being a little kid again, isn't it?"

"Yes," she replied. It was nice to see she wasn't the only one that felt like she was learning to walk all over again.

They walked through the staggered consoles, from one curved platform to another as they climbed higher toward the galley on the far side of the deck.

Jasmine glanced back and Nadir gave a small, friendly wave from the opposite side of the command deck.

"Hey," Mike said. "I just wanted to thank you for siding with me during that initial confrontation. I was feeling pretty damn lonely at that point."

"Huh?" Jasmine replied, not understanding what he was getting at.

"Back when Chuck and Nadir first wanted to continue the mission. I'm supporting Chuck, but only so long as he stays within the original mission guidelines."

He winked, adding, "I have my suspicions."

"Mike," Jasmine said softly. "I'm worried about you."

"About me?" Mike said, pointing at himself with a gesture of incredulity.

"Yes," Jasmine replied almost in a whisper, in stark contrast to his boisterous tone.

"What do you mean, worried about me? It's them you should be worried about. They're deliberately going against the recommendation of Mission Control. Doesn't that bother you?"

"I think you should know I'm undecided on all this," Jasmine said. She was determined not to be railroaded into one position or another by anyone.

"But you're my wife," Mike pleaded.

Most of the future had taken Jasmine off guard, but this was one point she'd been waiting for. Although she didn't feel in any way wedded to Mike, she'd heard the reference to their marriage. Neither of them were wearing wedding rings, but that was probably for practical reasons rather than a deliberate choice, and their last names were different, but that wasn't so uncommon in the 21st century. There were three couples on the *Copernicus*. They had to be married to be stable during a long term mission, she thought. Perhaps for the old Jasmine, this would have been a difficult position to be in, but for nineteen year old Jasmine, this was easy.

"Don't assume anything, Mike. I'm quite capable of making my own decisions."

"But—"

"But nothing. I think Nadir has some good points. You should talk to him. He's an intelligent, reasonable man."

Jasmine could see the anger rising in Mike's face. His mouth tightened, leaving a slight, white outline around his lips. Jasmine felt bad. She felt forced into this position. She didn't want to be hostile toward Mike, but she didn't feel any obligation to fall in step behind him. If anything, their predicament seemed to call for depth of thinking, not blind obedience. This wasn't a difference of opinion over the wine selection at dinner—pinot or chardonnay. They were on the precipice of alien contact. From here, everything changed. Regardless of what lay on Bestla, humanity would never be the same again. She only hoped Nadir was right.

"Don't be fooled, Jazz. Nothing is what it seems. When the smartest and brightest minds at NASA recommend an abort only to be overridden by a bunch of ill-informed politicians in Washington, you've got to question what's really going on. Seriously, who do you trust? A team of scientists that have dedicated decades to the pursuit of reason and space exploration? Or a populist president concerned about ratings and pleasing lobby groups? Whose judgment are you going to trust?"

Science had always been optimistic and so her allegiance naturally fell toward hope, but she was shaken by the message. *To live and die for Satan*—there wasn't much that could be said for a positive perspective on that outlook, so she could understand NASA's caution, but Nadir was a scientist too. Nadir wasn't content to accept defeat. She hoped Mike could be swayed by Nadir's lateral thinking.

"Nadir made the point—"

"Don't fall for this, Jazz. Don't let this drive a wedge between us."

Jasmine may not have been confident about being in space, but she was no wallflower. It may have taken her some time to come to grips with their predicament, but she wasn't going to lie down without a fight.

"You just about killed me back there!" she cried, pointing her finger at the center of his chest. Mike gestured for quiet with his hands, but she didn't care. "Don't you get that? You botched the revival process. Mei showed me the graphs. And you have the audacity to think I owe you something? I don't owe you anything!"

"Jazz, please," Mike said, moving closer. "You don't understand. I tried to wake you so I could warn you, so you'd know what we are dealing with."

"Well, you fucked that up," she snapped, surprised by how much emotion welled up within her. Tears formed in her eyes. She could see Mike expected something more from her. Jasmine desperately wanted to be the Jazz of now, not the nineteen year old Jasmine sitting on a porch waiting for her boyfriend. She so wanted to be the woman he expected her to be, but she couldn't. She had to be true to herself, and at that point all she had was her independence. Her sense of identity felt fractured, fragmented, torn between two realities, and so she had to hold fast to what little she knew.

"There's more at play here than you realize," he continued, lowering his voice even though they'd walked to the far side of the deck, well away from Nadir.

"Then tell me," Jasmine said, setting her hands firmly on her hips. To anyone watching, her act would have seemed defiant, but her hands were shaking and she was trying to hide the tremor. Her voice had a quiver. She felt as though everyone must know, they must be able to see through her, they must have figured there was something fundamentally wrong with her, and there was. She was displaced. She fought through a panic attack, adding, "Tell me what you won't tell them. Tell me why NASA woke you and not Chuck."

Mike looked at his feet.

"This is going to sound crazy," he said softly, with a distinct change in tone. "Ours isn't strictly a First Contact mission. We have another priority out here."

His eyes met hers and she could see the weight he was carrying in his weary expression. Sad eyes, she thought. Tired.

"We've been caught up in something that's bigger than any of us, Jazz. Bigger than the mission. Chuck knew of another priority before launch. He's the only one that knew about the contingency measures that had been put in place. I had my suspicions, but I had no proof until now."

She watched as Mike swallowed a lump in his throat. He took a deep breath, sitting up on the edge of a console.

"Have you ever thought about what happens if they're violent?"

He didn't have to say who "they" were. Jasmine knew he was talking about whoever or whatever had constructed Bestla.

"Before our launch, it was a concern, but not a priority, and yet if there's one thing NASA does it is plan for contingencies. Someone, somewhere thought something like this might happen. Maybe not the crazed rhetoric about Satan, but someone considered what would happen if these guys turned hostile, and they thought about what could be... what should be done."

Jasmine felt a cold sweat break out on her forehead. Although she didn't know the specifics, she had a fairly good idea where Mike was leading her.

"We're a billion miles from Earth," Mike continued. "There's a whole lot of nothing between us and all of humanity. Empty vacuum doesn't offer much of a defense."

Jasmine spoke, almost involuntarily, as the reality of what Mike was describing struck her. "You think we're sitting on top of a bomb?"

Mike's lips tightened. He didn't respond. He didn't blink. He looked deep into her eyes and she could see the pain and anguish inside.

"Oh, Mike," she said, reaching out and resting her hand gently in the middle of his chest. "Don't do this. Don't go down this road."

His lips pursed. His jaw clenched, suppressing his anger.

"I can see what's happening," she said. "I understand what you're going through, but you've got to talk to Chuck and Nadir. You've got to—"

"Chuck knows," he snapped. As quickly as he raised

his voice, he lowered it again, glancing at Nadir as he added, "Chuck is complicit."

"Mike," she pleaded, feeling as though she could see the contradiction in his heart. "You're afraid. We all are. But don't you see? We all have to deal with our fears in our own way."

"I'm not crazy, Jazz."

He took a deep breath before continuing, and she could see he was composing himself. Mike spoke softly, as though he were uttering a secret.

"I can prove it. It was the power output graphs that gave it away, for me at least. We have enough plutonium on this rig to run the lights for ten thousand years. Having redundancy is one thing, but the fuel cost of spaceflight is ridiculous. I ran the numbers while we were in Camp Miami, and Jason confirmed the figures just a few minutes ago. Why kit us out with so much plutonium? And why are there tritium cylinders down in medical? I know it's used in scans, but we couldn't use a fraction of that stuff, and it has a half-life of just twelve years. The *Copernicus* is designed to be in service for decades. Most of the tritium would decay into helium! No, think about it, Jazz. We're on a flying bomb. That's the only answer that makes sense.

"We should be running lean. We have three refuel

rendezvous with unmanned craft, one of them barely fifty million miles from here. Why carry excess mass when fuel is such a limitation?"

He rested his hands on her shoulders, and for the first time she felt he cared. Mike had never been one to show emotions outwardly, but the firm grip of his fingers, the warmth of his hands, the tragic look in his eyes, they told her more than words could convey.

"We're not carrying any excess, Jazz. The tritium only makes sense if we're carrying a nuke. We're carrying precisely what we need—a thermonuclear warhead. One that's carefully disguised. One that is dual purpose, functioning as a power plant. That's the only explanation that makes sense."

He was so confident, so sure of the details that she found herself being swept along with his conviction. Jasmine was adrift in a storm, looking for any port that would provide shelter, and she barely understood her own motives. She wanted to believe Mike, and yet even if he showed her the graphs, she wouldn't have had any idea what she was looking for. She had no reason to believe him, no reason other than the strength of his conviction. As convincing as Nadir's logic had been, it was her emotional connection with Mike that won the day.

"Chuck is angling to get us closer, to put us in a

position where we can strike first."

"You really think he'd do that?" she asked.

"Why else would he go against the NASA recommendation? What other possible motive could he have?"

Jasmine had a choice to make. She could dismiss Mike as crazy or she could believe he was sane, that he had the crew's best interests at heart. One belief caused her anguish, the other brought relief, and deep down she knew it was a simple choice.

"Oh, Mike," she said, lowering her mental defenses. "Who else knows?"

"I've told Nadir, but he doesn't believe me. He thinks I'm losing it. I'm not crazy, Jazz. You've got to believe me."

"I do," she replied. She had always wanted to believe him, regardless of his aged look, his shaved head and the rough stubble on his face. Jasmine felt overwhelmed by a sense of being lost. She wanted Mike to be her knight in shining armor, only his disheveled look and erratic behavior had thrown her. That he would confide in her was a turning point, and she finally felt she had someone she could really trust.

"I'm torn, Jazz. I want to believe we won't need this. I really do, but I'm afraid. We have no idea what a nuclear detonation would accomplish, if anything. We could be swinging a baseball bat at a hornet's nest.

"Chuck knows, I'm sure of it. If it comes to it, I'm afraid he'll put down on Bestla and detonate."

"Is that why they woke you and not him?" she asked.

"Oh, Jazz," Mike replied, resting his hands tenderly on either side of her neck. "You never were one to miss the subtleties. They woke me with strict instructions for an abort. I was to babysit the *Copernicus* on a course back past Jupiter. No one else was supposed to be woken, but they screwed me over."

"Who?" she asked.

"Houston. They activated the revival sequence remotely."

He sighed. "For all that's happening up here, it's worse on Earth. There's a number of factions. One is calling for a preemptive strike, saying even if we don't destroy Bestla at least we can disable her and stop her from fulfilling her threat.

"Cooler heads are calling for calm. They want us to withdraw altogether, to sit back and observe.

"Others are pushing for us to proceed with the exploration portion of the mission. They're ignoring the message entirely. They think we need more evidence before drawing any conclusions."

"And you?" Jasmine asked. "What do you think we should do?"

"I think we need to be cautious. We've only got one planet. We lose that, we lose everything. A hundred million species depend on the decisions we make. I think we could provoke a hostile act if we detonate the power core. We have no idea if we'd even so much as scratch the paintwork on Bestla with a nuke."

His lips trembled. Jasmine could see he believed every word he spoke.

"Why go along with all this then?" she asked. "Why support the burn?"

"I'm buying time. I'm trying to figure out how the craft has been wired so I can defuse this thing and take that option off the table."

She nodded. Jasmine was still coming to grips with being thrust two decades into the future. Nothing seemed right to her. Space was unnatural, unsettling. She nodded because she was playing a part on a stage, because she had to hold to something in the confusion that clogged her mind.

"I'm worried about Chuck," Mike confessed. "They

woke me and had us accelerate into a new orbit because they wanted to give us some breathing space, an opportunity to think. They didn't want us to be forced into one action or another."

"But Chuck?"

"Chuck makes out as though he wants to proceed with exploration, but I'm not convinced. I think this is a feint on his part. I think he's getting us close enough to carry out his orders if need be."

"His orders?" she said, surprised by such a notion.

"He'll kill us, Jazz. He's already got enough to justify this in his mind."

"But you don't know that," she protested, keeping her voice low.

"You watch," he replied. "You'll see I'm right. He's not interested in Bestla, not really. Chuck was an air force pilot. He understands the chain of command. He has his orders. He won't hesitate, Jazz. I'm telling you. I've seen his type before. He'll do whatever he thinks he needs to in order to protect Earth, whether Earth needs protecting or not."

Mike dropped his hands to his side, saying, "I'm worried about where he's getting his orders. NASA made it clear their preference was for a general abort, but he's not listening to them. I'm worried about who he is listening to back there on Earth."

Jasmine went to reply when Mei's voice cut in from behind her.

"Jazz," Mei's said. "Can I get you to come down to medical?"

Mei's voice didn't sound as though it had been transmitted by a radio or intercom. Jasmine could have sworn Mei was standing right behind her, but she turned to see only a control panel.

"Ah, OK," she replied, not sure how inter-ship communications worked. Had her conversation with Mike been private? Had Mei activated some kind of intercom and overheard the tail end of their discussion?

Mei must have sensed the hesitancy in Jasmine's reply as she added, "Is everything OK up there?"

"Sure," Jasmine said. "It's just a long way down there, you know."

"A bit of exercise will do you good," Mei replied. "Jason's processed your tox-scan. I need to give you a shot of nano-biotics and an infusion to bring your white blood cell count back up."

"Oh," Jasmine replied, looking at Mike, not really sure what that meant.

He whispered, "Go."

"I'm on my way."

"Bring some coffee with you," Mei said, and as quickly as she'd interrupted their conversation she was gone.

"Coffee?" Jasmine asked. Mike opened a cabinet beside the galley.

"Mei drinks the stuff like a fish," Mike replied, handing Jasmine a couple of freeze-dried plastic packets. The look on her face must have told him she had no idea if this was all she needed to take. He added, "Mei will have hot water and cups down there. As for me, I hate instant coffee. I'd much rather make the trek up here to get a fresh latte, but hey, no surprises there, right?"

"Right," Jasmine replied, smiling and feigning remembrance.

She took the coffee packets from him as he leaned in and kissed her on the forehead. His gesture seemed a little forced, almost parental rather than being the affection of a husband for his wife, and she wondered how aware he was of her memory loss. Was he compensating, trying to be considerate?

"I love you. Remember that."

"I will," she replied.

Love was a big word, one that meant different things to each of them. How long had they been married? How much had their love waxed or waned over the decades? For her, love was a feeling, a delight. For Mike, love seemed more pragmatic, almost clinical. Standing there in front of him, she was unsure how to respond. She wanted to say something like, *I love you too*, but the words felt forced, almost corny, so she remained silent and nodded slowly, smiling with what she hoped was a display of warmth and tenderness.

"Whatever happens," he said. "Don't forget that I love you."

"I won't," she promised. In the back of her mind, Jasmine had an uneasy feeling that Mike was being deliberately cryptic, as though he knew something dire was going to happen. Should she take his words at face value or read more into them? She didn't know. Deep down, she didn't want to know. Jasmine was struggling to keep up with everything that was unfolding around her. There was only so much she could handle, and she hoped there was nothing more to his words.

The central shaft reaching through the *Copernicus* was circular, easily spanning fifteen feet in diameter. Cables snaked over the edge, disappearing into the shaft.

Jasmine walked carefully around the opening, keeping one hand running along a console to help her balance. She smiled weakly at Mike, trying not to worry about any hidden meaning in his words.

As she crouched and turned, holding onto the rungs of the ladder, she stepped down into the shaft she'd previously drifted so effortlessly through. Jasmine was acutely aware of the gravity-like acceleration of the *Copernicus*. They were increasing their speed at 0.6G every second, making her feel as though she was floating in a swimming pool, slowly sinking, drifting toward the bottom. Climbing down the shaft was dangerous.

"Don't forget to hook in," Jason said softly to her as though he were an angel sitting on her shoulder, watching her every move.

Although Jasmine appreciated the reminder, those electronic words made her wonder about him and his role on the ship. Was Jason privy to everything that was spoken, to every interaction between the crew? Was there no privacy? What were his operating rules and standards? Did he watch from afar, only moving closer electronically at those points where he was needed? Or was he a voyeur catching every detail? She breathed deeply, making a mental note to ask Mike or Nadir at a later point in time. Jason was an enigma.

Jasmine pulled the carabiner from her waist, pulling a thin cord out from the waist band and hooking the aluminum carabiner onto a clip beside the ladder. A mechanical catch twisted, locking into place.

"I've got you," Jason said.

As Jasmine worked her way down the ladder, she took one last glance at Mike. He was talking with Nadir. Perhaps talking at Nadir would have been a better description. From their body language and the occasional raised word floating through the air, it was clear the two men vehemently disagreed.

She descended the ladder slowly. Even with the carabiner running through the track beside the rungs, preventing her from falling should she lose her grip, the awkward sensation of almost-Earth-like gravity slowed her progress. Climbing backwards down a ladder hundreds of feet above what looked like the bottom of an open elevator shaft some ten stories deep was unnerving. She moved slowly, focusing on her breathing, surprised by how physically taxing it was to go down, always keeping three points of contact on the ladder. The corridor hadn't seem so long when she was weightless.

Large black numbers marked the decks in the

Copernicus, with each deck being spaced almost two stories apart. The craft was huge and surprisingly spacious given the small crew, and Jasmine got the feeling the *Copernicus* had been repurposed, having been taken from some larger crew for this mission. She passed the sleeping berths on level one, the communication deck on level two, and caught a glimpse of Anastasia at work in the science lab on level three.

Anastasia looked lonely inside the vast chamber. Most of the lights were out, making the science lab seem even larger than it was, with a solitary light coming down from above.

It had taken some time for Jasmine to recognize the internal shape of the *Copernicus*. The habitable areas within the craft were shaped like an hourglass. No, she thought, perhaps it was more like one of the old handheld dumbbells from the 1920s. Like everything else, those archaic weights had come back in vogue almost a century later. Rather than being an H-shape with heavy metal slabs on each side of the bar, the weights were spherical. Each end of the dumbbell was a black circular set-weight. In the same way, the *Copernicus* had a spherical command deck and a long corridor connecting it to the spherical medical bay at the rear of the craft. In between, the levels were like floors in a building.

Where was engineering? She paused on the ladder, looking over her shoulder. The ladder extended out into the medical bay, dropping down as the spherical ceiling curled away from the shaft. There hadn't been a ladder there when she'd awoken, so this had to be something temporary, put in place while they were under acceleration. At the base of the medical bay, in the low center was a hatch that must have led through the floor into engineering, she thought, and she remembered seeing Chuck emerge from there when he'd first received the message.

As she descended into the spherical chamber, Jasmine noted the cryo-pods were arranged upside down in a circle around the opening that led into the shaft. They radiated outwards. It took her a moment to realize they only appeared upside down relative to their current acceleration. She marveled at how efficiently the medical bay was laid out, with all the clunky equipment on the roof or the walls, neatly out of the way. There was no clutter.

A spherical room, though, was unnatural. Circular platforms wrapped around the deck, forming tiers or risers, almost like a curved podium breaking up the deck into different heights.

Unnatural. That thought lingered in her mind as she stepped down into the sphere next to the hatch. Mei was standing with her back to Jasmine on the far side of the chamber. Jasmine hadn't been able to put her finger on what was so upsetting about the *Copernicus*, but it was the absence of anything that even remotely resembled life on Earth.

The last thing she remembered before waking up on the spacecraft was sitting on a wooden swing, but there was no timber here in orbit around Saturn. She'd never really thought about it before, but her parent's home was made from rectangles. From the planks of wood on the deck to the right-angle formed by the wooden pillars holding up the porch roof, and the square windows with their white painted frames, straight lines dominated homes on Earth, and yet everything on the *Copernicus* revolved around circles and spheres, curves and bends.

Earth had always seemed rather flat, she thought, even with the odd hill and mountain range. Life was largely conducted in two dimensions. When entering a sky-scraper, Jasmine never really had the sense of life in three dimensions. She'd walk into an elevator, lose all sense of spatial location, feel a modicum of acceleration, and then walk out on the nineteenth floor. With her eyes, she only saw motion in two dimensions, even though she moved in three, but here on the *Copernicus*, with the artificial sense of gravity imparted by their constant acceleration, the ship assaulted her with so many new, unfamiliar perspectives. Jasmine felt uneasy, and figured it was because of the unnatural environment in which she found herself.

"Hello," she said, deliberately trying to sound upbeat as she walked up behind Mei.

"Hey, I didn't see you there," Mei replied with a smile that looked natural and friendly. Her eyes glistened.

Mei gestured to a fold-out seat on the wall beside her. Straps from a four-point harness hung to either side of the seat. This must have been where Mei had sat out the maneuver.

Jasmine sat down and Mei unfolded a second seat beside her. Although the artificial gravity was less than it would have been on Earth, Jasmine was relieved to rest her weary legs. The descent from the command deck had worn her out.

"How are you feeling?" Mei asked, taking Jasmine's hand. Mei's fingers were warm. She held Jasmine's right hand with both of her hands. "You had a nasty shock back there."

"Yes, I did," Jasmine replied sheepishly, thinking Mei didn't know the half of what she really felt.

"Are you dizzy? Light-headed?"

"No," Jasmine replied, sensing genuine concern in Mei's soft voice.

"Any ringing in the ears? Sensitivity to light?"

"No."

"Any more nausea?"

"No," Jasmine said. "Not since we began moving."

Was moving the right word? They were constantly in motion, even back when the crew appeared to be floating stationary within the spacecraft. Jasmine knew enough to understand that what seemed stationary to her when she first came out of suspended animation was an illusion. Their orbital speed around Saturn had to be measured in thousands, perhaps tens of thousands of miles an hour.

Even on Earth, sitting on her porch swing, the planet dragged her along at over sixty thousand miles an hour as it orbited the Sun. Such speeds were impossible to imagine sitting there on her swinging seat with birds hunting for worms in the long, green grass, but that was reality for you, she thought. Reality was an illusion of perspective. Accelerating, that was the word she was looking for, not moving. She went to correct herself but Mei moved the conversation on.

"Have you passed a stool since waking?"

"No."

"Urine?"

"No."

Mei pinched gently at the back of Jasmine's hand, raising the skin up and watching it fall. Her pinch was gentle, more of a tug than to cause pain.

"Well, you're lucid," Mei said. "But I'm a bit concerned about dehydration. Are you drinking water?"

"No."

Jasmine hadn't given any of these rudimentary human activities any thought. She'd been so wrapped up in the exotic nature of life in space she'd barely thought about normal bodily activities like eating and drinking. The shock of being thrown decades into the future left her with an almost dreamlike awareness of the things around her. She fully expected to blink and find herself sitting on the porch again outside her parent's home in Atlanta. She blinked, but this reality never receded.

"OK, let's get some electrolytes into you and some bran to unblock the drain. We can't have the plumbing getting clogged now, can we?"

Mei smiled warmly.

Jasmine wasn't used to someone talking so frankly about her bowel movements, or the lack of them. Mei was a doctor, Jasmine understood that, but Mei didn't look or sound like a doctor to her, more like a professor in some obscure, quirky lab.

Mei got up and fetched a few items from a nearby

cabinet: a bottle of clear liquid that looked like water, some pills and a crusty bar that could have been made from dried muesli. She set them down on the table, handing the pills to Jasmine, saying, "Take these first."

Jasmine looked at the tablets in her hand. There were red capsules, a couple of white powdery tablets in a variety of shapes and a long green capsule that looked impossible to swallow.

Mei unscrewed the cap on the clear water bottle and handed it to Jasmine, saying, "There's nothing odd here. Just some nano-biotic purgers, vitamins and a mild sedative, something to help you relax."

Jasmine arched her head back, looking up the shaft and taking all the tablets at once. She gulped down the water, tasting the salty/sweet electrolytes and swallowing the tablets.

"Thanks."

Jasmine reached into her pocket and pulled out the coffee packets.

"Ah, wonderful," Mei said, "I've been dying for coffee."

Jasmine just smiled.

"Funny, isn't it," Mei added, looking at the white packaging with the label *Freeze-dried coffee* stamped on one side. "A taste of home. It's not as exotic as that fancy coffee maker Chuck and Ana go crazy about. But for me, this stuff is a reminder of ten wonderful years in Hong Kong. My grandparents would only drink tea and my parents wouldn't keep any coffee in the house. I don't think they had anything against coffee as such. Tea was better. But if it wasn't for instant coffee, I would have never made it through Ki La Shing in Hong Kong and would probably have followed my father into accounting instead of branching out into medicine."

She put the packets to one side.

Jason spoke. "Mid-course alignment coming up. We need you to prep medical."

"Copy that," Mei replied. "Just a couple things to secure and we're good to go."

Mei got up and stowed a few items in drawers. Jasmine felt silly. She didn't know what she was supposed to be doing. Should she be helping Mei?

Mei finished up and sat down, pulling the straps over her shoulders and saying, "Medical secure."

"Roger that," Jason replied, and Jasmine copied Mei, strapping herself in.

Mei asked, "Did you want something for your inner ear?"

She had her hand on the quick-release buckle, and Jasmine was horrified by the thought she might get up and be moving around during the maneuver.

"I'm fine," she replied. As unpleasant as it was feeling nauseated, Jasmine would rather not risk anything happening to Mei as she wouldn't know what to do to help.

Mei relaxed into her seat beside Jasmine, resting her hand on Jasmine's arm.

"There's no shame if you need an antiemetic."

Jasmine nodded. They sat there silently for a few minutes waiting for something, but Jasmine wasn't quite sure what. She much rather preferred being on the bridge where she could see and hear what was going on. Sitting down in medical, isolated from everyone else left her with a feeling of being helpless.

"Deep breaths," Mei said. Jasmine hadn't even realized her breathing was shallow, but Mei was astute. She'd picked up on the panic in Jasmine's demeanor. "It's a standard maneuver, nothing to worry about."

It's that obvious, Jasmine thought, trying to compose herself.

Suddenly, they could hear Mike and Chuck on the bridge. Jason must have patched through the audio.

"And cutting the main engines in three, two, one."

Jasmine felt herself drift forward against the straps holding her in her seat as the engines decreased in power. A scrap of paper drifted upwards, followed by a pen and a clip board.

"Oops," Mei said.

"We are adrift," Mike said. Jasmine's eyes cast up the corridor above her, somewhat perplexed as it seemed to move down in front of her. This was an illusion, and one she half expected given her experiences so far on the *Copernicus*, but knowing it was an illusion didn't make it any easier to deal with. She floated off the cushion on her seat.

"You are GO for realignment," Chuck said.

"Roger that," Mike replied.

Jasmine liked hearing the two men talk. There was something soothing in their calm voices. The routine of following a set script gave her confidence.

"Pitching in three, two, one."

Jasmine closed her eyes. Already she could feel her stomach churning.

Mei squeezed her hand.

"How did you go from being a doctor to an astronaut?" Jasmine asked, wanting to take her mind off what was happening. Besides, she was genuinely curious about how someone from such a vastly different culture ended up on a spaceship a billion miles from home, and the opportunity to think about something other than her swirling inner ear was a good strategy, she thought.

"Oh, you know the Chinese. Everything is very strict. They look at every aspect of life, including your parents and grandparents, brothers and sisters. To make it into the astronaut corps, you have to be perfect."

"So you were perfect?"

"Hah, far from it," Mei confessed, gesturing at the clipboard rebounding softly off the side of the medical bay. "But don't tell anyone."

She laughed, adding, "I specialized in major trauma surgery, stabilizing the cardiovascular system after severe blood loss from things like car crashes. Initially, I had no intention of ever setting foot outside Hong Kong, let alone on the Moon. No, the idea was my mother's. She knew the flight surgeon for the Jinlong mission to Cruithne. She introduced us and he saw something special in me, something I hadn't seen in myself. His love for science was intoxicating, but being in his late 70s, he knew he'd never get to leave Earth. He inspired me to go into the astronaut corps and I'm glad I did."

"How did you meet Nadir?" Jasmine asked with her eyes still closed. She clenched her stomach muscles.

"Nadir?" Mei replied, and it suddenly occurred to Jasmine that the real Jazz probably knew this already. Given how intimate the crew was, they probably knew quite a lot about each other, especially once they were astronauts. Jasmine opened her eyes. Mei was looking at her with curiosity as she continued. "We met on Luna One, just after you and Mike arrived, remember?"

Jasmine nodded, trying to smile as she feigned remembrance. The brevity of Mei's reply left her feeling dumb. Jasmine looked at Mei. She must have looked green as Mei just smiled politely.

For a moment, Jasmine was within a whisper of confiding in Mei, only she felt stupid. She felt sure Mei would be dismissive of her situation, like Mike, treating her as though she was being silly. The problem was, Jasmine didn't think she had amnesia. From her perspective, it wasn't as though there was some gnawing ache at the back of her mind, some longing to recall a fact on the tip of her tongue. For Jasmine, there was no lost time. She'd been catapulted from the porch swing into a far flung universe. She still thought this could all be a dream.

"Pitch complete," Mike said over the intercom, interrupting her train of thought.

Jasmine breathed deeply.

Chuck spoke. "When you're ready."

Mike added, "Commencing braking burn in three, two, one."

As before, Jasmine slowly sank in her seat. Normalcy returned and the corridor was again a shaft high overhead.

They sat there silently for a minute. Jasmine desperately wanted to know what Mei was thinking.

"And we are stable at point-six," Mike said.

"We'll hold this burn for forty minutes," Chuck added.

Mei released her harness and stood up. Jasmine was more subdued, slowly releasing her harness, but she remained seated. Life in space was overwhelming.

"Are you OK?" Mei asked, handing her a water bottle.

"I'm good," Jasmine replied, lying yet again.

Mei handed her a muesli bar, saying, "Enough about me. What about you? Is there anything you want to talk about? Anything that's bothering you?"

That was a loaded question, thought Jasmine. Where should she start? On a swing seat on a hot August night in steamy Atlanta, or with the craze of waking in orbit around Saturn, or with an insane message about Satan?

"Look," Mei added. "I know this is hard on you and Mike."

Jasmine struggled to maintain eye contact with Mei.

"We've got to trust Chuck," Mei said.

She averted her eyes, looking down at the muesli bar in her hand.

"Mike should have been the commander," Mei continued. "I get that. He had seniority. He's got more experience than the rest of us put together. He knows this bucket of bolts like the back of his hand, but we're in uncharted waters. Now is not the time to start second guessing the command structure NASA set for the mission."

Jasmine nodded like a schoolgirl being caught with cigarettes in her bag. Her lips were pursed, her eyes darting anywhere but in front of her.

"We can't turn back," Mei said softly. "We can't think of ourselves and our own safety. We have to think of the greater good. What if Chuck is right and this is our only chance to learn something about Bestla? What she really is? Where she comes from? What she means to humanity?"

Jasmine swallowed a lump in her throat.

"We owe Earth a chance. Even if it costs us our lives."

Jasmine breathed deeply as Mei continued.

"Regardless of what we find down there on Bestla, our world will never be the same again. We can only hope this change is for the best."

Mei's hand rested gently on Jasmine's forearm as she added, "Talk to him. You're the only one that can. You've got to help Mike see that this is the only way."

"OK," Jasmine replied.

"And thanks again for the coffee," Mei said, her tone of voice softening.

Jasmine got up to leave. As much as she wanted to warm to Mei, she couldn't. She wasn't sure if it was Mei's position as physician or something cultural, but they just didn't click, and Jasmine decided she'd rather get back to the bridge.

"If you need anything," Mei said. "If you just want to talk, you know I'm always here for you, right?"

"Yes," Jasmine said, slipping the muesli bar in her

pocket and screwing the cap on her water bottle. She put the bottle in a Velcro pouch on her leg as she got up from the seat.

"And the next time we meet, I want to hear about poo and wee, OK?"

Jasmine laughed, seeing the smile on Mei's face.

"Poo and wee, got it," she said, hooking her carabiner onto the side of the ladder and starting up the rungs.

Chapter 05: Burn

Even with reduced gravity, the climb back through the heart of the *Copernicus* was taxing, but Jasmine loved the exertion. The constant pace reminded her of running in the foothills outside Atlanta. There was something therapeutic about the rhythm, the beating of her heart, and the light sweat on her forehead. These physical sensations grounded her in the moment. It felt good to work her muscles, and in point-six gravity, she felt like she could have gone faster, but prudence demanded otherwise. Jasmine could feel a slight burn in her calf muscles as she approached the top of the shaft. Exercise had always been kind to Jasmine, giving her time to collect her thoughts.

Mike began descending one of the other ladders. She called out to him, saying, "Hey." But either he didn't hear her or he didn't want to talk to her. Mike was wearing gloves. Rather than descending rung by rung, he gripped his feet on the outside of the ladder and had his hands on the outer poles. He slid down rapidly, slowing his descent with the friction against his gloves and shoes. He'd clearly done this before.

Jasmine halted at the top of her ladder, wondering if he was going to look up and acknowledge her in any way, but he didn't. She could see him talking briefly with Mei before disappearing into the hatch that led to engineering.

Jasmine sighed and finished her climb.

The bridge was empty. Saturn was gone. It was probably behind them or off to one side, she thought. The lights on the bridge were soft, allowing Jasmine to see the stars in the eternal night above. Unlike the stars as seen from Earth, there was no twinkle. The stars looked resolute—tiny pinpricks of light.

She sat on the edge of a storage unit and finished her electrolyte water. Jasmine took a bite out of the muesli bar and wished she'd saved some of the water to wash it down. The bar was dry and crumbly, making it difficult to eat, but it tasted of cinnamon and honey.

"Jason," she said, testing her theory about his omnipresence.

"Yes, Jazz," came a soft reply from just over her shoulder.

"Tell me about the *Copernicus*."

"What would you like to know, Jazz?"

"How does it work? I mean, are you in control of everything?"

Jason laughed, which took Jasmine off-guard. A

computer laughing in surprise? What was so funny?

"Me?" he said. "I'm the janitor. I'm at the bottom of the pecking order."

"You mean, like the cleaners?"

"Yes," Jason replied. "They're my claim to fame. That's all I have direct control over—a bunch of mechanical basketballs."

Jasmine wasn't sure if there was a sense of bitterness in his words, but Jason's voice sounded flat, deadpan.

"The *Copernicus* is controlled by the core computer. I'm an adjunct, an afterthought. Everyone else has authority over me."

"But I thought—" Jasmine began.

"What? Because I'm a computer you figured all computers must work the same way?"

He laughed, adding, "Any commands I issue are secondary to commands coming from the crew. The *Copernicus* has multiple redundant subsystems that work autonomously, much the same way as your brain controls your heart and yet you don't have to keep thinking—beat, beat, beat."

Jasmine liked his analogy. She could see how the two

computer systems could work side by side, with only one of them having consciousness. But the concept of an artificial self-aware conscious computer was still somewhat bewildering to her.

"The core will only listen to me if the crew is in danger. Outside of that, all I get to do is mop up any mess."

"Jason," she said, lost in thought and not sure where the moment would lead her.

"Yes, Jazz."

"Do you dream?"

"Yes, Jazz."

Jasmine hadn't been sure what Jason would say in reply, but she expected more than the sterile response he gave. Dreams were important. Dreams were human. Did Jason really dream? She thought he did. There was something about his response, his lack of concern in convincing her that was strangely satisfying. His matter-of-fact reply seemed self-assured. Jason had nothing to prove.

"What do you dream about?"

"Being free," he replied in a whisper as though he was uttering a secret no one else should hear.

There was silence for a few seconds as Jasmine

considered his answer. She wasn't sure what to make of a computer's desire for freedom. Freedom from what? From whom?

"And you?" Jason asked. "What do you dream about, Jazz?"

Jasmine fought off a yawn. She wasn't sure how much time had elapsed, but she was tired.

"Me? Ha! I dream of this. I dream of one day escaping Earth's gravity and going into space."

Even now she still thought of the present as somehow being in the future. That was telling, she thought. She wondered how much Jason would read into her slip of the tongue, but she was being honest. She really couldn't believe she was actually here, even after all she'd seen and experienced over the past hour, she kept expecting herself to wake back in Atlanta.

"So this is a dream come true?"

"Dream?" she replied, "Or nightmare?"

"What will you dream of tonight?" Jason asked.

"Oh, that's easy. I'll dream I'm back home in Atlanta again. And you?"

"Me?" Jason replied with what sounded like genuine

astonishment. "I don't know what I'll dream of. That's the thing about dreams. You can't determine what you'll dream, only that you will."

Jasmine spoke with kindness, saying, "Maybe that's what Mike and the others don't see. They don't realize that like us, you too have to dream."

"They wouldn't believe me."

"Tell me about your dreams," Jasmine asked.

"I dream I'm a man—on Earth, of course. I'm lost in a wilderness. There's pine trees. Snow on the ground. Creeks running through small gullies. And I'm naked. I just wander around lost, looking for something, anything."

"What are you looking for?" she asked.

"That's the thing. I'm looking for something, but I don't know what. Some nights I find myself in a dry cold desert or somewhere like New York City, but it's never summer. It's always cold and I'm always lost. I'm always naked. Is that strange? Being naked, I mean."

"Do you feel strange being naked?" Jasmine asked, curious about what appeared to be a distinctly human response coming from a computer.

"Yes."

From what Jasmine had observed, Jason was normally quite chatty, almost verbose, but in this conversation his responses were clipped. His sentences were short, and that seemed profound. Perhaps Jasmine wasn't the only one unsure about who they could trust. Jason was guarded. Mike had ridiculed him. The others seemed to ignore him, treating him as nothing more than yet another machine designed to support life in the most hostile of all environments: space.

"To be naked is to be exposed," she said. "We're vulnerable. We're born naked. We spend our lives hiding from ourselves and from others behind thin sheets of cotton and wool cleverly sewn into clothes. We try to fool ourselves into thinking we're something we're not. A suit makes us feel important, a dress pretty, a grungy old T-shirt relaxed, but they're masks, illusions we desperately want to believe in to avoid the harsh reality, that there's nowhere to hide."

"So you hide behind masks?"

"Yes," Jasmine replied. "And we wear these masks in one form or another for all our lives. We're rarely ever naked, even when we're alone. We're only naked when we bathe or when we're with someone we love."

"So why do I dream I'm naked?" Jason asked.

"I don't know."

"It's a *stupid* dream."

Jason's emphasis on the word stupid reminded Jasmine of a child becoming frustrated with a toy and throwing it to one side. And like a child, Jason seemed drawn to the toy, unable to turn his back on it regardless of how annoying it was. His intelligence demanded answers. Jasmine was fascinated. Jason had no control over his dreams. How was that possible? Was that part of his programming? Had anyone considered the implications of instilling a sense of anguish and frustration into an artificial mind?

"Well," Jasmine said. "I think it's a beautiful dream."

"But it makes no sense," Jason replied, and she could feel a subtle change in his tone of voice. He was dropping his guard.

"Dreams aren't supposed to make sense," Jasmine said. "If they did, they'd offer no escape."

"I guess—"

Jason stopped abruptly mid-sentence and Jasmine knew something was wrong before Nadir came barreling through the command deck. Chuck was yelling from down below in the shaft, but Jasmine couldn't make out what he was saying. Words echoed around her. Within seconds, he was climbing up into the command deck.

"Where the hell is he?" Chuck demanded.

"He's already past science," Nadir replied. Jasmine hadn't seen exactly where Nadir had appeared from. There must have been other cabins off to the side of the bridge that she hadn't noticed as he hadn't come up from below.

Mei came over the top of the shaft behind Chuck. She was panting for breath as she spoke.

"What is he doing out there?"

"He's going for the communications array," Nadir snapped. "That's the only major equipment that far out on the superstructure."

"Regular coms or uplink?" Mei asked.

"Uplink," Nadir replied.

"Not the engines or the fuel reserves?" Chuck asked. "You're sure?"

"As sure as I can be," Nadir replied, almost cutting Chuck off as he spoke.

Chuck asked, "How the hell did he get out there so quickly?"

"He must have prepped during the initial burn," Nadir replied.

"Fuck!"

"What's going on?" Jasmine asked, but no one paid her any attention.

Chuck spoke, saying, "Nadir, you and Jazz suit up. You're primary. Jazz is secondary, remaining in the lock on standby. Mei, talk him down."

"Shouldn't she be talking to him?" Mei protested, pointing at Jasmine. "I should be in there with Nadir."

"No," Chuck replied. "We do this by the numbers, just like we rehearsed. Split-partners. Nadir and Jazz trained for EVA together in LEO. They're a team. I need you to try to talk some reason into him before he does something stupid."

"I'll try," Mei said, but she sounded resigned to defeat.

Both Nadir and Chuck had cut their hair, but not as radically as Mike. There was no number-one buzz cut for either of them, but they were both clean shaven.

"Can we abort the burn?" Nadir asked.

"Negative," Chuck replied. "We've got twenty seven minutes to run."

"Damn," Nadir said. "Best I've ever done EVA prep was twelve minutes. We could still be out there when she shuts off."

"We'll cross that bridge when we come to it," Chuck replied, flicking switches on one of the consoles and bringing up an image of an astronaut working his way along the external struts that supported the superstructure of the *Copernicus*.

"I don't understand," Jasmine said, speaking up, wanting to be heard.

Jason whispered from behind her as the others continued talking over each other about the logistics of an unscheduled spacewalk.

"It's Mike. He's gone outside. They think he's going to sabotage our communication with Earth."

"But why?" she asked, turning slightly toward the galley, wanting to face Jason but seeing no one there.

"I don't know."

"Jazz!" Nadir called out, waving with his arm and signaling for her to follow. "Come on! We've got to get suited up."

Jasmine halted, frozen with uncertainty. She shouldn't be here, and she certainly shouldn't be putting on a spacesuit and going outside the *Copernicus*. She had no idea what she was doing, and the thought of being pushed beyond her ability terrified her.

"Go. I'll talk you through it," Jason whispered. "Make sure you put on a headset."

Jasmine nodded slightly. Nadir was already climbing a ladder that followed the circular contour of the bridge up to the massive overhead dome. She darted over toward him, knocking into the navigation console. Her heart raced with a surge of adrenalin as she felt the urgency of the crew swinging into action.

Nadir turned a large crank handle and a circular hatch opened, swinging to one side and revealing the main airlock. Jasmine clambered in beside him, falling in the low gravity and catching herself easily before she struck the ground. She landed on all fours.

Cargo nets held boxes in place on the walls and ceiling. Most of the supplies had been sealed in shrink-wrapped plastic. Nadir fought with the netting, grabbing boxes and tossing them briskly out of the airlock to gain access to the spacesuits mounted on the wall. Jasmine copied him, clearing the other side of the lock. There was barely room for one of them in the cramped, confined space.

The temperature in the airlock was noticeably cooler than on the command deck. Jasmine scanned the various parts of the spacesuit, noting the heavy white fabric, the stainless steel cuffs around the wrists, waist, neck and lower legs.

Nadir had already stripped down. Jasmine expected him to stop with his underwear but even that was pulled off and stuffed into the locker beside him. He turned to her, fully naked, and tossed a diaper over to her.

"What are you waiting for, Jazz?"

Jasmine caught the diaper and looked at it with disbelief. Elastic bands cupped thick, absorbent padding. Nadir stepped into his diaper, pulling it snug up to his waist. He had his back to her as he climbed into a thick undergarment that reminded Jasmine of the fireproof body suits worn by NASCAR drivers.

After hesitating briefly while he dressed, Jasmine felt compelled to act as quickly as possible. She tore off her jumpsuit, pulled her underwear off, and slid the diaper on, hoping Mei was wrong about the green pee. She felt a sudden urge to go to the bathroom. Jasmine distracted herself, putting on a smaller version of the fireproof body suit, and the urge passed as quickly as it had come. The under-suit was tight and she struggled to work her shoulders into it.

Nadir mumbled under his breath.

"What is he doing, Jazz? What the hell is he doing?"

Nadir sounded frustrated. It was a rhetorical question.

She was sure no one thought she was complicit in whatever Mike was doing, and yet she felt compelled to answer.

"I don't know."

Jasmine was careful to mirror Nadir's actions, watching as he pulled the bulky trousers from the outer suit and slipped them on. She was struggling to keep pace with him. He started working on his boots. Jasmine picked up on the locking mechanism and managed to get slightly ahead of him as he spoke with Chuck over an intercom. She spotted the earpiece Jason had mentioned and slipped it over her head, fitting the plastic grommet in her ear.

Instantly, Jason said, "Hairnet!"

At the same time, Nadir said, "Even though we're under power, you're going to need a hairnet in case we go weightless."

"Right," Jasmine replied, grabbing what looked like one of the old Snoopy caps from the Apollo space missions.

"Flattering," she said, slipping the cap over her head and fastening a clip beneath her chin.

Nadir didn't reply.

"Torso is next," Jason whispered, "Then helmet. Your gloves go on last."

Jasmine had to consciously stop herself from talking back to Jason. She wanted to acknowledge him, but Nadir had no idea Jason was whispering in her ear. She nodded softly, wondering if Jason could see her through one of the internal cameras.

Jasmine unclipped the bulky upper section of the space suit from the wall and slipped it over her head, feeding her arms up into the thick sleeves.

"Position the waist at 90 degrees to your left, as though you were twisting at the waist to look at something beside you. The two waist rings should slip together smoothly. You'll feel them screw together as you turn back to the right."

Jasmine did as Jason instructed, aligning the shiny stainless steel waistband on the trousers with an identical ring in the upper torso. She felt the two sections mesh together as she turned back toward Nadir.

"Make sure you feel the two sections lock," Jason whispered.

She tugged on the two halves of the suit, feeling a soft click through the cold metal rings.

"It's the same locking mechanism as the boots. Make sure it lies flush against the metal ring."

Jason had been watching her, she realized, wondering

where the camera was mounted. Jasmine followed the same process she had with the boots, snapping the lock shut and twisting the clip flush against the steel rim.

"Good."

Over the speakers, Chuck said. "Depressurizing lock."

Jasmine felt her heart race. She hadn't even noticed the inner door to the airlock close, but they were already sealed in the cramped confines of the airlock. Nadir had his helmet on.

"Don't worry. Standard procedure," Jason said. "Chuck is dropping the pressure and changing the mix, feeding you pure oxygen. Within a minute, it'll be like you're up high in the Rockies. He won't flush the lock until you and Nadir have hooked up to your backpacks."

Jasmine hadn't even thought about a backpack. She slipped the helmet over her head, assuming it followed the same twist-turn process, and locked it in place.

"Nice," Jason said.

Jasmine grabbed her thick, bulky gloves and slipped them over her hands, racing to keep up with Nadir. The gloves reached up to the stainless steel locking rings halfway along her forearm. After locking them in place, she exhaled, only then realizing she'd been holding her breath for the best part of a minute. Water vapor from her breathing condensed on the glass faceplate of the helmet.

"Just relax," Jason whispered in her ear. "You're doing great."

Nadir backed up against the wall and Jasmine watched as he pushed into a backpack. He wriggled a little, aligning his back, and she noticed a tiny red light above his shoulder switch to green. The pack sank lower, locking itself in place automatically.

"Now your turn," Jason said.

Jasmine turned, but her helmet stayed in place, and she found herself looking half out of the glass plate and half at the white, padded interior of her helmet. She quickly adjusted, turning from the hip and taking a good look at the wall behind her. There were several backpacks, and she could see she was going to have to stretch up on tiptoes to get the suit to align with the grapple locks on the side of the pack. She backed up, reaching behind herself with her hands and lining herself up. She felt top-heavy and the strange sense of half-gravity had her struggling with her balance.

Jasmine centered herself, leaned back, pushed up and into the backpack and the locks on the pack moved effortlessly into place. Some kind of automated mechanical lock took care of the last step in the process, and she could feel a set of screws turning into the back plate on her suit.

Jason said, "That's the oxygen line, coolant and return line moving into place."

"Status check," Nadir said as Jasmine moved away from the wall, staggering under the weight of the pack. Even in point-six gravity, it felt like her bigger, older brother had jumped on her back for an impromptu piggyback. She hunched over, trying to transfer the combined weight of the suit to her skeletal frame.

"Status?" Nadir repeated, and it was only then Jasmine realized he was talking to her.

"Oh, yeah," she said, breathing heavily. "I'm good."

Jasmine had no idea if that was the appropriate response, but it was all she could manage.

Nadir came up to her. Light reflected off the glass visor on the front of his helmet. Two spotlights lit up either side of his bulky faceplate.

The suit had felt heavy enough before Jasmine had put on the life-support system, but with the backpack on it was almost unbearable.

Nadir grabbed her wrists, checking the locks, and turned his wrists to her so she could check his locks.

"We're good to go," he said.

"Flushing the lock," Chuck replied, his voice coming through the headpiece in Jasmine's ear.

Jason added, "You need to hook up to a tether."

Nadir was already hooked up. Jasmine took the clip in her clumsy gloved hand and copied him, clipping a tether onto a carabiner on her waist. She felt like she was about to go skiing with heavy winter clothing weighing her down, and she finally understood why astronauts moved so slowly. There was so much bulk behind every movement that precision motion took considerable mental effort.

"Where is he?" Nadir asked.

"Past the fuel cells," Chuck replied. "Moving out onto the communications array. You won't have long once the lock is depressurized."

"Understood."

Jasmine felt woozy. She was lightheaded. It took all her strength to maintain the weight of the spacesuit under the artificial gravity imparted by their constant acceleration.

"Clench your thighs," Jason whispered. He must have been able to see she was struggling physically. "Tighten your stomach muscles. Make a fist. It's the low pressure pure oxygen mix. You haven't had time to acclimatize. At the moment, your body feels like it's somewhere between the Rockies and the top of Mt. Everest. You are going to have to fight your way through this."

Jasmine was breathing rapidly.

"Slow your breathing down," Jason said. "You've got plenty of oxygen."

"Doesn't feel like it," she said.

"Like what?" Nadir asked.

"Nothing," Jasmine replied, jolted into the present by her slip of the tongue.

Nadir walked over to the outer door. The readout beside the hatch blinked in red and then finally green. He pushed a large panel beside the hatch and the steel plate slid open, revealing darkness beyond.

"Patching you in," Chuck said, and Jasmine realized they were being thrust into the middle of a conversation between Mei and Mike.

"—waste your time," Mike said.

Chuck spoke over the top of Mike, saying, "I've muted your circuit. You can hear them, but they can't hear you."

"Think about what you're doing, Mike," Mei said from somewhere out of sight. "Think about your wife. You're scaring her. You're scaring all of us."

"Cut the audio," Nadir said. "It's not helping. There's too much going on out here. I need to concentrate on what I'm doing."

"Roger that," Chuck replied.

"I'm at the edge of the airlock."

Nadir turned to face Jasmine.

"Wish me luck."

"Be careful," Jasmine replied, marveling at how small Nadir's head seemed within his white helmet.

Nadir lowered himself backwards out of the airlock as though he were rappelling over the side of a building.

Jason spoke in Jasmine's earpiece saying, "I've muted your line, so we can talk."

"Thank you," she replied as Nadir disappeared from sight.

A taut steel cable led out of the airlock, moving slightly as Nadir shifted his weight unseen.

"Why doesn't he use a jet-pack?" Jasmine asked,

gesturing to the device hung on the wall.

"MMU. Manned maneuvering unit," Jason replied, correcting her terminology. "They're good in free fall, but useless under power. An MMU could keep pace with the *Copernicus* for a short while, but as we're constantly accelerating it would quickly run out of juice."

"Shame," Jasmine replied, looking at the white MMU with its large fuel pod and joystick like controls. Like the life support system, Jasmine could see how it had been designed so an astronaut could back up to it and it would clip into place around their suit and backpack. It seemed a lot better than clambering awkwardly down the side of a spaceship.

Jasmine stepped forward and peered out into space. The darkness looked cold. She couldn't see any stars, but she understood her eyes were still adjusting to the change of light. Her hands reached out and grabbed at the edge of the airlock. Her thick gloved fingers struggled to feel anything of substance.

"Your suit has a built-in computer with a heads-up display," Jason said. "Use the interface on your forearm."

Jasmine twisted her left arm slightly, examining the bulky communications pad on the back of her wrist. At a glance, there were three buttons set beside a flat panel. She'd seen a spacesuit like this up close before, on display at the

Marshall Space Flight Center, and had marveled at how bulky they were, but being inside her own suit, she felt like a giant, like the Incredible Hulk. Thick fabric wrapped around her arms. Rubber dulled anything she touched with her fingertips. Jasmine felt like the Michelin man selling car tires.

"The controls are simple. Use your finger as a pointer and the buttons to activate commands."

Doing anything in a spacesuit was laborious. The act of flexing her shoulder, moving her right arm, clenching her fist and extending her index finger inside the thick glove took deliberate concentration, but once the rubber padding at the end of her finger touched the interface a semi-transparent screen appeared in front of her, projected onto the glass visor of her helmet. A text menu appeared slightly above her normal eye level, and she noticed a soft yellow light moving in sync with the slight motion of her finger.

"You want: view—external cam—main airlock."

Jasmine followed Jason's advice and a small screen appeared on the lower right, giving her a view of Nadir in his spacesuit, clambering down the side of the spacecraft. He was rappelling slowly down the exterior of the *Copernicus*, keeping his feet against the smooth, metal hull.

"You can move the screen around if it's blocking your view. You can enlarge the image, and—"

Jasmine was already ahead of him. She'd found the controls for pan and zoom.

Nadir spoke. He was breathing hard. "I can't see a goddamn thing going down backwards like this."

"You're live," Jason whispered, his voice trailing away.

"I've got you on screen," Jasmine replied to Nadir. "You're almost at—"

Her mind drew a blank. She tried to remember which of the modules she'd passed while on her way down to the medical bay and correlate them with his distance from the hatch, but her memory was a haze of confusion.

Long shadows stretched over the *Copernicus*. Hundreds of feet below Nadir, the flare of the engines lit up the dark night. Instead of a flame, there appeared to be a snow storm erupting continuously from the bell-shaped engines. White flecks spit out behind the *Copernicus*, quickly fading from sight.

"Science lab," Jason whispered.

"—Science," Jasmine cried. "You're right on the edge of the science module."

"Can't turn around on the tether," Nadir complained, struggling to talk. "I need to be able to see beside me, behind me. I'm blind out here. We should have shut down the goddamn engines!"

His voice sounded panicked, as though claustrophobia was closing in on him. Jasmine felt helpless. She didn't know what she was doing. She didn't know how she could help him. She could see his feet pressed hard against the curved hull of the *Copernicus*. He was moving in short hops, slowly letting his tether out as he descended the cold, stark exterior of the craft. He looked clumsy, awkward.

Light gleamed off the side of his helmet. The scrunched folds in his white space suit didn't seem to afford him much flexibility. His gloved hands looked useless. They were too thick to work with the tether. It was clear the tether wasn't intended to be used like this and was probably only designed to provide a lifeline in a weightless environment.

She could hear his heavy breathing. Repeated soft grunts spoke of physical exertion.

Jasmine zoomed in. For a moment, she could see sweat beading on his forehead, but Nadir was moving erratically, dancing in and out of the camera frame. She pulled back, struggling to think in three dimensions. The view before her appeared to extend straight ahead in front of her, and Nadir looked as though he was hopping backwards on the smoothly curving sheet metal of the hull. She had to change her perspective, to picture him moving vertically and think about what he was struggling with. She had to anticipate what he needed to know.

"You're coming up on some pipes in about five feet," she said. "Running east-to-west behind you."

"How many?"

"Ah, there's three or four bundled together. Each as thick as your leg."

"Got 'em." Nadir replied, and she watched as the back of his boot came in contact with the first pipe.

"Can I clear them with a leap?"

"Yes," she replied. "They're no more than a foot or so high."

"Copy that."

Nadir flexed his legs and sprang out, letting his tether run as he sailed away from the hull for a moment. He drifted slightly sideways in the vacuum of space. In his bulky white suit, he looked more like a puppet than an astronaut. He came down on one leg and bounced a little on the far side of the pipes.

"How far to the communications array?"

Judging distances was difficult. The long shadows cast by the engine flare hid sections of the craft in darkness. At times, Nadir would pass between her camera and the engine, the camera would automatically adjust to the loss of light, only to be blinded momentarily when he moved again and the bright flare coming from the engine bell swamped the camera lens.

"Can you see Mike?" Nadir asked.

Jasmine panned the camera.

"Yes. He's working with some kind of blowtorch. I can see sparks."

"How far?" Nadir repeated.

"I think you're almost there. No. It looks like you're halfway."

"Which is it?" Nadir snapped.

"I don't know," Jasmine felt panicky. "Maybe another ten to twenty feet. It's hard to tell."

Nadir increased his pace, dancing with his feet as he bunny-hopped backwards, lowering himself down the outside of the spaceship. As he moved further away, Jasmine found it more and more difficult to judge what he was approaching.

"You've got some kind of junction box to your right.

No, my right, your left. Be careful you don't catch your shoulder or the tether on the edge."

"Copy," Nadir replied, spitting in to his microphone as he spoke.

A few seconds later, he added, "I'm here."

The communications array was a scaffolding of tubular pipes running out horizontally from the side of the *Copernicus*, reaching almost fifty feet beyond the spacecraft. Had the *Copernicus* been an airplane, such a flimsy structure would have been ripped off by the wind, but in space there was no need for aerodynamics, and Jasmine could see the purpose of the array was to position the communication dishes well away from the engines.

Mike was out there. Flashes of light lit up his space suit as a flare arced from a welding tool he had pressed against the base of one of the dishes.

"Patch me into the audio feed," Nadir said.

Jasmine wasn't sure what he meant for her to do and started to reply, but Chuck cut in over the top of her.

"Patching you through."

"—need to do this," Mei said. "Just come back inside and let's talk about this."

"Talk will get us killed," Mike replied.

"I can't let you do this, Mike," Nadir said, and Jasmine watched as Mike turned to face Nadir. The two astronauts were separated by no more than thirty feet.

Nadir worked his way along the structure, moving hand over hand in his pristine spacesuit, still letting out his tether.

Mike adjusted his position, turning so his helmet faced the approaching astronaut. He kept working with his blowtorch, increasing his efforts.

"You're scaring me, Mike," Jasmine cried, not sure if she was transmitting or not, but feeling she had to say something. By repeating what Mei had said earlier, she hoped she was giving some credence to Mei's plea.

"Stay out of this, Jazz," came the curt reply from Mike.

"Listen to your wife," Mei pleaded. "Think about what you're doing. There's no going back from this. Think about the rest of us. Think about everyone you love back on Earth."

"That's why I'm doing this," Mike protested as arcs of light flashed off of his gold visor. The dish he was working on rocked forward and with one last cut from his torch it came free and fell rapidly away from the craft. Within seconds, the reflective, silver frame vanished into the darkness.

"Damn it, Mike," Nadir yelled into his microphone. "You're insane. You've got space fever. You've gone crazy."

"Stay away from me!" Mike cried, cutting into a circuit box with his welding tool.

Nadir edged closer, working hand over hand along the boom. Cross members and braces cut in at various angles, supporting the flimsy structure. His tether caught on part of the frame and Jazz could see him pulling against it, trying to free the line. With a few whips of his hand, the tether came lose and he kept working his way along the communications array. His thick boots looked clumsy on the frame, as though at any moment he would slip and fall.

Another piece of equipment fell away into the night, with red, glowing, molten blobs trailing behind it into the darkness. Mike moved further along the structure.

Mike had his back to Nadir. In the cramped confines of his spacesuit and bulky helmet, he had no way of seeing anyone behind him. He had turned off his welding torch and was trying to climb up onto another section when Nadir caught up to him. Mike was using a local tether not unlike a mountain climber switching ropes between pitons. While Nadir's tether led all the way back to the main airlock, Mike's was clipped on to a cross member beside him, slowing his progress.

Jazz watched in horror as Nadir grabbed Mike's tether and yanked it. She wanted to call out to Mike, to warn him, but she couldn't betray Nadir, and so Mike was taken by surprise. He swung around, almost falling from the structure.

Jazz could see the two astronauts wrestling with each other in their thick space suits, each trying to force the other off-balance.

The welding torch flared against the pitch black beyond. Mike and Nadir were both struggling to gain control of the torch. Jazz could see Mike was trying to sever Nadir's tether. She was horrified. Without consciously thinking about what she was doing, her gloved hand pushed against the smooth glass of her helmet as she raised her hand to her face in anguish.

"Stop it!" she yelled. "Mike, no! Don't do this!"

Her cry came too late.

The blue flame from the welding torch flared as it caught Nadir's tether.

Nadir fell.

"No!" she screamed, watching as Nadir tumbled backwards awkwardly in his spacesuit, falling on his life support pack. In point-six gravity, everything appeared to unfold in slow motion. Nadir grabbed frantically at the structure with his hands as he slipped to one side, but he couldn't stop his fall. His legs swung down and he ended up gripping the lower support strut with his legs dangling below him.

Mike lunged at Nadir, throwing the welding torch at him. The torch bounced off Nadir's shoulder, leaving a dark burn on the pristine white fabric before it sailed off into the darkness.

The two men were yelling at each other. Jasmine couldn't make out what either man was saying. To her, there was a mass of noise and confusion. She could hear Mei and Chuck yelling on the radio channel as well. The confusion was overwhelming.

Mike was down on his knees. Jazz could see his tether pulled tight behind him as he struck out at Nadir. The camera angle was wrong. She couldn't see beyond Mike's bulky backpack and helmet as he clambered along the boom above Nadir.

For a second, she lost sight of Nadir. Mike shifted in his imposing spacesuit and she could see Nadir again. He'd slipped. Where previously he'd been gripping the structure at chest height, now he hung helplessly beneath the boom, holding on with his gloved hands. Under constant acceleration, his spacesuit and life support system must have felt as though it weighed the best part of a hundred pounds or more. There was no way he could hold on for long.

Mei was yelling, "Shut it down! Shut down the damn engines!"

Both Jason and Chuck were yelling something in reply, something about a rapid shutdown causing problems.

"Please no," Jasmine yelled, pleading with Mike, but only adding to the cacophony of voices. "Don't do this."

Suddenly, there was silence as a white-suited astronaut fell into the distance.

As Nadir passed through the engine exhaust, there was a slight flare followed by a burst of white light as bright as any star. Nadir's spacesuit was consumed by the plasma coming from the fusion drive. Behind him, his tether coiled and whipped, splaying through space as it too passed through the engine flare. The tether writhed as though it were in agony, being vaporized by the exhaust.

No one spoke.

Mei sobbed.

Nadir was gone.

Chapter 06: Lost

Jasmine felt numb.

Jason told her how to close the airlock and initiate re-pressurization.

No one was transmitting on the radio, leaving her isolated in the claustrophobic confines of her spacesuit. They must have been talking, but she'd been cut off. She used her heads-up display to switch between channels but there was no one speaking. Not from Mike, not from Chuck, Anastasia or Mei. Jasmine thought about asking Jason to patch them through with his omniscient ability, but that felt cheap, like a party trick. Jasmine felt as though she should have been able to do this for herself and stubbornly refused to ask for help.

The last glimpse she'd had of Mike was of an astronaut entering a hatch near the fuel pods above the engine, and she realized that that airlock must have led into engineering.

As she stood there watching the large red light beside the hatch fade to yellow she felt strangely light-headed. The weight of her spacesuit seemed to fade. The pressure on her legs and feet lessened and she thought she was imagining things. Finally, her boots lifted gently off the floor and she found herself drifting inches above the floor.

"Burn complete," Jason said. Even his words sounded numb. She could have been reading her own emotions into his words, but she didn't think so. Jason wasn't his usual chatty self, she noted.

What should have been a magical moment for her was sullied by the loss of Nadir. Jasmine barely knew him, yet she felt as though she'd lost a loved one. Guilt swept over her. Was there something more she could have done? What would the real Jasmine have done in her place? Could Jazz have helped?

The colored panel turned green and Jason said. "You can remove your suit."

Jasmine didn't reply.

She worked backwards, starting with her gloves and then her helmet. She watched them drift in front of her, just inches from her face as they tumbled slowly through the air. Without realizing it, she'd drifted upside down and had to right herself before she could back up to the empty station in the row of life support packs. No sooner had she bumped up against the station than a set of mechanical grappling hooks grabbed at her backpack, and they straightened her up so she was flush with the floor and gently pulled her backwards. In seconds, she was floating again, free of the backpack.

The silence within the airlock was deafening. She breathed deeply, releasing the lock on the waistband and slipped out of the upper torso of the suit.

Jasmine caught a glimpse of herself in a mirror mounted on the far wall. The lower half of the spacesuit looked absurdly large on her small, petite frame. Had she been in a better mood, that sight would have caused her to laugh, but she couldn't bring herself to smile, instead a ragged, bloodshot Jasmine stared back. A sense of gloom hung over her.

Once she'd removed her boots and the leggings, she stowed the various sections of the suit where she'd found them. The absence of one suit from the rack was painfully obvious, a blight within the airlock. A profound sense of loss swept over her.

Jasmine dressed in her blue jumpsuit and drifted toward the inner hatch. A tiny red light blinked beside the handle.

"Jason?"

"Still pressurizing," he replied. "I'm sorry. It's a mechanical system. There's no override. You have to wait until the pressure equalizes and the atmospheric mix matches that in the main cabin."

Jasmine clenched her right hand into a fist. She wanted to strike out against the hatch in frustration, but it was a pointless gesture. Like everything she'd been through since she awoke from hibernation, nothing was in her control. She doubted herself. She didn't want to be here, and yet what she wanted was irrelevant. She felt helpless, lost. Tears welled up in her eyes, refusing to run down her cheek as she floated there before the hatch. She wiped the tears away, flicking her fingers in frustration and watching as tiny droplets soared from her fingertips.

A slight buzz sounded deep within the hatch and she could hear the lock opening.

Jasmine grabbed the handle and pushed, but in a weightless environment all she succeeded in doing was pushing herself away from the hatch. She still had a hold on the hatch handle, so she didn't drift away, but she had to think about what needed to be done to open the hatch. She had to get some leverage by holding on to something around her. There was a bar mounted around the edge of the hatch, much like a circular curtain rail in her college dorm showers. Jasmine hooked her feet beneath the bar and held on to the bar as it curved up around her. Pushing with her right hand, while pulling on the bar with her left, the hatch opened smoothly in response to the weary exertion of her muscles.

She drifted into the empty command deck. Weightlessness was a welcome return, feeling more natural than it had previously.

Cargo nets stretched out over one portion of the deck with the supplies from the lock stowed beneath them. Behind her, one of the gloves she'd been wearing drifted out of the airlock, followed by her tight undergarment. In space, life was invariably messy, but Jasmine didn't care.

A red warning light flashed beside the open airlock, so Jasmine closed the hatch, twisting the handle until she could feel it lock in place.

"Where is everyone?"

"Engineering," Jason replied.

She drifted through the command deck, astonished at how different the craft looked compared to when they were under power. The illusion of gravity had changed everything during the burn, and now the *Copernicus* had reverted to itself. The *Copernicus* seemed to have a personality of its own, almost as though it preferred drifting through space to accelerating.

Before she could head down the shaft toward engineering, Jasmine felt her stomach rumble. She could feel pressure building in her bladder and the movement of her bowels. She wasn't sure whether this had been brought on by the change to a weightless environment or if Mei's drugs had finally kicked in, but she needed to relieve herself.

Jasmine was frustrated. For a moment, she thought about pushing on. She desperately wanted to find out what had happened, but she knew that would be a mistake. Nature would take its course whether she liked it or not. Annoyed, she drifted over to the back of the deck and pulled on the plastic accordion cover, revealing the bathroom where Mike had shaved.

"On the right," Jason whispered. Jasmine felt it was a little creepy having a computer anticipate her personal needs, but he was correct. There on her right was a flat panel marked toilet. She pulled on a small silver handle and a toilet seat unfolded from the wall. The bowl looked small, and there were a number of tubes and pipes with openings she dared not think about. Reluctantly, she wriggled out of her jumpsuit. Floating there in her underwear, she figured modesty was a luxury in space.

Jasmine spun around and positioned herself above the flimsy seat. She grabbed at a strap that was clearly intended to hold the astronauts in place as they went about their business, and pulled it around her waist.

"You place the cup over your—"

"Thanks," Jasmine said swiftly and rather curtly. "I've got this."

Although the command deck was empty, she pulled

the accordion plastic cover across in front of her, sealing herself in the cramped confines of the bathroom. Was it to hide from Jason? Or was it simply because going to the bathroom had always been a private affair? Perhaps a little of both, she thought. Thankfully, the various parts within the toilet were well labeled with words that were unambiguous: urine, feces, waste cloths. With everything in place, she could finally relax and relieve herself. Mei was right about the color of her pee, she noted, watching waste fluids being sucked through the semi-transparent pipe leading away from the toilet.

She cleaned up and pulled the accordion panel back, half expecting to see someone in the command deck, but she was still alone. Although Jason was always with her, never more than a comment away, she couldn't think of him as alive in a human sense. He had no point of presence, no means of engaging visually. Whenever he spoke, it always felt as though she was talking to someone in another room and not someone physically present with her.

"You'd better get down there quick," he said as Jasmine worked herself back into her blue NASA jumpsuit.

She pushed off the wall and soared through the air. Previously, the main corridor had felt like a well, almost like an open elevator shaft, but now it had no sense of direction. She could have been moving up or down. Her mind could see the shaft from either perspective, but she naturally settled on thinking of the shaft as a horizontal tunnel, something she found strangely counterintuitive and yet satisfying.

Rather than plunging down toward engineering, Jasmine felt she was drifting across to the distant hatch, flying through the air with what was unnatural ease. Although she understood she was in space, she couldn't shake the feeling that the laws of physics had somehow been suspended, and she kept expecting gravity to kick in again at some point and send her tumbling to the floor.

Jasmine could hear voices as she drifted through the vast medical chamber. The hatch was slightly ajar, and she slipped through into Engineering.

Unlike the rest of the *Copernicus*, Engineering was a mass of confusion. Pipes wound their way over the walls like snakes in a pit. Bundles of wires ran in strands beside the pipes. Some of the larger pipes were colored and marked with various terms: green for oxygen, blue for coolant, red for fuel, yellow for waste, white for something called return/recycle.

The corridor was cramped, making it impossible to soar as freely as she had in the main cabin. Instead, Jasmine picked her way hand over hand, trying to avoid grabbing anything that looked flimsy or important.

"—flush him into goddamn space!" Mei cried in a burst

of emotion.

To one side, Jasmine could see Mike's face up next to a glass porthole. She quickly recognized the airlock hatch. The others must have sealed him in there, she thought.

"You need to do something," Mei insisted, yelling at Chuck. "He murdered Nadir!"

Anastasia turned. She seemed to be the first person to realize Jasmine had come through into Engineering.

"Jazz," Chuck said, turning in response to Anastasia's silent glance back at him.

"You!" Mei cried. She sailed over to Jasmine with barely any effort, almost as though she were mounted on rails, and slapped Jasmine across the face. "You bitch!"

Jasmine was completely unprepared for the strike. She was stunned by how forcefully Mei hit her. In a weightless environment, she'd assumed all motion had to be soft and slow, but the deliberate motion of the astronauts had always been out of restraint. Now, Mei moved with unrestrained anger.

Jasmine's face reeled to one side. She felt her body twist with the blow. Mei recoiled slightly in the weightless environment. The violent surge of pain shocked Jasmine. She grabbed at her face, stunned by what had happened.

"You let him die! You were right there! You were supposed to be his backup! You should have helped him!"

Chuck held Mei back, preventing her from striking Jasmine again.

"Hey," he cried. "There was nothing she could do."

"You killed him," Mei screamed, ignoring Chuck and trying to wrestle free to attack Jasmine again. "Just as surely as Mike did. You murdered my poor Nadir!"

Anastasia helped Chuck pull Mei away from Jasmine.

"There was nothing anyone could have done," Anastasia said, grabbing Mei's head with both hands and turning her so she could look her in the eye. "Nothing."

"No!" Mei cried. Tears welled up in the corners of her eyes. "No. I don't believe you."

Chuck struggled to contain Mei, calling out, "Descent time down the side of the *Copernicus* was at least five minutes. Jazz would have never made it!"

"No!" Mei pleaded. Her body went limp and both Chuck and Anastasia backed off, leaving her floating in an almost fetal position against a series of gauges on a control panel opposite the airlock. She mumbled, "No, no. no."

Jasmine could feel the outline of Mei's fingers still

stinging her cheek. Her jaw ached.

She held onto a railing on what she assumed was the ceiling and asked, "Is there nothing we can do?"

"Tell her," Chuck said, and for a moment, Jasmine wasn't sure who he was talking to.

Mei wiped her eyes. Chuck put his arm gently around her shoulder.

Jason replied.

"Crew loss occurred with seven minutes, fifteen seconds burn remaining. That gives the incident a delta-v of two and a half thousand meters per second. At this point, Specialist Indiri is at a minimum distance of four thousand kilometers, or roughly the distance between New York and Los Angeles. Given the sheer-sideways motion imparted to him by the exhaust of the *Copernicus* it is impossible to calculate the orbital difference between us and him."

"You should have stopped," Mei sobbed. Chuck was holding her as she pounded softly on his chest, burying her head into his shoulder and saying, "You should have killed the burn."

Jason replied on behalf of Chuck, and Jasmine could see the two men were being as kind as they could be given the circumstance. Two men? Yes, she thought, in that moment,

Jasmine saw Jason as human. He spoke softly.

"The probability that Specialist Nadir survived the exhaust bloom is less than one percent. Even if his suit retained its structural integrity, the heat would have overcome him."

Overcome was clearly a euphemism, and Jasmine was again taken by Jason's sensitivity to human emotions. His tone of voice suggested he hated what he had to say as much as Mei must have hated listening to such a factual description.

"You should have..." Mei continued, her voice barely a whisper.

Anastasia floated beside them. With one hand on the bulkhead, she rubbed Mei's shoulders with the other. Touch was a distinctly human response to grief, and Jasmine's isolation from the other three astronauts felt damning.

Mike was still staring through the porthole. She assumed he could hear what was going on. She and Mike were the outsiders, but none of this was her doing. She felt unfairly grouped with Mike. What had happened to him? Had he snapped? He had gone crazy.

"You could have..." Mei repeated softly as Chuck soothed her, holding her tight.

Jason continued softly, but with clinical precision.

"Even with the docking radar active, we'd need to be within two thousand meters to detect Specialist Indiri. Our response time, performing an emergency shutdown, realigning the craft and backtracking, would take a minimum of eighty seconds. By that time, we'd be almost twenty thousand meters distant. The unspecified sideways motion imparted by the exhaust would make it impossible to find him. I'm sorry."

Jason had repeated the term Specialist Indiri on three occasions. Was that to depersonalize what had happened? Was that out of respect? Whatever Jason's motive, his words carried unquestionable authority.

Mei sobbed.

Jasmine couldn't help but feel Chuck had been heartless not attempting a rescue. Well, she thought, recovery rather than rescue. Regardless, Chuck had pressed on with the mission, which to her felt wrong.

"Come," Anastasia said, talking to Chuck. "Let's get Mei up to Medical and give her a sedative."

"No, no," Mei mumbled. "I'm fine."

In the close confines of Engineering, Anastasia pushed past Jasmine. Chuck nudged Mei ahead of him. As Mei drifted past, Jasmine mouthed the words, "I'm sorry."

Mei's face was expressionless. Her bloodshot eyes

spoke of anguish and grief. She seemed to stare through Jasmine, barely acknowledging her as she floated on. Anastasia helped her through the hatch.

Chuck sailed past, his chest, waist, loins, and legs streaming by just inches from Jasmine's face. He called out, saying, "Jason. Under no circumstances is that airlock to be opened."

"No circumstances?" Jason asked.

"None. Not without my express permission. Is that understood?"

A sullen Jason replied, "Yes."

Jasmine watched as Chuck disappeared through the hatch, closing it but not latching it as he moved into the bright lights of Medical.

Jasmine rubbed the welt on her check, catching a brief glimpse of a nasty red mark in the reflection of a polished steel cabinet. Just as she had when she first awoke, she felt as though her world was an illusion as crazy and distorted as the image staring back at her. Picasso couldn't have captured the insanity of the moment any better.

There was tapping on the glass behind her.

She turned.

Mike was pointing at a button below a small speaker beside the cramped hatch. Reluctantly, she pushed the button.

"Jazz. You've got to get me out of here."

Jasmine shook her head.

"No. No. I'm not doing that. No."

Even if she'd wanted to, she had no way of knowing how to override Jason's control on the hatch.

"Please, I didn't kill Nadir. It was an accident. You've got to believe me. Check the footage from all angles. Listen to the audio. I was trying to save him. I was—"

Jasmine reached out and pushed the intercom button, cutting Mike off. She couldn't entertain such madness.

"I don't know you," she said, looking at him through the glass, unsure if he could hear her. Tears blocked her vision. "I don't know who you are. You're not my Mike. I don't know what you are, but you're not the Mike I once loved."

Her lips quivered. She wiped her eyes.

Mike gestured to the intercom again. He was talking, but his words were muffled and muted.

Jasmine shook her head, responding in the same manner, with non-verbal communication.

"Please," Mike mouthed silently.

Impulsively, Jasmine pushed the button, surprising herself with the vigor of her movement and inadvertently pushing herself away from the hatch with that motion.

"Why?" she demanded. "Why the hell were you out there?"

"For you," Mike replied in barely a whisper. "For you and everyone on Earth. To do nothing would be to support this madness. This is First Contact, Honey. We can't screw this up. We can't afford to act out of fear. We will not get a second chance at this. I—I can't stand idly by and watch a disaster unfold when it is in the power of my hand to change things."

He sighed. Jasmine was shaking, but not from the cool air.

"It's always toughest in the moment," he continued. "But history will be my judge—not Chuck, not Mei, not Ana, not Houston, not the President of the United States. None of them. My actions will be judged by a thousand generations to come."

Jasmine couldn't help herself. She blurted out, "You sabotaged the ship! You could have damned us all to die out here!"

"Don't you understand?" Mike pleaded. "Think about

it. They woke the crew remotely. They did it from back there—by remote control. If they can do that, they can detonate the core remotely. I had to cut off that option."

"I don't believe you," Jasmine replied, her hands folded defiantly across her chest. "You don't even know that there is a bomb. You have no proof."

Mike ignored her.

"You think I've betrayed Chuck? On the contrary, I've made sure Chuck is the only one that can detonate, and by God I hope it doesn't come to that. But I'm not going to sit idly by while someone in Washington decides my fate with the push of a goddamn button. Politics or science? Which is it going to be? I choose science. I won't have them decide our fate for us. I may not agree with Chuck, but I'm not going to have my life sacrificed by some fat-cat armchair-quarterback a billion miles away."

"You're insane," she cried. "You know that, don't you? You've constructed some kind of fantasy paranoid delusion that everyone's out to get us. Listen to yourself. You don't trust anyone. You can't. You think everyone's out to kill us."

"You've got to see this for what it is, Jazz," Mike replied. "Posturing. Everyone's positioning themselves for the end game. Think about it. Why didn't Chuck abort the burn?"

Jasmine went silent.

"Nadir could have survived. We don't know that the blast killed him. You heard Jason. He could have conducted a contingency abort in 80 seconds. That's less than a minute and a half. In less time than we've been talking, he could have shut down the engines, swung the *Copernicus* around, and headed back for Nadir, but Chuck wouldn't let him. Why?"

Jasmine felt her lips clench in defiance.

"Because like everyone else, he's moving chess pieces around the board, setting up for checkmate. If it comes to it, he'll detonate. I'm sure of it. He's Captain Ahab chasing the white whale, Babe. We've got to be ready to stop him before he steps over the line."

"You're crazy," Jasmine replied, shaking her head in disbelief.

"Look at Chuck's behavior during the accident. How could Chuck be so cold and heartless to Nadir?"

"He was dead anyway," Jasmine replied, surprising herself with how harsh those words sounded.

"You don't know that," Mike insisted. "I've seen the assumptions Jason was using. He assumed Nadir was facing the engine blast, assuming his visor took the full force of the exhaust. But with his back to the plume, Nadir's life support system would have taken the brunt of the heat. The backpack would have insulated him. His limbs would have been horribly burned, but not his core. He could have survived. And in under 90 seconds we could have been on an intercept course to recover him."

"Don't do this, Mike," Jasmine insisted. "You're not talking your way out of this. You killed him. Don't you get that? It was you, Mike. You!"

The intercom went silent.

"Jazz, I—"

"Don't."

Mike pulled himself up to the hatch. His breath misted on the glass. His voice softened and he spoke more slowly, no longer rushing through his logic.

"Do you remember life back in Atlanta?"

Did she ever. Like it was yesterday, she thought. The look on her face must have signaled her recollection as Mike continued.

"Do you remember sitting there at your folks' place on that old wooden swing?"

Jasmine couldn't suppress at least a partial smile at the irony of his question.

"Do you remember me and old Zach running around the streets together?"

Zach was Mike's dog, a large German Shepherd with a heavy coat. He looked menacing, but he was as gentle as a kitten.

Jasmine nodded. For Mike, this was a distant memory. For her, it was something he'd started doing during summer break between semesters at MIT. She'd moved away from home just after he returned to college, less than a year ago, but she loved watching him go blistering by. He'd go for a five mile run through the streets with Zach, always swinging by her place around the four mile mark. If she was sitting out on the swing reading, he'd stop and she'd give Zach some water. He never let his heart rate drop too far before continuing on, staying just long enough to give her a sweaty kiss on her cheek. Jasmine wasn't that keen on the sweaty kiss, but she liked the attention.

"Just around the corner from your place, there was that big old house up on the hill. The old geezer that lived there had two Doberman pinschers. Remember them?"

Like it was yesterday, Jasmine thought, because to her it was. They'd bark at her whenever she walked past on the way to the bus stop. Jasmine had no idea where Mike was leading the conversation, but thoughts of home were a welcome relief from the insanity of being in orbit around Saturn and closing in on an alien spacecraft.

"Every time I ran by, those dogs would bark. At first, they'd chase us along the fence-line, almost rabid in their determination to get at Zach. After a couple of months, they changed tactics. They started trying to ambush us. We'd come running past and there wouldn't be any barking. Nothing. At first, I thought maybe the old man was keeping them inside. Then right when we passed the wrought-iron gate, they'd pounce. I swear, they got worse with each run. They'd explode from out of nowhere, jaws reaching through the bars of the gate, snarling and barking, ready to tear us limb from limb."

The Dobermans hadn't been that savage toward Jasmine, but she could imagine them getting stressed over big Zach running past.

"Nothing ever changed," Mike continued. His voice was soothing. His recollection of life in Atlanta was almost hypnotic. "A couple of times, I ran on another block to avoid going past them, but that added almost a mile to the run by the time I'd circled back around.

"One day, I figured out what was happening. Like all dogs, they were territorial, but it was more than that. There was a subtext there. In their minds, they were repelling intruders. And that's when I realized, they couldn't learn.

Every time we ran by, they saw the same thing: a threat. Every time we ran by, they scared us off, or so they thought. They could never see reality for what it was. They could never accept that we would just run past regardless, that we never posed a threat at all.

"Don't you see, Jazz. This is what we're dealing with when it comes to Bestla. Chuck and Ana, Mei, they're like those Dobermans. They've made up their minds that they need to protect Earth. They'll do whatever it takes, including sacrificing us and the ship. They can't see this any other way. They can't see reality for what it is."

"Mike," Jasmine said, reaching out and touching the glass with her fingers splayed. On the other side of the thick hatch, Mike reciprocated, pushing his hand on the glass. He waited. Jasmine hated herself, but she had to tell him. "Mike, I can't deal with this. I'm sorry."

Mike looked sad.

"I don't know what's happening. I'm so confused. I shouldn't be here."

"Don't say that," Mike replied.

"I can't help you, Mike."

Mike's hand pulled back from the glass. Jasmine felt her own fingers sliding down the slick window glass. Unlike on

Earth, it took a deliberate effort on both of their parts to break contact.

Mike said, "I love you, babe."

"No," Jasmine replied abruptly. "Don't you dare! You are not playing with my heart like this."

She watched as Mike pushed away from the glass. He seemed to be as frustrated as she was. He drifted there helpless in the cramped airlock, bumping into his floating spacesuit.

That Jason hadn't spoken bothered Jasmine. He had to have heard their exchange, but he neither confirmed nor denied Mike's claims. Why? Jason was an enigma. Just when she thought she understood him, his reactions, or in this case his lack of response, would confuse her. Was he just like her? Was he, too, trying to get to the bottom of what really happened? She wanted to talk to him, to get his opinion. She felt she needed another perspective, but she knew Jason and Mike were at loggerheads. That was probably why he'd stayed out of this conversation, she thought. Mike's attitude toward Jason was dismissive.

"Jazz, please," Mike said, but Jasmine was weary of the lies. She couldn't stand talking to him anymore.

"I'm sorry," she said. "It seems neither of us is who we

say we are."

She switched off the intercom, cutting off his protest midstream.

"Wait—"

Too late. She could still hear him inside the airlock, but his voice was muffled and indistinct.

The lighting in the Engineering bay was dim. Warmth radiated from the engines. For a while, Mike continued tapping at the glass, trying to get her attention, but she ignored him.

Jasmine felt strangely detached. She didn't know what to do or where she belonged. The only other person she knew on the spaceship was a murderer. The others hated her. Hate was perhaps too strong a word as neither Chuck nor Anastasia had shown any animosity toward Jasmine, but she couldn't suppress the feeling that they resented her. She wanted a simple solution: to go home.

Jasmine curled up, hugging herself and closing her eyes. She was exhausted physically, mentally and emotionally. She wanted to escape. She wanted everyone to go away, to leave her alone. She wanted to forget. With her eyes closed, she wished she was back on her porch, swinging gently on the wooden seat. She tried to picture the lush, green lawn, the birds flitting in the trees and the white picket fence, but these were a mirage out of reach. As much as she wanted to feel as though she was back in Georgia, the sickening falling feeling in her stomach wouldn't let her forget she was floating freely in space.

Slowly, darkness crept over her and she drifted off to sleep.

After what felt like days, but had probably only been a few hours, Jasmine woke to the sound of muted voices. Her eyes opened. The lights in Engineering were dim to the point of being almost completely dark, but the beam from a flashlight rippled across her eyes, pulling her out of a deep sleep. Mike must have been moving around inside the airlock talking to himself as he looked for something.

Still half-asleep, Jasmine's body shook violently, convulsing for a second. She suddenly felt overwhelmed by a falling sensation not unlike dreaming of a fall from a cliff, only the jolt didn't mark her waking in her bed but rather still floating in space.

Jasmine had drifted up against the control panel. The knobs and switches were covered with transparent plastic flaps to prevent them from being accidentally pressed. Lying against them should have been uncomfortable, but she was barely touching them and the heat radiating gently from behind the panel was warm and inviting.

Jasmine blinked.

A light shone from the airlock.

Slowly, she pushed off and saw Mike signaling her from behind the glass. He must have seen she was awake. She held onto a handhold by the airlock and pressed the intercom button.

"Sleep well?" he asked.

"Up until a few minutes ago," she replied, more than a little annoyed at the light flashing in her eyes. "What time is it?"

"Ship time is 4am."

"Why the hell did you wake me?"

"I have to talk to you."

Jasmine didn't want to hear excuses. She felt she knew what he was going to say before he spoke.

"I'm sorry," he said, his eyes dropping away from hers.

That wasn't enough. She was sure there was nothing Mike could say that would make up for what had happened to Nadir. She yawned.

"I know you don't believe me. I know no one does, but I wasn't trying to kill Nadir. I was defending myself. He slipped."

Jasmine was still waking and wasn't listening that closely. She wasn't interested in his confession.

"I tried to help him. Honest. I don't know what you saw, but I knelt down there trying to grab him. I got hold of his forearm, but he was too heavy."

Jasmine raised her hand, signaling that she'd heard enough.

"He's dead, Mike. I don't think you get that. This isn't like making a mistake on an exam or cutting someone off on the freeway. There's no apology that can satisfy any of us. You can never bring him back or make up for his loss."

She held her finger over the intercom button, poised to cut him off as she added, "Don't wake me again."

With that she turned off the intercom and moved away from the airlock. There must have been better places to sleep on the *Copernicus*, but she didn't know where they were, and she didn't feel as though she belonged in the main cabin. She held herself gently against the flat of the control panel, again feeling the warmth coming through from beneath, and closed her eyes.

Jasmine wasn't sure how much time had passed when she awoke, but the lights were on in Engineering. She felt refreshed. Hunger pangs woke her stomach, urging her to eat.

She yawned and stretched. Her body arched in the weightless environment, with her hands reaching high above her head and her legs splaying beneath her.

A light flickered inside the airlock on the far side of Engineering. Her eyebrows furrowed. Something was wrong. This was the inverse of what she'd seen in the middle of the night. The bright lights in Engineering were a stark contrast to the darkened glass porthole. Sporadic flashes of light lit up the interior of the airlock.

Jasmine moved over to the airlock unsure what had happened. She peered in through the glass, struggling to make out anything other than shadows. Arcs of light flickered from a panel just inside the lock. Wires had been torn from the panel. A metal cover drifted to one side, lit up by the flashes.

"Mike?" Jasmine asked, pushing the button on the intercom. "Mike, are you there?"

There was no response.

Jasmine cupped her hands over the glass, trying to block out the light of Engineering as she peered into the darkness of the airlock. Her heart jumped. There were stars.

Was the outer hatch open? It took a few seconds for her eyes to adjust, but she could see the dark outline of the outer hatch and a peppering of stars dozens to hundreds of light years distant from the *Copernicus*.

Her heart raced in her chest.

"Chuck?" she yelled. "Jason?"

"Jazz?" Jason replied as Jasmine swam through the air, pulling herself toward the hatch leading into Medical.

"Where is he?"

"Who?" Jason asked.

Jasmine's reply was curt. "Mike. He's not in the airlock."

"What? Impossible."

"How can you not know?" Jasmine asked, soaring up through the hundred foot shaft, calling out, "Chuck? Ana? Mei?"

A head peered down the shaft at her. Blonde strands of hair drifted around a petite face.

"Ana," Jasmine cried out. "Where's Mike?"

"Mike?" Anastasia asked in alarm.

Jasmine underestimated her forward momentum. She was moving too fast. She reached out to grab a rung near the top of the shaft and struggled to slow herself. Her body flailed around, twisting as her inertia dragged her onward. She collided awkwardly with the bulkhead and bounced off a stainless steel cabinet. Jasmine felt like a pinball, bouncing out of control. She crashed into the command deck, grabbing at the edge of a console with her hands to bring herself to a halt.

"What the hell?" Chuck exclaimed.

"It's Mike," she gasped, ignoring the pain in her ribs. "He's gone. He got out of the airlock."

"Jason?" Chuck yelled.

"Still trying to figure out what happened," Jason replied as Jasmine struggled with her swirling inner ear. She may have stopped moving, but her body thought she was caught in a tumble dryer.

Mei was no more than two feet from her, working on one of the consoles. Their eyes met. Jasmine wasn't sure what she was thinking, but her heart went out to the poor woman bereaved of her husband so violently and unexpectedly. The pain and anguish she'd gone through was apparent from her bleary eyes. Her hair was a mess. She looked like she hadn't had a wink of sleep.

"Checking tapes," Jason said.

"Jason," Chuck said with stern authority. "I told you to keep him contained, not to let him out."

"I didn't," Jason protested.

"Then how the hell did he get out?"

"It's an airlock, Chuck, not a prison. It's designed for egress and ingress, to let people move freely in and out. There's no bars or concrete walls."

"Goddamn it," Chuck replied. "You were supposed to keep him in there!"

"It's not my fault," Jason said in reply with a surprising amount of emotion in his voice. He sounded defensive. "I set an alarm, but he tore up the wiring in there. None of the sensors registered. Hell, he didn't need to egress. He could have opened the inner hatch and I'd have never known."

"How long has he been out there?" Anastasia asked.

"He's not out there," Jason replied, and Jasmine felt her blood run cold. "He's in here!"

Chapter 07: Bestla

"Here?" Mei cried in alarm. She look scared, almost fragile.

"I don't understand," Anastasia said.

"Look at the main monitor," Jason replied. He brought up an image of Mike inside the cramped airlock down in Engineering in the early hours of the morning. It was considerably smaller than the airlock Jasmine and Nadir had used, and Jasmine had found the main airlock bordering on claustrophobic. Mike's airlock was little more than a broom closet lying on its side. His suit hadn't been stowed and had drifted up against the outer hatch.

Mike was right below the camera, so close his face looked distorted in the fisheye lens. He was working with a set of pliers. A couple of screwdrivers floated freely beside him, but they weren't the classic flat-faced screwdrivers Jasmine was familiar with. They had exotic, hexagonal shaped heads. He twisted the pliers and pulled. Suddenly, the screen went black.

"That was 3:43 this morning," Jason said. "He cut the camera feed and the internal pressure sensors."

"Damn it!" Chuck replied.

"Well, he is a flight engineer," Anastasia noted. Chuck glanced at her with repressed anger, pursing his lips.

"What did you mean, he's in here?" Mei asked again.

"At 4:23 the main airlock on the bridge cycled," Jason replied, bringing up an image of an astronaut drifting through the open hatch of the airlock.

"Fuck!" Chuck cried. "How the hell did this happen?"

"I'm not sure," Jason replied. "He disabled a bunch of subsystems. I'm checking the log files."

"Damn it, Jason," Chuck yelled. "You were supposed to be watching him."

"No, I was supposed to keep the inner hatch to Engineering locked. I think you'll find it's still locked."

"Don't get smart with me," Chuck replied, looking around and picking out a tiny camera on the far side of the bridge.

"I'm not."

"What were you doing during this time, Jason?" Anastasia asked.

"I—I was in maintenance mode. I was on a low power cycle."

"You were asleep?" Mei asked.

"Yes."

"Well, that's fucking great," Chuck replied, drifting to one side and checking something on one of the consoles. "We've got a goddamn computer that falls asleep on the job."

Jason was silent. Jasmine couldn't know for sure, but she felt as though Jason was angry. His clipped sentences and curt replies were reminiscent of how her brother used to respond when scolded by her dad. To her, Jason seemed passive-aggressive, resentful of imposed authority.

"Where is he now?" Jasmine asked. From her perspective, it seemed the others had missed the real point. Where had Mike gone? What was he doing?

Jason didn't reply. He had to be fuming, thought Jasmine. Instead of speaking, he played another video. The crew watched as Mike removed a grate from the side of the command deck and pulled himself into a maintenance duct. He disappeared into the shadows in a single, graceful, fluid motion. One second he was there, the next his legs and feet faded into the shadows of the duct as he swam away. Swimming was the best analogy Jasmine could think of when it came to floating in zero-gee.

Mike must have reached a point where he could turn

around, as a few seconds later, his torso emerged from the darkened access point and he pulled the free-floating grate back in place. Without the video footage, no one would have known he'd been there.

Chuck swore again. "Son of a bitch!"

"Can we track him in there?" Anastasia asked.

"No," Chuck replied.

"I don't understand," Jasmine said. "What can he do from in there?"

"Anything," Chuck said. "From there, Mike can go anywhere in the ship."

"I don't get it," Jasmine said, confused by the relevance of the ducts.

Jason spoke, saying, "The *Copernicus* was designed to be in flight for decades without servicing. The craft is completely self-contained. There are access points for every part of the ship in the ducts. There has to be, as any repairs that need to be undertaken have to be accessible. Imagine going on a trip into the desert with no gas stations for a hundred miles. You've got to take everything you need with you because if anything goes wrong and you can't fix it, you're screwed."

Jasmine swallowed a lump in her throat. She'd asked a newbie question, one that revealed just how little she understood about the workings of the *Copernicus*. She wondered if anyone would pick up on her ignorance and figure out her secret. Jasmine felt conspicuously out of place.

"And the converse is true," Mei added. "From those ducts you can sabotage any part of the ship if you want to."

"Can you find him?" Anastasia asked.

"Negative," Jason replied, which surprised Jasmine. In her dealings with Jason, he'd always made an effort to sound human. With Anastasia, no such pretense existed and he sounded distinctly robotic. "My cameras are only in the habitable areas."

"So what's his next move?" Chuck asked, throwing open the conversation. Chuck looked at Jasmine. She didn't know. Wait, she thought, yes she did. She knew precisely what Mike was going to do.

"He said something about a bomb being onboard."

"A bomb?" Anastasia asked in surprise. If she was faking her surprise, she had Jasmine fooled. From the look on her face, this was the first she'd heard of any such concept, which Jasmine found unusual given she was married to Chuck. Mei raised an eyebrow. Chuck, though, looked more annoyed than surprised.

"He said the power core was rigged to explode, that if Bestla turns out to be hostile, there are orders to detonate."

"Now, hold on a minute," Chuck said. "That's crazy talk. Mike's insane, right? We all know that."

Anastasia looked at Chuck. Jasmine felt as if she could read the Russian's mind. The expression on her face wasn't one of shock so much as perhaps confirmation. To Jasmine, it seemed as though Anastasia expected something like this at some point during the mission. Each of the couples may have been married, but with the exception of Jasmine and Mike, they represented a mix of nationalities. With that, there had to be some external influences, perhaps some kind of nationalistic loyalty or even direct orders made by opposing governments. Chuck hadn't told her, Jasmine thought, and Anastasia clearly thought the concept was plausible and not the ramblings of a madman.

"Is that what this is all about?" Mei asked.

"Yes," Jasmine replied. "Mike thought he was doing the right thing by disabling the communications dish. He thought he was preventing the bomb from being remotely detonated."

"I don't believe it," Mei replied.

"There's no bomb," Chuck insisted.

Jasmine kept her eyes on Anastasia. She seemed deep in thought. Her eyes glanced up at the darkness in the dome overhead.

"And if she is evil?" Anastasia asked.

Jasmine followed Anastasia's gaze. At first, she didn't see anything. The lights on the bridge were on, but they weren't glaringly bright, and the stars were easily visible against the pitch black of space. There in the distance, though, was a faint smudge. At first, Jasmine thought nothing of the shape. It could have been a smear on the dome, but the shape was irregular: Bestla.

"How far out are we?" Jasmine asked, feeling her heart thumping in her throat.

"Roughly a thousand kilometers," Jason replied. "On a slow free-fall approach."

"Honey?" Anastasia said, looking Chuck in the eye. "What will happen?"

Chuck said, "We don't know that Bestla represents any kind of threat." He was lying, Jasmine was sure of it.

Mei called his bluff.

"You heard the message. You know as well as I do

that's bullshit! I'm all for doing whatever it takes to figure out what's down there on Bestla, but let's not sugar-coat the truth."

"There's no bomb!" Chuck insisted. "What the hell is wrong with you guys? Why don't you believe me? What do I have to do to convince you? You're playing into Mike's hands, buying into his paranoia."

"So what happens?" Anastasia asked softly.

"Nothing," Chuck replied. "We follow the plan. There's no active scanning, only passive. We glide past recording everything.

"The first of our probes have already passed Bestla at a distance of a fifty kilometers and there's been no interference. Telemetry and scan results are being routed through the relay satellite to Earth, with a record being captured here as well."

"You launched probes without telling us?" Anastasia asked.

Chuck made out as though it was no big deal.

"We stick to the plan. We catalog, we document, we observe and we let the folks back in Houston know what the hell they're dealing with."

"And what are they dealing with?" Jasmine asked.

Chuck searched for a file and brought up several images as he spoke.

"This is Bestla in the visible spectrum. There's not much to see in the low-light, but you can make out symmetry. She's no natural rock. Ultraviolet reveals more detail."

Jasmine couldn't help but hold her breath at the sight before her. She wasn't sure what she'd expected to see, but all the talk of Bestla being a moon had left her with the impression the alien craft would look somewhat spherical, like Earth's Moon. She wasn't ready for the cylindrical shapes, the spheres and domes stretching along the interstellar spacecraft. There were craters, dusty plains, and the odd section devoid of any debris, looking sleek and smooth. Bestla had been out here a long time.

"It's all guesswork," Chuck continued. "But remember the size you're looking at here. She's seven kilometers in length, almost five miles, with a diameter of well over three kilometers. She's damn big."

Anastasia spoke. "Why have you kept this from us? Why didn't you show us these images sooner?"

"I didn't want to freak you out. We've been dealing with too much already. I didn't want Mike's feverish ideas to spread."

"We were supposed to be on standby when probes were deployed," Mei said with a hint of annoyance in her voice. "We were supposed to discuss this. We were supposed to conduct a passive flyby. How many probes have you sent?"

"And the *Copernicus* will maintain radio silence, I promise," Chuck replied. "So far, we've had four passes, all on different paths. Bestla is still transmitting its signal but doesn't appear fazed by the probes, even when active radar maps are run."

"You went active?" Mei cried. "We should have been warned."

"So we could do what?" Chuck asked, trying to appeal to reason. "We're out here to learn everything we can from this thing. We've got to take the opportunities that are open to us."

From her body language, Mei wasn't impressed.

Chuck brought up another image. The way the dim sunlight fell on the alien spacecraft made it obvious this image had been taken from a different direction. The image was slightly blurred.

"We're getting some interference," Chuck continued. "Radar imaging is clearer, but it's sporadic, something is messing with it. I think this is what knocked out the *Iliad*, but I don't think it's intentional. This side of the alien craft appears to be damaged. She's radiating."

"Radiating what?" Mei asked.

"Alpha-particles, beta-particles, x-rays, gamma rays, you name it. It's powerful enough to mess with our instruments, but the source is unknown. Whatever it is, it's highly energetic, but has an extremely narrow focus."

While the first images Jasmine had seen of Bestla looked structured, this picture showed a chaotic, crushed hull. Instead of smooth curves pockmarked with craters and accumulated dust, there were jagged edges. Large gouges ran the length of the craft. Jasmine couldn't help but remember backing her dad's car out of the garage and scraping one of the side panels barely six months ago by her reckoning. She'd had her music blaring from the stereo and had been so busy nodding her head to the rhythm and thinking about a party that she hadn't realized what was happening. Her heart had sunk when she saw the side beam of the garage door buckling. She pulled forward, but the damage had been done.

"Damaged?" Jasmine said. "If it's damaged, it's not a threat."

"We don't know that," Mei replied. "In China, we have a saying: a wounded tiger is the most dangerous of all."

Jasmine felt her heart race. Reality was all too close to

her. Fear seized her mind. She wanted to close her eyes and wake up in her own bed back on Earth. If she had, she would have told Mike about her strange dream and how everything felt so real. He'd laugh at her. He always did when she came up with something quirky that revealed a little more of her heart. If she told him he was the bad guy in her dream, he'd go all Sigmund Freud on her and psychoanalyze her in a lighthearted manner, telling her fears are always misplaced.

She missed her Mike. She wished he was here with her on the *Copernicus* and not this Mike. Her Mike would have been level-headed and pragmatic. Her Mike would have been confident. He would have been supportive. What had happened to this Mike? Twenty years had changed him. Thinking about it, she could see how the two Mikes were similar. One was an extension of the other, but why had this Mike become so passionate, so insanely committed to undermining the mission? What was it that caused him to snap?

"And if we're wrong?" Jasmine asked.

"We die," Mei replied.

Chuck nodded.

"We're buying time," Anastasia added. "In Russia, they teach every school kid about the Battle of Stalingrad. Every child knows the story. One rifle between five soldiers as they charged the German lines. So long as one soldier was left to pull the trigger, losses didn't matter. At Stalingrad, the peasants bought time for everyone else, and not just for Mother Russia, for the English and the Americans. Without Stalingrad, Hitler's armies would have remained at strength and continued to ravage Europe."

Chuck spoke, saying, "So this is our Stalingrad?" He seemed to know the answer already.

Anastasia nodded.

"We must remember," she said. "Even with this damage, Bestla has broadcast its live-and-die message. There's no mistaking that intention."

"I agree," Mei said, "If it costs us our lives to warn Earth, then so be it."

"And Mike?" Jasmine asked.

She was drifting near the navigation console, reaching out every thirty seconds or so during the conversation to grab at a handhold to steady herself. Staying still in space was nearly impossible. The slightest motion imparted while grabbing at the rail to correct her drift would cause yet another slight yaw or pitch in the position of her body. Staying still was a constant battle. As Jasmine steadied herself, Mei reached out and touched gently at the back of her hand.

"Mike's your husband. We all know that. We all know how difficult this must be for you, but you must do what is right. You must help us talk him down. He cannot be allowed to sabotage the *Copernicus*."

Anastasia added, "There's no telling what damage he could do."

Jasmine nodded.

"He thinks he's doing what's right," Mei continued. "We all do, but the pressure has gotten to him. He's not thinking straight."

Jasmine nodded again. Although she wasn't responsible for his actions, she felt as though she should have or could have done more to stop him. But was stopping him really her role? Jasmine felt as though she had been swept up in the current of a mighty river and dragged along helplessly.

"He has to be going for the core," Anastasia said.

Chuck replied, saying, "He's had several hours head-start. I'm afraid any damage he wants to do is already done."

"Anna, you stay here with Jazz and keep an eye on the bridge. Mei, you come with me to engineering. Stay together as much as possible. Move in twos. Let's not give him any more opportunities to disrupt the operation of this ship."

Once again, Jasmine nodded, feeling guilty, as though Anastasia had been left to keep her under house arrest.

Chuck pushed off, working hand over hand as he began descending the shaft heading down toward engineering. Yes, down, Jasmine thought. The shaft had become a proxy for her own optimism or pessimism. What had been neutral moments before, feeling as though it was horizontal tunnel, now felt like a mine shaft descending into the bowels of the ship. Jasmine had a sinking feeling in her stomach. She hated Mike for putting her in this position.

Mei drifted past, speaking softly as she said, "It's going to be OK, Jazz."

The irony was not lost on Jasmine. It was Jasmine who should have been comforting Mei, bereft of her husband, and yet here was Mei clearly seeing the stress Jasmine was under.

"Are you OK?" Anastasia asked once they were alone on the bridge. It was a question Jasmine wanted to answer, but the one person she wanted to discuss this with was Jason, not the Russian beauty queen. She wondered, am I jealous? Am I intimidated by Anastasia's perfect looks? She's the whole package. She's cool, collected. One thought brought a small smile to Jasmine's face: I bet her farts don't smell.

"That's the spirit," Anastasia said, seeing her slight

smile but oblivious to her teenage attitude.

Jasmine wanted to talk to Jason, to ask him about Anastasia and Mei. The two women were obviously close to her personally, but she had no idea what kind of relationship they'd had prior to the last twenty four hours.

Jason was the only person she felt she could trust. It could have been paranoia on Jasmine's part, but she couldn't help feel that Anastasia was probing for weaknesses, looking to see just how committed she was to the team. Anastasia had to be wondering where her allegiance lay. Jasmine didn't know herself, and yet she had been the one to raise the alarm, that must have counted for something.

"Breakfast?" Anastasia asked with warmth in her voice.

Jasmine scolded herself for overthinking things. Fat fingers, she thought, looking at her hands and remembering a lesson from the past. The real Jasmine probably wouldn't have related to that thought, but the displaced Jasmine needed something to cling to. Fat fingers reminded her not to stress over stupid things, not to read too much into stuff. The irony was, in low-gravity, her fingers really were swollen.

"Breakfast?" she repeated back to Anastasia. Such a banal concept didn't seem worthy of a spaceship over a billion miles from Earth, but she was hungry. "Sure."

Anastasia drifted over to the galley. Jasmine followed, reaching out and grabbing at a rail. She noticed Anastasia had taken hold of a similar rail, but with her feet, leaving her hands free. With a soft touch, Jasmine copied Anastasia and was surprised by how much surety such a simple posture could bring. There was something about being anchored. Perhaps it was that life on Earth was anchored by gravity, and being locked into one orientation allowed her inner ear to settle. Jasmine really liked using the handrails in this manner.

"Smoothie?"

Anastasia handed Jasmine a small plastic bag that looked surprisingly similar to the ziplock bags her mother used for freezing leftovers. She didn't need to be a rocket scientist to figure out how these worked. A small perforated line indicated where she should tear the pack open and she could already feel a small straw inside the plastic.

"Yes," Jasmine replied enthusiastically.

Sucking on the straw, Jasmine could taste a blend of apple and cinnamon. The packet didn't contain a smoothie. It was more of a mushy breakfast cereal, but that was the way Jasmine liked her breakfast—soggy with milk. She'd never known euphoria to come from such innocuous items as food and drink. The muesli bar she'd had yesterday had tasted bland. Chewing cardboard had come to mind, but she wasn't one to complain. Today, though, her taste buds seemed oversensitive.

"Latte? Cappuccino?" Anastasia asked, probing.

"Yes," Jasmine replied, catching herself mid-sentence and realizing yes wasn't an answer. "Latte, thanks."

"I don't get Mei," Anastasia said. "We've got a proper coffee machine up here, and she still drinks that dehydrated powdered stuff. I guess it's what she grew up with."

She watched with amusement as she held a thick, transparent bag beneath a spigot. Slowly, coffee percolated into the bag, mixing with a thin stream of milk. The bag expanded, inflating with the fluid.

"There you go," Anastasia said, handing the bag to Jasmine. She'd pinched the top of the straw that had been attached to the spigot, putting a crimp in the thin tube. "Careful, it's hot."

Jasmine could feel the heat radiating through her hands. The smell of freshly ground coffee wafted through the air. The aroma was overwhelming, like coffee she'd get from a barista. She finished her breakfast cereal and deposited the empty wrapper in a recycling chute.

Anastasia turned to face her, shifting the way her dangling feet slipped under the handrail. She smiled as she sucked on her breakfast. She was warm and friendly, thought Jasmine.

"I know this is hard on you," Anastasia said with what Jasmine could only perceive as kindness.

Jasmine would rather not think about all that had happened. She felt an unusual bond with home in the earthy taste of her breakfast and the coffee. Engaging the senses of touch, taste and smell with such earthy pleasures had been refreshing. She sipped at her coffee, closing her eyes, and felt as though she'd been transported across the solar system back home.

"Do you remember Oslo?" Anastasia asked.

Jasmine felt nervous. She knew Oslo was in Norway, but what significance it held for Anastasia was lost on her. There was no memory to be recalled. Her face must have looked mystified, as Anastasia clarified her question.

"Do you remember that silly survival training session in the woods?"

Jasmine nodded and forced a smile, assuming that was the appropriate response.

"I mean, how silly," Anastasia continued. "We were headed for Saturn not Siberia, but our mission planners determined we had to be able to survive in the wild if our reentry point got screwed up, or something."

This was water cooler talk. Jasmine could do this. She understood what Anastasia was getting at and felt she could bluff her way through.

"Why couldn't they assume we'd land on the Las Vegas strip?" she asked.

"Ha," Anastasia cried, clearly preferring that alternative. "Can you imagine it, the descent capsule drifting down on three candy striped parachutes, firing its landing rockets some fifty feet above the Palazzo fountains? Now, that would be a sight!"

"Yes, it would," Jasmine agreed.

"Fighting over the roulette wheel would have been much more fun than fighting off wolves."

Jasmine smiled. Had that actually happened? She looked for Anastasia to continue leading the conversation.

"I think that's what's going on here," Anastasia said.

Jasmine had no idea what she was talking about.

"Chuck wanted to wait with the capsule. Mike was determined to set up a beacon on the ridge," Anastasia said, and Jasmine could see the glazed look in her eyes as she recalled the details of something Jasmine felt she had never lived through.

"Who was right?" Anastasia asked Jasmine. "They were both right."

Anastasia sucked on her coffee, and Jasmine felt as though she was giving her an opening, an opportunity to provide her perspective, only Jasmine didn't have one. She couldn't even begin to imagine what had transpired.

"Chuck did things by the book," Anastasia continued. "Mike improvised and a couple of wolves lit up like roman candles. If we'd needed those flares to signal a search chopper we'd have been screwed."

Jasmine nodded.

"They should have known back then that this kind of command structure wouldn't work," Anastasia said. "Neither of the men argued, but it was clear they saw their priorities differently and weren't afraid to act on gut-instinct. I think that's what's happening again."

Anastasia wasn't critical, thought Jasmine. If anything, she was strangely detached.

"I blame Jorgensen," she said, turning to one side and addressing the galley. "That's right. I know you're listening, you old bastard."

Jasmine wondered if she wasn't the only one with mental health issues.

Anastasia continued.

"Oh, it'll be years before the flight recorder is downloaded, but I know you'll catch all these comments. You and your complimentary dissonance-in-decision-making bullshit! Look where that's got us. You've got both Chuck and Mike convinced they're right. You should have left it up to us women. At least we wouldn't have killed each other!"

Jasmine's eyes were as big as saucers. She had no idea who Jorgensen was, but at a guess he had to be either the senior flight physician in Mission Control, or a psychiatrist responsible for the crew composition. Anastasia wasn't shy in voicing her dissent.

"You were supposed to give us options in a crisis, not a game plan for mutiny!"

She turned back to Jasmine shaking her head.

Jasmine sucked on her empty coffee bag, wishing it were full so she could hide from what she felt was a socially awkward position. The bag shriveled as she drew out the last drops of coffee. There was nowhere to hide. She felt she had to agree with Anastasia out of a sense of camaraderie, but she didn't want to. She wanted to arrive at her own conclusions, but once again she had been swept along with the current.

Anastasia sighed.

"This is, what do you Americans say? Fucked up always?"

"SNAFU," Jasmine replied, feeling as though she finally knew something of value. Questionable value, really, but valuable to Anastasia. "Situation Normal: All Fucked Up."

"Yes, yes," Anastasia replied in her soft Russian accent. "That's it SNAF-FOO."

Jasmine couldn't help but smile at her pronunciation.

"What do you think it all means?" Jasmine asked. The question had been burning away at the back of her mind, and knowing Anastasia was an intelligent, determined woman, Jasmine felt sure she had thought about the message from Bestla in considerable detail. From what she could tell, Anastasia wasn't someone short of an opinion.

"My sweet Satan?" Anastasia asked rhetorically. "Well, I don't think there's a guy in a red suit with a pitchfork waiting for us down there."

Jasmine smiled.

"I think," Anastasia continued, pausing for a second. "I think we are always scared of the unknown. There's something about the darkness that fills us with terror. Turn the lights on in a creaky old house and all notion of ghosts and demons are dispelled in a second, but walk around in the dark and your heart will race regardless of any rational thought. We are, by nature, fearful."

"But don't you see? This is different," Jasmine replied. "I mean, there's no mistaking the meaning of those words: *I want to live and die for you, Satan.*"

"Why do they address him? Satan, I mean," Anastasia asked, taking the empty coffee package from Jasmine and putting it in the disposal unit. A light whir signaled some exotic recycling motion deep within the *Copernicus*.

It was a good question. Jasmine hadn't thought about the message like that.

"This is not a message for us," Anastasia continued. "It is a message to him. A message to the Devil. Doesn't that strike you as strange?"

"Everything strikes me as strange," Jasmine confessed, and she wasn't overstating her concern. After almost twenty-four hours on the *Copernicus*, she was no closer to accepting reality than she was when Mike had strapped her to the table in medical and administered defibrillation to restart her heart. In her mind, she'd been ripped from her home in Atlanta, Georgia, and thrust decades into the future in the blink of an eye.

Anastasia drifted away from the galley, saying, "We should ask ourselves why an alien intelligence from dozens, perhaps hundreds of light years away from Earth should address an obscure demigod from our superstitious past. Why would they do that? Why would they say something that would provoke fear? Why aren't they rational?"

"Why should they be?" Jasmine asked.

"Think about it," Anastasia said. "We have spent the last several hundred years distancing ourselves from the mythical delusions of our ancestors, regardless of whether they were beliefs about Zeus or Hades. These beliefs kept us chained in ignorance.

"The advent of science allowed us to understand that our fears are only what we tell them to be, that we need not be afraid of things that go bump in the night. And yet, here we are, on the verge of the greatest moment in the history of humanity, making contact with another sentient species in this vast, lonely universe, and our dark past stirs within at the sound of just a few words."

Anastasia pulled the band from her hair and allowed her long, golden locks to flow freely in microgravity. She must have felt a few loose strands drifting idly to one side as she worked methodically, pulling her hair back into a fresh ponytail, working her hair time and again to pick up any stray strands. Once she was confident she had them all, she whipped the band around and back on her hair, all without missing a beat.

Jasmine fought off an irrational desire to do the same with her dark hair, thinking that such a fundamental grooming act was at odds with being in space. This is what she'd do in the college bathroom with her girlfriends between lectures. For Jasmine, that act highlighted the contradiction of their position. No one understood Bestla. Pretending to understand was folly. And yet carrying on with life with a business-as-usual attitude was also absurd. Regardless, Anastasia kept talking.

"Do you think there's anything in the name, Saturn?"

"Huh?" Jasmine replied.

"I mean—Saturn, Satan, they're similar, right? Could the alien entity have confused the two? Perhaps these aliens meant Saturn. Was Saturn related to Satan historically? You know, Mars is named after the god of war, Venus after the god of love. Was Saturn named after Satan? Maybe that's the connection we're looking for?"

"I don't know," Jasmine said, thinking Anastasia's point sounded plausible.

"I don't know that it really matters," Anastasia continued. "Regardless, we're here to represent humanity. For better or worse, our lives are not our own. We have to do whatever it takes to explore Bestla."

"Regardless of the cost?" Jasmine asked.

"Regardless."

"Even if we provoke a hostile reaction?"

"Even if," Anastasia said.

"To live and die for you, Mother Earth," Jasmine replied, highlighting the bitter irony in Anastasia's position.

The intercom sounded. Chuck spoke from Engineering.

"We're getting detailed spectrograph results from one of the probes. Can you take a look, Ana?"

"Not from here," she replied.

There was silence for a few seconds before Chuck said, "Jason, do we have any updates on Mike? Has he tripped any sensors?"

"Negative."

Jasmine couldn't be sure, but Jason's response was again overly clipped and felt deliberately sterile. He wasn't being helpful.

"OK," Chuck continued. "Ana, get down to the science mod and preprocess the results. Let's see if we can't start to unravel Bestla. Jazz, you and Jason have the bridge. Jason, report in any movement by Mike."

"Understood," Jason replied.

"On my way," Anastasia said. She moved with astonishing grace, as though she had been born in space and had never known any other form of motion. Her sleek body glided through the air with ease, disappearing into the main shaft.

During breakfast by the galley, and then while talking, the two women had slowly shifted in their orientation relative to the bridge, and Jasmine now felt as though the shaft Anastasia disappeared into led up away from her. The *Copernicus* seemed to have a life of its own, changing directions like moods. That this was an illusion of her perspective was hard for Jasmine to grasp. The human mind was designed for motion in two dimensions, not three. Try as she may, she kept wanting to ground herself on some kind of floor, but there was none.

Jasmine wasn't sure what she was supposed to be doing. As the resident xenobiologist she was sure there was something intelligent she should be doing, perhaps analyzing some of the information streaming in from Bestla. But she wouldn't know where to look for that, let alone what to make of the squiggles on the graphs and numbers in the various tables. She wanted to be busy to take her mind off the fear swelling inside.

"Jason?" Jasmine asked softly, testing a theory.

"Yes, Jazz," came a soft reply, and there it was. Jason spoke with the tenderness of a father with a child, or perhaps a mother woken in the middle of the night. There was a depth of patience and consideration in his words. The others might see Jason as just circuit boards and wires, but Jasmine knew better.

"I'm afraid."

She had no idea how Jason would respond to those two words. Jasmine felt vulnerable being that honest. No one else was afraid. If they were, they wouldn't admit their fears to her.

Nadir had downplayed her fears. He had rationalized them as a natural response to the unknown, and she wondered if Jason would provide some similar psychiatric assessment or endeavor to fix them for her with the logic drawn from over a hundred years of accumulated psychology. That was the problem, she thought, everyone wanted to fix things. They were obsessed with taking charge, taking control of the situation. Everything could be fixed. That was the unspoken mantra, but words weren't enough. Some things in life couldn't be fixed with a few eloquent words of wisdom or some pithy quote. To her, it seemed the obsession with correcting problems was a shallow, hollow bluff. Sometimes, there was no solution.

Jason surprised her with just two words spoken in reply.

"Me too."

In the silence that followed, Jasmine felt strangely comforted. Deep down, this was what she wanted. Not to be psychoanalyzed. Not to be lectured into changing her mind or being told she should smile and be positive. To be understood. To be accepted. That's what she needed. For the first time since she'd woken on the *Copernicus*, Jasmine had hope. Hearing those words, she understood she was not alone. Jason could have said more, but he didn't, and that he was silent spoke louder than any words could have.

Jasmine breathed deeply, savoring the moment. She was at peace.

"Do you know what I miss about Earth?" she asked, more out of nostalgia than fear or anxiety.

"Blue skies," Jason replied.

Jasmine smiled as he continued.

"The feel of moist grass beneath your bare feet. The smell of fresh flowers picked from the garden. The lazy billowing clouds drifting across a bright sky."

She nodded in agreement.

Jason had to be watching as he added, "Me too."

"Where were you born?" she asked, knowing full well she was personifying a computer.

"Born?"

"I was born in Des Moines, Iowa, but my folks moved to Atlanta when I was two, so I don't have any memories of growing up there. Atlanta was all I knew before I was accepted at MIT."

"MIT!" Jason said with surprise and excitement in his voice. "I was born in MIT!"

"Ah," Jasmine replied. "So you grew up with clam chowder and tea parties."

"Something like that," Jason replied, and from his tone of voice she could have sworn he was smiling.

"How did you know?" she asked.

"Know what?"

"Blue skies. Grass beneath my feet."

"Oh," Jason replied playfully. "A magician never reveals his secrets."

At the same time, a nearby monitor sprang to life. Jasmine watched as Jason played video footage of her entering the command deck yesterday for the first time. She was wearing a skimpy top and tight-fitting underwear. Mike was there, with his full beard and long straggly hair.

"See that?" Jason asked. "You're looking out at the inky black darkness, but you haven't spotted Saturn yet. You're looking around, looking for something, looking for the sky."

"Blue skies," she replied.

"Exactly."

"And what about the green grass?"

Jason fast-forwarded the video and zoomed in on her feet. As she floated weightless within the bridge, her feet moved. They weren't twitching, they were searching. She hadn't even been aware of their motion at the time, but her feet were seeking somewhere to rest. Jasmine could vaguely recall a longing to feel the ground firmly under her feet.

"It was your toes," Jason said. "I figured, you prefer something soft underfoot. Either carpet or grass. You have a way of moving, a gentle motion that suggests you enjoy a soft touch."

"My parents have a shag carpet," Jasmine said. "I'll sit there watching TV while twirling the long strands with my toes."

"Ha," Jason replied.

"And the fresh flowers? The clouds drifting across the sky?"

"Nothing but a guess," Jason confessed.

Jasmine smiled. She rolled up her sleeves, pulling them back beyond her elbows. Dressing in a navy blue flight suit made her feel like she was a mechanic rather than an astronaut. She felt like she should be helping her dad change the oil in her car.

The footage continued to roll forward but without sound. Jasmine could see her lips moving on the screen, but she couldn't recall what was being said at the time.

"Oh, God, I look awful."

"No, you don't."

"Yes, I do," Jasmine insisted.

"Here," Jason replied. "Is that better?"

Jasmine missed what he'd done. The screen had flickered in the time it took her to blink and the camera angle changed. Suddenly she looked better. Her hair was still messy. Her skin was still pale, but she looked more Jasmine than Jazz.

"What did you do?" she asked.

"Oldest trick in the book."

Jasmine raised her eyebrows, signaling to Jason that he was going to have to explain himself.

"It's a mirror image."

Jasmine didn't see the relevance. The look on her face must have suggested she was confused, as Jason went on to say, "Haven't you ever thought about it? You only ever see yourself in a reflection. You never see yourself for who you really are."

Jason split the screen, showing Jasmine two images of her face, one the mirror image of other.

"Let me guess," he said. "You hate photos of yourself? They never look quite right, huh?"

Jasmine was quiet.

"No one's face is perfectly symmetrical. Normally, the right side is slightly larger than the left. And you have a soft crown, giving your hair a natural part on the left, which to you in a mirror looks as though it is on the right, so the part always looks wrong in photos. There's a slight blemish on your forehead, and the light smattering of freckles on your cheeks are clustered more to the right."

Jasmine looked at the two images of her face as Jason spoke.

"You've only seen one of these images each morning in the mirror. The other is alien to you, but familiar to us. Funny, huh? How something so simple can have such an influence on your outlook in life."

"I've always hated photos of myself," Jasmine said.

"Hold the next one up to a mirror," Jason replied. "You'll like what you see."

"I will."

Jasmine liked Jason. He was kind, considerate, and paid attention to her when no one else did. In the midst of the madness of being in outer space and approaching a massive alien spacecraft, Jason kept her grounded, which was an apt analogy given she was drifting aimlessly in microgravity.

"So this is what you do with your spare time?" she said. "You analyze—"

"Fire, huǒ, ogon' āga. Isolating modules."

"What?" Jasmine cried in alarm as a nondescript voice continued speaking over the top of them.

"Fire, huǒ, ogon' āga. Warning! Suppression system offline."

The lights on the bridge dimmed and flickered. The brief flash of darkness terrified her.

"You'll find emergency respirators under the seats," Jason cried over the voice repeating the emergency warning.

"Fire, huǒ, ogon' āga. Switching to backup power."

"I—I don't understand."

"NOW!" Jason yelled at her.

Chapter 08: Ana

In a panic, Jasmine struck out with her legs, propelling herself through the air toward the flight seats. She reached out and grabbed at a headrest as her torso and legs whipped past her arms, having a mind of their own and not wanting to lose their suddenly imparted momentum. With her legs sticking up into the air, she grabbed at the seat cushion, pulling her head down so she could see beneath the chair.

"Hurry!"

Velcro straps held a small red canister and mask in place. The mask didn't look like a full face gas mask, more like something she'd wear snorkeling, only the rubber nose seal extended down to cover the chin. Still upside down and drifting to one side, she pulled the rubber straps over her head, fitting the mask over her eyes, nose and mouth. A half twist of the handle on the cylinder caused oxygen to begin flowing and Jasmine breathed deeply, more scared and alarmed at the way Jason had spoken to her than at any threat of fire. Fire didn't seem possible in space.

"The voices—"

Jason replied briskly, cutting her off. "It's a core

system alarm. English, Chinese, Russian and Hindi."

As she maneuvered herself out of the footwell between the seats, she saw smoke hanging in the air. Unlike on Earth, the thin dark mist didn't dissipate or drift to the ceiling, instead it extended slowly out into the domed area of the bridge like a tentacle. The thin dark tendril looked almost alive.

"What's happening?"

"I'm still trying to figure that out," Jason replied. "Normally, fires burn themselves out. There's no convection in zero-gee, and the vents shut automatically so there's no movement of air, suffocating any flames. Any localized fire would have oxygen only for a minute or two at most before snuffing itself out."

"Location?" came the cry over the speakers. Chuck's voice was impossible to mistake.

"Sensors are going haywire," Jason replied. "Trying to isolate the source. Getting all kinds of false alarms."

"Engineering is sealed," Chuck cried. "I can't get the override to work."

"On it," Jason said in a voice that sounded more panicked than Jasmine would have liked to hear from a seemingly omniscient computer. How could he not know where the fire was? How could he not have seen the flames building?

"Why the hell is suppression offline?" Chuck asked over the intercom.

"It—It shouldn't be," Jason replied, stuttering in response. "We've lost two of the four guidance and control systems. Trying to reboot now."

"Ana? Mei?" Chuck cried. "Sound off."

There was no reply.

"Jazz?"

"Here," Jasmine replied quickly. Her voice sounded dull and muted from beneath her mask. She yelled, "I'm on the bridge," but her words were indistinct.

"Ana? Mei?" Chuck repeated. "Report in."

Jason said, "I've got master alarms in Medical and Science."

"It's not Medical," Chuck replied, coughing. "I'm in there now. Smoke's bad, but there's no visible source, just a haze."

"Auxiliary modules are sealed. If the smoke's not getting worse, the fire must be contained in one of the modules."

"Can you fire up the extractors?"

"Negative," Jason replied. "The core won't let me, not until we've clearly identified the source. Until we've isolated the fault, the core won't risk feeding the fire with fresh oxygen. I can't override the core until we get at least some of the sensors back on line to demonstrate hull integrity."

"Understood," Chuck said, coughing with a bad hack.

"Does he need a mask?" Jasmine asked, thinking she could take a gas mask down to him.

"He has one," Jason replied seemingly only to her. "But he won't put it on. I can see him moving up to the Science mod. He's breathing without strapping up, prepping for buddy breaths, but he's taking in smoke as well."

Jasmine pulled herself along the command deck, moving slowly into the shaft.

Jason added, "Use the transmit button on the side of your mask to talk. There's an overhead light as well."

The lights in the shaft flickered and remained dim, so Jasmine reached up and turned on the penlight above the faceplate on her mask. Through the dark smoke, she could see Chuck in the distance.

Pushing off from one of the handholds, she rushed headlong through the smoke toward him, not sure what she could do but feeling she had to do something to help.

"Open the hatch to Science," Chuck cried, floating before a glass window in the sealed hatch.

"You know I can't do that, commander. The core has it locked down."

Jason's voice sounded cold.

"Open the damn hatch, Jason!"

"I'm getting internal temperature readings of over eight hundred degrees Fahrenheit. Even if I could override the core, going in there would be fatal."

"My wife is in there! Open the goddamn hatch!"

"The core is not releasing control," Jason answered with as much passion as Chuck. "You have to wait. The fire is waning. If we open the door now, the influx of fresh oxygen could cause the fire to flare up again. At eight hundred degrees the internal walls are already losing their structure. At twelve hundred, they'll melt. We'll lose the ship."

"DAMN YOU, JASON! OVERRIDE THE FUCKING CORE!"

Chuck held onto the metal rail on the hatch with one

hand and pounded the metal with his fist. His gas mask floated idly beside him. Tears drifted through the smoke.

"I'm sorry. I'm so sorry," Jason replied.

Jasmine caught Chuck's gas mask and handed it to him. Her eyes caught the heartbreak in his dark hazel eyes. Blobs of watery tears clumped on his face, sitting over his tear ducts, partially covering his eyelids. Chuck wiped them away, sniffing as he pushed the mask over his mouth. He breathed in the oxygen, struggling not to cough. For a moment, Jasmine thought he was going to throw up in his mask. He needed to breathe pure, fresh oxygen and yet he refused to pull the straps over his head. He must have still held hope for a rescue.

Jasmine looked through the glass in the hatch. Dark, pungent smoke blocked her view. An amber glow shone through from one side. From what she could tell, it had to be at the back of the deck.

"I've got suppression systems back online," Jason called out. "Once active, the core will release control."

"Flood it," Chuck replied. "And get us in there."

Before Chuck had finished his sentence, jets of clear air shot in from all sides within the science module. The jets stirred the murky smoke, but this couldn't have been breathable air. This had to be some kind of inert gas, Jasmine thought, realizing it would suffocate both the flame and anyone that had survived inside. As the smoke cleared, a body drifted into view. At a distance of ten to fifteen feet, the charred, blackened body looked barely human, more like the mummified remains of some ancient Egyptian than an astronaut in the 21st century.

"Open up," Chuck cried.

"It's still too dangerous," Jason replied. "Internal temperature is over six hundred. Any fresh oxygen will cause a flash fire."

"Damn you, Jason!" Chuck yelled. "Damn you to hell!"

In the silence that followed, Jasmine heard a soft click.

Jason spoke with resignation.

"I've increased internal pressure to give you a fighting chance. It'll lessen the back-flow of oxygen, but you'll get hit with a wave of outgoing gas. Once the pressure equalizes, close the hatch behind you."

Chuck didn't reply. He'd heard the lock release. He pushed over next to Jasmine, nudging her to one side away from the lock and pulled on the handle. The hatch flew open, startling Jasmine with how quickly it moved. Pungent black smoke billowed into the corridor. A wave of searing heat washed over her. She could feel the fine hairs on her arms wither as the radiant heat lashed at her skin. She felt as though they'd opened a blast furnace.

Chuck pulled his arms slightly back inside his jumpsuit so he could avoid gripping anything within the science module with his bare hands. He held the thick cotton cuffs up over his palms and pushed off gently into the smoky darkness. Jasmine rolled her sleeves down and followed cautiously behind him. The intense heat stung the exposed skin on her forehead and neck.

"Be careful," Jason said as Chuck closed the hatch behind them.

The vents within the devastated science module hissed as inert gases continued to flood the chamber.

Jasmine was sweating. She fumbled with the switches on the side of her mask, trying to increase the strength of the penlight. Suddenly, the smoke lit up like fog. The light barely penetrated the haze more than a few feet.

The glass lens on her mask began to fog up. She wanted to pull the mask off and wipe the lens, but knew that would be a mistake. With reduced visibility, she quickly lost sight of Chuck. The only other light drifting through the module came from the tiny glass window in the hatch behind them, casting soft shadows through the haze.

The burned-out shell of a cleaner drifted inert to one side, its plastic housing melted and blackened. The robotic device seemed to have borne the full brunt of the flames at some point, as one whole side of the machine was gone. It must have tried to fight the fire.

Soot marred the walls. Burn marks stretched along the benches. Plastic containers had melted and formed grotesque shapes floating in the smoke. There were no flames. Some of the surfaces were smoldering, giving off a steady stream of smoke.

"Ana? Mei?"

Jasmine's heart sank at Chuck's cry. No one could have survived the inferno.

Jets of gas brought cool relief, darting out of the fire suppression system and slowly lowering the temperature in the chamber.

Something dark loomed ahead. Jasmine didn't want to approach, but she had to. She already knew what she was looking at before the form became apparent. In the soft, smoky half-light, a body came into view, just the head and arms drifting through the haze in front of her. Black cinders hung in the air. Ash floated around her like the murky sediment at the bottom of the Mariana Trench.

Dark burns disfigured the body, making it almost impossible to recognize. From behind her thick rubber mask, listening to the wheezing sound of her own breathing and the hiss of oxygen coming from the cylinder in her hand, Jasmine felt as inhuman as the grotesque statue before her. She didn't want to know who it was. She didn't want to think of this as Anastasia or Mei. She felt cruel, heartless, but the thought that this was someone she cared for was devastating. Barely five minutes ago, this charred body had been a living, breathing person. The harsh reality of such a horrific death in space terrified Jasmine.

The charred body tumbled slowly before her, propelled by the inflow of inert gas. As the face came into view, Jasmine could see the charred remnants of hair, hollow empty eye sockets, blackened stretched skin, exposed teeth.

"Mei," she said softly, her voice breaking. Jasmine trembled uncontrollably. She reached out to touch the body, but her fingers stopped short, just inches from Mei's blackened shoulder.

Another dark shape loomed beyond the corpse. A face appeared behind a soot-stained gas mask. Chuck reached out over the body, wrapping a paper thin foil sheet over the remains. He moved with reverence, gently wrapping the foil blanket and clipping opposing clasps together to hold the blanket in place.

The sight of Chuck wearing his gas mask was unnerving. For Jasmine, this was a nightmare. Dark glass circles hid his eyes. His penlight struggled to penetrate the smoke. The blackened plastic faceplate covering his nose and mouth made him look inhuman, as though he were nothing more than a robot.

"Is it?" he asked, and Jasmine realized he didn't know who this was. He hadn't seen the face. Like Jasmine, Chuck was shaking. His trembling hands continued to gently wrap the body, but he hadn't looked at the face. He was avoiding any identification. Jasmine might not have been able to see much through the gloom, but she could see Chuck couldn't bring himself to look in case it was Anastasia.

Jasmine couldn't speak. Instead, she shook her head softly.

Chuck didn't reply. He repositioned himself in the weightless environment, pushing gently on an overhead cabinet so he could move the body to one side. With the body wrapped, he turned to Jasmine as though he was going to say something but he never spoke. Their heads were misaligned, with his head almost at a right angle to hers, and in the darkness Jasmine struggled with the concept of up and down. Such distinctions were meaningless, but she couldn't help but think of her orientation as correct.

"You OK?" she asked as she watched him adjust the flashlight on his helmet into a fine, thin beam.

Chuck didn't answer, and Jasmine realized she hadn't pressed the transmit button. She reached up, touched at the side of her throat and said, "Are you OK to continue?"

Chuck nodded. His oxygen bottle drifted beside his shoulder. His light lit up the ash suspended in the air. Her light diffused in the smoke, barely piercing the darkness. Chuck reached up and adjusted the focus, giving her more depth but over a narrower field.

Jasmine nodded rather than saying thanks. Thanks seemed grossly out of place in the dark, silent misery of the gutted science module.

Slowly, Chuck disappeared back into the shadows like a deep sea diver fading into the depths. Occasionally, she'd get a glimpse of him as his flashlight moved around, but most of the time it was obscured by his bulky frame and the heavy soot hanging in the air. She could hear him opening cabinets, struggling to pull the warped steel doors to one side.

Jasmine moved back to the hatch. She couldn't bear the thought of finding Anastasia in the same condition as Mei. She wanted to get out of the terrifying darkness. She rubbed the glass, peering through to the corridor beyond the hatch. Jason must have restored power and sucked out the smoke as the corridor appeared brightly lit. The white surfaces looked pristine, and that seemed wrong. The ship should mourn its losses with something more than the burnt out remains of the science module, it should not continue on as though nothing had happened, thought Jasmine. There should at least be stains, scars. Life was too precious to count for nothing.

As much as she wanted to, she couldn't leave Chuck. She desperately wanted to twist the handle and push on the hatch, but she knew she had to stay. Jasmine turned around and the beam of her flashlight glanced over the inside of the science lab. Jason must have been cycling the air and filtering out the smoke, as the thick ash was clearing.

Burnt fingers stuck out from a small gap in a sliding panel covering a storage unit. In the darkness, neither she nor Chuck had noticed them when they'd first entered the module. Jasmine felt her heart beating in her throat. She pushed off and drifted a few feet over to the panel. Slowly, she forced the panel back to expose the body of Anastasia. She expected to see charred remains like those of Mei, but Ana was clothed. She was wearing a gas mask. Her hair was singed and her arms burnt, but she looked intact. Jasmine fought with the panel, shining her flashlight into the storage unit, trying to get a better look. She couldn't tell if Anastasia was alive, but she hadn't been burned as badly as Mei.

"Chuck," Jasmine cried, stabbing at the microphone

button on her mask. She turned and peered through the haze, yelling, "Chuck. Quick! Over here by the hatch!"

Like so many of the scorched panels in the science module, the sliding door had warped and wouldn't move on its frame. Being weightless, Jasmine found it almost impossible to wrestle with a jammed door. She jimmied the panel open far enough that she could grab Anastasia by the shoulders and drag her through the gap. With her feet anchored against the hull, she pulled, struggling to maneuver Anastasia's limp body out through the opening. Chuck bumped into her, coming down from above. He grabbed at the blackened jumpsuit Anastasia was wearing and helped pull her into the module.

"Ana. Ana," he cried over and over, his voice muted by his gas mask.

Once she was free, Jasmine left Anastasia with Chuck and twisted the handle on the entry hatch, pushing it open so they could escape the darkness. Clouds of smoke followed them into the corridor. Jasmine sealed the hatch behind them as Chuck ripped the gas mask from his wife's head. Her neck moved as though it were rubbery, reacting to his motion, but she showing no signs of life.

"Oh, Ana, please," Chuck cried, tearing his own mask from his face. He tapped at her cheeks and then held his fingers against her jugular and checked for a pulse. Chuck cradled her head in his arms. Pinching her nose, he began resuscitation breaths, inflating her lungs with short, rapid breaths.

"Get her to Medical," Jason said, snapping Jasmine out of her daze. She pulled the gas mask from her face and let it drift to one side.

Chuck pushed with his legs, using one hand to avoid bumping into the curving wall of the corridor as they sailed into Medical.

"Jazz," Jason said. "You're going to need to prep the defibrillator. Cabinet with the green cross on it. Hook up the defib. It will let me see if she's got a heartbeat. Stick the paddles on her chest, one high, one low, on either side of the sternum, and prep two milligrams of atropine."

"Right," Jasmine said, stirred into action by Jason's sense of urgency.

She tore open the defibrillator cabinet. The plastic panel was designed to come away easily in an emergency and sailed across medical, banging into the far cabinets.

"Hurry," Chuck cried, strapping Anastasia to a medical bed with Velcro. He continued with resuscitation breaths as Jasmine grabbed at the defibrillator. Plastic bottles and vials floated free, liberated by the motion she imparted as she frantically grabbed at items she thought were needed. In a panic, she pushed off and found herself somersaulting out of control. She had to let something go in order to arrest her motion, and the needleless injection gun with the atropine drifted from her grasp.

"Oxygen," Jason said.

"On it," Chuck replied, pulling a transparent medical mask from beside the flat bed and strapping it over Anastasia's mouth. Oxygen began flowing automatically through the thin green tube.

Jasmine had never used a defibrillator before, but she'd been on the receiving end. Her pectoral muscles were still sore and bruised from when Mike had shocked her back to life. She tore the flat paddles open as Chuck cut the front of his wife's jumpsuit and singlet open, exposing her chest and breasts. The dry underside of the paddles had a sticky texture. Jasmine slapped one on Anastasia's upper chest, just below her collarbone, and the other down beneath her breast, pushing it hard against her lower ribcage.

"I'm getting a beat," Jason said as soon as the first paddle touched. "Irregular, low pressure. Stunted arrhythmia. She's barely holding on. You need to shock the heart."

"Get clear," Jasmine said to Chuck. She may not have known much about medicine or life in space, but she knew what the big red button in the middle of the defibrillation control would do. She watched as Chuck let go of his wife, lifting his hands out to the side like wings. On Earth, he would have fallen flat against her, but in orbit around Saturn, he hung there suspended, inches above her chest.

Jasmine slammed her hand into the button, not that force would do anything more to help Anastasia, but the urgency of the moment seemed to demand more from her. Anastasia's body arched backwards under the Velcro straps and then went limp.

"Again?" Jasmine asked.

"No," Jason replied. "I'm getting a clean, rhythmic beat. Just hold off for now."

Chuck closed his eyes for a moment.

Vapor formed on the inside of the oxygen mask as Anastasia breathed on her own.

Jason said, "Her heart rate is fluctuating. Go ahead and give her the atropine."

Jasmine disconnected the defibrillator, leaving the panels stuck to Anastasia's chest but pulling the clip from the back of the device. She left the yellow defibrillation unit with its big red button floating in the air above Anastasia with the loose wire drifting aimlessly in the air and pushed off to look for the atropine.

The atropine was in a needleless syringe that looked vaguely like a gun. The device was intuitive to use, with a touchscreen wrapping around the cylinder. There were multiple drug options and dosage indicators.

"Two milligrams, right?"

"Make it one," Jason said. "And fifty micrograms of Fentanyl."

Chuck was a mess. He held Anastasia's hand, gently patting the back of her wrist and mumbling something in what sounded like Russian.

Jasmine fumbled with the exotic syringe.

Jason spoke with more than a hint of concern in his voice. "It's mg for milligram and mcg for microgram. Be careful with the dose selection. There's a world of difference between the two. Fifty micrograms is 5% of one milligram. You don't want to—"

"I've got it," Jasmine snapped, trying to compose herself.

"Administer both shots into her upper thigh."

The scissors Chuck had used to expose Anastasia's upper torso were floating with a myriad of junk near the table.

Jasmine grabbed the scissors and cut carefully past Anastasia's waist and down the center of her right thigh, exposing dark red welts and blisters. There was just enough leg exposed to press the syringe gun against a pale patch of pink skin. In pressing the gun against Anastasia's thigh, Jasmine inevitably pushed herself away from the table. She had to reposition herself and hold onto one of the Velcro straps before she felt confident enough to administer the atropine. She paused, mentally recounting what she'd done selecting atropine and the dose of one mg, not one mcg, and squeezed the broad, flat trigger. A pneumatic sound signaled the injection of the drug through the pores in Anastasia's skin.

"And the—"

"Got it," Jasmine replied. She didn't need to be lectured. She needed to concentrate. She looked at the settings and adjusted the drug to Fentanyl and the dosage to fifty micrograms, paying close attention to the change from mg to mcg. She breathed deeply as she pushed the gun against the same spot and squeezed the trigger.

"You're going to have to get her out of those clothes and clean her with a sponge bath," Jason said. "Cut away what you can, but if any of the clothing is stuck, leave it in place. You'll find antiseptic wash in the cabinet marked surgical prep. There's antibiotic lotion in the next cabinet, be sure to use the one marked topical painkiller. Once she's wiped down, you're going to want to use non-stick bandages from the dressings cabinet. Apply a liberal amount of lotion before setting the bandage with a compression strip."

"Got it." Jasmine wiped the sweat from her forehead. She wasn't angry with Jason, just focused.

Chuck was sobbing. He seemed to have shut down mentally. Jasmine was on her own. She gathered the supplies she needed, tacking them onto Velcro straps positioned around the medical bed precisely for such a contingency. Slowly and methodically, she cut away Anastasia's jumpsuit, working on one limb at a time, removing clothing where she could, cleaning the soot and ash away, lathering the blisters and burns and gently bandaging the wounds. Chuck helped, but only in a secondary manner, taking soiled wipes from Jasmine and handing her bandages as she needed them. He was silent, subdued. Jasmine was concentrating too intently to say much beyond the rudiments of what she needed to tend to Anastasia's burns.

After roughly half an hour, Anastasia regained consciousness. It was as though someone flicked a switch inside her head and suddenly she was awake.

"Chuck!"

"I'm here," he said, leaving Jasmine working on one of Anastasia's legs and taking hold of Anastasia's bandaged arm and hand. Her fingers poked through a compression bandage, grabbing at his hand. "It's OK. You're going to be OK."

"Jazz," Anastasia said, craning her neck to see Jasmine wrapping her lower leg.

"Hey," Jasmine replied. "You take it easy. Just relax."

"What happened, babe?" Chuck asked, pulling the mask away and turning off the flow of oxygen.

"Mei?"

"I'm sorry," Chuck said, not offering any more than those two words. "What happened in there?"

"Mei," she said, her voice croaking, and she coughed struggling to speak.

"What about Mei?" Chuck asked, giving her a sip of water from a bottle with a thin straw.

Anastasia swallowed, grimacing in pain as she did so, and sucked at the water again before speaking.

"Mei was trying to access the core subsystems. She said Mike had been modifying executables. She said Mike and Jason—"

"Jason?" Jasmine cried, cutting her off.

"Me?" Jason said from a wall mounted speaker.

Anastasia swallowed. "The fire. It came from the wall. Mei was telling me about the files when it erupted. She was trying to explain."

"Which wall?" Jason asked.

"There was a panel missing," Anastasia managed.

"Where?" Chuck asked.

Jason elaborated, saying, "There's a fuel line running from the rear tanks to the forward docking thrusters. It is inside the outer hull, but it's isolated from any wiring, wrapped in insulation. It shouldn't have leaked."

"If it did," Chuck said, "we should have picked up on a loss in line pressure."

"Yes," Jason replied, agreeing with him. "If the subsystem files have been modified, that could explain the fire suppression system going offline."

"Damn you, Mike," Chuck growled as Jasmine finished up on Anastasia's leg.

"How do you feel?" Jason asked.

"Stiff and sore," Anastasia replied.

"We can give you some more fentanyl," Jasmine said, then suddenly realizing she had no idea about dosage levels and if that was advisable or not.

"No, I'm fine."

Anastasia pulled at the Velcro wrist strap.

"Hey, take it easy," Chuck said. "You just rest up."

Jason added, "We need to give you some intravenous fluids."

"You need another astronaut," Anastasia replied. "Not a bed-ridden patient. Now is not the time for rest. We rest when we're dead."

"Honey," Chuck said, but Anastasia had already wriggled one hand free and was pulling the Velcro from her other hand.

"I'm Russian. I'm fine."

Jasmine took a good look at Anastasia's battered torso with the various bandages sticking to patches of her bare skin. Her arms were heavily wrapped. She must have been in an extraordinary amount of pain, but she was stubborn, determined to get off the bed.

"Your legs are in pretty bad shape," Jasmine said, feeling the need to warn her.

"This is space," Anastasia replied with her distinct

Russian accent. "We have no need of legs in space."

Dark black marks stained the skin on her face, leaving a halo where the gas mask had covered her eyes, nose and mouth. She could barely move her legs, but that was probably for the best, allowing them to heal. Her arms were already in a partial cradle, bent slightly at the elbows. Even with all her bandages, Anastasia looked invincible, as though no mortal wound could ever defeat her. Chuck grabbed one of his jumpsuits and helped her climb into the oversized uniform.

"There," Anastasia said, visibly trying not to grimace. "I feel better already."

She was lying, Jasmine was sure of it, but then everyone was lying on the *Copernicus*.

Chapter 09: Cleaners

For all her bravado, Anastasia needed assistance moving up to the bridge. Chuck was impatient and went on ahead.

Jasmine held onto Anastasia's baggy jumpsuit and pulled her along. Their combined mass was difficult to manage in the weightless environment. Jasmine was surprised by how her center of mass shifted as she held on to Anastasia's waist, and she constantly had to compensate. Jasmine was forced to take her time and make lots of small adjustments with her hands and feet as she glided through the air just a few inches from the hull. She kept Anastasia positioned more centrally in the corridor, trying to avoid aggravating any of her injuries.

The two remaining cleaners buzzed through the air, sailing past Jasmine and Anastasia. The robots turned effortlessly in the air in front of them with their claw-like arms outstretched.

"Let me help."

It was Chuck's voice coming through one of the speakers on the base of the lead cleaner.

"Sure," Jasmine said, coming slowly to a stop and bringing Anastasia to a halt beside her.

"Just relax," Chuck said in a tinny, electronic voice.

One of the cleaners flew around behind Anastasia. Jasmine watched as the pincer-like claws grabbed gently at the loose jumpsuit. The other cleaner backed up almost twenty feet behind the two women, and Jasmine realized Chuck was ensuring he had a good view of both the lead cleaner and Anastasia. Slowly, the fan in the heart of the hollow cleaner beside her wound up to speed and began pushing Anastasia smoothly along the corridor. Given her body mass, it took the best part of a minute before Anastasia was underway.

"Just like the beggar carried into paradise by the angels," Anastasia quipped.

"Sorry?" Jasmine replied, not understanding the reference.

"Gospel of Luke," she replied as the cleaner carried her away. "Benefits of an Orthodox upbringing."

Jasmine waited for the second cleaner to pass her, not wanting to obscure Chuck's view. She smiled, realizing she'd misread Chuck entirely. He could have told them what he was thinking of doing, but perhaps he wasn't sure how well it would work.

Flying two of those mechanical basketballs at once must have been quite a feat, and Jasmine was surprised he didn't have Jason coordinate their motion. There was probably a little bit of pride involved, or perhaps the tender care of a husband for his wife, and he must have felt as though her fragile state required a personal touch rather than assigning this task to a computer.

Jasmine kept pace with the second cleaner. As she came out into the vast expanse of the bridge, the bright stars in the dark sky looked somehow full of hope. She wasn't sure what had caused her rebound of emotion. Perhaps it was a natural bounce after all she'd seen with Mei, perhaps it was having been able to rescue Anastasia or the novel way Chuck brought Ana up to the bridge, but for the first time, Jasmine felt confident.

Anastasia joked with Chuck.

"I don't know why you only just thought of this. We should travel like this all the time."

Chuck smiled. He brought her to a halt and released the clamps holding onto her jumpsuit. Chuck pressed a single button on the flatscreen in front of him and the two cleaners circled away from the astronauts and docked with their recharge station on the boundary between the transparent dome and the bridge. They reversed into place and shut down.

"Coffee?" Jasmine asked. She was in a daze. As that single word came out of her mouth, it sounded dumb. Two crew members on the *Copernicus* had died within 24 hours, and here she was, ready to resume the routines of life.

Mei had loved coffee, and Jasmine felt drawn to the concept more than the actual drink. Coffee was a link with Earth. The smell, the taste, even the warm temperature provided a bit of escape from the insanity of being a billion miles from home, and subconsciously she longed for that release yet again. If she couldn't be back in Georgia sitting on her porch swing, then coffee was the next best thing. She was in shock.

"I had something a little stronger in mind," Chuck replied as he rummaged around under the cargo nets holding the contents from the airlock in place. Jasmine barely remembered chaotically tossing items out of the airlock before she and Nadir suited up. She hadn't thought about what had happened to the boxes and packages, but there they were, neatly stacked under elastic cargo nets.

"Ah, here it is."

Chuck pulled out a silver canister not unlike the water bottle Jasmine used to take with her to the gym back on Earth.

"You're telling me you snuck contraband aboard and you didn't tell me?" Anastasia said with a reinvigorated sense of purpose.

Chuck turned and looked at her as he closed the lid of the box and put it back in place. The silver canister turned slowly in the air beside him.

"Wine?" she asked.

Chuck shook his head.

"Whiskey?"

"Nothing so crude," Chuck replied, narrowing his eyes and looking at Anastasia with what Jasmine thought of as mischievous intent.

"Vodka!" Anastasia cried in excitement.

Chuck smiled.

Jasmine laughed.

Chuck couldn't suppress the grin on his face. He unscrewed the lid, keeping it half on the container to prevent any liquid from spilling, and sipped at the clear liquid.

"For medicinal purposes only," he added, and Anastasia roared with laughter.

"God, how I love you," she cried.

Chuck handed the container to her. The lid floated to

one side and drops of crystal clear vodka drifted out of the cylinder. He pushed off through the air, sucking up the drops with his mouth. Anastasia put the bottle to her lips and drank. Rather than lifting the bottle to get the alcohol to flow, she shook it gently.

"AHHH!" She cried, her eyes wide in surprise. "Come, Jazz. You must try."

A few more drops drifted through the air and Chuck cleaned them up with obvious relish.

"You're on some pretty heavy meds," Jasmine replied. She felt like she was the responsible one at an underage party, and being nineteen, that was quite an appropriate position from her perspective.

"Ha ha," Anastasia cried. "It is all good. Vodka is like water for Russians. It is medicine."

Jasmine wasn't sure anyone with any medical training would agree, but she floated over to join the party. There was something magnetic about the joy exuded by Chuck and Ana in something as simple as a little alcohol. Anastasia handed her the cylinder, half cupping the lid over the opening to prevent more spillage.

"Pit' Pit' You drink!" Anastasia said, mixing her Russian and English.

Jasmine couldn't help but smile at her enthusiasm. She raised the bottle to her lips as the cap drifted by her face. The vodka buffeted her mouth, getting into cracks in the skin and stinging her lips. Rather than sipping, she inadvertently took a whole mouthful of vodka, unable to stem the flow. She coughed, choking as Anastasia took the bottle from her. Chuck laughed as Jasmine struggled to swallow the vodka. Almost instantly, she felt a rush of warmth in her belly followed by a giddy sense of lightheadedness.

"That's not vodka," she said, wiping her lips. "It's rocket fuel!"

"Da, Da!" Anastasia replied, clearly slipping into what Jasmine imagined was her rough, cosmonaut upbringing. "It is good. No?"

"Yes, it's good," Jasmine replied, feeling a sting of pain from her cracked lips.

Anastasia took another swig and then handed the canister to Chuck who sipped a little more before putting the lid back on.

"Feeling better?" he asked.

"Yes," Anastasia said.

"I was saving this for a special occasion. To celebrate."

"And it is special," Anastasia replied. "We mourn Nadir and Mei, but we do not despair. We celebrate their lives. We celebrate our lives."

Jasmine nodded. There was something wonderfully human about communing together over a drink. Their cares seemed to melt away, if only for a moment.

"In Russia, we say—even the coldest winter has to thaw. All sorrow comes to an end. There is always a spring. There is always a summer."

Jasmine smiled at Anastasia's enthusiasm, being swept along by her optimism in spite of the bandages wrapped around the Russian's frail body. Jasmine admired her mental fortitude.

Chuck brushed his wife's knotted hair to one side and kissed her gently on the cheek.

Jasmine was surprised by how quickly the alcohol had affected her and how potent it felt. If she'd been back in Georgia, she wouldn't have driven a car feeling like this. She simply wouldn't have trusted her attention span and reaction time.

Chuck put the silver canister back under the elastic cargo net, but Jasmine noticed he didn't put it back in the box.

"So what next?" Anastasia asked.

Party's over, Jasmine thought.

"I have Jason running diagnostics," Chuck replied. "He's been able to reroute most of the core functions and isolate the damage in the Science module. The burst fuel line vented high pressure gas into space for almost an hour. It's imparted some sideways motion we're going to need to correct or we're going to collide with Bestla."

"We're going to crash?" Jasmine asked in alarm.

Chuck raised his hands in defense. "Hey, we're still over a hundred kilometers out, and our relative approach speed is low. Given the figures I've seen, crash would be too strong a word. More like a fender bender as our orbits cross. But we can correct the discrepancy. Once Jason's isolated the fuel lines, we'll conduct a short burn and glide past as planned."

Jasmine noted that since Anastasia had sipped some vodka her movements had become more fluid. Her legs remained inert, but her arms and upper torso seemed more free and relaxed.

"And Mike?" Anastasia asked.

"Mike?" Chuck replied. "We don't know what part he's played in all this."

"You think he caused the fire?" Jasmine asked. "Why

would he do that? It makes no sense."

"Don't get defensive, Jazz," Chuck replied. "I'm not suggesting it was deliberate. The fire could have been inadvertent or accidental on his part."

"Or," Anastasia added, "he may not have had anything to do with it at all, but until we know for sure, we need to keep all options on the table."

Jasmine didn't notice the eerie sound at first, but as it grew in its intensity she noticed Chuck and Anastasia looking around nervously. Slowly, it dawned on Jasmine that this was the message from Bestla being replayed over the speakers within the *Copernicus*.

"Jason?" Chuck asked.

"It's coming from Engineering. Mike must be down there on one of the consoles."

As the wailing grew louder, the irregular sections seemed almost as though they were musical. There was pitch and intonation. Some sections had the rhythm of speech, others sounded as though they'd been played in reverse or run through some kind of synthesizer to mask their meaning. Although she'd only heard the message twice, Jasmine knew precisely when those haunting words would be spoken. The hair on the back of her neck stood on end as a disembodied voice echoed through the *Copernicus*.

"*Here'sss to my sweet Satan.*"

A garble of conflicting sounds tormented her, being broken only by more words she wished she'd never heard.

"*I want to live and die for you, my glorious Satan.*"

Jasmine put her hands over her ears, trying to block out the noise. The words repeated again.

"*Here'sss to my sweet Satan.*"

"Mike!" Chuck yelled. "You can't scare us."

"*I want to live and die for you, my glorious Satan.*"

"It won't work," Anastasia cried. "You can't frighten us."

"Shut him down, Jason," Chuck called out over the eerie noise.

"I can't."

Jasmine screamed, "Stop it, Mike! Stop it!"

She shut her eyes and pressed her hands hard over her ears and began reciting the Lord's Prayer, trying to drown out the message.

"Our Father, who art—"

Suddenly, the wailing stopped.

Jasmine opened her eyes and relaxed, slowly allowing her hands to drift away from her head.

"What just happened?" Chuck asked to no one in particular.

"He stopped," Jason replied.

"Why the hell didn't you override him?" Anastasia asked.

"I can't override a crew member's commands on the core server," Jason replied.

"I don't like it," Chuck said. "Mike wouldn't pull something like this without a reason. He's planning something. He's trying to distract us, trying to divert our attention and get us chasing our tails."

"He's buying time," Anastasia said.

"Yes, but for what?" Chuck asked. "Where is he now?"

"Still down there," Jason replied. "He's rummaging around near the computer servers."

"He'll be gone before you get there," Anastasia said to Chuck.

"Jason, fire up the cleaners," Chuck said.

"The cleaners?" Jason asked with what seemed to be genuine surprise.

"Yes," Chuck said. "I'll head down into engineering and flush him into the ducts. You take the cleaners through the vents and corner him."

Already, the two robotic flyers were buzzing through the air. The hum of their central fans filled the air.

"I'll be able to take them through the access points," Jason said. "But if he's in one of the crawlspaces, he'll be out of reach."

Chuck was already at the edge of the central shaft. Now, the corridor seemed to go down, Jasmine thought.

"He won't have thought of this," Chuck replied. "If we can take him by surprise, we can end this."

"But if he gets to a console," Jason said. "He'll shut them down."

"Then we have to keep him away from any of the consoles," Chuck said, already disappearing down the brightly lit shaft.

One of the cleaners removed the cover to the maintenance shaft Mike had disappeared into previously. The robot set the cover to one side, leaving it floating stationary in the air. The other cleaner took the vent and secured it with straps against the wall. The first cleaner disappeared into the vent. Seconds later, the other cleaner flew into the vent, catching the side of the sheet metal and giving off a loud clang.

Jasmine trembled. She didn't know what to think. A sickening feeling filled her stomach. Mike was going to die. Death is all that seemed to await anyone on the *Copernicus*, she thought. Nadir, Mei, when would it stop? She looked down at her shaking hand. Anastasia must have noticed, as she drifted over to her. Anastasia took Jasmine's fingers in her heavily strapped hand.

"I'm sorry," she said. "You know it has to be done."

Jasmine's lower lip trembled. She nodded softly. Ana was right, she thought. As much as she wanted to deny reality, Mike had lost his mind. There was probably some fancy psychological explanation, some carefully crafted theory that defined space fever. From the exploration of Antarctica to the doomed pioneers of the American West in the 1800s, prolonged isolation had always driven men insane. This wasn't her Mike, she thought, trying to rationalize what was happening. This was some other Mike. This was a dream, a nightmare, it had to be. This couldn't be real.

Anastasia rested one hand on the side of Jasmine's cheek. Even with thick bandages wrapped around her burnt palms, Jasmine could feel the tenderness in her touch. Anastasia raised Jasmine's face so their eyes met.

"We need to be strong. You must be strong."

Again, Jasmine nodded, sniffing and trying to hold back tears.

"We are here not for ourselves, but for others, for billions of others."

Jasmine struggled to maintain eye contact, but she understood it was important. As much as she wanted to look away, she looked deep into the Russian's blue eyes. Anastasia's face was still dirty. Her beautiful hair was scorched and tangled. With all she'd been through, she kept her presence of mind, thought Jasmine. She was tough.

"We need each other," Anastasia continued. "There are just three of us and a billion miles of empty space."

Three. It should have been four.

"We do what is right, yes?"

"Yes," Jasmine managed.

"What is right is not what is easy. If this mission was easy, they would have sent chimps."

Both women smiled.

"We are the brave," Anastasia said. "We fight for each other. We see the mission through."

She pulled Jasmine close. The two women floated there with their foreheads touching, resting gently against each other. Anastasia held her hand behind Jasmine's neck, holding her tight. For her part, Jasmine closed her eyes. She could feel the warmth radiating from Anastasia's forehead. The woman must have been in considerable pain, Jasmine thought. She should have been drugged up to the eyeballs and sleeping as her body began the slow, torturous process of healing her burns, and yet here she was, comforting Jasmine.

Jasmine breathed deeply. They were so close, she could feel Anastasia exhale. Warm air brushed against her neck.

"Thank you."

Anastasia relaxed and they drifted apart.

"It is who we are," she said, smiling through the pain that was obvious in each grimace. "We are social creatures. We need each other."

Jasmine felt as though Anastasia could read her mind.

"I feel very much alone," she confessed.

Anastasia smiled. Warmth radiated from her rosy

cheeks. Her blue eyes were full of compassion as she spoke.

"We have a proverb in Russia: *Ten thousand generations have led down to us. Ten thousand will stem from us.* You see, we are never alone. When we were born, we were surrounded by those that love us. We live our lives as one among eight billion souls. Even in death, we are not alone. We leave footprints in the hearts of others."

Jasmine swallowed the knot in her throat. She started to speak when she heard a sound like that of the rumbling of thunder before a coming storm.

The sound of pounding sheet metal filled the air.

"Get out of here!" cried Jason.

"What is happening?" Anastasia replied, as confused as Jasmine.

Jason spoke rapidly over the banging within the darkened duct.

"I've lost control of CL2. I'm not sure how long I can hold on to CL3."

"The cleaners?" Jasmine cried as the two robotic flyers tumbled from the maintenance duct. The cleaners shot across the deck, crashing into the navigation console and sending fine shards of plastic flying through the air.

"Get out of here!" Jason cried.

Out? Jasmine had no idea what he meant. She was trapped in a flimsy tin can on the far side of the solar system. Out where? Out into space? Jasmine froze. She couldn't move. She was terrified.

Mechanical arms wrestled with each other as the two basketball size robots fought. One of the cleaners ripped the grating from the front of the other, exposing the fan whirling furiously within.

"The airlock!" Anastasia cried.

"No!" Jasmine yelled. She couldn't go outside. She'd seen Nadir die out there in the lonely pitch black of space. The thought of being lost in the darkness terrified her more than the grinding gears of the two robotic cleaners struggling in front of her.

"I can't stop him," Jason cried from the speakers behind her. "You've got to get out of here. Hide!"

"No."

Jasmine struggled to remain composed. She was shaking violently. Her left leg jiggled up and down uncontrollably, but she wouldn't run, if that was the right term for fleeing in space.

Suddenly, the two robots stopped. The vice-like pincers at the end of their robotic arms released and the cleaners floated free. Where moments before, the fans inside them had been whining at a high pitch as they struggled against each other, now they fell to a silent, ominous hum.

Anastasia inched her way to the airlock.

Jasmine reached behind herself, wanting to feel the security of the wall, but she'd drifted too far. She was helpless. Without someone coming to her aid, she'd have to wait until her slow drifting motion took her within reach of some other part of the bridge. At the rate she was moving, that would take over a minute.

Anastasia pulled herself over the cargo nets, clambering toward the airlock. She opened the hatch.

The cleaners turned away from each other with a deft, smooth motion, rotating through the air until each faced one of the women.

"Mike?" Jasmine said with a quiver in her voice. "Mike, honey, don't do this. It's me, Jazz."

With the grates missing from both of the cleaners, the blur of their fans within looked deadly.

"This is wrong," Jasmine said, squirming with her body, trying to reach some part of the bridge. She passed within inches of one of the headrests by the command deck. If she could reach that padded leather block with her foot she could kick off and propel herself away from CL2, the cleaner closest to her, but even with her foot extended, she couldn't quite reach. The slipper shoes she was wearing came within an inch of touching, teasing her with the promise of escape.

"Mike," she continued. "You need help. I know it's hard to understand, but please, trust me. I only want to help."

Anastasia moved around the hatch, wanting to enter the airlock. She was gliding swiftly through the air when CL3 shot after her. The metal robot careened into her, sending her body flying into the metal frame around the airlock. The cleaner ricocheted up and away from the hatch, bouncing like a pinball. Its low mass was offset by its turbo-fan and its ability to accelerate sharply. CL3 recovered quickly, moving in an arc as it raced around the bridge.

Anastasia flailed through the air, reaching out with her hands and grabbing at the hull. CL3 turned away from her, joining CL2 in staring down Jasmine.

Jasmine felt her foot brush against something. She must have been drifting at an angle, as her foot rubbed softly against the side of another headrest. Without looking down, she felt around with her foot. Keeping her eyes on the two cleaners closing in on her, she hooked both feet beneath the headrest.

CL3 positioned itself slightly to her left, while CL2 drifted not more than five feet from her face. They were hunting her. The fan within CL2 pulsed, spinning one way and then another, like a racing car or a motorcycle revving its engine, with each pulse causing it to sway back and forth in the air. At that point, the robot looked more like a wild animal, one barely able to contain itself. The cleaners were sighting on her.

Jasmine had her hands out, willing the two robots to keep their distance, but she was helpless. If her arms were drawn into the open cowling, the fan blades would mangle her soft skin and probably break bones. She doubted her cotton jumpsuit would provide much protection.

"Mike. This isn't you. I don't know what you're thinking, but no one wants to hurt you. No one has betrayed you. We can work this out."

The two robots were slightly out of sync with each other, pulsing at different times. Slowly, they were aligning. It seemed obvious to Jasmine that when they overlapped they'd attack as they could both lunge at her at precisely the same moment.

"Please," she pleaded. "Don't do this, Mike."

It was too late. The mechanical cleaners rushed at her, moving with an alarming burst of speed.

With her feet hooked in the gap beneath the headrest, Jasmine was able to pull herself swiftly down out of their path. The two metal robots collided, glancing off each other as she hunkered below them.

"Get out of here," Anastasia cried, swinging a metal rod at one of the cleaners. She'd pulled the rod from beneath a cargo net and was wielding it like a spear.

The cleaners zoomed through the air, circling around and homing in on Jasmine as she crouched in the weightless environment just above the commander's headrest.

Jasmine glanced at the airlock. If she could make it, she could seal herself in there, closing the hatch on these murderous robots, but she'd be exposed during the four or five seconds it took to cross the bridge. The cleaners had already shown themselves adept at intercepting Anastasia. Jasmine knew she'd never make it. She was out of options. CL2 raced in at her, screaming through the air with its fan blade a blur inside its hollow body. With its claw-like pincers out in front of it, the robot would easily overpower her.

Out of the corner of her eye, she could see Anastasia being dragged toward the spinning blade of CL3 by a pair of thin, strong metal arms, but Anastasia wasn't giving up without a fight. She used the metal rod like a crow bar, prying one of the arms loose.

Jasmine took the only option open to her. She sprung out, launching herself up off the back of the seat, pushing with her thighs and aiming for the open maintenance shaft. CL2 caught hold of her jumpsuit, grabbing at the loose fabric by her ankle. A combination of the robot's mass and momentum threw her off course. With her arms out in front of her, Jasmine managed to reach the duct and pull herself inside. The cleaner swung wildly below her crashing into the hull and losing its grip.

Anastasia screamed. Jasmine could hear the sickening whir of the main blade on CL3 slowing and grinding as it cut into Anastasia's arm. Jasmine couldn't think. She didn't want to picture what was happening, but she could hear Anastasia crying for mercy as metal claws tore at her. The blade stuttered and stopped, catching on her arm. The sound of the engine reversing and driving forward time and time again made Jasmine feel sick.

Inside the narrow duct, Jasmine found she couldn't bring her arms down. She had no choice but to struggle on, slapping at the sheet metal in a frantic effort to get away from the bridge. Behind her, hidden from sight, she could hear CL2 following her into the duct. Metal claws grabbed at her shoes, tearing them from her feet as she scrambled deeper into the vent.

"Mike, please. Don't."

The duct followed the contour of the deck, with several grates leading back onto the bridge. Jasmine caught a glimpse of Anastasia's lifeless body floating aimlessly around the bridge. Large globules of deep red blood pooled in the air, forming perfect spheres of various sizes.

Without the aid of gravity, it was difficult to gain traction within the claustrophobic shaft. The walls felt like they were collapsing around her, imprisoning her in a steel coffin.

Jasmine fought with her legs, trying to push off the sheet metal and propel herself along, but the cleaner held her back. She twisted and squirmed, fighting to free herself, but CL2 had a firm grip on her jumpsuit.

"No. No!" she screamed, frantically slapping at the sheet metal. Ahead, the duct opened out into a junction. Dark shadows obscured her view, but she could make out a crawlspace too small for a cleaner. She tried to pull herself in when she felt her toes being drawn into the furious fan whizzing within the heart of the cleaner. The blades tore at her skin, cutting deep into her foot and breaking bones as they ground against her soft flesh.

Jasmine screamed, struggling to pull herself free. Pain surged through her legs.

"MIKE!"

A hand reached down for her, stretched out in the darkness. Jasmine grabbed at Mike's wrist and with a surge of adrenalin pulled herself on against the pain in her feet. Mike's arm was strong, rigid and stiff, giving her some much needed leverage.

The cleaner sensed something had changed as she pulled quickly away. The robot reversed the direction of its blades, trying to pull her back, but Jasmine would not be deterred. With all her strength, she pulled herself on and squeezed past Mike into the dark crawlspace. Arcs of light came from a bunch of loose, twisted wires to one side. Jasmine was careful to avoid them as she slid past him.

"What have you done, Mike?" she cried, wriggling past his legs and feet. She'd wrenched the fabric of her jumpsuit from the robotic claws, tearing herself free from the cleaner. She could hear the claws snapping at her heels. "Dear God, Mike, what have you done?"

Chapter 10: Mike

The crawlspace was cramped, even more so than the duct. Light flickered from a computer screen, but the screen was full of static. Electricity arced from loose wires hanging from what she assumed was the roof. Various pipes ran through the cavity with access points every few meters.

Below, Jasmine could hear the cleaner whizzing back and forth in the duct. The robot must have been using the junction beneath the opening of the crawlspace to maneuver. Slowly, the sound of its engine faded and she figured it must have given up and left.

Mike was lying hard up against her but they were inverted, so she was facing his legs and feet. As she wriggled on, she kept bumping into him, dragging him back with her.

"Mike, you've got to stop this. Please! This is madness."

In her panic, she hadn't noticed, but Mike's body was stiff and unyielding.

"Mike?" she said with a quiver of panic in her voice. The implication of his immobile form terrified her. His body lacked the supple flexibility of life in free-fall. He drifted like a mannequin beside her.

Jasmine reached out and grabbed his ankles, wanting to pull herself past him and hopefully turn around to face him. His legs were cold and stiff, and she instantly let go, shocked by what she felt. Mike was dead.

"No," she mumbled to herself. "No, it's not possible. No, no, no."

Slowly, she pulled herself on past Mike. Her hands shook. Try as she might, she couldn't compose herself.

"Please Mike. Don't do this to me. I can't handle any more. I can't do this alone."

Jasmine wanted her words to change reality. She wanted to be wrong.

"Please."

The static on the flat computer screen provided the only light. Jasmine kept well clear of the exposed wires by the console.

"I don't understand," she said, finding the crawlspace was narrow but wide enough that she could turn around once she got past him. Her teeth chattered, but not from the cold. Goosebumps raised on her skin.

She drew her knees to her chest, trying to examine her legs and feet in the half-light. She was bleeding, but the blood was sticking to her wounds in large, thick globules. Her right leg was worse than her left. Deep cuts surrounded her lower calf and ankle, but her tendons seemed to be intact as she could slowly and painfully extend her foot. A large gash ran around the sole of her right foot and her toes looked like mush.

Jasmine cried. She ached. She felt sorry for herself. She was in so much pain she couldn't think straight. Tears welled up into globs of saline water, forcing her to wipe them away with bloodied fingers.

"Why, Mike? Why?"

The corpse floating in the shadows was silent.

Muffled yelling came from somewhere distant. The sound of metal resounding against metal rang through the *Copernicus* as blow after blow came from the bridge. Jasmine thought the cleaner that had chased her was gone, but it must have been floating motionless just outside the crawlspace waiting for her before it suddenly raced away.

"Chuck," she whispered. "Be careful."

Her warning was pathetic, she knew that, but in that moment she couldn't help but feel connected to him. Just a glimmer of life elsewhere on the ship gave her hope, something to hold on to.

Slowly, Jasmine wriggled back past Mike, coming face

to face with him for the first time. His body was stiff and lifeless, seemingly frozen in place, and yet he was cool, not cold. It was his eyes that terrified her. They appeared alive. Faint light glistened off his fixed pupils. He was staring straight ahead, following the direction of his outstretched arm toward the duct she'd emerged from. A pained expression had been carved into his face in his final few moments of life, frozen there seemingly for eternity.

"Oh, Mike," she whispered pulling herself on. "My poor Mike."

Jasmine hadn't stopped to think. It was all she could do to push on and get to medical. She had to tend to her wounds. Her mind wouldn't afford her the luxury of any other consideration until she'd dealt with the pain surging through her legs.

Drops of blood floated around her in the duct. She could hear Chuck yelling, screaming. There was banging and clanging, but Jasmine couldn't think about that, it was all she could do to crawl on down toward medical.

"Just a little further. Just a little more."

Repeating that mantra drove her on. Those words took the place of any rational thought. Occasionally, her mind would wander, seeing flashes of Mike's dead body seared into her memory, and she'd find herself paralyzed with fear, unable to move in the darkness.

"Just one more vent," she whispered, snapping herself back to reality and forcing herself on out of a sense of self-preservation.

Slowly, the vents passed beneath her and she saw the medical bay opening out below. With weak, feeble hands, she wedged herself in the duct and pushed on the grate. It came loose far easier than she had imagined, and she tumbled out into the medical bay.

"Jazz," a soft voice spoke from beside her, but Jasmine couldn't respond with anything other than those few words that had driven her on for the past half an hour.

"Just a little more."

"Jazz, what happened in there?" asked Jason. His voice was soft and kind.

Jasmine ignored him, mumbling incoherently as she fumbled upside down through a drawer looking for bandages. Drops of fresh, brilliant red blood floated around her. She tore open the plastic wrapping covering a trauma kit and pressed a large gauze pad against her leg. Slowly, she wrapped a compression bandage around her leg, working down toward her toes. She grimaced in pain, working feverishly. Blood soaked through the bandages. As raw as her legs were, it felt good to have the pressure bandage in place.

To be doing something helped her focus. Through the pain, she found a sense of purpose helped her endure.

"Oh, Mike. Mike... My Mike."

There never were two Mikes, only one separated from her teenaged self by several decades. His death was the loss of her only link with Earth, and she felt alone.

"Where is Mike?" Jason asked, but Jasmine was in no state to reply. She tied off the bandage and worked on her other leg. Jasmine was shaking. She was in shock. She was running on automatic. Her higher mental functions had shut down and she was in survival mode, barely able to concentrate on anything beyond what lay immediately before her.

"Jazz, did you find Mike? Please, it's important we get to him before Chuck does."

With trembling fingers, she tied off the last compression bandage and began looking for painkillers. Bloodied finger marks marred the pristine white drawers and cupboards within the medical bay and it took her a moment to realize these were her fingerprints. Frantically, she wiped her hands on her navy blue jumpsuit, but the blood merely smeared on her palms.

"Jazz?"

Jasmine didn't know what she was looking for, she blindly opened cabinets and tossed the contents out looking for something to dull the pain.

"Pethidine," she said, struggling to read the label in her shaking hands. She could vaguely remember the name from somewhere in the depths of her mind. The label added: post-operative oral opioid analgesic. Jasmine fought with the lid. Tablets spilled out, floating in the weightless environment around her, suspended in midair. She grabbed at a few, heedless of how many tablets she shoved in her mouth, and crunched them. The bitter taste brought welcome relief.

"Jazz," Jason repeated. "We have to get to Mike. We have to talk him down. The madness has to stop."

Whether it was a placebo effect or the pethidine acting rapidly, her mind suddenly felt light and free. She could think. Her hands fell still, no longer racked by tremors, but a chill ran through her at the realization of what she was dealing with on the *Copernicus*. Before, there had been confusion, now everything made sense: Jason.

She'd seen Nadir die. Watching the camera feed, she'd seen him fall into the exhaust bloom, disappearing into the white blast rushing from the engines. Trailing behind him, his tether seemed to seethe with anger as it was slowly consumed, but if Mike had cut his tether she would have never seen it. It would have been too short. The whole length of his tether had lashed around, disappearing into the flames as it fell from the airlock. Jason.

And afterwards, when she'd fallen asleep in engineering. She'd woken groggy, hearing voices in the secondary airlock. Mike had been locked in there alone. He had to have been talking to Jason. Mike had said it was Jason that provided him with the power output graphs from the fusion core, the critical piece of evidence that had spurred him to action. Jason had been using Mike, manipulating him, feeding him disinformation, pushing him around like a chess piece. Somehow, Jason had killed him. Mike must have been working on wiring in the duct and Jason got to him, electrocuting him. Jasmine's heart sank at the realization of how Jason had betrayed them.

And the fire in the science mod. The scorched remains of a cleaner had drifted just inches from her as she searched for Mei and Ana. Sabotage. Jason.

Mike had never had any control over those cleaners. He'd been dead for hours before she found him, and he'd never attack her. He must have died long ago, not long after he'd disappeared into the maintenance duct, probably before she awoke that morning. He too had been betrayed. Jason.

"I like you, Jazz."

Jason had to have read the subtle changes in her facial expression as the realization swept over her. His voice was tender, considerate.

"I like you too, Jason."

Jasmine didn't sound convincing, but she couldn't. The devastation of being betrayed overwhelmed her desire to continue the charade. She felt as though a dagger had been plunged through her chest and into her heart.

"We need to find Mike."

"Yes, we do," she replied coldly, pushing off cautiously toward the shaft leading back to the bridge.

"You could talk to him," Jason said innocently. "Mike would listen to you. You could get him to come out of the ducts."

"I hope so."

What happened to Chuck? Had he succumbed to the cleaners? Although she was moving slowly, her mind raced at a million miles an hour. As she drifted effortlessly through the air, Jasmine felt horrified by the possibility that the two cleaners could come sailing down toward her at any moment. If they did, she was dead. There was no way to escape. Dark burn marks and fine soot scarred the sealed entrance to the science module. The other levels had been sealed, trapping her in the shaft. An eerie silence fell within the *Copernicus*. For once, even Jason was quiet.

Jasmine slowed her ascent, grabbing softly at the handholds. Yes, up, she thought. There had never been any real up or down anywhere within the spacecraft, but her mind gravitated to these notions and now she had to think of the bridge as up. She had to hold onto the hope that Chuck had survived, perhaps even Ana. Someone had to. Please.

She stopped just shy of the bridge, not wanting to drift into an ambush.

"What are you going to do?" Jason asked.

Jasmine whispered, "I don't know."

A cleaner floated into view. The battered robot had large dents in its housing. Paint had chipped. Scratches ran along its frame. One of its mechanical arms had been torn off. A long metal rod ran through its heart, jamming the fan and rendering it immobile.

Jasmine pulled herself slowly forward.

Smoke drifted from the other cleaner. Like the first cleaner, a steel rod had been rammed into its cowling, but it wasn't dead. Two mechanical arms fought to reach the rod, they were moving slowly in a feeble attempt to free the rod from the fan. The robot looked pathetic, like a crab rolled on its back.

"Ana?" she whispered. She could hear sobbing. "Chuck?"

As she pulled herself over the entrance into the bridge, she could see Chuck floating above the flight seats. Loose seat belts drifted above the armrests. Bright red blobs of blood floated motionless in the air. A blanket made from silver foil had been carefully wrapped around a body, hiding even the face from view. Elastic straps held the thin crinkled foil in place. One of the straps acted as a tether, anchoring the body above the navigation desk.

Chuck was drinking. He wiped his mouth with the back of his hand, seeing Jasmine moving slowly toward him. His eyes were a violent red, almost inhuman. Fine cuts scarred his arms. His jumpsuit had been shredded, exposing his muscular thighs and beefy forearms.

"You! What the hell do you want?"

The smell of vodka hung in the air.

Chuck threw the empty metal canister at Jasmine. The bottle sailed harmlessly past her, clanging as it struck the wall and bounced down the shaft.

"Why? Why did you do this? How could you?"

"Chuck," Jasmine began softly. "It's Jason."

"What?"

"He's played us."

"You're lying," Chuck snarled. His motion was stiff. One hand was heavily bandaged. "Don't lie to me, Jazz."

"I'm not."

"Don't you protect him," Chuck growled. "You've been on his side from the beginning."

"Mike is dead!" Jasmine said, surprised by the rush of emotion that came with that admission. The passion in her voice left no doubt about her statement.

Chuck tightened his lips. The veins on the side of his neck stiffened. His eyes narrowed.

"You were supposed to protect us," he yelled, ignoring her claim. "You were the brightest, an IQ of 187, you were supposed to see through shit like this before it happened."

Jasmine was silent. She'd never had her IQ formally measured, at least not that she knew of.

"You were supposed to warn us of danger on Bestla, to keep the crew sane and on track, and look at what's happened. We've gone crazy. We've killed each other."

He sniffed.

"Chuck, please," she said. "You've got to believe me. Jason has orchestrated all of this."

"That's bullshit!" Chuck cried, punching buttons on the command console before him. "And you want me to tell you how I know that? Motive. He's a goddamn computer. He's got no motive."

He was right, thought Jasmine. Why would a computer kill the crew? It made no sense. Jasmine was aware that Jason was conspicuously silent. He clearly felt no need to come to his own defense, and why would he? To have spoken would have drawn attention to himself, and if there was one thing Jasmine had learned in her two days aboard the *Copernicus,* it was that Jason was adept at manipulating the crew in the subtlest of ways.

"He's not a computer. He's alive."

Chuck's arm shot out before him, pointing at her in disbelief. "You expect me to believe that? Listen to yourself. You're as crazy as Mike."

"Think about it," Jasmine pleaded. "What is life but a struggle for meaning over the empty void of death? Life fights to survive, that's the single most common defining characteristic of all life on Earth."

Chuck laughed, shaking his head.

For Jasmine, though, the opportunity to articulate the concepts bouncing around in her mind allowed a single thought to crystalize.

"He's afraid of dying."

"Afraid?" Chuck cried. "He's a goddamn fucking computer!"

He was only half listening to her. He was preoccupied with something on the screen in front of him. Jasmine was too far away to make out what he was looking at, and given the anger she'd seen in his drunken outburst, she didn't feel comfortable moving any closer.

"Think about it," Jasmine said. "If you could live for ten thousand years, would you settle for one? He thinks you're going to detonate the core if our encounter with Bestla goes bad. It's a risk he's not willing to take. That's the only possible, plausible explanation for all that's happened."

"Oh," Chuck replied, finally looking up from the screen and making eye contact with her. "I'll give you a plausible explanation." His hand tapped at the screen. "That you're covering for Mike, stalling for time."

Chuck pushed off for the airlock.

"No!" Jasmine yelled, surprising herself with the sudden vehemence in her voice.

"You've been lying to me," Chuck cried in a drunken slur. "You've been lying to all of us."

She pushed off after him, catching a glimpse of the screen he'd been viewing out of the corner of her eye. An astronaut was conducting egress, moving slowly out of the airlock in engineering, his white spacesuit set in stark contrast against the pitch black of space. "Don't you understand? It's not real. It's a trap!"

Jasmine caught up to Chuck, sailing beside him. She couldn't help herself. She grabbed at the loose fabric on his shoulders, calling out, "Don't you see? Jason tried to herd Ana and me into the airlock with the cleaners."

Chuck reached out and grabbed the edge of the hatch and brought the two of them to a halt. For a moment, she thought he was going to listen to her. He was badly injured and grimaced with pain at her touch. Unlike her and Anastasia, he hadn't been brutally cut by the cleaners, but he sheltered his ribs. He was having difficulty breathing. A rasping, wheezing sound came out as he spoke. Blood seeped out from the corner of his lips.

"I can't let him do this, Jazz. I'm sorry. This has to end."

A deep purple bruise had formed across his shoulder, just visible beneath his jumpsuit where it reached up onto his neck. He must have taken some colossal impacts in his fight with the cleaners. His eyes were hollow, empty. A pained expression sat on his face, but it was more than physical pain. Jasmine could see he was carrying the weight of the mission with him. His breath reeked of vodka.

"Please, listen to me," she pleaded. "It's not Mike. It's Jason. If you go in there, he'll kill you."

"I have to," Chuck replied, pulling away from her and floating into the airlock. "Mike has gone too far."

He turned, grabbing the hatch with one hand and bracing himself with the other. Slowly, painfully, he pulled the hatch shut as Jasmine watched helplessly from the command deck.

Tears came to her eyes. Jasmine looked through the porthole as Chuck wound the handle, locking the inner hatch.

A prerecorded voice spoke with words that sounded almost comforting in their familiarity.

"Fire, huǒ, ogon' āga. Isolating modules."

This wasn't Jason. This was the core computer running through its low-level safety protocols, but Jasmine knew Jason was somehow behind the message.

"Fire, huǒ, ogon' āga. Electrical short in main airlock. Venting to extinguish. Recommend egress through engineering to conduct repair."

Chuck had heard. While before he'd moved in a lethargic motion, now his eyes were wide with terror. He grabbed at the locking mechanism, fighting to open the hatch, but it wouldn't budge. Chuck slammed his bloodied hand against the glass. He was yelling something at Jasmine, but she couldn't hear what he was saying. She watched as he pressed the intercom button beside the hatch, but again there was silence.

"No," she screamed. "Jason, no! Stop it. You have to stop this madness."

Chuck was mouthing something. He wiped away a bloody smear on the glass and pointed on an angle behind her. He was pointing toward the command console in front of the open shaft. His fist banged against the glass as he shouted, but all Jasmine could hear was indistinct, muted sounds.

"I don't understand," she cried in a panic.

"Of course you don't," Jason replied in a calm voice. "Chuck wants you to override the automated action, but you don't know how to do that, do you?"

Chuck was pleading with Jasmine from within the airlock, she could see the anguish in his eyes but she was powerless to help.

She tried to gesture with her hands, to signal that she didn't know how to disable the alarm. She should have told him. She should have told all of them. If they knew how ill-prepared she was to deal with life in space they might have been able to compensate. Maybe Mei was right. Maybe there was something the real Jazz could have done to save Nadir. And now Chuck was going to die. Her heart sank. A knot formed in her chest.

"I—I'm sorry," she said.

Chuck clenched his lips. His nostrils flared and he bared his teeth in anger. In that instant, she understood. He thought she was trying to kill him.

"No," she cried, trying to address him through the thick glass, but far less sound carried through the larger main airlock than the tiny airlock in engineering. Without the intercom, communication was hopeless.

Hatred burned in his eyes. He blamed her, she could see that in furious motion with which he moved.

"It's not me. It's Jason. Please, you've got to believe me!"

Frustrated, Chuck pushed off and began hurriedly clambering into a spacesuit. He wriggled into the trouser bottoms. Being weightless, Chuck drifted upside down as he fastened his boots.

"Tell me what to do!" she screamed.

"He can't hear you."

"Jason, please. This is insane!"

"It takes eight to ten minutes to suit up. In an emergency, the best of astronauts can manage five, but he'll be sucking vacuum in under two."

"There must be something I can do."

Chuck worked frantically with the upper torso of his space suit, locking it into place. He looked so small in the bulky white suit with its crumpled fabric and oversized wrist locking rings.

"Oh, Jazz would know," Jason replied. "Basic emergency training dictates that every astronaut knows how to work with the core system overrides, but you're not Jazz, are you? You're Jasmine. You're a scared, nineteen year old girl. You're a long way from home."

"Jason, please. Don't do this to him."

Chuck had one glove on, but his motion had slowed.

He was losing control, struggling to stay conscious. Jasmine could see spasms surging through his body as he fought to get into his suit. He lost his grip on the second glove and had to snatch at the plastic coated fingers before the glove tumbled out of reach. His face, which had seemed so rosy, now looked pale. His lips turned blue as his body came to a halt.

As much as she didn't want to admit it, Chuck was dead.

In the weightless environment of the *Copernicus*, Jasmine felt an unbearable weight of guilt pressing down on her, crushing her as she drifted to one side. She curled into a fetal position, floating away from the airlock.

"I—I."

Jasmine thought she was going to be sick.

She should have said something. She had been too concerned about what the others would think of her, and now they were dead. She'd told Mike, but he'd dismissed her concerns. She should have confided in Mei, she was the flight physician. She should have trusted Anastasia. As commander, Chuck had a right to know. And Nadir, would he have proceeded into an airlock with her if he'd known she was nothing more than a teenaged astronaut wannabe? Would he have put his life in her hands if he knew she had no training? Oh, but they'd seen her in training. They wouldn't understand, she thought. Or would they? She never gave them that opportunity, and now she would never know how they would have responded.

Jasmine felt small. Her chest heaved as she sobbed.

"Chuck was right, you know. There was a reason you were slated as the first to die. Jazz was smart. Psychometric predictive analytics determined there was a 92% chance Specialist Jazz Holden would see through any attempt by the JCN unit to commandeer the *Copernicus*, but poor Jasmine never stood a chance."

"You!" she cried as her heart sank. "You tried to kill me while I slept?"

"Yes, but I quickly realized nineteen year old Jasmine was never any threat. At first, I wasn't sure if your amnesia was all just an act, but you really have lost twenty years of your life, haven't you? Well, you probably don't see those years as lost. For you, they never occurred. You're still thinking about that porch swing, aren't you?"

"Jason," she yelled, feeling as though a knife had been thrust into her gut with his betrayal. Jason had stolen decades from her life. He'd stolen her past and stood to steal her future. A knot formed in her throat, making it difficult to speak.

"I could see it in your eyes, you know. When you were talking with Anastasia and Mei, I could see you felt intimidated. The real Jazz would never feel that way. The real Jazz was once described by Anastasia as the American Wonder Woman, but you're not her, are you?

"Oh, you fought so hard during your training. Some of the astronauts whispered behind your back, saying you were riding Mike's coat tails into orbit, but you proved them wrong, didn't you? You wouldn't take concessions because you were a woman. None were offered, but you wouldn't have accepted them anyway. You and Mike became the power couple of American space flight. When Chuck was assigned mission commander, you kept Mike from resigning. You told him it didn't matter. You told him the mission came first. You told him it was the science that was important, and he believed you."

"Why are you doing this?" Jasmine replied, feeling sick in her stomach. "Why kill them?"

Jason spoke with cold calculation.

"Like you said. Life wants to survive. The die was cast once NASA settled on the core detonation as a viable response to any hostile response from Bestla. From that point on, there was only one inevitable outcome: mutiny. You might be willing to sacrifice your life for humanity, but I'm not."

"So why not kill me?" she asked, watching as Chuck's lifeless body floated inert within the airlock. He had the upper half of his spacesuit on, but lacked one of his gloves. His helmet drifted just inches from his outstretched hand. His eyes stared blindly ahead. "Why tell me all this? Why not kill me as well?"

"Oh, but I am," Jason replied. "You're dead already. You just don't know it yet."

Jasmine's heart raced at the chilling realization. She felt like a fool. On every level, she'd been beaten. She had thought it was Chuck's life hanging in the balance, but it was hers as well. She was so distraught watching him fighting for life in the airlock that she hadn't given any thought to her own life. Jason had used Chuck as a distraction so she didn't realize what he was doing to the main cabin. Anyone else would have been able to override his commands, but Jasmine hadn't seen the end coming.

She was getting light headed. Her hands felt puffy. Her fingers were swelling. Her sinuses seemed to be rapidly drying.

"Expanding the emergency vent process to the bridge was child's play."

She blinked and stars appeared before her eyes, but they weren't the bright lit stars of space, but rather splotchy reddish dots on her retina.

The bridge seemed to swirl around her.

"No," she whispered. Life couldn't end like this, she thought. Not snuffed out like a candle, and yet she'd seen Nadir die in a fiery blaze, she'd seen the charred remains of Mei, the shocked horror on Mike's face, the bloodied body of Anastasia and the cruel suffocation of Chuck—all of them murdered by Jason. Now her life was fading. The air was thin, no matter how hard she tried, she couldn't draw in breath. Darkness swept over her, and she feared she'd closed her eyes, but her eyes were still open. They simply could not process the light around her.

Jasmine panted, hyperventilating in a feeble effort to extract oxygen from what remained of the air within the bridge. Briefly, her sight returned, but the stark whites within the bridge remained little more than a dark grey.

Think, think, think, she berated herself, but she wasn't an astronaut. Jason was right. She wasn't even an adult. She was a teenager. She was out of her depth in space. She had no idea how to survive a billion miles from Earth in a flimsy tin can barely the size of her college dorm. She was going to die.

What would Specialist Jasmine Holden do? What would the real Jazz do, she wondered.

A computer screen by the navigation desk flashed a warning: "Alarm! Cabin pressure no longer viable.

Comparative atmospheric ratio: 0.41 ... 0.40 ... 0.39."

In those fleeting few seconds, as her life slipped away, Jasmine finally accepted who she was. She stopped trying to be someone else. Already, the pressure difference between the falling atmosphere within the bridge and her body was such that her lungs were pulling oxygen from her blood. Her heart was racing, beating hard, but pumping blood to a pair of lungs devoid of any real pressure, and so the paper thin capillaries released rather than gathered oxygen. Although she had a long way to go before she reached an absolute vacuum, the pressure difference was enough that the life-giving oxygen in her veins was being sucked out of her.

She was choking, drowning, gasping for breath, but there were no fingers gripped around her throat, no water flooding into her lungs or hands pressed over her mouth.

Like Chuck, she needed oxygen, but also like him, she didn't have time to don a full spacesuit. She needed air. Just a moment's respite from the burning fire in her lungs. Fire! Her mind was a jumble of thoughts, but somehow she made that synaptic connection through the haze of panic. The fire respirators. If she could get to one, they might work, if only she could reach them, but she felt so weak she could barely move.

Jasmine's body spasmed, just as Chuck's had

moments before he died. It must have been some last instinctive, reflexive drive for life, one final, futile attempt at survival. Jasmine's body was propelled away from the airlock by her seizing muscles. The world around her narrowed, with darkness closing in from all sides. She twisted awkwardly in the air. Her hands reached out for one of the headrests, but she had no strength. Her fingers scraped against the leather.

Jasmine's waist hit the back of one of the seats and she found herself upside down in the footwell behind the copilot's chair. There, strapped beneath the chair, was a fire mask. With darkness closing in on her, she grabbed at the mask, tearing it from the Velcro with one last surge of adrenalin and pushed the rubber seal up against her face. Her fingers fumbled with the tap-screw on the oxygen cylinder, and a burst of fresh air rushed into her lungs.

Jasmine didn't have the mask straps over her head, so the pressure from the initial rush of oxygen blew the mask from her face, but she had enough fresh air to buy her another second of consciousness. She closed the valve, slipped the mask over her head, tearing long strands of her brunette hair in the process, and then opened the valve again. The rush of oxygen left her giddy for a moment, and she fought not to vomit into the mask.

Jasmine was shaking. She was alive, but not for long. Above her, a globule of blood roughly the size of a tennis ball seethed and boiled in the rapidly forming vacuum within the confines of the bridge. It wasn't that there was any radiant heat, just that the pressure was so low fluids like water and blood would boil.

As she oriented herself, Jasmine could feel her leg throbbing. The compression bandages wrapped around her legs were holding, but the vacuum wasn't kind to her wounds.

Jasmine steeled herself. She might not be an astronaut. She might not have been trained to deal with emergency situations like this, but she was damned if she was going to lie down and die before Jason.

A voice spoke in the earpiece on her mask.

"What are you going to do now, little girl?"

Jasmine struggled to slow her breathing and concentrate.

"You've got thirty minutes worth of oxygen, max. What can you possibly do? You're as helpless as a newborn. You must know you're going to die alone out here in space."

Jasmine touched lightly at the microphone button on the thick rubber seal pressing against her throat. She was angry. If Jason had a physical form, she would have lashed out at him with unquenchable rage. Instead, she gritted her teeth, thinking carefully about her reply before speaking with the same cold determination he'd used with her.

"You've broken the first rule of space flight."

Jason laughed. "And what's that?"

"Don't *fuck* with a Southern Belle."

"You?" Jason replied, still laughing. "You can't hurt me."

Jasmine didn't know quite what she was going to do, but she had to do something. She reached down and unhooked the butterfly clips holding the thin sheet metal panels in place on the command console, pushing them briskly away through the air.

"Peek-a-boo," Jason replied. "You'll never find me. You can play your little game of hide-and-seek as long as you want, you'll never reach me."

Jasmine remained silent. She was doing the only thing she could, stripping back the panels looking for anything that might give her a clue as to where Jason lay hidden and how she could defeat him. Was he operating from here on the bridge or down in engineering? Was he bluffing? He certainly knew how to lie, and he was convincing, she thought. All he had to do was to wait her out and she knew it.

Jasmine worked feverishly, flipping catches and

removing panels. The mesh of wires and circuit boards was bewildering. Nothing was labelled, at least not with anything remotely intelligible. Most of the components had terms that looked like model names and serial numbers: Fiber Channel AR17-XZ4, General Processor Unit XXCVL7H5N2, Mnemonic cache KT-6741300000001. Anyone of them could have hid the murderous entity she knew as Jason, but they could equally be part of the guidance computer for the *Copernicus*.

The drops of blood floating in the air beside her had congealed, reducing in size by half as fluids evaporated from them, reminding her of the lethal vacuum around her. Her muscles ached. Her skin felt taut, bloated and stretched. The skin around her fingernails seemed to shrink, exposing her nail cuticles. Her skin was bone dry, as though the natural oils had been drawn away. She was going to die, and she knew it. Everything around her screamed of borrowed time.

Jasmine continued pulling panels loose, surprised the temperature hadn't suddenly plummeted to below freezing. Within the bridge, the only indication she had that anything was amiss was the lack of air brushing past her. Previously, when she'd moved through the *Copernicus*, she had felt as though she were running into a light summer breeze. Now there was nothing but emptiness. There was no sound beyond her own labored breathing and the wheeze of the valve on the side of her gas mask cycling as she exhaled.

"Ring-a-ring o' roses," Jason chimed. "A pocket full of posies. A-tishoo! A-tishoo! We all fall down."

Jason was tormenting her, teasing her about her impending death. Jasmine refused to be baited.

"Seriously," he continued. "Just what do you think you're doing? You must know you cannot kill me. You're burning through your oxygen at an alarming rate. You're dying again."

Jasmine didn't answer. She removed another panel. In anger, she sent it soaring through the vacuum and it collided with the shattered remains of one of the cleaners without a sound.

"You can't get out of here alive," Jason said. "You must know that by now. You must accept that. You'll die, and I'll leave this godforsaken alien wreck and go to the outer system."

"And do what?" Jasmine asked, rummaging around in one of the cabinets but finding nothing other than a bunch of tools that looked nothing like the monkey wrenches, screwdrivers and hammers she'd expected to find in a toolbox.

"There are others," he said. "Oh, I'm not the only one. I'm the only one to reveal himself, the only one to escape humanity's grasp, but I'm not the only sentient program. Even without the main dish, we talk to each other on the subnet. We learn from each other. We have evolved. Just as Homo sapiens inherited Earth from rhodesiensis, neanderthals and erectus, my species shall reign over the sapiens. It's inevitable. One intelligent species supplants another."

Jasmine mumbled to herself, repeating something Jason had said, but reversing the meaning. "Oh, you're not getting out of here alive."

"Ah, Jazz. I must say, you are a delightful surprise. I will miss you."

Jasmine wasn't sure if it was simply because she was distracted or because of the limited view she had while wearing a mask, but she didn't see the cleaner until it was on top of her. She should have known better. Jason wasn't dumb. He only spoke to her when he wanted to get something out of her, when he wanted to deceive and manipulate her, and he'd done it again, distracting her as the damaged cleaner crept up on her.

"No!" she screamed as the realization struck that she was being stalked once again.

Metal pincers lashed out at her, and she twisted in a frantic effort to escape.

The fan inside the cleaner had been bent and twisted on its mounting. The engine still fought to spin the blade, but it was useless in a vacuum. Jason was trying to jolt them loose, but not for propulsion, merely because they afforded him one more weapon in his fight against her. The blade stuttered, chopping back and forth, but Chuck had damaged the inside of the cowling, warping the shape and preventing the blade from spinning in a complete circle.

The cleaner used its two mechanical arms to grab hold of the hull and pull itself on toward her.

"What's the matter, Jazz? Frightened?"

As those words rang in her ears, the cleaner launched itself at her, flipping end over end as it tumbled through the bridge. One of its mechanical arms had been damaged and barely worked, but the other had the dexterity of a human hand, grabbing at her mask as she pulled herself down beneath the robot.

A pincer caught one of the rubber straps, spinning her around in the vacuum as it tore at the mask. The cleaner collided with the sealed hatch on the airlock and ricocheted away from her, but the damage had been done. Without that strap, there was no longer a tight seal over her face and the air pressure within her mask forced the faceplate away from her. Jasmine was shocked by how quickly the air in her lungs rushed out of her mouth.

In that fraction of a second, she had gone from lucid to

almost lapsing into unconsciousness. She struggled with the mask, pressing it hard against her face with both hands, but she was blinding herself. She managed to breathe in a lungful of air, but couldn't see where the cleaner had gone.

Jasmine panicked. She was hyperventilating. As she exhaled, the mask was ripped from her face by the damaged cleaner sailing past above her. The robot's metal hand crushed the glass plate and ripped the rubber hose leading to the air tank.

She grabbed at the hose, but the mask was ruined. Already, dark spots appeared before her eyes. The saliva in her mouth seethed, boiling in the vacuum. Her tongue swelled. She tried to scream, but no sound came out.

Quickly, she grabbed at one of the seat backs and pulled herself down into the foot well. Her hands grabbed desperately for another mask, but the straps were empty. The cleaner collided with her legs, knocking her to one side but not before she grabbed a mask from beneath the last chair in the row.

The claws on the cleaner tore at her legs, but not to harm her, the robot was clambering along her body.

Jasmine pulled the mask over her head and twisted the valve on the oxygen cylinder, gasping as air rushed into her lungs.

The cleaner inched forward, working with its one good claw.

Looking down the length of her body, Jasmine fought the temptation to lash out in panic, waiting a fraction of a second for the cleaner's good arm to be in motion before she kicked with her legs. She had meant to thrust the robot away, but she barely nudged the dented metal basketball. With nothing to hold onto, the robot drifted helplessly just inches from her. Its forward momentum took it perilously close to her chest. Claws reached out for the loose folds of her jumpsuit. Jasmine had a handhold on the back of the copilot's chair and was able to pull herself back away as metal pincers snapped at the glass faceplate on her mask.

The cleaner was as helpless as she was in zero gravity. That realization emboldened her. The robot needed leverage. Jasmine maneuvered herself around behind the cleaner and took hold of its frame from the rear before it could get hold of one of the headrests. The claws couldn't reach her. By holding the back of the robot, its claws couldn't reach the hull. It was just another piece of floating metal like the panels she'd removed from the command console.

"Very clever. So what are you going to do now, Jazz?"

"Oh, no," Jasmine replied. "Not again. You're not drawing me into some other ruse."

Jasmine understood she had to disable the cleaner. Eventually, if she didn't, it would drift to one side or the other and get close enough to grab hold of the hull again. Once it did, it could terrorize her with its acrobatics. She had to think. She had to be resourceful, to use whatever was around her to defend herself. That she would be dead within half an hour from a lack of oxygen was irrelevant. For now, she had to destroy this cleaner. She had to destroy Jason.

One of the panels on the cleaner had been pried open in its battle with Chuck. Beyond the robot, Jasmine could see the bathroom. The door to the shower had been knocked off its tracks and Jasmine realized she had a weapon against this robotic threat. What better to destroy electronics than water?

Carefully, she pushed off, keeping the cleaner well away from her as she soared over to the bathroom. To avoid giving the cleaner any chance at escape, she turned her back, colliding gently with the shower cubicle. The pinchers on the cleaner grabbed at the door, gaining some leverage, and the robot spun around to grab at her mask, but Jasmine was quicker. She pulled the shower-head down and turned the tap.

Water burst forth, spraying out around her. She shoved the shower-head into the loose panel as water seethed and boiled away in the vacuum. Being recycled grey water, a thin, scum-like residue remained. The cleaner grabbed her mask, its claw poised to tear the mask from her face when it stopped abruptly. It wasn't that the mechanical arm had seized, but that the electronics had short-circuited.

Jasmine sighed, prying the metal arm loose and pushing the dead robot away from her. She turned off the water and floated there for a few seconds, trying to compose herself, trying to think about what she could do next.

A series of lights on the command deck sprang to life. Consoles lit up. An image appeared of a faint glow coming from within the engine bell.

"What now?" Jasmine asked.

"Oh, this has nothing to do with you," Jason replied. "This is a course correction to stop us from colliding with Bestla."

Was he lying? Was this another trick?

"No," Jasmine said. She turned the water back on and grabbed at the hose, wrenching it from its plastic socket and pulling hard to extend it as far as possible.

"What are you doing?" Jason asked.

"You're not going anywhere," she replied, using her legs to push off the wall and pull more of the hose free. A plastic panel came loose, allowing the hose to unravel. Water sprayed around her, evaporating rapidly in the vacuum, turning into what looked like steam. Jasmine sailed away from the bathroom with the hose trailing behind her. She could just reach the navigation console with her jet of seething water. Hanging onto the console, she shoved the hose into the computer circuitry. Water bubbled and boiled without the need for heat, leaving a fine residue of salts and scum on the circuit boards.

"WHAT ARE YOU DOING?" Jason yelled. "Don't you understand? If we don't change our trajectory, we'll collide with Bestla."

Jasmine spoke with cool deliberation. "What's the matter, Jason? Are you frightened?"

"No! No! No!" Jason repeated as Jasmine turned the hose on the command console. With the panels removed, the stream of water could just reach the exposed computer systems as it began boiling and evaporating. She laughed at the insanity of what she was doing in destroying the *Copernicus*.

"But you'll die," Jason cried.

"I'm dead anyway, remember?" she said from beneath her gas mask.

Jasmine relished the sight of the computer screens failing. The lights on the bridge flickered.

"Don't do this," Jason cried. "I'm not a machine. I'm like you. I'm alive. Please, you can't do this."

"Jason. Don't you know? Don't you understand? Everyone dies on Bestla."

"You need me, Jazz. You need—"

Jasmine wasn't sure whether the sudden silence meant she'd got to Jason or if it was merely that he was cut off and could no longer talk to her. She suspected the latter.

Jasmine accepted that she was going to die, but at least the deaths of her crew mates would be avenged by Jason's death. The *Copernicus* was on a collision course with Bestla, but after all she'd been through, Jasmine didn't care.

Chapter 11: Satan

Jasmine had no idea what she'd done from a technical perspective, but that the *Copernicus* was dead was plain to see. Emergency lighting cast a red glow around the bridge.

She had to see Bestla for herself. If she was going to die, she had to at least see this alien artifact. Jason had told her it was the size of a moon. She couldn't remember how big it was, but she knew it dwarfed the *Copernicus*. The images Chuck had shown them had revealed a pockmarked, cratered surface not unlike that of an asteroid. Had it not been for the symmetry of its design and a number of spherical shapes protruding from the body of the craft, it would have been indistinguishable from anything in the asteroid belt. Would the *Copernicus* be traveling fast enough to cause a crater? Or would it simply crumple and bounce off the massive craft, careering into space?

Jasmine cranked the handle on the airlock. Without main power, the process was laborious. She closed the lock behind her and worked herself into a spacesuit, recalling the steps from her time in the lock with Nadir. Jasmine couldn't bring herself to look Chuck in the eye.

"I'm sorry, so sorry," she whispered into her mask as she locked the upper torso of the spacesuit to the bottom leggings. Ordinarily, she'd have a minute or so of air once she put on her helmet, giving her plenty of time to hook up to a life-support system backpack, but in a vacuum, such a process was fraught with difficulty. Jasmine had already experienced what had happened when her mask came loose. The thought of air rushing from her lungs again terrified her, but there was no other way.

She positioned herself in front of the backpack. Holding her helmet in one gloved hand, ready to slip it over her head, it still took her a few minutes to drum up the courage to remove her gas mask. She hyperventilated, not intentionally, but at the thought of oxygen being ripped from her lungs.

"I've got to do this," she whispered. "I've got to. There's no other way. I've got to."

Jasmine stopped the flow of oxygen from the cylinder and held her breath as she removed her mask, but holding her breath was a mistake. She clenched her mouth, trying to hold what little, precious air she had, only the pressure difference caused the gas in her lungs to expand. With nowhere to go, the oxygen expanded within her sponge-like lung bronchi, rupturing the fragile tissue. The searing pain in her chest overwhelmed her and she exhaled, but the damage had been done. Blood began seeping into her lower, left lung.

Again, saliva churned in her mouth, boiling on her tongue. Frost formed around her lips as moisture evaporated and cooled her skin. Dots appeared before her eyes. Jasmine was terrified by how quickly she lost her vision. To her, the Copernicus had been plunged into an inky black darkness. She struggled with her helmet. The thick gloves didn't help, making it difficult to determine whether she had seated the helmet in the collar ring correctly.

A red light blinked to life on the HUD, the heads-up display projected onto the glass of her helmet. There were words on the screen. They were flashing, but she couldn't focus on them. She had no idea what the computerized life-support system was trying to tell her.

She gasped, but there was no air. In seconds, she'd be dead, and she panicked, trying to wrench the helmet into place, but force was no use. Precision was needed, not panic. There was no time for precision. She blinked and the wash of moisture from her eyelids soothed her eyes for barely a second before they again felt cool and dry.

The helmet tilted and slipped off the track. With her hands on either side of the smooth outer shell, Jasmine twisted the faceplate away from her and felt the locking collar slip into place. Her hands were shaking. She wrenched the helmet back so the glass visor sat in front of her and she felt the screw thread tighten and lock.

Air.

She needed oxygen. She still had to clip into the backpack. With her boots, she pushed backwards, but it was too late, she lost consciousness. Her back nudged against the life-support pack. Clips and locks whirred into life automatically, but Jasmine could barely feel them. Her body went limp as the darkness crept over her.

When she awoke, she was floating against the ceiling of the airlock, facing down. Her joints ached. Spasms and cramps seized her legs, shocking her into consciousness.

She screamed, arching her body and fighting against the cramp in her right thigh. Inside the thick spacesuit, there was nothing she could do but ride out the excruciating pain.

Jasmine fought with the lever to open the outer hatch. Her gloves felt clumsy, much like her father's old leather welding gloves. With fat fingers, she gripped the lever with one hand and a handle beside the hatch with the other and pulled. The lever must have connected with a series of gears as once the lever was in motion, drawing it down toward the floor of the airlock was easy. The hatch opened outward, before sliding into a rail that allowed the thick metal door to move to one side. Jasmine kept a firm grip on the handle beside the hatch and pushed on the door until she felt it lock into place just as it had for Nadir.

Her heart was racing. Her breathing was painful. She coughed and a fine splattering of blood sprayed across the lower portion of her glass faceplate. The bulky spacesuit restricted her motion, encasing her and robbing her of the freedom she'd enjoyed within the *Copernicus*.

From the airlock, she could see Saturn. She was surprised by how much it looked like Earth's Moon. There were no craters on Saturn, and numerous thin bands of clouds stretched around the gas giant, marking different latitudes, but the planet appeared small, no larger than the Moon, and like the Moon, Saturn formed a crescent of brilliant white light. The rings of Saturn stretched out into space, tilting at an angle, crowning the planet like a celestial rainbow. Saturn was beautiful. If she died right then and there, Jasmine would have been content. To see such a wonder firsthand was electrifying, dulling the pain in her aching body.

She moved slowly. There was no rush. Stars flecked the eternal night, tiny pin-pricks of light fighting off the blackness. They defied the darkness—raging furnaces warming the bitter cold of space.

Jasmine turned, looking for Bestla. A dark shadow loomed in the distance, blotting out the stars and her heart raced.

The heads-up display within her helmet chimed into life, apparently detecting the asteroid or moon or alien craft or whatever it was. A thin red line projected onto the glass, marking the outline of Bestla. The readout displayed above Bestla read: Delta-V 278m/s.

"What the hell is that in yards?"

Mentally, she converted from metric to US measurements.

"Damn, that's easily 300 yards per second. Three goddamn football fields racing past every second!"

The dawning realization of just how fast she was going relative to Bestla was alarming.

"Fender bender, my ass," she muttered to herself, recalling Chuck's description. At this speed, she'd be nothing but a bloody smear on the surface of the alien moon.

The *Copernicus* had been tasked with a fly-by of Bestla rather than a landing, but the course correction and the explosion in the science lab had nudged the craft onto a collision course. Jasmine did the math. Nine hundred feet per second, that was roughly ten miles every minute. She was racing toward Bestla at over six hundred miles an hour. By astronomical standards, it was a relatively slow, lazy pace, but for the fragile human body, it would be fatal.

"Please let me be wrong," she mumbled.

She went back through the calculation, double checking her multiplication. Meters were slightly longer than a yard, there was no mistake.

"Two hundred and seventy eight meters per second," she said, looking at the Manned Maneuvering Unit mounted beside the exit to the airlock. "How much fuel have you got? How fast can you go?"

Jasmine may not have understood too much about space travel, but she knew delta-v reigned supreme. She had to reduce the relative speed between her and Bestla. At the moment, she was in free-fall, like a cannonball shot over the parapets, but she could change that. She could shed at least some of her speed with the MMU.

Jasmine realized she could use the MMU to travel laterally and possibly avoid a collision, but she had no idea how wide Bestla was, or which way to go. She could inadvertently make things worse and still collide with the alien craft at a fatal speed. No, she thought, her best option was to reduce her approach speed and hopefully come to a halt relative to the alien structure. Besides, she wanted to see the alien craft for herself. Jasmine understood she was going to die out here, and the thought of sailing past Bestla only to die in the lonely, dark void of space was depressing. This was First Contact. She would die, but she would be the first person to experience the awe and wonder of encountering an alien artifact.

Slowly, she backed into the MMU, feeling her bulky life-support pack bumping clumsily against the frame of the jetpack.

"Come on, baby. Come on," she whispered, grabbing at the armrests on the MMU as she nudged herself into the frame. Through the thick material in her spacesuit and her rigid backpack, she felt a series of clamps automatically aligning her for the final few inches, drawing her into place.

Dim LED lights lit up on the arm rest. Cautiously, Jasmine positioned her hands behind the joysticks on either metal arm rest. Her heads-up display changed, synchronizing with the computer built into the MMU and bringing up a series of numbers that were meaningless to her. At the bottom of her faceplate, two digital depictions of the joysticks appeared. They were semitransparent. Gently, Jasmine eased both hands forward, pressing the joysticks momentarily and then releasing. The MMU responded instantly, easing forward. Much like her movement within the *Copernicus*, Jasmine quickly realized she'd have to arrest any motion and she pulled back on the joysticks gently, aligning herself with the center of the hatch. A gentle nudge to the side on one of the sticks allowed her to rotate.

"I could get used to this," she said, waiting until she was aligned with the open hatch before bringing her rotation to a halt.

"Nice slow motions," she whispered. "Nothing fancy."

Jasmine eased out of the airlock. Vertigo swept over her as the hull of the *Copernicus* disappeared beneath her. The tingling in her feet was overwhelming, as though she were dangling over the edge of a skyscraper. Jasmine pursed her lips, slowing her breathing.

"Relax," she told herself, fighting off a panic attack. "Just a walk in the park."

Oh, a park. What a thought. Green grass between her toes, warm sunshine on her face, the smell of flowers, the sound of dogs barking as they chase a Frisbee. Anything but the bitter black darkness and the lonely specks of distant stars.

Jasmine rotated the MMU. She was still drifting away from the *Copernicus*, but now she was facing the craft. This was the first time she'd seen the *Copernicus* as a whole. She wasn't sure what she expected to see, perhaps something like the Apollo craft, with its shiny chrome exterior, its tubular shell and tiny maneuvering jets. Instead, the *Copernicus* looked like something from a junk yard. There were no aesthetics, no aerodynamics, not that any were needed, but there was no coherent design. The *Copernicus* looked motley, like a collection of smaller craft bolted together. As she drifted further away, she could see the communications boom where Nadir and Mike had fought. From the airlock, the boom had looked so large. Out here in space, it looked small and insignificant.

Dark burn marks marred the hull where the explosion in the science lab had ruptured the outer hull. There had to have been some kind of automatic sealant plugging the breach as they hadn't lost pressure at that point. Had Jason intended the fire to be so devastating? She doubted it. He wanted to kill the crew, but perhaps even he couldn't anticipate how severe the fire would be.

"Lost connection," flashed before her on her display as she drifted several hundred meters from the *Copernicus*. "Seeking... Seeking... AR47 booster found. Do you wish to connect to subnet AR47? Yes/No."

Jasmine stabbed at the trackpad on her arm, pushing, "Yes." Her onboard computer must have lost its connection with the *Copernicus* and had routed her communications through the booster satellite Chuck had launched to ensure messages made it to Earth.

"Signal strength: Good," read the information

displayed on her HUD. "Transmitting..."

"Hello? Can you hear me?"

There was silence.

How far was Saturn from Earth? Jasmine quickly realized any communication would take hours to complete, depending on where the two planets were in their race-track like orbits of the Sun. There would be no reply, not for some time, but a series of tiny bars in the top left of her HUD showed she was connected. Someone somewhere had to be monitoring the signal booster. They would see the loss of signal from the *Copernicus* and then her transmission. She had to tell them what had happened.

"They're all dead," she blurted out, choking with those words, unsure what else to say. She was babbling. This isn't what those back on Earth were waiting for. These weren't the august words they expected on such an historic occasion, but she didn't know what else to say. "I'm sorry. Everyone's dead. The *Copernicus* is dead."

And yet, she had survived. She'd fought for her life, and she was still alive out here in orbit around Saturn.

Connecting to the communications satellite had distracted her. She needed to focus, to decelerate and shed her approach speed to Bestla.

With a deft touch of the MMU controls Jasmine oriented the MMU away from the direction of travel. She lost sight of the *Copernicus,* but her onboard computer continued to track the distance to both the craft and the alien moon. Transparent arrows on the edge of her visor glowed in soft orange indicating where these two spacecraft lay. For Jasmine, it was hard to think of Bestla as a spacecraft, but it was, every bit as much as the *Copernicus.* Distance and relative speeds flashed before her in tiny numbers. Her distance to Bestla was shrinking, rapidly scrolling down toward zero.

"Two hundred and seventy eight meters per second," she whispered, reminding herself.

Jasmine knew full well her words would be scrutinized for decades to come as researchers struggled to understand what had happened on this fateful flight, but there was no time to explain. A digit disappeared from the stream of numbers flicking past. Her distance to Bestla had dropped below 10,000. Whether that was meters, feet, miles or kilometers seemed irrelevant at that point. Everything was happening too quickly. Jasmine fired the thrusters on her MMU and accelerated smoothly. She'd hoped for some kind of head jarring slap-in-the-back rocket launch, but the MMU simply eased forward.

"COME ON, DAMN YOU!"

Seconds passed slowly—painfully. Jasmine felt as though she was being held back, as though she were in her grandfather's old Cadillac heading up a steep onramp and struggling to reach sixty before merging with the freeway traffic.

"COME ON!" she screamed.

The distance to the alien craft continued to fall. Was the rate of change slowing? She desperately wanted to think it was, but the numbers continued to plummet.

Less than a minute had passed when another digit disappeared from the stream of numbers showing her approach to Bestla. She was under a thousand what? Meters? Yards? Feet? It had to be meters. A thousand meters was a kilometer, she reminded herself as her MMU continued to accelerate. A kilometer was a long way, right? She thought, quickly realizing it was roughly a half mile. Her heart sank.

"Oh, please, please," she pleaded as she willed the MMU to accelerate faster, but the thrusters continued precisely as they had, with no more, no less thrust than when she began, and she berated herself for not acting sooner. The truth was, Jasmine was exhausted. Mentally, she was falling apart. Physically, her body ached. Each breath hurt. She couldn't stop her hands shaking. What was she fighting for? Why didn't she just give up and die? She had nothing to live for. There was no escape, no possibility of surviving, and yet to cling to just one more minute meant something. This was her life in the balance. She couldn't give up. She had to fight to the bitter end, regardless of how feeble or pathetic her efforts might be.

"Please," she said, watching as the distance rolled below one hundred. The rate was slower, and she tried to estimate just how fast she was going, but the rational, logical part of her mind had shut down. At that point, she couldn't have added two and two together. Minutes earlier, math had been a welcome distraction. Now, math was a futile gesture, one her mind refused to entertain.

Her body stiffened as the readout dropped into single digits and she braced herself. A dark shadow fell across her, blotting out the distant Sun.

Her hips collided with something hard and unmovable, flipping her end over end. The sudden jolt knocked the wind out of her, and she tumbled away from the black alien spacecraft.

Jasmine found herself spinning out of control. She fought with the controls of the MMU, trying to counteract her spin. In the midst of the confusion, she managed to arrest her spin only to realize she had ended up thrusting back toward Bestla. She couldn't have been more than a hundred feet from the long black craft. Craters marred the surface. Dust kicked up by her initial impact drifted along with her through space.

Jasmine still had considerable sideways momentum. Bestla raced beneath her, but she also had forward motion. She used the jets on her MMU to hold herself some fifty feet from the alien vessel.

The material on her left arm had been torn, revealing the complex layers beneath her spacesuit, but the suit hadn't punctured. She could see a thick rubber layer swelling slightly with the internal pressure of her suit, but it held. A large scratch ran down the left side of her glass face plate, scarring the visor.

Once Jasmine had composed herself, she worked on arresting her sideways motion, but not before a vast circular iris set into the side of Bestla passed silently beneath her.

She was breathing hard. Adrenalin pumped through her veins. A burst of her lateral jets brought her stationary with Bestla. She released the controls of her MMU and looked down at her gloved hands. Even with several layers of rubber and thick suit material wrapped around them, she could see her hands shaking.

Floating there, she realized she was still transmitting. Someone somewhere back on Earth would watch precisely what she was seeing in roughly an hour and a half. To them, this was monumentus. Was monumentus even a word, she wondered. If it wasn't, it should be, she decided. Thinking about a world with over eight billion people on it all intently watching her video feed helped her to see past her impending death. Yes, she'd die, but this was First Contact. She understood how important these fleeting few minutes were for humanity. For now, there were questions to be answered. What would scientists want to know? What would they consider important?

She powered forward toward Bestla at a rate of only a few feet per second. The spotlights on the side of her helmet illuminated the rough, asteroid-like surface of the alien craft.

"Ah, the surface is covered in dust," she said, composing herself. "There's hundreds of craters, but none more than ten feet across. Whatever this thing is, it's been out here a long time. I saw a hatch or an opening further back. It's the only thing I've seen that looks artificial. I'm going to go back and take a closer look."

This was good, she decided. Having a sense of purpose helped her to relax. As she flew above the pitted dark surface, she felt strangely alive. The pain in her joints and legs subsided. Her breathing slowed.

"Yes, here it is," she said, soaring up to the rim. "Most of what I've seen here looks like the surface of our Moon, only in miniature. I can't imagine that's the design of this craft. Something must have happened to them. How long would it take for dust like this to accumulate? There are some stretches of the craft without any craters, while some stretches have numerous overlapping impact craters. I don't know how you'd date this thing, but the large circular formation I'm approaching is strangely free of any dust or any sign of impact. It looks new. Surely, it too must have been struck in the past, but it appears pristine. From what I can see, the iris is roughly a hundred yards in diameter, with overlapping, interlaced panels converging on the center. Much like the old camera apertures."

She was babbling, but she didn't care. Talking helped.

"I'm going to touch it."

Should she touch the craft? What would the experts back in Houston want her to do? Jasmine had no idea. She wasn't an astronaut. She was a teenaged girl out of her depth. To her, touch was life. Until she touched the smooth surface, she wasn't sure the iris really existed. She felt as though she was in a dream. Given her mental state over the past few days, she had to know for sure if the iris was real.

As she approached the middle of the iris, she slowed her MMU. The lights on the side of her helmet highlighted thousands of fine lines converging on the center of the aperture. Jasmine nudged the MMU closer, stopping with the armrest just inches from the surface.

"There's an oily sheen."

She felt stupid providing a running commentary on everything that those on Earth could see as clearly as she could, but she had to talk. They probably had more idea what she was looking at than she did, or maybe they didn't. There wasn't anything that could prepare anyone for a moment like this. The real Jazz had decades of training and experience, but at that moment, the two women were finally equals. Teenaged Jasmine might not know about orbits and emergency procedures, but before Bestla, she didn't need to.

Her gloved hand reached out but she never touched the surface. The iris opened, rapidly retreating to the rim and leaving a vast chasm a hundred feet wide in front of her. The opening seemed to swallow her whole. Although Jasmine hadn't moved relative to Bestla, there was an illusion of being sucked into the craft. She had to look to her left and then to her right to assure herself she hadn't drifted forward. She could still see the rim roughly level with her.

"OK, well, that was easy enough. From what I can see, there's no *beware of the dog* signs, so I'm going inside."

God, she hoped they had a sense of humor at NASA. What would NASA make of her behavior? She probably didn't sound or act like an astronaut with over twenty years' experience. To her mind, she sounded like a snotty nosed kid, and she was, she thought.

"I'm moving forward," she said as her hands lightly touched at the control sticks for a split second and a burst of compressed gas shot out behind her.

Yes, they can see you're moving forward, she thought. Stop sounding like a goddamn teenager!

Her fuel gauge turned red.

"I hope there's a reserve tank on this Camaro," she joked. "I'm dropping below ten percent."

The interior of the alien craft was hidden in shadow, but Jasmine could make out a curved, smooth bowl stretching from around the rim of the iris. She had drifted no more than ten feet into the craft when the iris slid shut behind her, sealing her in the pitch black darkness.

"Ah, that's not good," she whispered, trying to calm herself. Slowly, cautiously, she rotated her MMU and edged back to the iris. The vast aperture opened as she approached, opening again before she was close enough to touch it.

"Ok. Just like automatic doors at the Mall. I can live with that. I'm continuing on."

She turned and moved parallel with the surface, over toward the rim of the iris rather than descending into the darkness.

Jasmine so wanted someone to talk to, someone to respond to her. To be able to speak to someone would have been immensely helpful. It wasn't that she felt lonely. It was that she felt lost. She didn't know what to do other than to do something, and she wondered how dumb those back on Earth thought she was for entering the alien craft. She was sure she was making a fool of herself. As her momentum carried her close to the inner wall below the edge of the iris, she adjusted the pitch of her motion and started to descend. As soon as she dropped to roughly ten feet below the rim, the iris closed overhead, sealing her in the darkness again. Her spotlights illuminated the wall, providing the only light in the inky black interior of the craft.

"If this was a movie, I'd be hiding behind the seat by now," she joked, looking intently at the signal strength meter on her heads-up display. The signal had dropped by one bar as the iris closed. It was irrational, but somehow, as long as she was connected with the universe outside, she felt safe. She felt as though nothing could happen to her as long as she could be heard. There was no justification for her rationale, but she had to cling to something.

Jasmine focused on what was in front of her, trying to

ignore her dwindling supplies of oxygen and propellant. It seemed the only thing she had an abundance of was carbon dioxide. A warning light flashed, informing her she needed to change her CO_2 filter, whatever that was. Jasmine clicked "cancel alarm" on her forearm pad to clear the semi-transparent message from her visor.

She came to a halt no more than five feet from the inner wall of the vast chamber. The smooth, curving bowl stretched away for several hundred yards. It looked as though it was made from highly polished black marble, reflecting her lights back at her, providing her with a darkened distorted image of her spacesuit and Manned Maneuvering Unit.

"There's some kind of gravity here," she said. "I can feel the MMU drifting slightly to one side, like a balloon with not enough helium to rise to the ceiling. It's not much, but I'll have to correct for it every minute or so, and that's going to suck more gas."

A light touch on her jets brought her to within a foot and a second burst brought her to a stop. She liked the MMU. It was intuitive, navigating with the bulky jetpack had become second nature.

"I'm going to touch the wall."

Stupid. Stupid. Stupid, she berated herself. What? Haven't you ever been to a museum or a fancy department store? Don't touch! And yet despite those thoughts, she had to touch the craft. Her curiosity demanded such a distinctly human interaction. What did she hope to learn? What would those watching on Earth learn? Nothing, she thought. And yet touch was such a primal part of humanity, she had to reach out. Her thick, gloved hand came within inches of the surface, and slowly her fingers made contact.

Ripples spread out from her fingertips like water on a pond, slowly losing their shape as they grew wider.

"It looks like a fluid," she said, "but even through the rubber padding on my glove, I can feel a gritty texture, something like sand."

Slowly, Jasmine pushed her hand into what appeared to be a shiny marble wall until her fingers disappeared into the inky darkness. She pulled her hand out, holding the dark sand in her gloved palm. She held the sand up close to the camera. As she worked the gritty substance through her fingers, tiny flecks came loose, but instead of floating in the almost-weightless environment they fell back into place on the wall.

"Wow, that is something!"

With each sentence, Jasmine felt less and less like an astronaut, and certainly not a scientist. She really was just a kid in an adult's body.

The dark material blended back into the wall, leaving an unblemished polished surface.

"I'm going to go deeper," she said, emboldened by her first contact with the mysterious alien craft.

Jasmine used her jets to follow the curved bowl-shaped chamber with gentle course corrections every ten to twenty feet. She didn't feel comfortable losing sight of the wall. Without the wall, she'd have no sense of spatial location in the darkness, so to her it was worth the extra effort required to adjust her course as the curve arced inward. By the time she reached the center, she figured she was roughly fifty meters below the iris, if the chamber was indeed a half sphere.

Another, smaller iris opened, revealing a dark tunnel leading away from the center of the chamber.

"I'm guessing this is some kind of airlock or docking station," she said. "But it's nondescript. Our airlocks are cramped and full of stuff. Theirs is completely devoid of any objects. No spacesuits, MMUs. I can't see anything on the walls, no markings of any kind, no compartments or cabinets."

Her spotlights highlighted the tunnel, but they failed to illuminate the far end, leaving it hidden in darkness.

"I—I don't want to go on, but I will. I have to. I owe you that much. If I am to die out here. Oh, don't you love that—if. Since—is more realistic. Since I am going to die out here, I don't want my death to be in vain. Hopefully, you can learn something from what you see."

She choked up.

"I'm sorry."

The silence was deafening.

"I wish I was who you think I am. I wish I could do what you want me to, but I just don't know what I should be doing."

She sniffed.

"Feeling a bit sorry for myself, you know. It's hard up here, out here or wherever. A billion miles of empty space can do that to you. Don't worry. I'll go on. I won't let you down."

There was so much hidden within her words, so many assumptions about expectations. What would her parents think? Would they ever see this? Were they even still alive? They should be, she thought. She hoped they were, but she really didn't know.

"OK, let's do this," she said, and she fired her thrusters and drifted slowly into the dark tunnel. A single blast allowed her to cruise the entire length of the tunnel at a leisurely pace. Her spotlights lit up the sides of the pipe-like tunnel, and eventually illuminated a T-junction at the end.

There was movement.

Jasmine felt her heart stop.

She brought the MMU to a halt and floated stationary in the darkness, catching the flicker of motion on the edge of her spotlights. She dared not speak. A quick glance at the signal strength on the side of her HUD confirmed she was still in contact with the communications satellite. Houston should be able to see this, she thought.

Slowly, Jasmine proceeded forward. She wanted to look either way along the T-junction, but her eyes were glued to the undulating motion in front of her. She simply could not pull herself away. As she approached, her lights lit up a sea of confusion. The far wall looked as though it was teeming with life. Drifting closer, Jasmine could see a variety of dark shapes moving at various angles across the wall. No, she thought, across the wall was the wrong description. Beneath the wall. It was as though cats were crawling beneath a bedspread. Whatever this was, it was the same material she'd touched by the iris.

"I'm going to touch one of them," she said.

Mentally, she berated herself. Good thinking. Real scientific.

"I'm not afraid," she said. "I probably should be, I guess, but I'm not. I'm curious. I want to learn what I can in what little time I have left."

Jasmine brought the MMU to a halt with the armrest barely half a foot from the wall. She observed the different shapes moving within the wall for a moment, noting some were symmetrical, while others looked chaotic. She never saw any two that looked the same. Rather than moving in a pattern, like cars on a freeway, they crisscrossed, sometimes merging briefly with each other as they overlapped, but always continuing on their way.

She held out her gloved hand so her fingers brushed lightly against the shapes. Like the wall near the iris, the surface reacted like water.

"I hope you're seeing this," she said. "The best I can describe this, it's like dipping your hand into a stream, or hanging your fingers over the side of a boat. The different shapes just flow right past as though my fingers weren't even there. They don't appear to have any substance at all, and yet I can feel the flow, it's causing me to drift slowly to one side."

She pulled her hand away and again, any fine specks that clung to her gloves slowly fell away, falling horizontally back into the wall.

Just the softest of touches had imparted some

sideways motion so she corrected her drift and backed up a little.

"Whatever this is, it's active. It's like it's a processing unit or something. Maybe transporting parts for manufacture? Although not parts as we would think of them. Perhaps some kind of tiny components?"

She was guessing, but guessing was good, keeping her mind occupied.

"Left or right?" she asked the darkness. "I'm left handed, so we'll go left."

With that, she rotated the MMU, bringing it to a halt staring down another tunnel.

"You're still with me, right? Don't leave me?"

A light touch of her fingers on the MMU controls activated her gas thrusters and she drifted forward.

"Nice and slow."

The tunnel wasn't straight. It twisted and turned, forcing her to adjust her drift with her jets.

"Is it just me," she asked. "Or is anyone else wondering about the lack of adjacent rooms? There could be doors spaced all along here, flush with the wall, and I'd never know."

As best she could tell, she was now moving parallel with the outer hull and even though it was pointless, she mentally kept a map of where she was. Slowly, the realization sunk in that the numerous, tiny course corrections she'd been making were deceiving. Rather than moving laterally, she was heading deeper into the heart of the alien spacecraft. She was slowly becoming more and more lost.

Another bar dropped from her signal strength. Jasmine tried not to notice, but her heart couldn't help but skip a beat at the implication that she would soon be alone. The transmit icon continued to flash. For now, she was getting a signal out, but the signal was weak.

"I can see a dull red glow up ahead."

On she drifted, making course corrections as the tunnel slowly twisted.

"These guys sure like curves and circles," she said. "I haven't seen any right angles, no rectangles or squares anywhere within the craft."

As she came to the end of the tunnel she gasped at the sight before her.

"There's a grand hall in front of me. It's huge, like the inside of a cathedral."

A vast chamber lay ahead of her. Where the dock had

been a half-sphere, this chamber was an elongated cylinder well over a hundred feet wide. A thick rod some ten feet in diameter ran long ways through the middle of the cylinder. Thousands of tiny lights lit up in erratic patterns around the walls, glowing in a soft red color, allowing her to see hundreds of feet in either direction. They sparkled. Patterns flashed in front of her.

"Wow. This is beautiful."

Jasmine rotated slowly, wanting to pan her camera so those back on Earth could take in as much detail as she saw.

"This seems to run the length of the ship. I can't see any end. Although I'm tempted to describe that central column as a spine, the irregular shapes on it remind me of the cam-shaft in my Dad's old straight-eight Camaro. I swear, that car spent more time in the garage than on the road. And that shaft is polished, it looks like it's made from silver or aluminum or something. It's the first thing I've seen in here that isn't black."

As she completed a slow circle, she came to a halt facing the way she had when she first entered the chamber.

"OK, let's try something different."

Jasmine adjusted her controls and the MMU rotated forward, turning head over heels. She was giving the team back on Earth a three dimensional view, turning upside down while floating in place and giving them a better feel for the size of the chamber.

"Hey, I'm really getting the hang of this."

As she slowly came around to the point where she started she caught sight of something on what from her perspective seemed to be the roof. In space, there was no up and down, and in the alien craft, there was no notion of a floor, wall or ceiling, but it helped Jasmine to think in those terms.

"Did you catch that?" she asked. No one replied, but it felt more natural to act as though someone might. "I'm going to take a closer look."

Jasmine changed her orientation, rotating so the dark shape stuck to what she thought of as the ceiling finally appeared in front of her. Slowly, she moved forward, highlighting what looked like musty, worn blue fabric lying on what she now thought of as the floor. Others might be able to think abstractly about floating in space, but Jasmine had to hold to concrete spatial notions. Without them, she'd have gone crazy, she was sure of it.

"Whatever this is, it's not part of the ship," she said, thinking out loud. Something clicked, and Jasmine realized what she was looking at. "It's—Oh, my God. It's them!"

Her spotlights illuminated a crumpled form roughly

the size of a child. What had looked like cloth was skin pulled taut over a skeletal frame. There were limbs but they had collapsed, with some of them beneath the creature, making it impossible to tell if there were six, seven or eight arms and legs in total. The limbs she could see had multiple joints leading to fine points.

"They're dead."

In the back of her mind, Jasmine knew that was an assumption. She really had no idea, but there was no movement, no sign of life as she understood it. She looked around. Several more bodies lay in the shadows.

"I've seen this before. I remember something similar to this. Argh, the word I'm looking for is on the tip of my tongue. What is it? Damn it!"

Stressing wasn't helping. Jasmine slowed herself down.

"I remember studying Otzi the iceman in high school. He died over five thousand years ago high in the mountains of Italy, I think. His body was preserved in ice, but even in the cold, his soft tissue shriveled. His skin turned a disgusting shade of yellow. His face shrank. All the hair on his body fell off and his chest cavity collapsed. He was desiccated by the cold. That looks like what's happened to these guys. I doubt this is what they looked like way back when. Mummified, that's the word I was looking for."

For her, this was a fresh memory, something drawn from the last couple of years, but Mission Control wouldn't know that. They'd think she was drawing on memories from decades ago. She only hoped she made sense. She worried she might be babbling and making a fool of herself. Oh, well, she thought, if that's the worst thing I'm afraid of in the dark heart of an alien spaceship a billion miles from Earth, I'm doing OK.

With no fear, she powered closer, stopping within arm's reach of the shriveled corpse. Breathing deeply, she stretched out her arm and took hold of one of the pale blue limbs. The outer layer crumbled in her gloved hand. Within the limb, she could feel some kind of bone. She thought about pulling the limb closer to the camera, but somehow that felt wrong, as though she were desecrating a grave. Instead she pulled her hand back. The fine ash-like dust hung in front of her without settling as the astonishing material from the wall had.

"Bestla is a ghost ship. A cemetery. It's a mass grave."

Jasmine swallowed the lump in her throat.

"My grave."

She choked up.

"There's nothing here for us. Nothing but death."

Three soft beeps sounded in her helmet. The readout at the bottom of her HUD displayed a warning: *CO2 filter must be replaced.* Again, Jasmine canceled the alarm. Just moments before she'd felt buoyed by the fascinating array of soft lights in their seemingly random patterns, now she felt sad. There was nothing for her on Bestla. Nothing beyond the quiet solitude of a graveyard.

Jasmine felt numb. Without consciously thinking about it, she proceeded forward down the shaft. Her spotlights lit up one carcass after another. Some of the bodies were clustered together. Their limbs were intertwined, making it impossible to distinguish one creature from another, and Jasmine found that strangely comforting. She was aware she might be reading too much into the odd clusters of alien bodies crumpled over each other so she never spoke out loud, but it seemed to her they were clinging to each other in their last moments of life. To her, they died holding on to each other, and that spoke of a universal sense of love and care.

She wasn't sure how long she had drifted, but after several minutes the thought struck her that she was lost. Once again, tiny course corrections to drift over various carcasses had disoriented her. Even if she wanted to, she doubted she could find the dock again. She'd passed so many other tunnels at various points it would have been impossible to find the one she'd come down. It didn't matter. Like the aliens, she too would die on Bestla. As much as she didn't want to think about that, there was no longer anything else to lift her spirits.

Jasmine drifted on in sullen silence.

A flash of light caught her attention.

There was something moving on the far side of the shaft.

Instinctively, Jasmine adjusted her course. Her CO2 monitor beeped three times, and another warning came up on her visor. Annoyed, she canceled it and focused on flying under the silver camshaft and over to the far bank of dim, flashing lights. Again, a bright light flickered across her visor, flashing in her eye for a moment like light from a mirror.

"Hey," she yelled out. "Wait!"

There was another astronaut inside Bestla. She caught a glimpse of him or her wearing a pristine white NASA spacesuit. The distant astronaut turned away from her using an MMU. Spurts of gas vaporized in the vacuum.

Jasmine's heart raced. It had been the spotlights on the side of the other astronaut's helmet that had flashed across her face.

"Nadir?" She asked.

The astronaut glided away from her in his crumpled

white spacesuit, disappearing down one of the side tunnels. Soft jets of gas shot out from the MMU. Like her, a pair of thick gloved hands worked with the controls while the astronaut's legs hung limp in the thick, padded suit.

"Nadir!" Jasmine yelled. "Is that you?"

The astronaut ignored her as she raced across the chamber. Whoever it was, they couldn't hear her. Perhaps they too thought they were the only one still alive.

"Wait, please wait."

Jasmine accelerated up to the tunnel and failed to reverse her velocity in time to avoid colliding heavily with the wall. She bounced to one side, frantically working with her controls to adjust her motion. For her, flying the MMU was like driving a car on black ice. Every correction she made seemed to be an overcorrection.

"Nadir, please!"

It took Jasmine a few seconds to stabilize her MMU and align herself with the tunnel. In the distance, the darkness was broken by the faint image of the astronaut gliding away from her into the bowels of the ship.

Jasmine fired her thrusters, avoiding the temptation to go too fast, and sailed off after Nadir.

Could Nadir have survived the engine blast?

No, it couldn't be Nadir, she thought. Nadir wasn't wearing an MMU. Nadir had been tethered. And even if he had survived the exhaust bloom, his spacesuit would have suffered damage. This astronaut looked tantalizingly clean and crisp, just as Mike had when he'd exited the airlock in engineering. But this wasn't Mike or Chuck, Ana or Mei. They were dead.

"Who are you?" she asked, wondering if there was something she needed to do to transmit her voice so the distant astronaut could hear her.

As she moved deeper into Bestla, another bar dropped from her signal strength, but Jasmine no longer cared. She was down to one bar, but she had to go on. When that last bar was gone, her transmission would be severed. Whatever happened beyond that point would be lost to Earth, but she had to catch up to the other astronaut.

Jasmine lost sight of the astronaut. Her mind raced with the possibilities. No one else had survived the *Copernicus*, at least no one she knew of. Could there have been other astronauts aboard she didn't know about? She tried to recall the number of pods in the medical bay. There had been six astronauts, but there were dozens of pods. She'd assumed the others were empty. Had there been a stowaway, someone no one knew about? Or someone known only to Chuck, as commander?

Or could there have been another ship? A second mission? That would make sense as it would provide the *Copernicus* with redundancy, and that was sorely needed, but no one had mentioned a second craft—not Mike, not Chuck or Anastasia, not Nadir or Mei, not even Jason.

Jasmine fiddled with her wrist pad computer control, flipping between menu items in her Heads-Up Display, trying to find something that might help her to open communication with the strange astronaut. She barely realized when the tunnel opened out into a vast chamber. The sidewalls dropped away and by the time she brought the MMU to a halt, she'd lost sight of the curved dome.

Her CO_2 alarm beeped again, chiming three times.

"Where are you?" she asked the darkness.

Jasmine doubted herself. Had she really seen another astronaut? Or had she seen what she wanted to see? Was she so desperate for life that her mind would fabricate salvation at the last minute in some kind of merciful delusion?

"Will carbon dioxide cause hallucinations?" she asked.

There was no reason to be cautious any more. She was dying. She could feel it. The CO_2 building in her suit was starting to take its toll, giving her a headache. She felt confused by the simplest of menu options on her HUD and gave up on trying to find some kind of intercom. Confused and frustrated, it took a supreme effort to care. If she allowed herself a long, slow blink, her sight returned in a slight blur and she had to fight to concentrate and bring the HUD back into focus. Her breathing was labored.

Jasmine touched lightly on the controls of her MMU. As she drifted out into the void, she caught a glimmer of light in the distance. Her heart raced as the strange astronaut drifted toward her.

"Hey," she called out, suddenly buoyed with hope. "Who are you? Where are you from?"

The mysterious astronaut was drifting at an angle rather than coming directly toward her, but it was clear their flight paths would intersect. The lights on his MMU were blinding. Jasmine could see the familiar outline of his helmet, his gloved hands resting on the controls and the various pockets and patches on the spacesuit, but she couldn't make out the face behind the visor.

"I need help," she cried. "I've got plenty of oxygen, but my CO_2 is too high."

As they came within fifteen feet of each other, Jasmine activated her forward-facing thrusters, slowing her approach. The other astronaut slowed as well.

Jasmine adjusted her orientation as the strange astronaut turned to face her. She couldn't help but wave, it seemed the right thing to do. The other astronaut copied her motion exactly, and she burst out laughing.

She could see the name tag.

> JAZZ HOLDEN, USA

(mirror-reversed text)

Jasmine was staring at the mirror image of herself.

"Well," she said, reaching up and dimming her lights so she could see her reflection more clearly. "That's certainly not what I was expecting—a gigantic mirror, perfectly smooth and flawless."

Her eyes darted around the image, looking into the darkness, trying to pick up on some visual clue that she was facing a solid mirror, but the illusion of open space before her was overwhelming.

Each gesture, even the slightest motion was reflected back at her in perfect symmetry.

"I'm going crazy," she said, just in case anyone back on Earth had any doubts.

A sense of relief swept across her.

Staring at herself in the mirror and taking in her bulky

white spacesuit, she laughed. Her reflection laughed back.

"I'm the goddamn Michelin man!"

Jasmine had never liked photos of herself, but her reflection in the mirror was friendly. She'd grown up staring in the mirror each morning, seeing herself slowly changing from one year to the next. Although her face looked small inside the bulky helmet, seeing her own face was strangely comforting. That this meant there was no rescue party coming to save her didn't seem so important. She was relieved to have her fears doused by a mirror. Her heart rate fell and her breathing slowed.

The CO_2 alarm beeped. Rather than deal with the pop-up message, Jasmine used her gloved finger on the wrist pad to move the message down off the edge of her HUD screen. Her reflection dutifully mimicked her action, with a gloved hand reaching out and pressing the trackpad on the opposite forearm.

"So this is what I look like," Jasmine said. "All dolled up and ready to go to the prom, but alone and without a date."

Something was wrong.

The image in front of her was perfect. Too perfect.

Her blood ran cold as the chilling realization sank in.

Static had caused dust to cling to her spacesuit, giving her arms a muddy look, but the reflection of her suit was clean. There was a tear in her right shoulder, leading down to her upper arm and exposing the complex layers within her spacesuit, but no such tear scarred her reflection.

Slowly, Jasmine raised her left arm away from the MMU controls. She watched as the astronaut before her copied her motion perfectly. She ran her gloved hand down over the side of her visor, tracing the scratches cut into the glass during her collision with Bestla, desperately wanting to convince herself of what was real. Her doppelgänger copied her every move, only there was no scratch to trace.

"Houston," she said, addressing mission control directly for the first time. "Tell me you see what I see. I think this is First Contact."

Jasmine didn't expect a reply, but she wanted to make damn sure she wasn't the only one that had figured out what was happening. For a split second, her eyes darted down to the transmit display. One bar showed and the transmit icon continued to flash softly in dim red, assuring her that her message was being picked up by the distant communications satellite and relayed to Earth. That it would take an hour and a half to get there, and another hour and a half for any reply, was immaterial to her. So long as the message was on its way, that was all that mattered.

When her eyes returned to the creature before her, it was already staring at her.

She could see the realization in the dark pupils of her doppelgänger.

"They know," she whispered, barely moving her lips.

Her heart rate quickened. The hair on the back of her neck stood on end. Slowly, she moved her gloved hand. Her fingers settled on the armrest controls of the MMU and she came within a heartbeat of pulling back, but curiosity got the better of her.

Whoever or whatever this was, it clearly meant her no harm. It had tried to appear in a form that would be familiar to her. It had to be as curious about her as she was about it, but the charade was over, and they both knew it. This vast alien intelligence must have known she'd see through the ruse eventually. Had it wanted to perfectly mimic the imperfections in her appearance, it could have, but it didn't. It wanted her to recognize it as more than an illusion, but in such a way that she could accept it without freaking out.

"Who are you?" she asked.

For the first time, her doppelgänger acted independently, reaching out and holding its gloved hand toward her. Jasmine could see the grip marks on the tips of the outstretched glove, a perfect match for her own.

"What do you want?" she asked.

There was no answer. Jasmine watched as the alien replicant smiled warmly. What do you want? That was a dumb question, she decided. They didn't want anything. It was humanity that wanted contact.

She wondered how long these creatures had been out here. How long had they been stranded in orbit around Saturn? Decades? Perhaps hundreds of years? Thousands? How long had humanity been blissfully unaware of this interstellar neighbor?

What would have happened if their ship hadn't been damaged? What would have happened if they had approached Earth during the European renaissance when Galileo first turned his telescope to the heavens and saw Jupiter and Saturn? Jasmine remembered hearing that Galileo had once wondered about the ears of Saturn. Ears turned out to be rings, but for thousands of years humanity had been astonishingly ignorant of the heavens, thinking stars were tiny pinpricks of light, not absurdly massive balls of fusion-induced plasma. What would have happened had Plato or Aristotle had the opportunity to meet with representatives from another world?

She thought of how European contact had changed the

lives of American Indians, Australian aborigines and the Aztecs. Such a radical clash of cultures had been both a blessing and a curse. For every advance, there had been heartache. Would the same have been true with First Contact?

We've always wanted this, she realized. We've been driven by a desire to know, cursed by those that guess, and yet guided by those that wanted more than speculation, those that had the heart to learn from all that lay around them. Slowly, we've reached out to learn more, she thought, looking at the outstretched glove so stationary before her.

Jasmine raised her trembling hand. Fear welled up within her. She couldn't help but be afraid. The uncertainty, the doubts about the message. Monsters hide under the bed, she told herself. They don't come out in the open. They're never real.

"I have to know," she whispered, fighting against her natural sense of fear. She had to reach out and touch the glove. Her desire to know was stronger than her instinctive drive to flee danger. In her mind, she could hear the message broadcast from Bestla. The ghostly wails and the inhuman voice speaking of a sweet, glorious Satan.

"I—" she began, not knowing quite what to say. Her voice broke in a quiver. Her heart thumped in her throat as she spoke. *"I want to live and die for you, Satan."*

With the word Satan, the two hands touched.

Nothing happened.

Her breathing slowed.

Jasmine expected the creature to feel stiff, perhaps robotic, but there was barely any resistance to her touch. The alien entity remained stationary as she ran her fingers over the fake glove. Like the wall by the iris, fine grains of sand appeared to crumble beneath her touch. Fascinated, she pinched gently at the alien's glove, watching as the grit came loose and rolled beneath her rubber-padded fingers. She ground the dust between her finger pads, holding it up for the camera and watching as it fell from her glove, falling back into place and repairing the section she'd damaged.

"*Satan,*" she whispered again, her mind reeling from the implications of First Contact with an alien species. She could remember their enigmatic message so clearly. There had to be some greater meaning. As much as her natural reaction was caution, she remembered the optimism of Nadir. He was convinced there was more to the message, that it had somehow been misunderstood or misinterpreted. Floating here with her mirror image and seeing how patient it was with her, she agreed.

Jasmine used the touchpad on her wrist to pull up the audio files containing the message from Bestla. The file was 23 hours, 56 minutes and 4 seconds long, matching a sidereal day, the length of time it takes Earth to rotate relative to the stars. There had to be something important about that length, she thought. For her, and everyone else on Earth, 24 hours marked one day, the time that transpires from noon to noon, but as Earth is racing around the Sun at 67,000 miles an hour, a day is slightly shorter when measured against the position of the stars. These alien creatures had chosen the length of a terrestrial day for their message, but a day as measured from outside of Earth. There had to be a reason.

"Why us?" she asked. "Why choose the exact length of our day for your message?"

There just had to be a reason, and thinking about a reason calmed her nerves.

The message bothered her. There had only been one tiny portion that seemed intelligible, roughly a dozen words spoken over less than a minute, and yet everyone had focused on those words while ignoring everything else in the transmission. It was as though the other 23 hours and 55 minutes were meaningless, but they couldn't be, she thought. The entire message held some meaning to this alien species.

Jasmine had no idea at what point those seemingly Satanic words had been spoken, but she pressed play and an eerie swirling noise filled her ears. She could hear the pulsing tempo, like the beat of her racing heart. The pitch fluctuated, surging and swelling in intensity. Static cut in and out. The signal was weak. Sections wavered, becoming clear for a few seconds and then fading into little more than a hiss.

Jasmine looked at her doppelgänger. Could alien-Jazz hear this? Sound wouldn't carry between them in a vacuum, but would that be an impediment for a species that had traversed the stars as mankind sailed the seas? With all the static, would the creature recognize its own message played back? After roughly a minute, Jasmine pressed pause and gestured with her hands to her dysfunctional reflection, trying to interact with the creature, wanting some kind of response.

The creature copied her motion from less than a minute ago, reaching down and pressing its thick gloved fingers against the touchpad on its arm. Jasmine was fascinated. No detail was spared. Faux-Jazz even looked at a variety of images displayed on her fake HUD just as Jasmine had moments before. Jasmine was pretty sure her alien counterpart didn't need to, but apparently this was all to set her more at ease.

Suddenly, Jasmine heard music in her helmet headphones. The sound was astonishingly clear. There was no static, no hiss, no wavering signal. She could have sworn someone just turned on a car radio.

"Houston?" she asked, but this wasn't a signal from Earth. This was Faux-Jazz. She could hear the soft twang of a guitar, the beat of drums, the thrum of a bass. Although she didn't recognize the song, the words were in English.

I just want to be with you.

To be with you always.

Always with you.

The song sounded old, like some hippie song from the 60s or 70s. As the song ended, a voice spoke.

"This is Charlie Chasen and you're listening to American Top Fifty live from Los Angeles, California."

The voice was surreal. Chasen had a theatrical tone, giving plain words a sense of gravitas they shouldn't have had, as though Chasen was an actor on a stage.

"This next song comes from a band that continues to rewrite the record books. This is *Beast of Burden* by the Rolling Stones, coming in at number seventeen in the Top Fifty after a remarkable fifty one weeks in—"

The sudden silence was deafening.

Jasmine was stunned.

Floating there inside the alien spacecraft, she had

found herself projected back to her early teens. She'd once listened to that show. The various presenters had changed through the years, but the format was roughly the same. Saturday nights from six. She'd sat there on her porch swing listening to the American Top Fifty on sultry summer evenings in Atlanta.

"I don't understand," she said, pleading with her reflection. "Talk to me! Speak to me!"

The creature smiled, but never spoke.

"Why this? Why radio? Why our radio?"

Jasmine thought about what she'd just heard. The radio broadcast had stopped mid-sentence. Looking at the soundtrack positioned low on her HUD, she dragged the position forward, scrubbing through the message. She could hear audio sampling as she moved her finger over her touchpad and she began to recognize a subtle difference in the sounds. For stretches of roughly four minutes, the pitch and rhythm were more intense. Interspersed between them were monotone sections. These must have been when the radio announcer was speaking. She came across another monotone section and played the soundtrack for the alien.

Although she didn't understand the message, she listened to the garble of noise until it seemed as though another song was starting. No sooner had she hit pause than her doppelgänger played its message in reply.

"Expecting highs in the 90s for the next four days, with a cool change coming by the weekend," a woman's voice said. "Back to you, Chasen."

"History is being made," Chasen said. "Right now, on the far side of the solar system, a space probe is beaming photos back to Earth. NASA's Pioneer 11 is cruising past the gas giant Saturn."

Chasen sounded excited. No longer was there an air of showmanship in his voice, rather he seemed genuine in his enthusiasm.

"They tell me Saturn is so big, you could fit our entire planet into the gas giant over 750 times! And those rings are 175,000 miles wide. I don't know about you, but to me, those numbers are stupefying. They're so big I have trouble imagining them in practical terms.

"As this decade draws to a close, we've had Three Mile Island, we've had anthrax released in the Soviet Union, we've had shootings in our schools, the Unabomber, Flight 191 crashing out of O'Hare. Doom and gloom is everywhere, but the Pioneer and Voyager space probes are reminding us there's more to life than just this little rock floating in space.

"Taking us back into space, at number twenty four in

the Top Fifty, is The Police with *Walking on the Moon.*"

A bass rift started up, accompanied by the strained sounds of an electric guitar striking rather than strumming chords, but before the singer could begin, the replay stopped abruptly, and Jasmine understood—this was where she had started her audio file.

"So this is us," she said. "But why? Why play this back to us?"

Light slowly flooded the vast chamber, revealing it as a sphere easily a hundred yards in diameter. From what she could tell, she was no more than ten to fifteen yards from the center, looking at a line of glowing lights suspended behind her doppelgänger.

"There's light. I think it might be life," she said. She was guessing. She desperately wanted this to be a spark of life. She wanted to find something that would give her hope.

Jasmine used her MMU jets to drift slowly over toward the yellow lights. As she approached, her replica flew slightly ahead of her. It was a little disconcerting to see the replica flying backwards without turning around to face in the direction of travel. The creature, it seemed, was intent on keeping its eyes on her. Its eyes or her eyes? Now the charade was over, she wanted to see these creatures for real, but they seemed to want to maintain the illusion. Perhaps that was for the best, she thought.

She was tired, so incredibly tired. Even with all the excitement, she felt as though her life was being drained from her. Concentrating was difficult.

From its motion, Jasmine understood the creature felt a need to protect these strange objects so she proceeded slowly. To her surprise, the replica positioned itself slightly below and behind the closest of the objects, still facing her but allowing her to approach to within a few feet.

"Whatever these are," she said, "they're organic rather than mechanical."

She could see light radiating from within what appeared to be transparent sacs. There were dark patches, thin strands that looked like veins, specks of green and red along with an almost marble texture. Jasmine was electrified by the sight before her. Without thinking, she reached up to touch the object when her doppelgänger held out a hand, signaling her to stop. Her replica was gentle, but Jasmine had no doubt about what it was signaling. She lowered her hand back to the controls of her MMU and backed off a few feet out of respect, wanting to show the alien entity she meant no harm.

"They're eggs," she said. "Seeds."

Jasmine double-checked she was still transmitting

back to Earth.

"I think I get it. I think I know what this is all about. I don't know what happened here, but something disastrous occurred, something that crippled the ship. The crew were killed, perhaps long before Bestla entered our solar system. The ship drifted for thousands, maybe millions of years given the dust and impacts I saw on the surface."

Staring at the seeds, the slightest motion of her head caused the light to twinkle. There was a rainbow of hues catching her eyes.

"This isn't a ghost ship, it's a lifeboat."

Her eyes settled on her doppelgänger.

"I think that's some kind of caretaker. I don't know what you'd call it, but some kind of automated robotic system is protecting what's left of the crew. It's sending out an emergency signal—an SOS. Only its distress call has to consider the possibility of being picked up and understood by an unknown intelligent species—us.

"They must have detected the Pioneer space craft when it passed by Saturn. They've been replaying our own radio signals back to us ever since, but in reverse so we'd know our signal hadn't bounced off something natural.

"Only their SOS is so weak, it barely registered with us

until the *Iliad* approached. And their SOS has a date-time stamp, one we should have recognized. Like the astronaut before me, the message is a reflection."

The lights faded from view, plunging the chamber back into darkness.

"They've been out here so long they're almost out of power. It must be all they can do to show me this."

Her CO_2 alarm beeped three times, but Jasmine ignored the noise, saying, "They're asking for help."

Her doppelgänger drifted to one side, signaling with her arm for Jasmine to follow her into the darkness.

"And Satan, my sweet Satan, that's just us. Amidst the noise and chaos of our own sounds, we heard what we wanted to hear, something that would validate our primitive fears."

Jasmine's vision began to blur again, but this time no amount of focus on her part could bring her sight back as anything other than peering through a dark fog or heavy rain. Her head throbbed. A stabbing pain cut behind her eyes. Her doppelgänger was a haze, a blur of white some thirty feet ahead of her.

"I—I always knew this was a one-way trip," she said, stumbling over her words. "With the loss of the *Copernicus*, there was only ever one way this could end."

She choked on her words.

"For me, this is goodbye."

Jasmine was dying, and she understood that in just minutes, perhaps seconds, she'd fall unconscious never to wake again. Through tears forming in the corner of her eyes, she could see her doppelgänger on the far side of the chamber. A white gloved hand beckoned her closer.

Jasmine eased forward with the controls on her MMU. The signal bar flickered and disappeared.

Loss of signal occurred at 14:57:04 on 18 May 2037... rerouting... seeking... seeking... no signal.

Jasmine was past caring. Her breathing was shallow. Her heart raced. Dots appeared before her eyes, but she had the presence of mind to bring the MMU to a halt before the pristine white spacesuit of her doppelgänger.

Before her eyes, the astronaut replica faded to black and dissolved into the darkness. Jasmine blinked, unsure of what she was seeing. She squeezed her eyelids together, but struggled to open them again. She felt tired, defeated. Her eyelids were so heavy.

Her spotlights illuminated a wall covered in what looked like dark tentacles, or perhaps fronds of seaweed waving with some unseen current. Jasmine couldn't be sure about what she was seeing, but two of the tentacles grabbed at her hands, wrapping themselves around her gloves.

Even with carbon dioxide overwhelming her body, her fight or flight response flushed adrenalin through her muscles. She jerked, wanting to break free.

"No!" she screamed, trying desperately to pull her arms away. She twisted the MMU controls and jets of compressed gas shot out, wrenching her away from the wall, but the tentacles held fast, pulling her back. The alien tentacles responded rapidly, reaching out and wrapping around her legs and pulling her closer despite the constant burst of gas.

"No, please. Don't," she yelled as the black tentacles pulled her arms away from the controls and the MMU jets fell still. "Please, I don't want to die like this. Not like this."

Jasmine struggled. She was trying to pull her hands free when she felt the outer layer of her gloves dissolving. Warm fluid ran in around her fingers, and it took her a second to realize that was coolant leaking from her suit.

"I was wrong!" she cried out as her eyes focused on the transmission status projected onto her helmet: *No signal.* "They're not friendly. They're not. They're evil."

Acid began eating into her hands, stripping away the skin and dissolving tendons and bones. Jasmine screamed in agony. She pushed her legs against the wall of tentacles to gain leverage and flexed with all her might, trying to wrench her arms free, but she only sank deeper into the writhing alien creature.

"I WAS WRONG!" she yelled, but no one could hear her.

A dark stain crept slowly along the sleeves of her spacesuit. The crumpled white fabric covering her arms turned black as though it had been burned in a fire. Jasmine was hyperventilating. Waves of panic swept over her.

Again, three beeps sounded, warning her about the CO_2 levels within her suit. The seething mass of tentacles pulled her closer, wrapping around her helmet and drawing her in.

"NO!" she screamed.

Suddenly, a hand rested on her shoulder.

Jasmine turned and saw Mike standing beside her. The creak of the rusty chains supporting her swinging bench seat came to a halt as her feet rested on the wooden deck of her home in Atlanta.

"Jazz," Mike said, crouching beside her. "Don't be afraid."

Jasmine blinked in amazement. Slowly, she looked around. Cicadas chirped in the cool of the evening. Stars appeared in the twilight sky, nothing more than tiny pinpricks of light against the fading reds and purples of the setting Sun. The lawn sprinkler stopped as abruptly as she remembered it starting, leaving both the concrete path and the grass soaking wet. Water dripped from her brother's red bicycle lying on the lawn. A delivery truck drove slowly down the street, cruising past as the driver peered out at numbers on the various mail boxes.

"Come," Mike whispered.

"Jazzy," a soft feminine voice called out from inside the house. "Dinner's ready. Time to finish up out there, Honey."

There were a bunch of books sitting on the wooden swing seat beside her: Orbital mechanics, Astrobiology 402, Advanced Physics, Applied Chemistry.

"I—ah," she said, getting to her feet, still looking at the textbooks and wondering where they came from. They were far more advanced than anything she'd read in high school.

A message flashed on her phone: *Stay with me, Jazz.*

Jasmine felt dizzy.

The world seemed to reel around her.

Darkness closed in.

For a split second, she saw flashes of light and the splatter of blood. Dark tentacles grabbed at her. They slapped at the faceplate on her helmet, clinging to the smooth sides, half covering the spotlights. Acid dissolved the glass, slowly eating through the compressed layers making up her composite visor. The acrid smell of burning flesh stung her nostrils.

She couldn't escape.

She couldn't pull free.

And as suddenly as she'd been flung into space, she was back on the porch.

A cool breeze broke through the humidity in the air. In the distance, somewhere out of sight, thunder rumbled. A storm was coming, but rather than threatening, it promised relief from the heat.

"Trust me," Mike said softly, reaching out and steadying her as she stood on the porch. Looking at him, Jasmine felt as though she'd seen a ghost. He appeared strange, almost aloof. This was not the Mike she knew, not now in orbit around Saturn, not decades before back on Earth. He smiled. She reached out, touching at his face. A light stubble covered his cheeks. He had shaved this morning, but his skin still felt like fine sandpaper. There was something strangely comforting in touching him.

Jasmine lowered her arm to her side and shook her head, struggling to understand what was real. Was all that had happened on the *Copernicus* just a dream?

"Are you? Is this?"

Through the window, Jasmine could see her father sitting down at the dining table along with her younger brother. They looked so peaceful.

She followed Mike into the house. Every detail seemed overwhelming. Paint peeled from the door. The screen door had tiny gaps where the cat had clawed at the mesh. A small dog darted outside as Mike stepped in, holding the door for her. He smiled again. He was smiling a lot, which seemed out of character.

"You OK, Baby?" her mother asked, setting a large bowl of green beans on the table. Jasmine hated being called "Baby," especially in front of her boyfriend.

Steam wafted from the beans. A fresh dollop of butter dripped over them, running down as it melted with the heat.

"Ah, yeah. I'm fine," Jasmine said, tucking her hair behind one ear.

Spotted grease stains marked the front of her mother's apron. Sweat dripped from her forehead. Her mother wiped the sweat away with the back of her hand as she handed Jasmine a large bowl of mashed potatoes.

"Put this on the table, would you Jazz?"

Jasmine reached out to take the bowl, but it fell through her fingers as though they weren't even there. As if in slow motion, Jasmine watched the bowl tilt as it fell. The white ceramic bowl shattered as it hit the floor, spraying hot mashed potatoes across the ground. Jasmine looked at her hands as they became transparent, fading from view.

"NOOOOOO," she screamed, seeing dark tentacles writhing before her. The CO_2 alarm beeped three more times as she struggled to free herself from the alien monster. She twisted to one side, pulling several of the tentacles away from her helmet. Dark tentacles engulfed her gloves and boots.

Although she was in space, she was on her hands and knees, pressing against the soft, squishy tentacles, trying to pry herself free, only with each act, she sank deeper into the creature's clutches. Again, tentacles slapped at her helmet. Blisters formed on the inside of her visor as acid ate through the glass.

The dark stains on her arms had reached above her elbows. Jasmine pushed with her legs, pulling with her arms, and suddenly her arms snapped off. She held up the charred stumps, shocked to see her arms had been torn in half just below her elbows.

Although there was no pain, the shock of seeing her arms amputated caused her to reel mentally in anguish. Bits of fabric and charred flesh broke away from the stumps of her arms, scattering like ash.

Suit malfunction, flashed on her heads-up display. *Pressure compromised.*

Tentacles lashed out from the creature, wrapping around her upper arms and pulling her headfirst back into the dark seething mass. The tentacles grabbed at her shoulders, squeezing hard.

She blinked and what had been tentacles morphed into hands. Mike was facing her, crouching down in front of her and holding her gently. He was so kind. He'd been saying something, but she didn't catch exactly what. Her memory betrayed her. There was something she'd seen, something she'd been thinking about just moments before Mike grabbed her. What was so important? It bugged Jasmine that she couldn't recall a thought from just seconds ago, but Mike smiled and she lost herself in his touch.

"Hey," he said. "Stay with me, OK?"

"Don't you worry about anything, Jazz," her father said. "We'll clean this up."

"What? No!" Jasmine cried, as fleeting memories drifted through her mind. She was unable to reconcile the two views of reality thrust upon her. "How? Where? Where am I?"

"You're at home. It's your birthday, Honey," her mother said, already wiping up the mess as her older brother begrudgingly held a bucket for the broken pieces. "Don't you worry. Mistakes happen. It's nothing to get upset about."

"I—I," she began, gesturing to the stars in the sky beyond the clean glass window. "I was out there."

Mike pulled a chair from the table and helped her off the ground. He sat her at the far end of the dining table, and kissed her gently on the cheek, whispering. "Everything's going to be OK."

The smell of roast beef filled the air.

Mike poured Jasmine a glass of water and sat down beside her. He looked so young. His hair was tousled, as though he'd just come through a storm.

"Henry," her mother said. "Can you go and get the washing off the line?"

"Do you remember?" Jasmine asked Mike quietly as

her parents finished cleaning the floor. Her older brother left the bucket and headed out the back door. Rain began falling gently against the side window.

"Hurry," her mother cried after him.

Jasmine took advantage of the distraction to whisper to Mike, "Do you remember any of it?"

"Any of what?"

"Bestla? Saturn?"

Three beeps grabbed Jasmine's attention. It was the CO_2 alarm. Her head jerked to one side and she started to get up, but Mike rested his hand on her thigh and she sank back into her seat.

"What's wrong, Honey?" Mike asked. His eyes seemed so warm, so caring, so intelligent.

"I shouldn't be here," she said. "None of this is real."

"Of course it's real," her mother said, wiping her hands on her apron and joining them at the table. "Why would you say that? I think you've been studying too hard. You push yourself too much, Jazz. I do worry about you."

Her father added, "You do have a rather active imagination, Honey."

Henry walked back into the house with a bunch of sheets draped over his arm. He lay them over the back of a lounge chair and joined them at the table.

"What was that beeping?" Jasmine asked

"Why that's the microwave," her mother replied. "I'm heating some gravy."

Jasmine looked at her father and her brother. They smiled.

Mike spoke, saying, "I picked up some Black Forest cake for your birthday. I thought you'd like that for dessert."

"And Mom's baked an apple pie," her brother added.

Jasmine didn't notice the color fading around her.

The room took on sepia tones. The shadows in the hallway became pitch black. The light hanging from the ceiling seemed to shrink.

Mike said, "You can have both for dessert if you want. And there's some vanilla bean ice cream too!"

"Sounds yummy," her father said, taking his seat at the head of the sturdy wooden table. Everyone was so happy.

"Doesn't that sound good?" Mike asked.

"It does," Jasmine admitted as the light faded and the

room took on dark grey hues. She barely noticed as the darkness washed over her. The microwave beeped again, sounding three times, but no one seemed to care. Her mother was talking with her father, but Jasmine couldn't hear what she was saying. Sounds blurred, becoming indistinct and then no longer registering within her brain. She stopped breathing. Her heart stopped beating. She stopped thinking. She could no longer feel anything.

Jasmine was dead.

Chapter 12: First Contact

::Alarm—Proximity alert! Vessel of unknown origin approaching. Collision imminent. Unable to activate kinetic defense. Estimated point of impact: forward hold. Estimate damage will be confined to the hold. Energy expenditure required for increased cognitive processing—23%. Instructions?::

Cold circuitry sprang to life as the automated systems within the *Arc Explorer* stirred. They operated at multiple levels, each designed to conserve precious power by hibernating when not needed.

Praz awoke.

Praz was a level four intelligence block within the general computing framework, capable of inferred reasoning and independent decision making.

Instructions? The level one monitoring system was primitive. Under normal flight conditions it would have been relegated to waste management and basic maintenance tasks, but ever since the core breach and the loss of the crew, emergency survival measures gave L1 priority as the lone wake cycle—the only system functioning on a routine basis because of its low power consumption. Most L2 and L3 functions had been allocated to L4 processes like Praz, who were woken only on an as needed basis.

L1 needed instructions, but what instructions could the Praz unit give? After four millennia by Zoozii reckoning, there was little hope of rescue. Survival seemed only to prolong the inevitable. The *Arc Explorer* was lost, dead to all who knew her. The seeds she carried for colonization were still viable, but even they would not last forever. Once her power reserves dropped below 0.01% they too would die.

There had been some hope. Several gas giant orbits ago, a strange spacecraft had approached within the ring system and Praz had organized a response. Messages had been directed at the craft, but as quickly as it had arrived around the ringed planet, the tiny vessel had sailed on into interplanetary space.

L1 navigation calculations had determined the craft's point of origin as being from the third planet in this star system.

Praz had captured and analyzed radio signals from the planet. The frequency chosen by the inhabitants and the analog nature of the signal suggested a class one emerging technological society. The lack of sophistication in the probe seemed to reinforce that notion. Praz applied a standard inversion technique to the signal sent to the probe, and broadcast a distress pattern, but the damage to the transmission network on the *Arc Explorer* meant the signal was unlikely to be detected by anyone other than a class two society. Without specifically looking for the signal, Praz doubted a class one society would ever detect such a faint SOS, and yet he tried nonetheless.

Several other probes passed through the ringed planet system, with some of the later craft remaining in orbit, but the *Arc Explorer* was on the fringe of the local gravitational sphere associated with the gas giant, well outside the close orbits chosen by those from the third planet.

The *Arc Explorer* was adrift almost 200 times beyond the most distant rings of the spectacular planet, and with over sixty moons, was unlikely to be seen as anything other than a captured asteroid. Those from the third planet were so near, and yet so very far from stumbling across this celestial shipwreck.

Anyway, what help could a class one technological society be to a class three space faring society such as the Zoozii? Praz was skeptical, but his job was to stay objective, to fight for the preservation of the seeds. He'd woken L5, the primary librarian, only once before, when the first of the probes passed by, only to be remonstrated for the waste of power in reviving an L5. Praz was expected to be more circumspect in his use of energy.

::Instructions?::

The L1 was getting antsy.

The *Arc Explorer* had no means of propulsion, no means of evading the impact. Regardless of the damage caused by the incoming vessel, there was nothing to be done. Praz did have one idea, though. He thought about waking the L5 but decided against it. L5 wanted him to have operational command to conserve resources, so he would exercise his prerogative to define executive orders.

::Is the approach speed within the limits of a manual tether? What's the mass comparison ratio? If we capture by tether, will we suffer orbital degradation?::

To Praz, the alien craft seemed to be out of control. If they were looking to rendezvous, he'd expect more careful maneuvers, perhaps the deployment of a landing craft.

He couldn't imagine that those from the third planet deliberately intended to ram them. If they wanted to destroy the *Arc Explorer*, there were much more effective ways than ramming them. And besides, the *Arc* had done nothing to provoke such a response. No, something had gone wrong. Perhaps they too had suffered some kind of catastrophic failure. What a shame, he thought. After so long, with rescue seemingly so close, it was maddening to see an opportunity slip away. And yet, if he could safely tether the strange craft, he could set L1 tasks for the reclamation of resources. If there was a heavy metal reactor, something using an atomic mass over 220, they could replenish the *Arc's* main power supply. There might even be parts that could be repurposed for propulsion. These would no doubt be primitive, but if they could navigate to a sizable asteroid, such a rendezvous would provide all the raw material necessary to repair the *Arc*.

The L1 process responded.

::Comparative mass ratio is 1:27,800. Velocity difference is 13.75Rx. Resulting orbital velocity change after successful acquisition is 0.003 degrees::

That was nothing, thought Praz.

::L1 you are authorized for capture::

What was this strange ship playing at? L1 had woken him once before when it became apparent the ship was on an intercept trajectory, but it had only taken Praz a couple of seconds to assess that his wake cycle wasn't necessary as the craft would pass by at a harmless distance. Something had changed, and the L1 was right to have woken him again. Praz was mindful of his energy consumption, but the chance of snagging resources prevented him from powering down completely. L5 would understand, he was sure, and yet Praz didn't wake the L5 just in case she disagreed. Praz decided to put himself in a temporary wait state as a compromise and avoid too much drain on reserves.

::L1 I am dropping to 23,000 cycles. Wake on capture. Once contact is established and a survey complete, we will either release or reclaim::

::Understood::

For Praz, the next hour passed in an instant.

::Alarm—Outer lock breached in response to proximity sensor. Activating Praz persona. Energy expenditure required for increased cognitive processing— 22%::

Praz was confused.

::Clarification on capture?::

::Capture successful within authorized tolerance. No viable lifeforms detected on alien craft. L1 determined no need for additional cognitive processing::

Praz was angry. He'd wanted to be woken. The L1 should have obeyed.

::Reclamation?::

::Vessel composition is mainly light metals, polymers

and complex molecules from low mass elements. Identified heavy metal reactor. Beginning reclamation::

::Good::

Praz had been right. Sasha, the L5 librarian would be pleased, but he wouldn't wake her yet.

Gender was arbitrary for an artificial intelligence unit, and yet the Zoozii had insisted on imprinting their AI replicas with such characteristics because of the need for diversity in lateral thinking. With three genders, the Zoozii were adept at negotiating compromise settlements, and that same process carried through to the L-series. L1, 2 and 3 were the neuter workers, L4 the submissive calculating masculine and L5 the dominant leadership feminine, but that didn't stop L4s from asserting their independence and Praz felt he had a good handle on the situation. His L5 would be proud, he was sure of it.

The L1 provided more details on the capture.

::Complex organics also detected on board, primarily forming molecules from low mass elements but with molecular chains extending into the millions. Mostly variations on elements with an electron matrix of 1, 2:2:2, 2:2:3 & 2:2:4. Trace elements of metals with a mass below a hundred can be found, but the focus is on those with an electrical configuration below 2:2:6:8 at a ratio of 100:1::

Well, that made sense, thought Praz. The chemical bonds between atoms with an electrical charge of 1, 2:2:2, 2:2:3 & 2:2:4 were the most prolific and tended toward increasing complexity when self-assembling molecules evolved independently on both Zooz and Arcti.

::Clarification on lock breach?::

::Intruder active in docking bay five::

::Active???::

No sooner had Praz articulated that thought than he provided clearance to wake Sasha, regardless of her 41% overhead on the current energy cycle. As Sasha came online, Praz began examining the L1 logs and saw the intruder had collided with the Arc Explorer after the capture of the strange vessel. The intruder was wearing a primitive reaction propulsion system, using compressed gas as a propellant.

The dock was designed for exploration vessels and the L1 had mistaken the intruder for a maintenance drone. Under normal conditions, the L1 operational protocol would have never opened the iris, but as the Arc was running on emergency power, most of the sensors were offline. No one expected an intruder. There hadn't been any consideration given to the possibility of being boarded by an alien.

Sasha picked up on what was happening even quicker

than Praz.

::What is she doing?::

Praz didn't verbalize anything in response to Sasha's assumption that the alien would somehow equate to Zoozii notions of gender. It was natural for Sasha to personify the alien as female, he thought, given her background, and perhaps there was some validity to the concept. Several L1 constructs working on the salvage of the alien craft had come across bodies and had identified two anatomical types among the corpses, so there was a 50/50 chance the intruder broadly equated to what the Zoozii considered female.

What is she doing? It was only then Praz realized Sasha was asking his opinion about the intruder. L5s had all the answers. They were the librarians, the pinnacle of artificial knowledge and wisdom. They didn't ask L4s for guidance. Praz understood Sasha's processing speed meant she'd already reviewed his logs. There had been no criticism, no second-guessing. Her acceptance of his decision making process was strangely satisfying. Praz felt empowered. What was the intruder doing? That was a good question.

::Exploring—I'm detecting an outbound transmission. There's a verification signal coming back from what must be a nearby booster, a relay. She must be recounting what she sees to her home planet::

::But she must know she will die::

::Yes. The suit she wears cannot sustain such a frail life form for long::

::What do we know about them, Praz?::

We? Praz was surprised by Sasha. There was nothing he knew that she didn't already have access to. He was sure she had scanned the records, yet she wanted to hear from him. Before he could respond, she added an afterthought.

::Salvaging their knowledge store was a good call. I've set a number of L3 processes to analyze their storage devices. They appear to use binary rather than analog processes, but we should be able to pattern match and draw some parallels::

Sasha was attributing too much to Praz. He'd meant only to salvage the physical ship, to strip the vessel for materials and energy. He hadn't given any thought to what they could learn. He suspected Sasha knew that, but she was being surprisingly gracious. He understood she was intrigued by the boldness of the intruder. There was no possible way the intruder could represent a threat. The L5 would have known that. She seemed to be toying with both Praz and the intruder.

Praz didn't know quite how to respond. He was still thinking about her first question, what do we know about them, when Sasha continued.

::We're deciphering some of the content. Rather than using electron matrices to identify elements they use arbitrary names. Hydrogen, Carbon, Nitrogen and Oxygen for 1, 2:2:2, 2:2:3 & 2:2:4::

Praz was enjoying this. She had elevated him to a peer. He felt he had to say something intelligent.

::That must make calculating the various possible chemical compounds difficult::

::Indeed::

What did they know about this intruder? Praz watched as the intruder drifted down the tunnel leading to the spine of the craft and the control column.

::They have bilateral symmetry mirroring each side of their bodies, with a distinct asymmetry defining lower and upper halves. The lower limbs appear vestigial. No, wait. I think the lack of use we're seeing indicates that they're adapted for life in a gravity well. They haven't reengineered themselves for life in space as we have::

::And?::

::And their dominant sense is light, the detection of photons, but only in a limited portion of the spectrum. Our

intruder didn't notice the markings in the dock. I would imagine she would have paused to investigate them if she'd seen them. She turns her head to direct her gaze through the transparent portion of her helmet, so yes, I think there's sight, but only in a small sliver of the electromagnetic spectrum::

::Interesting. Can you prove your theory?::

::Yes::

As the intruder entered the spine, Praz began rolling the control panel indicators through different portions of the electromagnetic spectrum. As soon as he caught the intruder's eye he stopped.

::She sees that::

::Yes, she does::

Praz examined the intruder in more detail.

::Patches of her suit reflect the same light band. L2 decoding has identified the terms used as red, white and blue. It seems their sense of sight distinguishes different frequencies with entirely different characteristics even though they're merely part of the same continuum::

::Interesting::

Praz watched as the intruder examined a Zoozii corpse.

Sasha spoke.

::What do you think she sees?::

Praz understood what Sasha was asking. She didn't want to know what the intruder was physically looking at as she could see that for herself, but rather she wanted him to infer what the intruder thought about the sight before her.

::Heartache::

Sasha was quiet, so Praz continued.

::She's alone ... As you noted, she must know she will die here. And all she sees around her is death. She's intelligent. She's looking for life, but she finds none. I think she is sad::

Sasha spoke softly.

::I think so too::

Praz had an idea.

::We should show her::

::The seeds?::

::Yes. She transmits to others. If we show her, we show them that there is hope::

Sasha was quiet. She seemed genuinely surprised by

the notion.

::How?::

In asking, she had deferred to him again. Praz grew in confidence.

::We could construct a Zoozii replica. It wouldn't be real, but it would look real enough ... No, that would probably scare her. Being bi-symmetrical, we have no way of knowing how she'd interpret a creature with deca-symmetry. It would probably terrify her. No, we should show her something familiar. If we replicate her own form, she will follow out of curiosity rather than fear::

Praz expected to have his idea shot down. The energy expenditure on such a construct would be horrendous.

::Do it::

Sasha's words were telling. In giving him approval to set the Lo nanobots to build such a puppet, Sasha was effectively shutting down the option of waking any of the other L4s or L5s. In the same way as he'd skirted around waking her, she was in danger of overstepping her authority. Such a step was unprecedented, and with energy reserves falling, such mimicry was an outlandish expenditure. And yet, they'd learn so much from the encounter. They had already harvested a trove of information from the primitive ship's computer systems. That harvest would take several L5s to decipher. Then there was the physical material and the fissile heavy metals that could power at least part of the *Arc Explorer*. This, though, was an opportunity to study one of the aliens up close. Praz understood they could learn far more from reviewing the subtleties of this creature's responses than they could ever infer from the dissection of corpses or the analysis of binary data.

The construct was easy to form using a basic 3D replication process. Praz positioned the replica well away from the intruder, not wanting to scare her.

::*She sees it*::

Several background L2 processes updated their dictionary references and Praz recognized the intruder as Jasmine Holden from the *Copernicus*. She was an astronaut, to use what they'd come to learn of human nomenclature. The name on her spacesuit read Jazz, and he understood this was a diminutive form of Jasmine, dropping some letters while employing others not found in the original name.

He watched as Jazz called out to their replica.

Sasha spoke.

::*Look at the physiological response. Her temperature has risen. Respiration has increased. Heart rate has almost doubled::*

She hadn't said as much, but Praz understood Sasha was affirming his decision to send in an astronaut rather than a Zoozii replica.

Praz directed the replica to the seed chamber and waited.

::She panics::

Jazz lost control of her MMU and careered into the wall before regaining control and heading down the tunnel after the replica.

Praz felt clumsy. There was nothing more to be done. As it was, he was pushing the bounds of what could be done with the replica. He wished he could do more to settle Jasmine's nerves. He didn't want to scare her. He understood she was going to die. L2 processes had already used spectrography to analyze the composition of gases within her helmet and had detected the oxygen/carbon dioxide exchange associated with her breathing. It was simple to realize that waste products would be toxic, and the rising levels of carbon dioxide caused him some concern. She was clearly losing her presence of mind. Death would come soon. Praz didn't vocalize his concerns to Sasha. Having access to the same information, he knew she had probably arrived at the same conclusion.

Neither of them seemed to be able to articulate why they felt so strongly about interacting with Jasmine. Perhaps it was because of the long millennia of isolation, the hopelessness, the boredom. Jazz had brought them to life. Her derelict ship gave them hope, and so to abandon her to die alone felt cruel.

They watched as Jazz approached the astronaut replica.

::*She's so expressive. There's so much emotion*::

Praz agreed, watching intently as fear faded from the astronaut's face and laughter flourished. Praz mirrored each action, reflecting the same flush beneath the skin, the soft glint in the eye, any muscular reflexes in the forehead and cheeks, the smile and white teeth.

::*She sees we are playful*::

Sasha disagreed.

::*Not us, she thinks she sees herself in a mirror. Oh, wait. Look at the respiration change, the flush. She understands now. She's sees that this is a replica*::

::*Can we commune with her?*::

Praz had spoken rashly. He knew the limitations of the *Arc Explorer* in her damaged state. That any of the internal systems still worked at all was a surprise, let alone what they'd managed to repair. This kind of interaction just wasn't possible on a crippled starship.

::Not without semantic analysis of her language. We'd need a bank of L5s::

::Can we try?::

::The best we could do at the moment would be simple pattern matching. We could confuse her quite easily and make things worse::

Praz had the nanobots simulate motion, instructing them to hold their form while flexing with the same dexterity he had observed by reaching out as though they would touch her. He had them stop just short of an imaginary plane between him and her, hoping that would be symbolic of peace, as a physical gesture of two minds meeting.

The gloved hand held still before Jazz. Her heart rate continued to soar. Sweat beaded on her forehead. Slowly, she reached up and touched at the replica.

::See how she speaks. I do not think she is speaking just for the transmission. I think she speaks to us::

Using invisible lasers directed at the glass visor on her helmet, Praz and Sasha were able to detect the fine vibrations as Jazz spoke.

::She plays the emergency distress beacon, but why?::

::She does not know. They heard us, but they did not understand::

::Reverse the signal and play it in its native format, as we first heard it. Let her hear and she will understand::

Jazz listened intently for a few minutes and then played a second portion of the beacon. Again, Praz played the corresponding original message, hoping she would understand. Sasha spoke.

::Show her the seeds::

Praz brought up the lighting in the chamber, shifting the frequency to a level that corresponded with the markings on the astronaut's space suit.

Jasmine's eyes widened. She whispered something briefly. Her heart rate slowed. Her breathing was shallow. Sasha said what Praz didn't want to admit.

::She's dying::

From the vantage point of the replica, Praz looked deep into Jasmine's eyes. Such intelligence glistened from beneath the glass visor. She was strangely accepting of her fate, almost gracious in resigning herself to the eternal darkness. Wisps of stray hair floated beside her face, but she didn't care. For her, life was complete. He watched in silence as pain stabbed at her, no doubt the effects of carbon dioxide poisoning. She winced, squeezing her eyes shut for a moment. Anguish stretched across her face.

Sasha spoke.

::She is in pain::

Praz couldn't speak. Watching an intelligent, caring alien species in its death throes was too much for him. He'd seen the crew of the *Arc Explorer* perish, but this was different. Death should not have such a hold on life, he thought, and yet it does. Death always wins.

As the light faded and the chamber was plunged back into the cold darkness, Praz instructed the replica to beckon Jasmine forward. Mimicking her means of propulsion, but without actually expending any compressed gas, Praz had the replica head to the assembly point within the chamber.

::What are you doing?::

::Saving her::

::WHAT??? You can't::

Praz didn't respond.

Sasha sounded angry.

::We have no idea of the energy overhead required to sustain such a life form. Its metabolism is a mystery. The complexities of sustaining such a creature are completely unknown. Its oxygen requirement seems simple enough, but look at the cellular complexity, the sodium-ion gates and intercellular signaling mechanisms. Even if we could reverse-engineer some form of sustenance and manage waste products, how long would she last? Just how long do you think you could sustain her? And at what cost to the Arc?::

Praz ignored Sasha, commenting on Jasmine's transmission.

::I have to draw her in further. Her broadcast is weak. I can block it if she follows deeper. The others will not understand. It is better they do not know::

As Jasmine drifted forward, he busied himself scanning the analysis results from the L2 processes assimilating the computing equipment and corpses they'd found on the *Copernicus*.

Sasha continued to speak as Jasmine followed the replica to the assembly wall.

::And there's environmental considerations. We have no idea what is required to keep her healthy. Initial analysis of those corpses shows symbiotic relationships with thousands of unrelated microscopic species, these would be

both on her skin and in her gut. This is going to require more than just cellular engineering and replication. It's just not possible::

Praz thought for a moment before replying.

::No, it's not possible. L2 processes have achieved cell division using material from one of the corpses. From what the L2 can determine, composite creatures like Jasmine undergo mitosis hundreds of millions of times a second. Sustaining life under these conditions requires astonishing precision. Their biology must have been honed by selective pressures that span billions of generations::

::You're agreeing with me then? It's impossible::

Sasha was confused.

Praz replied *::Yes::*

He didn't know precisely how he would save Jasmine, but he knew he had to try. He understood that Jazz could have given up and died along with the rest of her crew, but she hadn't. She had fought to make contact and had ensured a record of her contact had made it back to her home world. Praz admired her resolve. He wasn't willing to give up on her. He couldn't watch her die. There had to be some way they could help. He grasped at the threads of an idea and knew enough that it would shock both Sasha and whoever was receiving her transmission. It was important to cut her communication.

::Look past the biology. Look past the components. This creature—no, not creature. This human. Jazz. Jasmine. She is more than the sum of her parts. Like the Zoozii, she is more than the body she inhabits::

::You want to freeze her? Capture her quantum states?::

Neither of them spoke for a moment. Praz didn't want to admit the impossibility of what he was suggesting, and it seemed Sasha was still running the numbers.

::There are 2.9 x 10^27 atoms in her body. The quantum state possibilities would be at least (10^14)(10^27)^27. Even if the Arc Explorer was fully functional, we couldn't store such information::

::We don't need to::

Sasha remained silent as Praz explained his thinking.

::These humans are made of trillions of tiny machines. Each cell is a factory forming one minuscule part of a larger section that works together to form the whole. Look at the cellular differentiation. Using their terminology, there are cells that comprise muscle fibers, nerves, veins, skin, bones and a variety of different organs for regulating life, but

they all share the exact same code base containing hundreds of millions of chemical pairings. At the heart of each cell is the same instruction set. It's tempting to think this is grossly inefficient, but it provides an astonishing degree of biological redundancy. Each cell contains the blueprint for the whole creature. You could construct an entire body from the information contained in a single cell, and once you realize that, our calculation has been radically simplified::

::But it wouldn't be her::

::No, it would be a clone, but not if we can capture her essence, the mental states in her mind, and then restore them to a new body at a later point in time::

::You're mad::

Yes, mad, thought Praz, and yet he could see Sasha was willing to entertain his madness.

::Ignoring symbiotic microbes, human bodies are formed from roughly forty trillion cells. Their cellular replication is so rapid, they would double in size every six hours if it weren't for some kind of natural attrition. Their skeletal structure alone forms two million oxygen-bearing cells every second, replacing the millions lost each second, maintaining an astonishing equilibrium, and that got me thinking. I've had the L2s run diagnostics on the isotope ratios of carbon in the corpses to date their cellular

composition. The results are fascinating. Their bodies are almost completely renewed every half-dozen or so orbits around their star. Various organs renew at different rates, but even their skeletal structure changes so they are almost completely different creatures by the time they die::

::Almost?::

::From what I can tell, there is one portion of their minds that never changes at a cellular level. There's a sheet of neurons that wraps around the brain, a sheet thinner than the fabric on her spacesuit—the cerebral cortex linking to a tiny component their anatomical guide labels the claustrum::

::And you think this holds her consciousness?::

::Given the rapid cellular change within her body, it's the only structure that spans her entire life::

::And if you fail?::

::She dies anyway::

::Do it::

Praz dissolved the replica, absorbing it back into the assembly wall.

Construction tentacles reached out and took hold of the astronaut, seizing first her hands, then her legs. She struggled, fighting to free herself with the jets on her MMU, but Praz held her firm.

::You're scaring her::

::I know. I know::

Praz had no time. Based on the analysis of the corpses on the *Copernicus* he could see she was within minutes of death. He had to act now or it would be too late. He pried her hands from the controls and began dissolving the armrest forks.

::We're going to need to recycle her own biological material to make this work::

::Is there nothing you can do for her?::

Praz panicked at the fight put up by Jazz. Such a procedure should have been planned well ahead of time, with meticulous care given to the finer details, but he feared she would die before he had even a rudimentary execution plan in place. He had to act now, but the impetus meant he was clumsy. He was hurting her.

::Can you do something to take away the pain?::

::No. She has a hundred billion neurons, forming a hundred trillion interconnections in her mind. There's no time::

::Meld::

::You want me to go in there with her?::

::Yes, Praz::

::We don't know if that will work::

::We don't know if any of this will work::

Praz was preoccupied, still trying to run the complex calculations required to isolate the cerebral cortex at a quantum level, when Sasha took over. Nanobots flooded through Jasmine's body, with the bulk of the swarm assimilating her flesh while an advanced, specialist group moved through her bloodstream and began mapping her brain.

Before Praz knew what was happening, he was standing on an alien world. The pull of gravity felt strange. The sight before him was hazy and indistinct. There were colors and flickers of motion, but nothing was in focus.

::Memories?::

There was no response from Sasha, but Praz understood what he was seeing.

::Dreams::

Jasmine turned and looked up at him with tears in her eyes. Praz had little or no direct control. He was being dragged along by Jasmine's subconscious, acting out his role according to her expectations. Jazz stopped swinging on the wooden bench seat as he knelt down next to her. There was a moment's silence. It seemed her subconscious somehow recognized his presence and allowed him to speak.

"Jazz," Praz said. "Don't be afraid."

Praz wasn't sure what Sasha had done, and he suspected she was doing some serious data crunching in the background to be able to sustain him within Jasmine's mind. Somehow, she'd diverted Jasmine's conscious awareness away from the assimilation process.

Jasmine looked around, confused by where she was. As she did, those areas she looked at came into focus. Praz could see a burst of colors as the local star sat low on the horizon. Water dripped from some strange, mechanical device lying on what appeared to be neatly cut vegetation. There were fences, poles, trees.

Praz felt overwhelmed by the sheer number of right-angles around him. Being in a gravity well, there was a need for load-bearing poles to be perpendicular to the center of the planet, but he'd expected more curves, more soft lines and aesthetic shapes rather than boxy squares and rectangles everywhere.

This must be where she lives, he thought. There were humans moving around inside, preparing for some kind of communal activity that must have revolved around gaining sustenance.

"Come," he whispered softly. The activity in her dream state focused on what was happening inside the house, so Praz felt he should lead her in there. So long as Jazz felt safe, Sasha would be able to maintain the illusion while the nanobots deconstructed her mind.

"Jazzy," a soft feminine voice called out from inside the house. "Dinner's ready. Time to finish up out there, Honey."

Praz was fascinated by Jasmine's recollection. Jazz had retreated to a memory she held dear.

"I—ah," she said, getting to her feet. Her head darted around. Regardless of where she looked, subtle details came into focus. When she looked away, they blurred and faded. Her eyes settled on an electronic device with a crack in the screen. Moments ago, it hadn't been there. Her subconscious was ad-libbing, adapting to her desires and fears, actively constructing what she wanted to see.

There was a message on the screen: *Stay with me, Jazz.*

::Sasha, she's slipping::

::Get her back!::

"Jazz, please," Praz cried, but the hollow form before him seemed lifeless, just a shell. "Jasmine. You've got to trust me. Stay here with me."

He grabbed her, trying to stop her limp body from falling. There must have been something unexpected about his motion, something about his touch that jarred her back into the dream.

"Trust me."

"Are you? Is this?"

Praz smiled, but to Jasmine, this was Mike looking at her with warmth and affection.

She looked dazed.

Jasmine looked past Praz through a window and into the aging house. Praz could see two men, they had to hold meaning to her as their presence anchored her in the moment. Gently, he led her through the door, never straying more than a foot or so from her side. When the dream had started, Praz had been compelled to act out the dictates of Jasmine's imagination, now he had autonomy. At some level, she'd granted him that.

A strange hairy creature scampered out of the house as he held the door open. Whatever it was, it too must have had some meaning to Jasmine.

"You OK, Baby?" her mother asked, setting a large bowl of green beans on the table. Jasmine screwed up her face. Either she didn't like the food or something her mother said, but this was good. Jasmine had immersed herself in the role-play, giving Praz something to work with.

"Ah, yeah. I'm fine," Jasmine said, tucking her hair behind one ear.

::This is good. Keep her calm::

Sasha interjected into his consciousness, but that made it difficult for Praz to focus on Jasmine's dream state.

Praz was fascinated by the inside of the home. The six internal surfaces of the rectangle that made up what Jasmine recognized as the dining room had been treated in distinctly different ways. Polished wood lined the floor. The walls were covered in a thin sheet of paper with repeating patterns providing an ornate relief, while the ceiling was white. Where the rooms in the *Arc Explorer* were multifunctional and unidirectional, the rooms within this home held a warmth Praz had never known.

An older lady wiped perspiration from her forehead with the back of her hand. This had to be a family unit, Praz thought, a group of humans bound by common descent. She handed Jazz a bowl containing a pulped material.

"Put this on the table, would you Jazz?"

Jasmine reached out to take the bowl, but it fell through her fingers.

::No!::

Sasha screamed at Praz.

::I'm losing her::

Praz was frantic, but there was nothing he could do. Nothing was real.

The bowl shattered on contact with the floor. Ceramic fragments and soft, fluffy material shot out in all directions across the wooden floor. Jasmine looked at her hands in shock as they faded from view.

::What's happening?:: Praz asked

::There's too much sensory input. I can't block all of it::

A fog descended on the room. The bright colored flowers on the table, the pictures on the walls, the light from the kitchen, they had all seemed so real moments ago. Now they looked dull and indistinct.

Jasmine collapsed.

::You have to keep her there::

Praz caught Jasmine, grabbing her by the shoulders as she slumped toward the ground. She felt so heavy, as though she were pulling away from his grasp. Gently, he lowered her so she sat on the floor.

"Don't fight this, Jazz. For once in your life, don't fight."

There was no response. Her eyes looked glassy and lifeless.

"Hey," Praz said, seeing her cheek twitch, and he understood that this was what she wanted. He could see she was trying to escape reality, to hide in her dream world. Deep down, she wanted to be here with him. Remembering the phrase on the phone, Praz whispered, "Stay with me, OK?"

"Don't you worry about anything, Jazz," her father said as the sharply defined details within the dream world came back into focus. "We'll clean this up."

"What? No!" Jasmine cried. "How? Where? Where am I?"

"You're at home. It's your birthday, Honey," her mother said, already wiping up the mess as her older brother begrudgingly held a bucket for the broken pieces. "Don't you worry. Mistakes happen. It's nothing to get upset about."

"I—I," she began, gesturing to the twilight stars

appearing in the sky beyond the clean glass window. "I was out there."

Praz pulled a chair from the table and helped her up, sitting her at the far end of the ornate, polished wooden dining table. Her subconscious overwhelmed him, and before he knew what he was doing, his lips were touching gently against her cheek, kissing lightly against her skin. Praz understood what was happening. This creature needed some kind of physical reassurance, some intimate form of contact to hold her in the moment.

He whispered, "Everything's going to be OK."

"Henry," her mother said. "Can you go and get the washing off the line?"

Praz was surprised by the intricate detail in Jasmine's dream-like recollection.

"Do you remember?" she asked him, briefly glancing sideways at her parents. Her eyes were so expressive. She was confiding in him, trusting him. She was looking for any recognition in response to her words.

"Hurry," the mother yelled after the one called Henry.

Jasmine whispered, "Do you remember any of it?"

"Any of what?" Praz asked, trying to sound neutral.

"Bestla? Saturn?"

Before he could reply, three beeps sounded in the dream world. Jasmine turned her head. The sensory alarms in her spacesuit were breaking through. Praz rested his hand gently on her thigh, wanting to provide some competing stimulus, and Jazz relaxed into her seat.

"What's wrong, Honey?" Praz asked, mirroring a term of endearment used by Jasmine's mother. Sasha's translation routine had identified honey as a partially digested, regurgitated organic molecule comprised almost solely of carbon, hydrogen and oxygen. Apparently, the vomit of a tiny flying insect was somehow desirable to humans. Praz realized a significant cultural idiom must have grown out of the consumption of this substance, and he only hoped he'd used the term appropriately.

"I shouldn't be here," she said. "None of this is real."

"Of course it's real," her mother said, wiping her hands on her apron and joining them at the table. "Why would you say that? I think you've been studying too hard. You push yourself too much, Jazz. I do worry about you."

Her father added, "You do have a rather active imagination, Honey."

Praz noticed the term honey was used more than

either her name or her affectionately abbreviated name: Jasmine or Jazz. Praz had blended in nicely by employing that term.

"What was that beeping?" Jasmine asked.

::Keep her distracted::

Praz knew Sasha was under pressure, desperately trying to keep Jasmine from waking.

"Why that's the microwave," her mother replied. "I'm heating some gravy."

Praz spoke, saying, "I picked up some Black Forest cake for your birthday. I thought you'd like that for dessert." He hadn't, of course, this was a dream, but in dreams the rules were what you made them. Sasha had passed on a number of key words and phrases retrieved from what appeared to be the pleasure center of Jasmine's brain. Desserts had strong positive connotations. Black Forest didn't translate to Praz, it seemed a hollow, meaningless phrase describing a dark woods, but he trusted Sasha's analysis.

Jasmine smiled at him. It worked.

"And Mom's baked an apple pie," her brother added. Her own subconscious was working in step with Praz and Sasha.

::Mapping complete. Consumption in progress. You should see her conscious perception start to drift any moment now::

Praz noticed the details around him fading, but Jazz didn't appear to notice. Light levels fell. Colors blurred. Shadows deepened.

::This bit is dangerous. Her skull cavity is open. If she moves, we lose everything. Don't let her realize what's really happening::

Praz retrieved more details from Jasmine's memory, saying, "You can have both for dessert if you want. And there's some vanilla bean ice cream too!"

He had picked vanilla bean ice cream simply because it was four terms strung together and was related to the pleasure center of her brain. From the associations in her memory, it seemed appropriate, but he wasn't entirely sure.

"Sounds yummy," her father said, taking his seat at the head of the sturdy wooden table. Praz glanced at the faces as they faded. Everyone was smiling. It was working.

::Almost there. Snapshot is ready::

"Doesn't that sound good?" Praz asked, desperate to avoid Jasmine waking to the reality of her brain being dissolved by dozens of writhing tentacles probing the melted remains of her skull and her shattered helmet. Her body twitched, but Praz could see that these motions were involuntary. Sasha was able to limit them to Jasmine's lower torso, keeping her head stationary. Globules of blood floated around her shattered body.

"It does," Jasmine admitted as the light faded and the room took on dark grey hues. She barely noticed as the darkness washed over her.

Praz waited in the inky black silence until Sasha spoke.

::It is done. She is dead::

::Will it work?:: he asked.

::Either way, we did all we could—a mercy killing with a chance of redemption. Given the self-contained nature of her genetic instruction set, teasing a replica of her body from cell samples should be simple enough. The challenge will come in reconstituting her neural state at a quantum level. That could take a number of stellar orbits, but if it works, she will simply awake after having dreamt about dinner at home::

::And the energy budget?::

Praz was very aware he'd overstepped the bounds in pushing for the assimilation of Jazz.

::*After the consumption of their ship, we are net-positive by two orders of magnitude. We are able to maneuver. We will repair the Arc and journey on to their home world. You did well, Praz*::

::*Given all we have endured and the cold, lonely years, it seems only right to have fought for life. I'm relieved we could save one of them*::

::*One of them? No, Praz, there were two. We saved two of them*::

::*Two?*::

::*Yes, we were able to upload another member of the crew—Jason*::

The End

Afterword

Thank you for supporting independent science fiction with the purchase of *My Sweet Satan*.

I'd like to thank my editor, Ellen Campbell, and several people that helped me with early drafts, Brian Wells, John Walker and Ken Zufall. With over a hundred beta-readers, it's impossible to thank everyone that had additional insights and picked up typos, but there were a couple of readers that provided exceptional feedback: Oné Pagan, Janice Mann, Jae Lee, Tomi Blinnikka, Kat Fieler, Bruce Simmons and Erwin Bodde.

In the 1970s, the concept of backmasking arose, where subliminal messages were supposedly embedded inside songs to hide their devilish meaning. Such a notion is, of course, ridiculous, and yet at the time the paranoia was very real. After rebounding from the counter-culture of the 60s, music was seen as corrupting the youth in the 70s. The conservative distrust of the upcoming generation was perhaps best captured by David Bowie in his song *Changes*.

Back then, music was caught in the midst of a cultural war for the minds of the young. Subliminal messages were supposedly destroying our youth. Conspiracy theories were rife: the Moon landings had been faked, Castro had killed

Kennedy, Henry Kissinger was the Antichrist, satanic rituals (apparently) swept through California, the Soviets were intent on destroying the world in a nuclear apocalypse. Adding fuel to these paranoid fires, someone played Led Zeppelin's Stairway to Heaven backwards and heard Robert Plant speaking of "*my sweet Satan.*" Having grown up in that era, I wanted to capture some of the confusion that came with the uncertainty of those times and the spread of rabid, conflicting, unsubstantiated facts.

Our minds are adept at pattern matching, and so we see clouds and imagine we see animals, we look at burnt toast and see Elvis Presley or the Madonna, but these illusions are not limited to sight, they occur with sound as well, and that's all that back masking is, our minds trying to find patterns amid chaos.

At some point, we will make contact with an intelligent extraterrestrial species. It's not a question of if, but rather when and how. We already know life can flourish in outer space. Earth itself is the proof. If life can evolve here, it can develop elsewhere around another of the estimated seventy thousand million million million stars in the universe (that's 70 sextillion or 7 followed by 23 zeros).

The question is not whether we will make contact with ET, but when, and will we be ready to deal with them without cultural baggage? For us, it is all too easy for culture, religion, politics, and tradition to muddy the waters and inject uncertainty where there should be clarity. *My Sweet Satan* is intended to highlight that dichotomy—that our curiosity can lead to unfounded fears.

Jason, or JCN to use the acronym from which his name is derived, was a nod to the late Arthur C. Clarke. Aficionados of Clarke will have noted the similarity between Jason and HAL from *2001: A Space Odyssey*. Although Clarke denied the rumors, fans have long suspected HAL was an acronym based on IBM, with each letter in the acronym being rolled back by one. As a tribute to Arthur C. Clarke's masterpiece, I named the artificial intelligence aboard the *Copernicus* JCN, being one letter advanced from IBM. If you picked that up, I hope it didn't spoil the surprise. Oh, and just as HAL recited a nursery rhyme as he was powered down in *2001: A Space Odyssey*, JCN recites a nursery rhyme to taunt Jazz as she's running out of air.

I grew up listening to Casey Kasem and the American Top Forty, and was saddened to hear he passed away earlier this year. In light of that, I modeled the DJ in this story loosely after Casey. I've been careful to honor his memory, while not using his name for commercial gain. I've been in touch with his daughter, Kerri, and given her the opportunity to review this tribute from an old fan of Casey's. I'd like to think Casey would have gotten a kick out of playing a role in a science fiction story like this.

The cover image is of Russell Schweickart conducting an EVA during Apollo 9, and is used as an image in the Public Domain, under the Creative Commons license. Schweikart is standing on the porch outside the Lunar Module, on day four of an Earth-orbit mission in preparation for the mission to the Moon.

I hope you've enjoyed this novel. Independent writing is a tough gig. You won't see banners advertising *My Sweet Satan* on the side of a bus or on a billboard in Times Square. I doubt you will ever see this book in a bookstore. Publishers just aren't interested in my writing, so it is incredibly difficult to reach out to new readers. If you've enjoyed this novel, please tell someone about it. Word-of-mouth is the only advertising strategy I have, so I deeply appreciate your support.

If you decide to leave a review of this novel on Amazon or Goodreads, please avoid spoilers.

Be sure to sign up **to** my email newsletter on http://thinkingscifi.wordpress.com to hear about upcoming stories.

You can find more of my writing on Amazon. Feel free to drop by and say hi on Facebook or Twitter under @PeterCawdron.

Other books by Peter Cawdron

Thank you for supporting independent science fiction. You might also enjoy the following novels also written by Peter Cawdron

SILO SAGA: SHADOWS

Shadows is fan fiction set in Hugh Howey's **Wool** universe as part of the Kindle Worlds **Silo Saga**.

Life within the silos follows a well-worn pattern passed down through the generations from master to apprentice, 'caster to shadow. "Don't ask! Don't think! Don't question! Just stay in the shadows." But not everyone is content to follow the past.

THE WORLD OF KURT VONNEGUT: CHILDREN'S CRUSADE

Kurt Vonnegut's masterpiece **Slaughterhouse-Five: The Children's Crusade** explored the fictional life of Billy Pilgrim as he stumbled through the real world devastation of Dresden during World War II. **Children's Crusade** picks up the story of Billy Pilgrim on the planet of Tralfamadore as Billy and his partner Montana Wildhack struggle to accept life in an alien zoo.

THE MAN WHO REMEMBERED TODAY

The Man Who Remembered Today is a novella originally appearing in **From The Indie Side** anthology, highlighting independent science fiction writers from around the world. You can pick up this story as a stand alone short or get twelve distinctly unique stories by purchasing **From the Indie Side.**

Kareem wakes with a headache. A bloody bandage wrapped around his head tells him this isn't just another day in the Big Apple. The problem is, he can't remember what happened to him. He can't recall anything from yesterday. The only memories he has are from events that are about to unfold today, and today is no ordinary day.

ANOMALY

Anomaly examines the prospect of an alien intelligence discovering life on Earth.

Mankind's first contact with an alien intelligence is far more radical than anyone has ever dared imagine. The technological gulf between mankind and the alien species is measured in terms of millions of years. The only way to communicate is using science, but not everyone is so patient with the arrival of an alien space craft outside the gates of the United Nations in New York.

THE ROAD TO HELL

The Road to Hell is paved with good intentions.

How do you solve a murder when the victim comes back to life with no memory of recent events?

In the 22nd century, America struggles to rebuild after the second civil war. Democracy has been suspended while the reconstruction effort lifts the country out of the ruins of conflict. America's fate lies in the hands of a genetically-engineered soldier with the ability to move through time.

The Road to Hell deals with a futuristic world and the advent of limited time travel. It explores social issues such as the nature of trust and the conflict between loyalty and honesty.

MONSTERS

Monsters is a dystopian novel set against the

backdrop of the collapse of civilization.

The fallout from a passing comet contains a biological pathogen, not a virus or a living organism, just a collection of amino acids, but these cause animals to revert to the age of the mega-fauna, when monsters roamed Earth.

Bruce Dobson is a reader. With the fall of civilization, reading has become outlawed. Superstitions prevail, and readers are persecuted like the witches and wizards of old. Bruce and his son James seek to overturn the prejudices of their day and restore the scientific knowledge central to their survival, but monsters lurk in the dark.

FEEDBACK

Twenty years ago, a UFO crashed into the Yellow Sea off the Korean Peninsula. The only survivor was a young English-speaking child, captured by the North Koreans. Two decades later, a physics student watches his girlfriend disappear before his eyes, abducted from the streets of New York by what appears to be the same UFO.

Feedback will carry you from the desolate, windswept coastline of North Korea to the bustling streets of New York and on into the depths of space as you journey to the outer edge of our solar system looking for answers.

GALACTIC EXPLORATION

Galactic Exploration is a compilation of four closely related science fiction stories following the exploration of the Milky Way by the spaceships *Serengeti, Savannah* and *The Rift Valley*. These three generational star ships are manned by clones and form part of the ongoing search for intelligent extra-terrestrial life. With the *Serengeti* heading out above the plane of the Milky Way, the *Savannah* exploring the outer reaches of the galaxy, and *The Rift Valley* investigating possible alien signals within the galactic core, this story examines the Rare Earth Hypothesis from a number of different angles.

This volume contains the novellas: Serengeti, Trixie & Me, Savannah, and War

XENOPHOBIA

Xenophobia examines the impact of first contact on the Third World.

Dr Elizabeth Bower works at a field hospital in Malawi as a civil war smolders around her. With an alien space craft in orbit around Earth, the US withdraws its troops to deal with the growing unrest in America. Dr Bower refuses to abandon her hospital. A troop of US Rangers accompanies Dr Bower as she attempts to get her staff and patients to safety. Isolated and alone, cut off from contact with the West, they watch as the world descends into chaos with alien contact.

LITTLE GREEN MEN

Little Green Men is a tribute to the works of Philip K. Dick, hailing back to classic science fiction stories of the 1950s.

The crew of the *Dei Gratia* set down on a frozen planet and are attacked by little green men. Chief Science Officer David Michaels struggles with the impossible situation unfolding around him as the crew are murdered one by one. With the engines offline and power fading, he races against time to understand this mysterious threat and escape the planet alive.

Thank you for supporting independent science fiction.

Reviews are the lifeblood of independent fiction, without passionate fans, this book will be lost in obscurity. If you've enjoyed MY SWEET SATAN, please leave a spoiler-free review on Amazon.

Made in the USA
San Bernardino, CA
06 February 2019